PARA
BELLUM

SIMON TURNEY

PARA BELLUM

HEAD
ZEUS

An Aries Book

First published in the UK in 2023 by Head of Zeus
This paperback edition first published in 2024 by Head of Zeus,
part of Bloomsbury Publishing Plc

9 7 5 3 1 2 4 6 8

A catalogue record for this book is available from the British Library.

ISBN (PB): 9781804540336
ISBN (E): 9781804540299

Cover design: Ben Prior/Head of Zeus

Printed and bound in Great Britain by
CPI Group (UK) Ltd, Croydon CR0 4YY

Head of Zeus
5–8 Hardwick Street
London EC1R 4RG

WWW.HEADOFZEUS.COM

For Cat and Mark, Harry and Poppy.

"*Ubi aliud accessit atrocius, quod arsuras in commune exitium faces furiales accendit.*" (There another, and more atrocious, thing was done, which kindled the frightful torches that were to burn for the destruction of the state.)

Ammianus Marcellinus, Roman History 5.4

Sic vis pacem, para bellum. (If you seek peace, prepare for war.)

Paraphrased from Vegetius, De Re Militari, Book 3

Flavius Focalis heard his decanus bellowing an order, a hoarse and desperate cry in the press, lost amid the tumult of war. Ofilius had a powerful voice that could suppress any commotion, and yet here, in this disaster, it was little more than a whisper of hope. Focalis tried to turn to see the man, to see if he was gesturing, had some great plan for survival, but there was neither room nor time. If he took his eye from those before him, he would die, and there was no doubt in him over that.

The Thervingi warrior roared as he brought down his long, straight blade, hammering at Focalis' shield, leaving great rents and dents in the brightly painted surface, numbing his arm with shock after shock. He struggled, heaving Sallustius – who was so close the two kept clouting one another – away in order to bring his own sword to bear. The battering on his shield continued unabated, and he took it as stoically as a dead man standing could, waiting for the moment he knew would come, as long as he survived long enough to recognise it. Then it came. The warrior, exhausted by his own relentless assault, paused for breath, bringing his sword back and up.

Focalis struck. His blade swung out, almost taking Sallustius' arm with it in its passage, and slammed into the

Gothic warrior with as much force as he could manage in the limited space. It was enough. He felt the contact with the chain shirt, felt the momentary resistance and then the slight give as the ribs inside broke, driving shards of bone into the man's lungs, a blow that would kill him, if not immediately.

As the man gasped and looked down, staggering back until he bumped into another of the growling bastards, Focalis took the opportunity to look around. He could see his own mates now, fighting hard for survival, all still standing by some God-sent miracle, and Ofilius roaring commands that no one could hear, let alone obey. But he could also see the purple standards ahead, where the emperor Valens struggled, surrounded. Victor and his Batavians had been striving to reach the beleaguered emperor, but the Gothic tribes were too numerous and too determined and had cut them off, so that the reinforcements had been forced to retreat, just like all the other commanders who had made their attempts.

Then he saw it, just as he'd known he would. Arrows flew all across the battlefield, as well as spears, thick in the air anywhere the Gothic archers knew they could loose without endangering their own tribes. But this one arrow carried doom, a black-feathered shaft sent by some demon to fell the light of the world.

He saw it plummet. Saw, in a gap in the press, the emperor look up, eyes widening, unable to move in time. Saw the arrow thud into Valens' chest.

Focalis knew he was dreaming. It was an old dream, almost comforting in its dark misery, a long-time companion of his sleeping hours, his only bed-mate since the passing of his wife three years before. He knew it was an old memory, relived in the darkness. He knew he could wake if he really tried, drag himself out of it, but he did not. Some men carried sin like a second skin, coating them and impossible to shed. Flavius Focalis would do penance all his days for his sins. They all would. He did not deserve to wake free from this nightmare.

They had fought for so many hours, even when it was clear the battle was lost. Even now he swung the sword with an arm robbed of all strength, a blow wrought by will alone, the will to survive and the will to wound those responsible for this day. Perhaps the one most responsible was already paying the price, though.

As they had been forced back across the field of battle, he had seen the emperor and his guards, the standards still high, manage to break free of the press – but, unable to make it to anywhere safe, still cut off by more Gothic warriors, they had taken shelter in an abandoned building. Valens had lived that long, and only that long. The colours went in, marking the last stand of the emperor, but it had been moments only before the Goths had fired the building, and the emperor had been roasted in his own makeshift tomb. Focalis felt his lip curl. If there was any justice, Valens had lived through the arrow wound long enough to burn. This was his fault, after all. His, and the general Lupicinus. And Ofilius. And Focalis. And the others. It was all their faults.

Another blow carried through purely by will, and a Goth of the Thervingi fell away, screaming and clawing at his ruined face. Few of the bastards wore helmets, and Focalis had thanked the Lord for that more than once as he took clear targets in the press.

Now they were almost back to Hadrianopolis, just one small band of survivors. It was like that all across the field. The army of Rome was gone, just small clutches of desperate refugees fighting to find a way out. Still, they all lived. That alone was a miracle. All eight of their tent party of the Legio Prima Maximiana still stood, though some cradled wounds and others had limbs hanging limp or dragging. But they were sinners of the worst order and cursed men, and their survival was no boon. God was preserving them for a fate of His own worst design, Focalis was sure.

The walls of the city were in sight now, but that was little comfort. They could seek safety there, but when the Thervingi and the Greuthungi and their Alani allies managed to clear the field of Roman resistance they would surround the city of Hadrianopolis and probably burn it to the ground with every living soul trapped inside. No, into the city was not the way to go. If the tent party of Aurelius Ofilius was to survive to face their God-given punishment, they would have to lose themselves in the wilds.

He turned, for another Goth had run at him, and he lifted his sword and shield in exhausted arms, ready to fight on against the impossible odds...

This time, Flavius Focalis awoke, the hair standing proud on his neck, his flesh prickling with anticipation. The threat had changed – had become real. The desperate fight of the old dream, even in his subconscious, had morphed into that preternatural warning that something was not right.

The room was dark, apart from a sliver of moonlight that lanced its way between the window shutters and cut across the blackness to leave a line of white across to the far wall. The air was chilly, though the cold sweat dampening Focalis' brow had nothing to do with weather or temperature. There was silence. The house was quiet, not even the slaves and servants were about at this time. Even the dogs slumbered in blissful ignorance of anything amiss.

Silence.

Darkness.

Focalis lay still, listening, eyes blinking once, twice, trying to rid his mind of the tattered remnants of the dream, even as the dying scream of the emperor in his fiery tomb echoed around his skull. It was quiet and it was dark and nothing was happening. Except something *was* happening. He could feel it. The silence was just *too* quiet. The stillness just *too* still. There is a certain type of nothing that is the deliberate result of someone trying not to be noticed, and this stank of such deception.

His head moved, a fraction at a time, just in case he was being observed, trying not to ruffle the covers, eyes dancing across the darkness, straining to pick out any features. Slowly he began to make them out, deeper black within black, a shadow of a desk in the abyssal darkness, the vague shape of a cupboard. He knew the room well enough to be able to assign a mundane shape to every black-on-black outline he could see, and satisfied himself that nothing was altered within the room. The danger had not reached this far yet, but he could feel it in the house, sense its presence and its approach.

Knowing that at least here in his sanctum he was safe, he rose now, blankets and sheets falling away, sloughing off like a shroud as he slipped out of the bed, bare feet falling to the thick fleecy mat below. He made fists with his toes in the rug, willing life into his old feet as he rose, his tunic dropping back into its natural shape from where it had twisted around him in the dream state. It was no sleeping tunic. He slept in his soldier's clothes, had even done so before Flavia had passed into God's grace. Lord, but she had scolded him over that habit. He was retired now, long years retired, and done with the army. Why did he need to cling to his old life so? What would she think now from her place with the angels, if she saw that his habits had extended to keeping his sword now jammed between the bed and the little cupboard beside it, unsheathed just in case.

That was one thing Ofilius had been sure to drill into them all. The decanus had made his men aware that death was only one mistake away, and only a fool slept with his weapon out of reach. Of course, Ofilius clung to the old gods, but still his lessons had value, and he was the man who had carried them through that debacle at Hadrianopolis.

His hand closed on the ivory hilt, fingers sliding comfortably into the worn-smooth grip, and he lifted the long spatha with practised ease, the blade almost an extension of his arm. He toyed with the idea of fastening his belt around his middle and pulling on his socks and boots, but that would take critical time, and there was more to worry about than just his own survival.

There was Martius.

With a quiet, calming breath, and shivering slightly in the cold, he shuffled across the rug and took a wide step across the marble floor to the thinner mat of wool in front of the door. Flavia had complained endlessly that they had paid for some of the most expensive marble in the world, and some of the most glorious mosaics, and he had largely covered them over with grubby, flea-ridden rugs. But this day had to come eventually, and the rugs and mats were not about comfort, but about silence. A footstep on marble or mosaic made an unmistakable sound, whether it be bare foot or hard boot. A footstep on a rug was muffled into silence. She had never understood that, but then she did not believe that her husband's sins were deep enough to damn him the way they had.

Silent, on the mat, he reached out to the door. The pivots that turned in the sockets when the door opened and closed were greased weekly by the house's slaves, and so made no sound, just like every other door in the house. Flavia had wanted the door to open out into the corridor, but he'd put a stop to that. The door had to open inwards. If it opened into the corridor, its opening was more immediately visible to anyone out there, and the door itself could hide anyone approaching. Inwards hid nothing.

Sword ready, Focalis pulled the door open in one swift, fluid movement, dipping his head out just far enough to put his eye to the corner and look that way. Only one way. He'd been careful there, too. Their room was the last in the corridor and there was only one approach, but, because he also knew the dangers of being trapped, the window in their room was low enough to effect an escape.

The corridor was empty. Dark, though not as dark as his room. A series of mats stitched together ran along the left-hand side of the corridor. An interloper might not notice them and would likely walk the marble floor, his footsteps betraying his approach, but as Focalis now moved down the passage he stuck to the mats, making no noise as he approached the heart of the house. There, at the rather old-fashioned atrium, lamps still burned, and the glow of gold lit the far end of the corridor, gleaming from the marble floor and the colourful, expensive mosaic that surrounded the central pool. No mats there. Focalis wanted to know if someone had entered that room at the centre of the house. Passing two other doors on the way, he peered in the gloom at the handles and at the base. Neither were open, and no light was visible beneath. The single tiny pebble remained in place on each handle, mute evidence that nobody had opened it. He passed those rooms silently, heartbeat increasing now with the heightening sense of danger.

Footsteps.

Quiet, being careful to be quiet. Gentle and whispering on the marble ahead, either just out of sight in the atrium, or in one of the rooms leading off.

Martius had to be safe. The boy knew enough to keep his door locked, for that had been a habit Focalis had drummed into his son every day and every night of the past six years. *Open it only when the clear sounds of normality are audible beyond it, or when you hear your father's voice.* Simple instructions, and Martius was far from daft. He had his mother's brains, though he'd been cursed with his father's looks.

His steps became lighter now, almost infinitesimal, a gossamer whisper on the mats as he approached the atrium and its footsteps. Light leather shoes moving quietly in small steps, he reckoned, and just out of view to the left.

The girl's sudden cough, feminine and gentle, saved her life. As Focalis reached the corner and leapt, she issued that muffled cough, and at the last moment, the sword that was coming up for a killing stroke lowered again. Instead, knowing now that this was one of the house's staff about night-time errands and moving quietly so as not to wake the master, he stepped out into the golden light of the room and grabbed her from behind, sword hand coming round her waist to pull her close as his free hand went over her mouth and stifled the gasp of fright.

Before she could recover and scream, hand still over her mouth, Focalis stepped round her so she could see who it was. As recognition and confusion dawned in her eyes, he let go of her, put a finger to his lips in a silent command for quiet, and then pointed back along the dark corridor to his room and mimed walking with two fingers. She obeyed, passing out of sight.

Focalis' pulse was pounding now with unbearable tension.

He settled in the room, backing into a corner so that he could see all approaches, feet slapping almost inaudibly on the marble. He was faintly irked that the girl's receding footsteps masked any other quiet noise in the house. As they disappeared, all he could hear was his own breathing.

Shield.

That was an idea. He could go warn Martius, but the boy should be safe for now, and a shield was as valuable in a fight as a sword. He padded across to the office doorway, where he would sit of a morning and go through the accounts, wishing Flavia was still alive, for she had a much better head for figures than he. The room was in darkness, just the glow from the atrium creating a golden strip of light across the floor.

He could see his shield hanging on the wall behind his chair, the brightly painted red and yellow circles glaring like some baleful eye. Again, it was only that strange sense that saved him. He took one pace into the room and knew that something was wrong. Indeed, he should have been more careful, checking the room before entering, but he had stupidly assumed that with the girl busy in the atrium, no one would be hiding in the vicinity.

He ducked on pure instinct as the sword cut out of the darkness, flashing in the golden light of the doorway, its wielder unseen in the dark to the left of the door. The owner gave a grunt of frustrated effort as his well-planned and well-executed attack failed only because of his target's unexpected caution. Focalis leapt into the room, slipping from the streak of golden light into the darkness beyond. For just a moment nothing moved, the two figures – and they were only two, the Roman was sure – hidden in shadow on either side of the golden glow, unable to make one another out.

The intruder took a single step to his left and Focalis narrowed his eyes, picturing the office in daylight, placing the man in the image, mentally strafing the darkness with his gaze, remembering every carefully placed item. His hand reached out behind him, his fingers touching the timber of a cupboard top and spidering across it until they touched cold, soft leather. The sling would be of little use right now, but his hand moved on and touched the pottery bowl, then closed on one of the lead bullets it contained. They were leftovers from his army days, each missile painted with a pithy and often crude suggestion as to what his victims could do to themselves. He lifted the heavy lead bullet and hefted it as he heard another step and adjusted his mental image. The man would be close to the office desk now. He was edging slowly around the room, not quite into the light, but close enough that when he struck it would be from an unexpected direction and closer than anticipated. Not closer than anticipated for a man as prepared as Focalis, however.

He pulled back his arm at chest height, like he had all those days down by the river teaching Martius to skip stones while Flavia laughed and read her precious books. When he threw it, he threw it hard, and angled upwards instead of the straight line of a skipped stone.

He was rewarded with a thud and a grunt as the stone connected with the intruder, but by then he was moving. With just two barefoot steps he leapt, crossing that streak of golden light in a flash. He hit the man hard and drove him back, across the office desk, tablets and pens and papers scattering and falling to the floor as the intruder snarled some insult in that guttural language for which Focalis had been waiting. Not that he had ever doubted who the intruder was, but it was oddly comforting to have it confirmed by the Gothic oath.

He gave the man no chance to rally. The Goths, no matter what tribe they might be, were dangerous warriors, more so individually than the Romans, whose strength had always come from disciplined formations rather than sole ability. Goths fought every fight as though they were alone and hell awaited should they fail, and this one would very likely best Focalis if he gave the man a chance.

He'd known the sword would not come into play immediately, for his plan had been to flatten the man against the desk and trap him, and he had done just that. Instead, his sword hand came up, blade raised, tip pointing to heaven, and came down hard, the pommel smashing into the man's head.

He cursed at the clonk. The bastard was wearing a helmet. Few of the Goths seemed to do so, and he'd not been prepared for it, yet seemingly his luck was holding. The pommel had struck the brim of the man's helmet with the clank of iron on bronze, but had slid off and smashed into the man's face, either nose or eye. The Goth cried out now in pain, all efforts at subtlety forgotten as he fought for his life. Pulling back the sword, snarling an oath to God, Focalis' free hand located the man's damaged face, his questing fingers finding the broken nose, feeling the warm, sticky blood. Then they found his eye, the Roman's hand bunching into a fist with the thumb extended. He felt the thumb meet damp resistance, and then felt that resistance burst, causing a fresh scream of agony from the man pinned beneath him. The Goth was ruined, but he was not yet done, his free hand coming up to his face in horror, assessing the damage in the dark even as his sword flailed, hoping to hit his assailant through sheer chance.

Focalis was already off the stricken man, though, taking one step back, bringing his sword level at his waist, ready for the strike. He thrust. He knew, even in the dark, where the man was, knew the height he was at, for he knew this office and his desk so well. His sword clinked momentarily on the hem of the man's chain shirt before passing beneath it and into the deadly region of his groin. It mattered little where the blow landed now. The arteries at the top of the inner thigh were a kill, the bladder and groin itself were a kill, and with no protection, the blade would find no resistance. He felt the spatha, two and a half feet of tempered Noric steel, slide deep into the man's body, passing through his pelvis and deep into his torso. Blood washed over Focalis' hand, and then again as he gave the sword a half turn, mincing the man's insides before drawing it free with a fresh slosh of warm liquid.

He took three steps back.

The Goth was shaking wildly as he slid from the desk and fell to the floor, tumbling into that golden strip of light where he thrashed in dying agony. His left eye was gone, his nose flat, the whole face coated with gore, and as he shook and bucked, a pool of blood grew rapidly around him.

Focalis looked down at the man.

He'd been expecting this moment for six years, since the dreadful deed, and even more so for the past four years since that hell on earth at Hadrianopolis. It had begun. This was just the opening act, too, and even that would not be limited to just one man. Breathing heavily, he turned. Gone was the stillness, the silence, the dark. The Goth's cries during their struggle would have woken the entire household, and even now he could hear shouts of alarm and the patter of many footsteps.

Focalis stepped from the room back into the atrium, blinking in the light, eyes darting this way and that, half expecting another Goth. He could hear activity everywhere now, and knew that he must look a sight. He stepped over to the small impluvium where the water rippled only slightly with the fresh flow of water from the pinecone-shaped fountain in the centre. Between the ripples, slightly distorted, he could see his own grisly face looking back up at him. Was it his imagination or was his reflection wearing an accusing expression? He looked at the stubbly chin, the unruly hair, the weathered, tanned, wrinkled face and wondered when he'd gone grey. He'd not really registered it happening.

Knowing how the girls of the household would react to

him like this, he knelt, cursing age as he did so, and pushed his sword under the surface, letting the water carry away the blood and gore of the kill. Leaving it submerged, he scrubbed his hands and forearms, and then sloshed pink water across his face, cleaning off the offensive matter there. There was little he could do about his clothes, for the tunic was military white with the rondel insignia and showed every stain, let alone the huge splash of blood that was slowly working its way across the weave. Retrieving his sword, he stepped into the now deep-pink pool and used his free hand to scrub off the blood.

A polite cough made him turn.

Otho, the doorman, was standing at the edge of the entrance vestibule, wearing a distraught look.

'No one came past me, master, I give you my word.'

Focalis nodded, waving away the slave's concerns. 'He sneaked in some other way. They're treacherous bastards, the lot of them.' He pointed to the office. 'What's left is in there. Move him into a corner and close the door. God alone knows what the girls will think if they stumble across him.'

As Otho bowed and moved towards the office, Focalis threw a finger out to the man. 'And when you've done that, gather everyone and get them outside to the gardens. You should have a good view and room to run if necessary.'

The doorman made no attempt to argue and went about his work.

Martius. It was all about Martius now. In truth it always had been. Focalis deserved anything that was coming to him, and he knew it. They all did. They were all wrapped in shrouds of sin that no amount of prayer or priestly forgiveness could remove. They were stained and would remain so until hell claimed them. In that, Focalis rather envied his old decanus, for Ofilius' refusal to accept Christ into his heart meant that he felt no guilt at what they'd done and expected no retribution. Focalis was prepared to burn in the pit for his sins.

But not to allow Martius to suffer. The boy had had no part in it. He was six years old, then, and only eight when his father had staggered, wounded and hollow, back from the greatest loss in Rome's history at Hadrianopolis. Martius had stayed home with Flavia, as was right, and was not stained with blood and sin. And that was why Focalis would not lay down and accept the fate that he knew he deserved. They could kill him and burn him and it would only be right, but they would not stop with Focalis, and he knew that Martius would be a second target for them, even if only one of convenience. He had even thought of sending the boy away for his own good, but somehow, with Flavia gone and Martius his only link to her, Focalis couldn't do that. And so the boy had been in danger, and now the old soldier must fight on, one last time, to save his heir.

Somewhere off towards the balneum – the small private bath house – there was a scream, and Focalis galvanised into action. He'd known the Goth would not be alone, but it seemed that all attempts at subtlety, at a surgical attempt to cut the corruption of the master out of the flesh of the house, had been abandoned, and the interlopers had begun a general slaughter.

'Shit.' He'd insisted on a small private mercenary force the day he'd come home, but that was one thing Flavia had flatly refused. She had married a soldier, and that was her curse, but she would not let him fill her home with other fighters. He should have done so after she died, of course, but it had never seemed right. Every time he thought about it, he could only see her admonishments, her wagging finger, and he'd put it off. Now he was paying the price. Only he and Otho were really in any position to defend themselves, Otho having been a pit fighter before Focalis had bought him and introduced him to a quieter life, conveniently not letting Flavia know the man's past until she'd decided she liked him. Every other slave and servant in the house had been bought or hired by his wife, and they were all delicate, educated, peaceful and quiet. And right now a group of vengeful Thervingi would be carving and battering their way through them.

In moments he was running, dripping wet, towards the corridor that led to the other wing of rooms. As he turned the corner, he was both relieved and irritated to see Martius coming the other way, tunic belted neatly, leather shoes clean and trousers tidy and pressed. His dark curly hair was wild, but that meant nothing. Just like his father's, no amount of combing ever tamed that mop.

'Why aren't you in your room?' he grumbled as the boy skittered to a halt.

'I heard all the commotion. The household is up, Dad.'

'Because they're being killed. We're under attack, boy.'

Martius frowned. 'What? Why?'

'I'll explain when we have time. Right now we need to get moving.'

His son's gaze had strayed as he spoke, taking in the stains on his tunic, and Martius' eyes widened as he looked up at his father. 'Are you…?'

'I'm fine. Have you got your sword?'

'No, it's in my room. I'll go back and get it, Dad.'

'No. You're dressed already and we're not separating

again. You can have my spare sword. Back to my room so I can finish dressing.'

'And then we report this? Ride into town, yes?'

'Fuck, no. No time, boy. And this is far from over. We need to get out now. Come on.'

And he turned and ran, his son at his heel. Just like Hadrianopolis, the Goths were closing in now, preparing to trap their prey. Flavia would admonish him for not thinking of the staff, but Christian charity was not in order tonight. Focalis had no sympathy to spare for anyone else. He had to get them to safety.

Passing back through the house, the pair bumped twice into panicked-looking slaves and directed them to the gardens and Otho's watchful eye. However many interlopers there were, it seemed highly likely they would be in the house now and looking for Focalis, so outside would be safer by a clear mile. At the bedchamber, he set Martius on watch at the doorway while he gathered his things and swiftly slipped on socks and boots, fastened his belt, and grabbed the secret pouch of solidi, a veritable fortune in one small bag, kept behind a loose tile for this very eventuality. Two old military cloaks and he was done. Preparing to leave the room, he quickly dipped into a tall cupboard and produced his spare sword, nothing fancy, but it had a handle and a pointy end, which was all a sword really needed.

'Quick stop for my shield and we're out.'

Martius, still looking frightened and confused, nodded, belted on the proffered sword, then turned and followed him.

'Who are they, Dad?'

'This is not the time, boy. Just stay close and keep your eyes and ears open.'

Now he pounded along the passage, ignoring the strip of mat down the side. The time for subtlety was past. As they neared the atrium once more, he could see shapes falling across the golden floor in the doorway – a shadow-play of death, for someone just out of sight was fighting for their life. Turning without a word, Focalis signalled his son for silence and then jogged left onto the mat, deadening the sound of his approach.

Nearing the corner, he held his sword up ready. The shadows told him the fight was over. He saw the shape of one of his slaves slip to the ground, dying, as the victor looked this way and that. For only moments he would have the advantage, taking the man by surprise, and so he leapt without further pause. The Goth was standing with his back to Focalis by pure chance, sword held low by his side, dripping blood onto the expensive marble. A Roman sword, he noted in passing, one of so many stolen during that debacle. In a heartbeat he was behind the intruder. His sword came up until the blade rested against the man's throat apple. The spatha was razor-sharp. Another lesson learned from Ofilius through the years: a dull blade was a worthless blade.

The Goth made to move, but realised his peril when even this slight jerk drew blood from his neck as Focalis' other arm came round to hold him tight.

'How many?'

The Goth gave a snort and replied something in his own tongue.

Martius was there now, keeping a safe distance from the fight, fondling the pommel of the sword at his side. The boy had had four years of training, and was as competent with the blade as any legionary recruit in his first year, but he had never had cause to try his skills for real, and the nerves were evident in his eyes.

'I know you understand me,' Focalis hissed at the Goth. 'If you want this easy, answer me.'

'Six,' grunted the Goth.

'Where?'

'Fuck you.'

Focalis shifted the blade slightly, drawing another bead of blood, but the Goth remained silent. 'Martius, break one of his fingers.'

'Dad?'

'Just do it, boy.'

As the lad gingerly stepped closer, Focalis hissed, 'Hurry. I can't take my blade away or he might get free.'

Mouth clamped into a straight line, eyes scrunched into a wince, Martius reached out and grasped the Goth's little finger. The man tried to fight him off, but Focalis drew another warning drip of blood. With a crack and a gasp of horror, Martius jerked the man's finger to a right angle with his hand. The Goth gave a gasp, which only served to lacerate his neck a little more.

'Where are they?' Focalis repeated.

'You will kill me.'

'That's a given, but it can be quick, or it can be very slow. Martius, break the next one.'

This time the boy was quicker, the snap joined by a pained yelp.

'Where?'

A rumble arose from the Goth's throat. 'Four in the house. Two with the horses on the road.'

Without another word, Focalis pulled his sword across

the man's neck, pressing hard, cutting deep into artery and windpipe. The man jerked and fell, gasping, pink bubbles forming in the cut as he reached up to his own neck fruitlessly. Focalis ignored him and ran across the atrium, beckoning to Martius. Pounding into the office, he retrieved his shield from the wall this time. He turned to find his son staring down in horror at the ruined body of the first kill in the shadowed corner.

'Dad?'

'Two gone. Four still out there.' Crossing to another cupboard, he pulled it open and found four martiobarbuli, clipping the weighted darts to the holders on the inside of his large, round shield.

'We could call for the guards from town, Dad. It's only two miles.'

'No time.' Bending the finger with the ring key on, Focalis dropped his shield, reached down to the chest in the corner and unlocked it, lifting the lid. Inside lay the family's funds, divided up into equal bags of lesser silver coins. He took four and threw them to Martius. 'Tie one to your belt and keep the others ready.' With that, he grabbed six and rammed them into a satchel nearby, slinging it over his neck before gathering up his shield again.

'We need to get the horses, but we need to make sure they're all gone before we leave. Life lesson for you there, boy: never leave an enemy behind you.'

Martius frowned in confusion. 'But if they're all dead, why the horses? Why leave at all?'

'Because this is just the beginning. There will be others. And we have places to go. Come on.'

He dipped out of the door into the atrium again and ran

towards the peristyle, Martius at his heel. Before he could reach the open garden a figure stepped out of the darkness, blocking the doorway. The Goth wore a shirt of bronze scales over his sleeved tunic and heavy trousers. The sprays of blood across his front spoke darkly of the fate of another of the house's staff, and the man grinned and said something clearly confrontational in his own tongue.

Not even breaking his stride, Focalis tucked his naked blade beneath the armpit of his shield arm, ripped one of the darts free and pulled it back, casting it underarm, an unorthodox throw, but one he'd used more than once in his time. The dart, a foot-long length of ash with a heavy lead weight and a wicked point at one end, was meant to be part of a cloud of such weapons cast up into the air in battle to fall like a deadly rain into an enemy unit. Years earlier, Focalis had realised that the missiles could also be used in a very similar way to a skimmed stone, on a more level trajectory.

The dart slammed into the grinning face of the Goth, smashing the bone and digging deep with its deadly point. The man fell away with a cry, mortally wounded, though it would take him some time to die.

Good.

The two leapt the dying Goth and ran into the peristyle, where Focalis made for the doorway that would lead them out into the open grounds outside the house. It really was a grand house, more suited to nobility than a common soldier. Martius had once asked how they'd afforded such a place. Focalis had fobbed him off with a tale of Flavia's monumental dowry, which was at least *part* of the truth.

Emerging into the open, Focalis drew himself up short. Otho was standing not far away, a hammer in his hand, coated with blood and gore. The doorman's left arm was hanging limp and bloody, but he had got the best of it, for a dead intruder lay at his feet with a misshapen, crushed skull. Half a dozen of the staff stood around looking pale and terrified, eyes raking the darkness for the next threat, and Focalis realised with a sinking feeling that this was all the survivors. Eighteen slaves and servants in the house, and seven had lived through the attack.

And the attack was not over yet. There were still two out there somewhere, with their horses. Focalis stabbed his sword into the lawn for a moment and then dipped into the satchel at his side, withdrawing four of the bags of coins. Stepping forward with a nod of understanding to the wounded doorman, he thrust a bag at him.

'The house is clear, but more will come. This should see you somewhere safe and set you up. There's a bag for each of you.' With that, he gestured to Martius, who produced the other three. As they moved around the survivors, handing a bag of coins to each, Focalis addressed them all. 'Get your things. In my office the chest is open. In there you'll find documents of manumission for you all. You're free. Take the gold and the papers, and the horse and cart from the sheds, and head for Augusta Traiana. Don't stay there, though, just in case. Get transport onwards. Head for somewhere big you can lose yourself in, Thessalonika or Constantinopolis.'

The slaves stared in dumb shock, while Otho nodded his acceptance and gratitude, but there was no time to talk further. Focalis gestured to them. 'Time is important. Go.'

With that, he turned and peered into the darkness. He could see no sign of the other two Goths. The track that led down to his country estate met the main Traiana road on the other side of a sprawling copse of trees. That would be where the Goths had dismounted, being careful to hide their approach from anyone awake in the house. They had left their horses there and come quietly on foot the rest of the way. That meant that the two remaining men may well be unaware that their task had failed. It would be some time before they became concerned – unless, of course, they had particularly sharp ears and had heard the distant commotion.

'Come on.' Pulling his sword free and remembering the time he'd once planted his blade in the grass on campaign, which had led to a tongue-lashing from Ofilius and a clip round the ear, he turned and ran to the stables.

There were two horses, his and Martius', and their tack and harness were close by. Leaving Martius on watch at the door, he dropped his shield, wiped and sheathed his sword, and hurriedly prepared the animals. As he toiled he could hear his son working his way up to a question.

'What is it?'

'These men. They're Goths.'

'Yes.'

'Aren't we at peace with the Goths, Dad?'

'It's a bit more complicated than that. Yes, the empire is at peace, but not me specifically, and not with all Goths, either.'

'What's going on, Dad?'

'There isn't time now.'

'You keep saying that, but if I'm in the dark and I don't know what's happening, how can I help?'

Focalis sighed as he cinched a strap. The boy was going to have to hear the whole sorry tale at some point, but this was most definitely not the time. 'Some years ago, me and a few friends were involved in something bad. *Real* bad. I've been

23

trying to make amends for it ever since, but I'll never manage. I learned an important lesson that day, though.'

'Don't do bad things?' Martius offered, Flavia's mild but avid Christian morals showing through in her son.

'No,' Focalis replied frankly as he worked. 'Never leave a job half done.'

'Where are we going, Dad?'

'I told you, I wasn't alone. My tent-mates were there too, and they're in danger. We have to find them all. I've always thought I'd be the first. I've made myself the easiest to find, so hopefully they haven't got to the others yet.'

'This is frightening me, Dad.'

'Me too, lad. I've been expecting this day for years, yet I still find I'm not ready. But we will be. When we find the others, we will be. And you are more ready than any lad your age. By ten you could hit the three killing points on a body and ride a horse like a professional. And your archery's coming on, too. Which reminds me. Get the bows and a quiver each. They're in the store next door.'

Blessedly saved from any further uncomfortable questions, Focalis finished saddling the horses and led them out of the stalls just as Martius reappeared with the bows and quivers. As Focalis tied his shield to the harness and checked the animals over, his son fastened the bows and quivers on for travel.

'How's your Parthian shot?' the old man asked as he pulled himself up into the saddle.

Martius shrugged, following suit. 'Not bad. I hit a target two times in three.'

'Better than me, then,' Focalis said with a grim smile. 'Come on.'

They walked the horses across the garden and then out of the gateway onto the dusty track. 'There will be two men at the junction,' he told Martius. 'Two more Goths. They might not be too alert. I suspect they're bored and inattentive. Leave them to me.'

'Dad, I know how to use this,' Martius argued, patting the sheathed sword at his side.

'I know.'

'And the bow.'

'I know. But this is my fight for now. Let me deal with them. If I fall, then you'll have to be ready.'

With that, he kicked his horse into a trot and the two began to work their way up the slope towards the wood that hid the junction with the main road. As they neared the trees, Focalis motioned for his son to slow and fall back, while he kicked up into a gallop. Pounding out ahead, he reached for one of the martiobarbuli behind him, still clipped to the shield, removing it with difficulty and hefting it.

Moments later he had rounded a bend and was between the trees, the junction in view. Sure enough there was a small group of horses just on the track, close to the main road. The man in the atrium had been truthful at least, for two men waited here. One sat astride a horse beyond the riderless horses, while the other was busy at the roadside, urinating into the trees. Their bored-sounding conversation changed instantly as the mounted one noticed the enraged Roman riding at them at speed. The urinating one snarled an oath and tried to fasten his trousers.

The decision was easy. The mounted man was too far away and on the other side of the horses. The other was an easy target. The weighted dart hit the pissing man even as he finished fastening himself and turned, slamming into an unarmoured chest, breaking bones and throwing him back into his own steaming patch of undergrowth.

The other rider was sharp. He had realised in an instant that the men at the villa had to be gone for Focalis to be here, that his relieved companion would be of little help, and that his odds of surviving the fight were at best level. Cursing in his guttural tongue, the Goth let go of the gathering of reins he held and clapped his hand, kicking out at the horses, sending them scattering in an attempt to put the beasts between him and Focalis, blocking the track. Having done all that he could, the Goth wheeled his own mount and trotted back towards the road, picking up speed.

'Oh no you don't,' Focalis growled. For just a moment, he contemplated trying another dart or reaching for the bow, but decided against it. The man was a fast-moving target some distance away. The dart would miss, and he'd never been that good with a bow. He would have to do this the old-fashioned way.

The Goth was already trying to put distance between them, out onto the main road and turning right, making for the city. Focalis gritted his teeth. This was going to hurt, but he had no choice. He'd never catch the man if he had to push his way through the milling horses. Instead, he jerked with his knees, hauled on the reins and turned the horse off the track. With a crunch, the hooves pressed down on the prone shape of the pissing man, who, if he wasn't already dead, would be now.

The animal fought him. It didn't want to go into the woods, but Focalis was determined, and long ago he'd been trained to master a horse in a manner that few soldiers could. In a matter of heartbeats he was in among the pine trees, hunched over as thin branches whipped him mercilessly from both sides. The animal was suffering too, he could hear it, but he was calling out soothing words and phrases of encouragement, known only to a master equisio. The horse didn't like it, but it did it anyway. Beast and rider pounded across the carpet of needles, those thin branches leaving lines of red on the flesh of both man and horse. Then suddenly there was moonlight ahead, and Focalis burst from the woodland onto the main road spitting out foliage and cursing the God-given abundance of the land.

The Goth was just two horse-lengths ahead now, for Focalis had cut diagonally through the small wood and emerged right behind him. The man turned, eyes wide with surprise, and put his heels to his horse. The two men rode hard, the lead trying to gain as much distance as he could, the rear desperate to catch up. The gap remained constant as they rode, and Focalis narrowed his eyes as the Goth realised he was not getting away and decided on a new tactic. He had a short spear with him, meant for stabbing rather than as a lance or javelin, but he now sacrificed the attempt at extra speed in order to turn in the saddle and heft the spear.

He was good – Focalis could see that just from the man's posture and the way he held the spear. But he was also foolish. The angle was wrong. He was aiming for Focalis, where a sensible man would aim for the horse to take him down. The Roman shifted his weight slightly in the saddle, lifting his right knee ready. He came closer now, ever closer as the Goth slowed, ready to throw, concentrating on his cast and no longer on an attempt to escape.

He threw.

It was a good throw, if a foolishly directed one. Had it been aimed at the horse, Focalis would have had to jerk the reins left or right out of the weapon's path and would sacrifice any hope of catching up. Instead, the short spear arced through the air on a direct path to Focalis himself. At the last moment, with a barked command, the horse dipped its head and he slid from the saddle, right hand grasping the leather horn to arrest his fall, right knee still up over the leather seat. He slipped down to the horse's side, pressed against its ribs and shoulder, face buried in its neck, holding on for dear life.

The spear whispered through the air where he had been, and the moment the danger was gone, Focalis hauled with all his might, pulling himself upright into the saddle once more. Everything ached. He was far too old for such playful manoeuvres these days, and he knew it. Still, at least he wasn't dead, so *there* was something after all.

He had the advantage now. He had not slowed throughout all this, while the Goth had dropped back every step. In moments he was on the man. As the enemy rider struggled to gain speed, pulling his blade free with difficulty, Focalis let go of the reins, pulling alongside the Goth, his left hand closing around the Goth's own, which gripped the sword hilt. With a grunt of effort Focalis pressed down, forcing the sword back into the sheath it had not quite left. They were too close now for swords to be much use. Instead, his right hand quested around behind him until it found the shield, bouncing and clonking on the horse's haunch, then closed on one of the three remaining weighted darts. He pulled it free from its clip and turned in the saddle, using his knees to keep the two of them close, keeping his weight on his left arm to hold the enemy's blade in its sheath.

His right hand came round with force and the sharp,

two-inch-long triangular point of the dart slammed into the Goth's neck. The man gave a strange gurgling shriek, and Focalis pulled the weapon free, tearing a large part of the man's throat out with it. He couldn't afford to keep losing darts.

He pulled aside, letting go of the Goth's sword arm, and slowed as the stricken rider made desperate sounds, his horse tottering this way and that, out of control and in a panic. He came to a halt, breathing heavily, recovering his composure as the Goth died in the saddle, swaying with the gait of the horse, who ambled around, directionless. He became aware after a while that they were not alone, and turned to see Martius sitting astride his own horse some short distance back up the road.

'Where did you learn to fight on horseback, Dad?'

Focalis sighed. 'I wasn't always a legionary, lad. Once, some time ago, I was something else. We all were.'

The boy sat staring at him, the next question unanswered. It would have to remain so for now. An idea had been working its way into his mind as he recovered from the fight, and he gestured to the boy.

'Help me. I want his shirt.'

His own chain armour was back in the house, buried somewhere in a store room with the bulk of his old army gear. With the six intruders now dead, they would probably be safe heading back, but now they had to move. Every wasted hour put the others in more danger. As Martius helped him drag the Goth from the horse and then peel the chain shirt from him, the boy continually failed to meet his father's gaze. Finally, as the old man lifted the shirt to examine it, the lad broke the silence.

'Are we ever coming back, Dad?'

Focalis answered with a noncommittal grunt. An hour or so ago he'd been fast asleep and dreaming horrible but at least familiar dreams. Now here he was on the road, half the house staff dead, his first fight in four years a brutal but touch-and-go success, with a panicked and shocked son repeatedly battering him with questions, the answers to which were all unpleasant. He'd been avoiding talking about all of this for six years now, and even Flavia had accepted that it was a subject best left alone.

Still, now the matter had sort of risen up and smacked them round the face, he was going to have to tell him at least some of it, and soon. It was unfair to keep the boy in the dark when his own life was in danger, and yet there was a selfish little part of Focalis' soul that shied from it. Flavia had accepted him, what he was and what he had done, for she was an exceptional woman – but Focalis would never forgive himself, and Rome, God and the weight of history would curse him forever. Right now, despite everything, Martius still looked up to him. The moment he learned the truth, would he still do so?

'Is this about Hadrianopolis?' the boy pressed.

Again, Focalis answered with a grunt. Let him think that for a while.

'Are we coming home?' the boy pressed again.

Focalis fought a moment of irritation, and turned as sympathetic a look as he could muster on his son. 'I don't know,' he answered frankly. 'Maybe. One day. It depends a lot on what we do next. These bastards won't stop coming until there are none of them left.'

The boy's eyes widened, and Focalis chuckled despite

himself. 'Not Goths. God, boy, but there are millions of *them*. *These* Goths serve one man. They are Thervingi.'

'But the Thervingi are part of Rome now,' Martius said, brow creased. 'They protect our border. The treaty…'

'Not *all* the Thervingi. Listen, I will tell you everything when I can. When we have time. When we're safe.' *If we're ever safe again…*

There was silence for a time as Focalis tucked the heavy chain shirt into one of the saddlebags, and then the two of them pulled themselves back up into the saddle.

'What way?' Martius asked.

'Away east. This bastard was heading for the city, so there'll be others there. We have to take a bit of a loop and then head for a friend.'

As they finally began to walk their horses along the road, heading away from both the house and the city they had called home all Martius' life, the boy took a deep breath.

'Alright, if you won't tell me everything, at least tell me about the people we're going to find.'

Focalis nodded. That at least was fair. 'There were eight of us, a tent party. We were once in a cavalry regiment, but something happened, and we ended up in the legion at Hadrianopolis. Still the same eight of us, though. We were close. Closer than most families. We've sort of kept in touch since Hadrianopolis. The nearest is our decanus, my old boss, Aurelius Ofilius. He's the hardest man I ever knew. If anyone knows what to do next, it'll be him.'

Martius' silence spoke volumes. The brief explanation had raised more questions than it had answered. Well, good. If the boy was musing on new ideas it would keep him quiet for a bit. Right now, Focalis needed to think. Ofilius was two days' ride away, and he was the nearest of them. But what were they going to do even if he managed to get them all together? Fight a new war?

He just hoped that Ofilius would have the answer to that.

2

The settlement had no name, no real importance. Likely on official imperial maps it had some designation in the form of a name or a number, for an imperial courier station sat at the near edge of the small hamlet, but that appellation was reserved for the official installation and not the small cluster of houses that lay beside it, between it and the small, brown river that tumbled past in the evening light.

'Is it safe?' Martius asked, trepidation painting his face in the failing light.

'Nowhere is truly safe now, lad. But as yet even allied Goths serving the empire don't have access to the imperial courier service, so they won't be found in that way station.'

He looked ahead and sized the place up. It was probably a mansio, a full official overnight stop and horse exchange for couriers and high officers, but it was a rather small example. Focalis had stayed at a few in his time, but not one on such a minor scale. The village was too small to be hiding a unit of Goths, and they would not have permission to stay at the mansio, so the place should be safe.

And that would be a relief. They had ridden all day, but had been nervous and careful throughout. They had taken the main roads, but at the first sign of more than a single cart or a travelling couple in the distance, they had ducked off the road and found shelter until the voyagers passed. Twice they had waited for military units to pass by: one a tent party of Roman auxilia and the other a small group of Gothic limitanei, both armed and armoured much the same, but the former bearing a banner that announced their status.

They had moved as fast as they dared, but already they were falling behind Focalis' planned journey. He'd hoped for two days to their destination, but at the careful rate they travelled, it would be two nights and three days.

He looked up. The grey clouds were moving with impressive speed and he felt sure he could sense just the slightest moisture in the air, suggestive of rain on the way, which could come at any time with those racing clouds. Whether it was safe or not, they had to find somewhere for the night out of the weather, and they had eaten nothing all day, thanks to their sudden departure, so they could both stand a good hot meal.

'Dad, if it's only for officials, how will we get in?'

Focalis patted the satchel at his back. 'I have a few tricks up my sleeve, and if they don't work, a Roman can usually get access by flashing enough gold. Come on.'

As the moisture in the air continued to thicken with the darkening clouds, the pair walked their tired horses down towards the mansio. This was no grand edifice in three wings, but a simple two-storey building with a small courtyard and a stable, just about big enough for a wagon and horses, and a tiny balneum a short way down the slope. They approached the gateway to the courtyard, which sat open, and as they reined in and dismounted on the damp flags, a boy of perhaps nine summers came skittering out of a dark doorway, bowing his head. Quickly, Focalis removed the packs he needed from the horse, and without a word the lad reached up, took the reins – eyes lowered at all times – and led the horses off into the stable.

They watched him go, then turned to the door of the main building. Shouldering his kit-bag and satchel, Focalis pushed open the door, a blast of warm, sweaty air hitting him in the face. He blinked in the oily smoke of braziers, tallow candles and a small fire, and pushed his way in. The main room had a small bar, replete with inbuilt bowls for foodstuffs and three large amphorae behind, a surly-looking man with a squint watching them as he rubbed a cup sort-of-clean on his greasy apron.

The room was empty other than the proprietor, whose eyes were twitchy and suspicious.

'Yes?'

Focalis swung his satchel round and opened it. Moments later, he was fishing out a small tube, which he opened to reveal a document on vellum. This he held out for the man, who took it and unfurled it, peering myopically at the small text. Focalis held his breath for a moment. The man did not look impressed, but they had to stay. They needed shelter and food. The document was genuine, signed by a senior officer in an elite unit and sealed with that unit's seal, but it was also six years old. There was no official limit on its usage, and it should still be good, but the age made it questionable in the eyes of the suspicious.

'Who'd you steal this off?' the proprietor grunted, without looking up from the papers.

'It's mine, and it's valid, and you know it.'

'These things are easy to forge.'

The tip of the man's tongue protruded for a moment,

moistening his lips. Focalis sighed and reached into one of the bags of lesser coins they had taken from the chest. No point in letting the man know they had good gold, or the price would rise drastically. 'Here,' he said, tipping out four small silver coins.

'That's almost the price of a meal.'

Focalis leaned close to the man, trying to ignore the stench of his breath, his eyes narrowing dangerously. 'Given that I have every right to free board and food, along with any travelling companion, I would take the coins and be fucking grateful if I were you.'

The man recoiled. He did not look at all happy, but he did sweep the coins off the bar and into his hand, suggesting that a deal had been struck. He recovered his poise in a strangely oily, ophidian move.

'Welcome, domine. And to your man, there. We have three rooms, but one of them is occupied and another needs cleaning.'

Focalis nodded. The man would not want to waste two rooms if he could avoid it. 'That's fine. We can share if there are two cots.'

'I will have it all arranged for you. Tonight's meal is lamb stew and fresh bread. We're only a small place, so we don't offer a menu.'

'Lamb stew will be fine. Is the balneum up to temperature? I'd like to wash before we settle into the room anyway.'

The man nodded. 'Furnace was lit an hour ago. Should be nice and warm.'

Chewing his lip, Focalis reached into the pouch again and slid two more silver coins onto the counter. 'Any interesting news to pass on, before I go?'

The man was warming to them with the exchange of coins. He gave a shrug. 'Never *any* news here.'

'What about groups of Goths?'

'They're all you ever see on the road, now. Don't know why we fought a war against them. Theoretically we won, but now there are more Goths in the empire than ever. Maybe if we'd lost they'd have pissed off home.' He spat in disgust.

'Would you have seen a group yesterday,' Focalis asked, 'on horseback? Half a dozen of them?'

The man tapped his lip in thought, his left eye intent on the bridge of his nose while the right held the visitor in its gaze. 'Seen plenty of 'em, but none on horses, not for a few days.'

Focalis nodded. Then the attackers had come from Augusta Traiana, as he'd suspected. That meant they'd approached the house from the north or north-west, which gave him hope, as it suggested Focalis had been their first target and he may still have time to get to the others first. Moreover, if the attackers had not come through here, their chances of dangerous encounters the next day were drastically reduced. They may not have to be so careful, and that meant they could move faster.

'Balneum is down the steps from the courtyard. It's locked, but here's the key.' The man dropped a heavy iron key into Focalis' hand, and then nodded. 'Meal in an hour, room should be ready by then too.'

Focalis thanked him and then retrieved his papers, slotting them back into the tube and then the satchel, fastening that and sliding it round to his back again. With a gesture to his son, he turned and went out through the door they'd first used. The rain had begun now, just a gentle drizzle, but sufficient to soak a man gradually, so they hurried through the damp air to the steps and skittered down them. The door unlocked easily and they slid inside, hanging the key on the hook in the changing room. There were three small niches for clothes, one for each guest room, but knowing that one room was empty, they disrobed and used one niche each. As they slid with relief from their travelling gear, Focalis could almost feel Martius waiting to ask a question.

'What is it, lad?'

'What was that document, Dad?'

'Authority to make use of the state courier system, including horse relays and mansios.'

'Where did you get it? They don't give that to soldiers, do they? You said the Goths wouldn't get in, and *they're* soldiers.'

'I've had it a long time. We all have them. Enough questions for now.'

With that, he grabbed a towel from the rack, slipped on a pair of wooden clogs and clopped away into the baths, though he took the sheathed sword with him. He heard Martius clonking along behind him, accompanied by the determined and pointed silence of a boy wanting to press for information and holding back with difficulty. Such a small place had no slaves or attendants, but the balneum was clean and well stocked, and in the next room, sweating in the heat rising from the floor, Focalis leaned his sword against the wall and retrieved a strigil and a small jug of oil from the shelf. In moments he was oiling up and scraping away the dirt of the day. Martius followed suit, and Focalis could feel the lad looking expectantly at him every time his back was turned.

'Alright,' he said with a sigh, turning as he worked on his left thigh. 'Such authorisation is not given to common soldiers but, as I said earlier, I wasn't always a legionary. All of us, our decanus included, were moved into the legion in the build-up to that mess at Hadrianopolis. Valens needed to move his manpower around. Until then, we were part of his scholae palatinae.'

He heard the sudden sharp inbreath. The scholae were the elite horse units of the emperor, the modern descendant in many ways of the ancient Praetorian cavalry that had been disgraced and disbanded by the great Constantine. At least the surprise would shut the lad up for a while, and hopefully stop him asking uncomfortable questions. The next one, of course, would be why they were moved from an elite unit into a standard legion, but with luck he could stave that one off for a while. In silence he finished scraping himself down, dropped the strigil in the bucket, replaced the jug and used the bowl of warm water in the corner to sluice the used oil into the gutter at the corner.

He hovered in the door, once he'd collected his sword and towel. Even here, nominally safe, it would be better for them to stay together. Once Martius was done, the two of them moved through into the hot bath and slid with sighs of pleasure into the water, the scant remnants of oil on their skin spreading out and giving a multi-hued sheen to the surface.

There was to be no respite, though, for Martius was making those noises again, preparing for more questions. Perhaps he should just tell the lad everything now and get it over with. He was, indeed, wondering how he would start the sorry tale when he became aware of footsteps in the outer room. His gaze darted to the sword standing against the wall. It would be within reach if he threw himself bodily across the floor, and for a moment he contemplated leaping out and retrieving it, but the footsteps paused, and then changed as their owner slipped into the other pair of wooden bathing clogs. Focalis relaxed a little. His enemies were cunning, but he couldn't imagine them stripping down and changing shoes just to sneak through a bath house. He looked across at the door and after a few moments, long enough for a man to quickly scrape down the dirt, the new arrival stepped into the doorway.

He was a small, rodential fellow, with a pointed nose and a three-day growth of black beard. His hair was thick and black, cut close to the scalp in the current fashion. The man acknowledged their presence with just a nod, then crossed to the other side of the bath and slid into the water, politely keeping out of their way so their legs did not entwine in the small facility.

'Evening,' the man said as he leaned back against the side, then his eyes fell on the sword standing by the wall and his brow rose in surprise, though he swiftly recovered. A man armed was hardly a surprise these days, even in a bath house in the middle of nowhere, and this man and his son could hardly be bandits, especially staying in a government place.

Focalis found himself relaxing a little, for the man was naked and unarmed, clearly the mansio's other guest. Best of all, he had interrupted their conversation, which frustrated Martius, but rather relieved his father.

'Hello. Passing through on business?'

The man scrubbed his short hair, dipped beneath the water for a moment, then came up, spitting out a mouthful with no apparent care for the slight sheen of oil on the surface. 'Yeah. I'm on the long run from Serdica to Constantinopolis. You?'

Focalis gave what he hoped was a nonchalant shrug. 'Just

heading to Suida on business. Nothing on your scale. That's a long run.'

The man nodded. 'Shit of a run. And it might not be so bad were I able to stay in the big places, but the service ain't what it was, and they cut back on costs wherever they can. This place is like a palace compared with where I was *last* night, though.'

Focalis gave a low chuckle. 'At least it's free.'

'It needs to be, when the rooms are already taken by fleas and the wine tastes like feet.'

Another laugh. Even Martius was smiling now, the seriousness of earlier fading in the good-natured banter. As Focalis lifted himself from the water a little on his elbows and then lowered himself into a better position, the man opposite them frowned.

'That's some nasty bruising.'

Focalis looked down. He hadn't really registered the bruises that he'd taken from the various clashes around the house and on the road. After a lifetime of battle, he only paid attention when it needed a surgeon's needle. Bruises and aches were nothing. He shrugged. 'Bit of a set-to last night.'

'You're not on the run, are you?' the man asked, eyes narrowing, darting meaningfully to the sword by the wall. Just when Focalis was about to cough out some feeble comment, the man burst into laughter. 'Just kidding. But you do look like you've been in the wars. Old and new.'

'Ex-army,' Focalis confirmed. 'But I got into a bit of a slapping match with a mouthy Goth yesterday.'

'I hope he looks worse,' the man said, with feeling. 'They're a surly lot. Can't count the number of times I've had to come off the road and ride round units of Greuthungi or Thervingi who won't move even for the emperor's own couriers. Six years ago they'd have had their backsides kicked clear across the river and into their own hovels for such behaviour.'

'I hear you, friend. So you're on imperial business then?'

'Right from the governor's palace, mate. Letter from the vicarius to the imperial palace at Constantinopolis. Probably something to do with the rogue king. He was last seen in Serdica.'

Focalis' ear pricked up.

'Rogue king?'

'You been hiding under a rock for the past month? That bastard Fritigern. Seems that part of the peace deal was his removal from power. He fought it for a while but even the Goths kicked him out. He pissed off into the wilds with his men. There's a rumour the vicarius wants to put a price on his head, but he'll have to get imperial permission.'

Focalis rubbed his face, trying not to show too much interest at the name Fritigern. Not that he wasn't expecting something like this – and it explained a lot about the timing. Glancing left, he could see Martius with a calculating look in his eye, on the edge of piecing something together just from their expressions. Damn it, but he was going to have to do some explaining after all. Heading it off for now, in company, he nodded to the courier.

'You think the letter you carry is the vicarius asking for permission?'

'Given the timing, it seems likely. Might be a good thing if the emperor agrees to it. Most of the Goths will abide by imperial rule, but that maniac would never make a citizen.'

Focalis nodded again. *Quite.* 'We'll see you at dinner? I

think I'll turn into a prune if I stay in here much longer, and I hate prunes.'

With an easy smile that took some mustering, he began to climb out of the bath, Martius following him, vibrating with the need to ask questions again. The courier said his farewell and slumped back into the bath, enjoying his relaxation, raising an eyebrow again as Focalis retrieved his sword from the wall on the way out. As the two travellers passed back into the changing room, Martius spoke in a low voice.

'We should have used the cold bath.'

'I've reached the limit of my sociability just now, boy.'

Hurriedly, the pair dried and dressed. Had they had adequate time leaving the house, they would at the very least have a spare set of dry, clean clothes, but their precipitous departure had forbidden them even that, and so they unhappily slid back into their cold, dirty travelling gear, vowing that the first town they came to they would pick up a few essential supplies.

Up the steps in the rain, being careful of the slippery stones in their climb, and then back across the courtyard and through the inn door, Focalis emerged into the main room with its welcoming warm, smoky air, to have his world explode.

Two men stood at the counter talking to the owner, each clad in a chain shirt, but wearing the trousers of the Gothic peoples rather than the shorter, more civilised legwear and puttees of a Roman. Their heads were bare and their matted brown hair was longer than any Roman style, their beards full. Surely they had no authority to be here, *especially* if they were part of Fritigern's exiled warband?

Despite the lurch in his stomach at the sight, Focalis was a man in control, always, and not once did his step falter as he took all this in, though he heard a nervous shuffle of Martius' feet behind him. Keeping his expression neutral and letting his eyes play around everything, rather than keeping his gaze away from the Goths, he walked on through the room and gestured to the owner. The man looked up over the Goths' shoulders, and Focalis caught the look in his eye. He was no happier about these arrivals than Focalis, clearly.

'Your room's ready,' he called. 'Last one on the floor, I'll have your dinners brought up shortly.'

Good man. Focalis made a mental note to tip him a few more coins in the morning for his quick thinking. As they made for the simple wooden staircase, Focalis listened in. The two Goths were arguing their case for a room for the night, despite this being a government stop. They were adamant that he must have a spare room, and their coins were as good as any legionary's, citing as common knowledge that these places would supplement their income with unofficial travellers if the recompense was high enough. Focalis left them to their debate. The owner might be no great lover of the empire's new sector of society, but coin was coin, and he would be stupid to turn down business in an out-of-the-way place like this.

As they reached the second floor and strode down the single corridor, he noted the three doors. Wet footprints were just visible at the first door, evidence that either the mansio's staff or the courier had been in and out of the room since Focalis arrived. The second door was resolutely shut and untouched, while a key sat in the far one, awaiting the pair of them. He cast up a mental prayer that the owner's xenophobia was strong enough to turn away the Goths. Whether or not they

44

were allied to Fritigern, Focalis really did not want them in the room next door.

A few moments later they were in their room, dumping their bags on the floor and looking around. There was a single window, glazed with warped, faintly blue-coloured glass, a single brown drape ready to pull across it and block out what light there was. This Focalis did, shutting out the cold, wet and increasingly dim world outside, trapping them in their one room for the night. Food would arrive soon, the owner quite rightly guessing that Focalis had no desire to sit and eat with the new arrivals if they stayed.

'Won't they think it odd that you'd rather eat here than downstairs?' Martius asked, as if plucking the thought from his head.

'No. I'm clearly an old soldier, and anyone retired now fought in the war. Nobody would expect a veteran, who'd waded through the blood and bones of his mates fighting Goths, to want to sit and eat with them a few short years later. They would get the same treatment from most old soldiers. They're used to it. And they might be perfectly safe and legal citizens, anyway. Not all Goths are our enemies, lad.'

'When are you going to tell me what's going on, Dad? You keep saying now is not the time, but right now we have nothing *but* time.'

Focalis nodded. He'd been thinking about that in the bath, and had all but settled on telling a half-truth. The story without some of the detail, painting the event in the best possible light.

'Alright. What do you know about the Goths?'

He'd never brought up the subject at home, and Flavia had had the good sense not to do so in Focalis' presence. Had she said anything about them while he'd been away fighting the war? Had his tutor told him anything? He'd have learned some of the basics from hearsay, no doubt, for though their house was isolated enough, the boy had attended lessons in the town, and they visited the market weekly.

'They crossed the Danubius six or seven years ago,' Martius said. 'Some new tribe was driving them south, I understand. They asked to settle in Roman lands but everything went wrong and there was an argument. The emperor led a campaign against them, but it all went wrong at Hadrianopolis and...' The lad tailed off, aware that this was the point when his father had come home from the war, dragging a wounded leg, covered in blood, some of it his own, his eyes haunted, his time in the army done forever.

'That's a summary, I suppose,' Focalis replied with a sigh, and slumped to one of the two simple cots, gesturing for Martius to do the same. The boy sank to the bed opposite, his eyes sparkling with the quest for understanding. Focalis scratched his neck.

'In those early days there were a lot of troubles and a lot of misunderstandings. The Goths were refugees in the empire, but they were also a proud warrior people. Those two things don't go too well. I was in the scholae with my mates in those days. We were riders for the emperor, but at the time we were on detached duty serving his general Lupicinus at Marcianopolis. There was a big misunderstanding, and a stupid mistake was made. I killed an important Goth, Martius.'

The boy frowned. 'It was war. Surely you were allowed?'

'This was before the war.'

This was the cause of the war. He pushed that nagging little detail back down where it belonged and continued.

46

'I killed an important Goth – a friend and ally of Fritigern, king of the Thervingi. I say *I* killed him, but it might be more accurate to say *we* killed him. The eight of us were at him and his guards, and at least three of us managed to land a blow on him. *One* of us killed him.'

'And this is the same Fritigern the courier was talking of downstairs? The king?'

Focalis nodded. 'He's had other matters to attend to since then, fighting the war against first Valens and then Valentinian, and since the peace treaty was agreed last year, he'll have been constrained. I had hoped that he wouldn't dare come for us after the treaty, in case his actions undid the agreement and plunged us all back into war again. I hadn't counted on this. If Fritigern has been deposed as a king and is now a renegade, then he and his men won't feel bound by such matters. It seems our old friend has decided that the time has come for revenge. The eight of us are in danger. His men will come for all of us.'

'And what will we do?' Martius breathed. 'Even if we find all of them and get your unit back together, what will we do? How many men does Fritigern have?'

'I have no idea, but he was a popular king, and he led a successful campaign in the war. There will be plenty of the Thervingi, and even the Greuthungi, who might decide to follow a renegade war leader rather than accepting an uneasy and unprofitable peace. I don't think he'll run out of men to throw at us any time soon.'

'So we're going to spend the rest of our lives on the run and fighting these men?'

Focalis sagged a little. 'This came sooner than I expected, but I've always known it would happen. That's why the house has been prepared these past few years, why I sleep with a sword. That's why you were trained with blade and bow when your friends were still playing with toy chariots. I'd limited my planning to getting you and your mother away and to safety, and then when she passed on, just you. Beyond that, I don't know, but I do know that Ofilius, our old decanus, has been working on a plan for years, and Sigeric, one of the others, will have been helping him. When we find them, there will be more details. For now we just have to gather the lads.'

He straightened at the sound of staff approaching along the corridor with their dinner. 'Right. Now to eat heartily and get a good night's sleep. Tomorrow could be a long day.'

3

He could tell that Martius was impressed, and rightly so. Suida was an impressive place. The new town clustered on the southern slope of the hill, a mismatched and unplanned collection of houses and shops, warehouses and taverns, a small river looping around to the west, while the old city with its thick, high white walls and magnificent gates stood on the crest, looming over the landscape. Suida had held off attacks by the Thervingi three separate times during the war, its military commander receiving a personal commendation from the emperor for his service. As though it were a legion, the city had been given the epithets 'fidelis' and 'felix', the faithful and the lucky.

The weather had held that afternoon, scudding clouds repeatedly threatening fresh rain without delivering it, the air chilly but clear. Focalis and his son had slept well that night at the mansio, and had risen early, slipping away before anyone else was up, bar the mansio's staff who provided them with a snack for the journey. They had left a generous tip for the owner, for helping them avoid the Goths the previous night.

At a small town, around about noon, they had managed to purchase a few supplies, including fresh tunics and cloaks and a bottle of wine, and they had made excellent time on the main road all day, reaching Suida as the sun slid towards the horizon.

'Where will we stay?'

Focalis shrugged. 'I don't want to impose on my old boss, so we'll find an inn somewhere. I've not been here for years, but there'll be plenty, for sure. First things first, though, we need to find Ofilius.'

'Have you been to his place before?'

A shake of the head. 'He only moved here after Hadrianopolis, when we all went our separate ways. Used his money to start a tannery and leather shop. The saddles we rode here on came from his place, a Saturnalia gift a few years ago. I've exchanged messages with him at times over the last few years though, by private courier.'

'If you were only two days apart, why have you not visited?'

Focalis sighed. 'Various reasons. We don't like to bring up the past. Meeting up reminds us of Hadrianopolis, and no one wants to remember that. Because some of us disagree over things we've done. And because we all had in the back of our minds that one day Fritigern would have the time and opportunity to come and settle an old score, and the fewer connections there were between us, the harder it would be to find us all. *I* made no effort to hide, because I was the fittest of us all and the best rider, and I stood a chance of getting to the others and warning them when it happened. Ofilius is larger than life. He couldn't hide if he tried. The others, though, they've all but disappeared unless you know where to look.'

Martius nodded, a touch of uncertainty in his manner. 'So do *you* know where to look for him?'

'He'll have a house, but it's still business hours, so he

should be at work. His workshop is off near the river on the lower slope, I understand, on the edge of town.'

'Isn't that a bit out of the way?'

'Best place for a tanner's. You'll appreciate that when we get there, believe me. Come on. I want to be talking to him before nightfall. Act natural. There may well be Goths here anyway, as some settled in the area, but most of them will be perfectly safe. Just keep your eyes and ears open as we move.'

They rode towards the outskirts, where a few shacks lined the road, children playing with a ball in a field off to one side, a mangy-looking dog lying in the road and barking at them as they passed, not quite raising the energy to actually get up. As the road began to rise very slightly, the buildings became tighter-packed and of a higher quality, the town proper clustering around them. Between the houses, Focalis could see glimpses of the small river, and so turned at the next corner and followed the contour of the lower slope just above the flow as it passed around the south and west of the hill.

He smelled Ofilius' place long before he saw it, the acrid stink of old meat and urine hanging in the air like a rancid miasma. He almost laughed at Martius' expression, the young man's face pale, eyes wide as he tried to breathe in tiny gasps to limit exposure to the smell. The old soldier became serious again as they closed on the place, though. A frontage with a single door, and beside it a wide and high gate into what had to be the tanning yard, but both remained firmly closed, no sound of activity issuing from within.

Focalis felt the first stirrings of unease, even though a cart and oxen sat in the street, a bored-looking teamster picking dirt from beneath his fingernails in the driving seat, the cart itself empty. The sun was still up, and other shops in the town had been open as they passed. It was, as he'd noted, still business hours. That Ofilius' place was closed seemed odd. His hand rose in a sign, warning Martius to be alert and to stay close, and the older man, hand going to sword hilt, rode slowly closer to the cart.

As they approached, the teamster turned at the sound, still messing with his nails, and registered their existence with a bored look.

'Good afternoon, friend,' Focalis said as he came close enough for conversation and reined in.

'Is it?'

'I think so. Is Ofilius around?'

'Bloody hope so. I was supposed to collect a consignment half an hour ago.'

Focalis' unease failed to dissipate. 'You've had no answer?'

'No. Knocked and tried both doors a dozen times. But then Ofilius is a bugger for messing people around. Maybe he forgot about the job and went home early. Or maybe he's wallowing in a tavern after losing at dice again. I waited three hours once while he drank himself stupid. I'll stick out the hour and then give up. He'll have to find another carter. I'm not pissing about like this. I have other jobs.'

Focalis glanced at Martius, who was also showing concern, then back to the teamster. 'You know where he lives?'

'Not really. I'm not from Suida. Somewhere up there, though. Wherever it is it'll be showy, the bastard,' he added, gesturing up to the walls of the old fortress-town on the hill.

'You might as well go to your other jobs,' Focalis advised him. 'When I find Ofilius I'll let him know.'

The man gave an unconcerned shrug and slowly began to move his empty cart on down the street. Once he was moving,

Focalis turned to his son. 'I don't like this. Not that he's wrong. Ofilius was a soldier through and through. Worked hard and played hard, and now that he's retired he won't have to make sure he has a clear head in the morning. But still, I want to find him fast.'

'How do we do that?'

'Somewhere up in the old town, the carter reckoned. Ofilius is not the kind of man to blend into the background. He's huge and loud, and wherever he is, he's always the centre of attention. Ask around enough and someone will be able to direct us.'

Tense now, the pair turned their mounts and passed back through the town to the main junction, where a carved stone grotesque spat a constant stream of crystal water into a fountain basin, and then turned and began the climb towards the walls. There was still at least an hour until sunset, and the streets were in that odd changeover time when shops and shoppers still abounded, but the evening drinkers and whores were already out and about. They climbed the hill on tired horses and passed through the open gateway of the old town, two men from a local unit on guard, looking uninterested and tired. A few buildings along the street from the city gate, an alleyway to one side was signed for a livery stables, and Focalis pointed to it.

'Let's get the horses stabled for the night. It'll be easier moving around on foot now, and horses tend to draw attention. Let's not tempt fate.'

Leading Martius inside, he found the proprietor and paid for the two animals for the night. As the staff took them away to stalls, Focalis called over the owner.

'I'm looking for a man.'

'Oh?'

'Ofilius. Ex-army. Runs a tanners in the lower town. Know him?'

The man snorted. '*Everyone* knows him, flash bastard.'

Focalis smiled. That sounded about right. His earlier fears were abating a little. Things sounded more normal up here, and there was no alarm registering in the stable owner's voice. 'Know where he lives? Or where he drinks if he might be there?'

'Sure. Go to the old forum in the middle, then turn left down the Decumanus. You'll find a tavern called the Scorpion about halfway down. He could be in there. If he's on a bender, he'll be there. If he is, tell him I'm still waiting for my new harnesses. If he's not there, take the second right just inside the walls. You can't miss his house. It's about halfway down the street, and it's the only one with columns.'

'Thanks. Make sure our kit is stored somewhere secure, and I'll make it worth your while. We'll be back for the horses in the morning.'

With that, he and Martius left the stable and moved off through the old town. With the traditional planning of such an ancient place, Suida was built on a grid, with main streets in the four cardinal directions, meeting at a forum in the centre. As they reached that heart òf the city, a market was in the final stages of packing away for the day, while men stood around the doors of taverns laughing and shouting. An archaic temple of Rome and the Augustus stood in pride of place by the basilica, though a more recent church had been raised deliberately close by, so as to overshadow it. Few citizens would visit the temple these days, but it remained intact and proud, where many had gone, for to remove a symbol of the imperial cult was to risk insulting the emperor. Ignoring market, citizens and temples alike, they turned, pulling their cloaks tighter about themselves, and strode off down the western street.

As he moved through the town, Focalis' gaze flipped back and forth between every face they passed, looking for any hint of malice or any sign of enemies. Half a dozen times he saw men in armour and with beards, but each seemed to be of local origin, none of them resembling the Goths of Fritigern. Still, he remained on the alert as they walked. Once more away from the easy familiarity of the stable owner, the sense of disquiet was growing again within Focalis, and his gaze populated every darkened doorway with imagined enemies.

The Scorpion was precisely the sort of dive that Flavia had always told him to stay away from, and, naturally, exactly the sort of dive that had been popular with their unit. The sign beside the door had a picture of an old-fashioned soldier in white with a scorpion emblazoned on his shield, the sign of the Praetorian Guard, gone for almost a century now, the forerunner of Focalis' own unit. And Ofilius'. Men inside laughed and sang, and the smell of roasting meat and cheap wine flooded out into the street. It was clearly a soldiers' bar, and the chances of any Goth frequenting it were small. Still, Focalis was on his guard.

'Watch yourself here. Keep one hand on your purse and the other on your hilt. Should be fine, but you never know.'

With that, he stepped in through the doorway. The place clearly catered for veterans. A sign above the bar reminded everyone that Suida was *fidelis* and *felix*, a throwing axe stuck into the timber between the two words, whether by design or accident, Focalis couldn't guess. One side was occupied by the bar, its dimpled surface filled with small treats and saleable items, the stone wall behind it obscured by amphorae of wine and casks of beer. Another wall was largely taken up with a fireplace which roared with golden heat, a huge stack of logs beside it. The other two walls were decorated with trophies, smaller versions of the official ones visible in great cities or near old battle sites, formed of captured armour, shields and weapons. He wondered how often the city's garrison was called out when some drunken idiot started playing with the trophies and using the weapons.

The place was smoky and warm and dingy. Focalis stopped just a few paces inside to look around. Martius halted behind him, an air of intrigue about the lad. The majority of raucous activity stopped at their arrival, arm-wrestling matches pausing with fists entwined and muscles bulging, dice clattering across tables and left where they lay as the owners turned to the door. What the patrons saw evidently put them at ease, for they went back to their leisure a moment later. Focalis was quite clearly a veteran himself, and any old soldier could recognise a kindred spirit. Martius raised a few eyebrows, but with Focalis there, no one was going to argue.

He could see no sign of Ofilius in the room, but to be certain, he threaded his way between tables to the bar and called over the owner.

'What'll you have?'

'Maybe later,' Focalis replied. 'I'm looking for Ofilius. He been in?'

The man shrugged. 'Last night. *All* night. Had to shove him out on his arse in the small hours. Not today though. Probably sleeping off his sore head. Any normal man who drank what he did last night would be busy searching high and low for what was left of his liver.'

'Thanks.'

'No problem.'

With that, Focalis pushed his way back across the room, picking up Martius and stepping out into the street, eyes going to every shadowy recess in sight, making sure they were all clear.

'He could be at home, hung-over. It would explain a lot. Too hung-over to be bothered with a cartload of leather. And his staff wouldn't be able to get in and work if he didn't turn up. We need to go find his house, then.'

They walked on, following the directions the gate guards had given them. As they turned into that final street, a quieter one on the edge of the walled upper town with no one wandering around, he fixed on the house ahead. The man had been right. You couldn't miss Ofilius' house. The rest were of cobblestone to the level of the windows and timber above, mostly single-floor. The old decanus's house spoke of opulence. The whole building was of the same white stone as the city walls, two storeys, with a pair of pristine columns flanking the door. This far from the centre there were no shops built into the street-facing walls of the houses, and all was staid and quiet, no movement or noise in the street.

Focalis felt a flood of relief as, even at this distance, he could see the faint glow of lights in the place. The house was at least occupied. He picked up the pace, a slight smile finally reaching his face. It had been four years, and he'd missed the bastard, both the hard taskmaster in the field and the loud braggart in the bar.

'Dad...'

He slowed again, turning. Martius had stopped. He followed suit with a frown.

'What?'

'Dad, there's someone there.'

Instinct took over, and Focalis immediately hurried his boy over to the side of the street, dipping into the shadows between two buildings.

'Where?'

'I just saw a shape. In a doorway opposite the house.'

Focalis leaned out and looked down the street. He'd been so focused on Ofilius' house that he'd not fully taken in the surroundings, which was stupid, given how observant he'd been through the rest of town. His guard had dropped with the relief that the house was occupied. Now, though, he saw the figure. Martius had the sharp eyes of youth, and Focalis probably wouldn't have seen the man even if he'd been looking. He was lurking in a deep recess between houses, and it was only occasionally, as he stretched or changed position, that a limb showed black in the evening light, giving away his location.

'Who is he?' Martius breathed.

'No idea. But whoever it is, he's watching Ofilius' house and trying not to be noticed, so he's definitely up to no good. Is he alone, though?'

He sucked on his lip, trying to decide on the best course of action. He tried to picture a bird's eye view of the street. The houses on that side would be built butted up to the city walls, just as they had been on the street where they'd entered the city. The place was packed in tight. That meant that no one could be watching the back of the house, and there were narrow alleys here and there between the houses, such as the one where they now lurked, but they were too narrow for windows to open onto, for there would be no light, and a place like the one Ofilius had built would not have a side door into such a dingy space. That meant there was only one way in or out, which meant only one place to watch.

Logic suggested that the man in the shadows was alone, though he could not definitely rule out the presence of another, especially in the alley at the far side of Ofilius' house. A direct approach was dangerous, then, for if the man was *not* alone, Focalis would be presenting his back to the others.

Ofilius could not know about the watcher, surely? The man who had commanded their tent party with an iron hand, drilling into them all the life lessons that had kept them alive over years of war, would have removed a watcher like that, if he knew about him. No matter how much he might let himself go of an evening, the Ofilius Focalis knew was never more than a step from being in parade stance.

Decision made.

He turned to Martius. 'Stay here and stay back, deep in the shadows. Don't even show in the street until I call for you.'

'What are you going to do, Dad?'

'Best you don't think on that, lad.'

The boy shuddered and Focalis clamped his hand on Martius' shoulder, squeezed once, and then turned and walked away. As he reached the edge of the street, he glanced left. Again, for now, there was no indication of the lurker, which suggested that he was back in his hiding place and watching the house intently. Quickly, Focalis counted the number of buildings between him and the watcher and estimated the distance. Suida was built on a very regular grid pattern, after all. Trusting that the man was concentrating on the house, he stepped out into the open and moved across the street, swiftly but carefully. Once there, out of sight of the watcher, he turned and retreated along the street the way they had come, once more counting houses and paces and adding them to his totals. At the corner, he turned left and then shortly thereafter left again, into a street parallel with Ofilius', a single block closer to the forum. There, he moved his way down, at speed but keeping to a regular pace. One thing that two decades of marching and parading with a unit will teach a man is how to keep a very regular step and estimate distances. As he moved, counting, he periodically looked down the occasional dark alleyways. A few were dead ends, one house deep. Others cut right across the block to the street he had just left.

It was with some satisfaction that when he had counted off the number of houses, he found he was within a half-dozen error margin for steps too. Slowing, he approached the mouth of the shadowed alley of the watcher. There he stopped. It took a few moments to see the length of the narrow passage and to identify the slight movement at the far end. Just as he'd hoped, the place the man lurked was an alley that cut through from street to street.

He listened carefully. Above the general background hum of a living, active city, there were two noises insisting themselves. The wind created an almost continual whispering, and somewhere along the alley, water from one of the recent rainstorms had pooled and was dripping down into the darkness with a regular repetitive 'pat, pat, pat'.

Carefully, Focalis reached up and removed his scarf, then tied it around his leg, pinning his scabbard to it and preventing the sword clonking as he walked. He was not armoured and his shield was still on his horse. Reaching down, he removed his dagger from its sheath, a long, straight blade with a simple, well-worn leather-bound hilt.

Ready, he began to move down the alley, slowly and lightly. Each footstep he timed with the pattering of falling water, a pace to each drip, largely masking the sound, especially with the wind whispering around them. Moving with the grace of a dancer, he swiftly traversed the alley. As he passed the centre point, he found the dripping and made sure to move along the far side of the alley so that his body did not dampen the sound for the waiting lurker.

He could see the figure now in silhouette. The man still had his back to the alley, eyes on Ofilius' door. As he moved, Focalis could gradually make out more detail. The man wore no helmet, nor chain shirt. He had a sword at his side and a tunic that could belong to anyone. What gave him pause, though, was that the man's legs were encased in well-fitted breeches that terminated below the knees, where leg wrappings began all the way down to the boots. He couldn't quite see the detail clearly, but the outline shape was unmistakable, and it suggested a Roman, not a Goth. Doubt began to assail him even as he paced carefully forward. Could there be other reasons men might be watching Ofilius' house? Of course there could. Something to do with competition in the leather trade, angry losers from dice games, or even just thieves eying up a prosperous house. And killing a Roman citizen was dangerous, not to mention sinful. He wracked his brain for a solution, and hit upon one as he closed.

He was no more than five paces from the watcher.

As he took the next step, his grip tightened on the knife in preparation. He opened his mouth.

'Gawaknan.'

'*Wake up,*' in the tongue of the Goths.

The way the man turned told him everything he needed to know. The man understood him, even if he simultaneously registered both surprise and alarm. He spoke the Goth tongue, and it was a rare Roman who could do so.

He leapt. The man had been so unprepared for him that he only had his blade a hand-width from the mouth of his scabbard before Focalis was on him. His left arm went over the man's shoulder, around the back of his neck, pulling him forward onto the blade held in his right. He stabbed upwards, the long knife entering the man's belly just below the bottom rib, but angled so that it cut upwards behind the ribcage, finding the heart with the practised ease of the trained killer.

The Goth died in his arms, gasping, arm jerking as he still tried to draw his sword. Focalis let him fall to the grimy alley floor and used a foot to nudge him back into the deeper shadows. He untied the scarf around his leg and used it to clean the blood from the knife before sheathing it. The scarf would wash. A moment later he stepped out into the street and scanned the surroundings.

There was no movement and no sign of alarm in the alleyway opposite, beside Ofilius' house. The watcher had been alone after all. Had he not been, any ally would by now be running at Focalis. Stepping out into the open, he looked back down the street and gestured to where he'd waited earlier.

'Martius.'

His boy emerged from their hiding place and hurried up the street to join him. He looked his father up and down, perhaps surprised not to find him coated with gore. Then Martius looked into the alley, but could see only a vague lump on the ground in the darkness.

'It's done. He was one of Fritigern's, I'm convinced.'

'And he was alone? Weren't there six sent for *you*, Dad?'

'He's alone *here*, probably not in the town. If I'd been more alert I'd have looked for watchers down at his tannery. I'd be willing to wager there were a couple there if there's one here. They've not been here long, I reckon. I think they're still trying to find him. The ones down at the tannery had probably pulled back safely out of sight while the carter was there. But there will definitely be others in the city. We need to be really careful, lad. But for now, let's see if Ofilius is at home.'

Crossing the street, he approached the door between the rather ostentatious columns and reached for the knocker, which he couldn't help but note had been made from a two-and-a-half-pound ballista ball. Lifting it, he clacked it against the bronze plate hard, three times. There was an extended silence, and then, finally, footsteps. His pulse, which had been racing since they arrived on this street, began to slow a little with the relief that someone was coming, and it was no Goth, else there would have been no one watching the door. After some time, the door cracked open.

There could be no doubting that this was Ofilius' doorkeeper. A soldier knew the quality of the man he put in charge of his threshold. Otho had been selected by Focalis, and he'd had endless confidence in the man. This fellow, chosen by their former leader, was astoundingly big and astonishingly ugly. The muscles in his arms were a match for Focalis' thighs, and the man's flesh was such a criss-cross and patchwork of scars and burns that very little plain flesh remained. What there was held the remnants of tattoos, most of which were made illegible by scar tissue. What this man had originally been, Focalis couldn't guess, but he'd hate to meet him in a dark alley.

'I'm here to see the master. We served together.'

As confirmation of this, he lifted his sleeve to show the tattoo on his right bicep, an eagle gripping the sun in its talons, the number II below. Ofilius had the same tattoo. They all did. The doorman looked him up and down, a hungry predator sizing up the meat value of prey, but then gave a single, curt nod. 'Wait here,' he said. No messing about. Focalis did just that as the door closed to a crack.

But his hearing was perhaps better than the man thought, for he could hear an exchange beyond the almost-closed door.

'Mumble mumble mumble, master.' The doorman sounded unsure.

'Mumble mumble business.' A female voice, sharp, authoritative.

'Mumble mumble mumble *scholae*.'

'Mumble.'

He'd not quite caught that last bit, but if questioned he would be willing to wager the word had been 'truth.' There was a pause, and after a few moments two sets of footsteps going in opposite directions, the heavy, male ones back towards the door, which opened with a creak once more.

'Master Ofilius is not here,' the man said.

Alarms began to go off once again for Focalis. Maybe he was in hiding, for he knew Fritigern's men were around? The old bastard might be a bit showy and loud in his civilian life, but the moment he strapped on a sword and rammed a crest into the holder, he was all business, and he was the best there was. Absence was no guarantee of disaster.

'Where is he,' Focalis asked, voice flat and calm, but carrying just a modicum of menace, his eye holding that of the big man.

'I don't know.'

'This is important,' he insisted.

The doorman harrumphed, then looked over his shoulder, Focalis suspected to make sure that very authoritative woman wasn't in earshot. He turned back. 'The master was at the morning feast today. Apparently it was a special occasion.'

'Morning feast?' Martius asked, confused.

Focalis held up a hand to forestall any further discussion, addressing the doorman again.

'He's still a Leo, I bet? Been looking to be sponsored up to Perses for years.'

The man gave him a suspicious look. Focalis shrugged. 'Where's the cave, then?'

He tried to ignore the baffled look Martius was giving him. The doorman seemed to consider this for a while, and then folded his arms. 'Just inside the north gate. Road to the right. Between a wine warehouse and a brothel, opposite the summer baths.'

Focalis smiled grimly. 'It's true what they say, you know? Nothing is worse for the body than bathing, sex and drink, but nothing makes life worth living like bathing, sex and drink.' He became serious once more in a moment. 'He went there this morning, and you've not seen him since?'

'No. But sometimes the master continues to drink after the ceremony, and goes out around town with the others, or they just sit in their cave and get hammered. I've had to go in and carry him out before now. They're secret, and outsiders aren't allowed in, but it seems to be alright if it's to collect a pissed-up initiate.'

'Thank you, my big friend. With luck we'll have your master back here shortly, but be prepared. He will likely want to move on quickly. And keep an eye out. Your house was being watched from across the street by a Goth with a grudge. You know the tale?'

The man gave a nod, his face hardening. He did. And he was Ofilius' man through and through.

'Then keep an eye out and have the staff on alert. Things could get nasty fast.' With that, he turned, and he and Martius strode back along the street.

'What in God's name was all that about?' the lad asked, after the door was closed and they had moved on.

'Ofilius and his temple.'

'What?'

'Local Mithraeum. They have ritual meals and they're not always in the evening. Never been to one myself, but I've known some of their lot, including Ofilius, to hit a three-day bender after one of their big religious feasts.'

The lad stared at him. 'Your boss was a *pagan*?'

'Now now, lad. There's no law against worshipping whoever the hell you want in this empire. It's one of the things that always made us great. Most of the people you meet now are wearing the cross, or the fish or the chi-rho and such, but I remember a couple of decades ago when I wasn't sure the Church of Peter were going to survive. Christ, lad, but just before you were born we had Julian on the throne, and our kind were almost outlawed again. And you've never fought a war, Martius. It's easy to espouse high morals when you've only ever known comfort. But in the press of battle, when there's only one mistake between life and shitting round a Persian blade, you'd be surprised where men turn. I've known avid Christians who've poured wine offerings to Jupiter Optimus Maximus before a battle. And Mithras is not so far removed from us, to be honest.'

'Dad, every command of his you followed, your *soul* was in danger.'

'But in fairness, Martius, no one was ever trying to stick a sword through my soul, and Ofilius saved my skin more than once. Things are different in the army. You have to understand, lad.'

His son's eyes narrowed. 'Tell me you've never prayed to these demons, Dad.'

'Son, I've prayed to every name from Jesus to Isis to Fuck-it-all and back when times were bad. I fought for Julian. He might have had us renounce Christ, but what an emperor he was, Martius. Maybe if we still had his like, and Zeus throwing around thunderbolts, the empire wouldn't be in the shit it's in.'

Martius was giving him odd looks.

'When we find Ofilius and the others,' Focalis said sternly, 'keep opinions like this to yourself.'

'There are other pagans in your unit?'

'Not as such. But in the army you'll find men who kiss the cross and yet drink for Mithras. Sometimes the lines blur. Now come on. We have to find this Mithraeum. I have a feeling we're in a race now with Fritigern's men, and we want to win.'

They picked up the pace then, hurrying through the streets of Suida, using the grid plan as a guide to move in a more or less north-easterly direction, zigzagging rather than taking the long way round via the central square. The light was fading fast, and the changeover in the streets from the daytime world to the night-time one was well underway. Shops were closing, bars opening, children were inside now, whores, beggars and drunks out. They reached the cardo not far from the north gate, which was being closed for the night by the guard. Suida was faithful and lucky, but it was not going to trust its survival to chance in a world where tribes crossed the river without fear, and emperors died on the field of battle. Suida survived the war because it was careful as well as lucky, and so the gates were closed at night.

Ignoring the gate, they took the road opposite that led along the inside of the north walls, lined mostly with warehouses and shops on their left, a variety of buildings on the right. Not bars, though, in this less salubrious area. The bars would be closer to the centre.

Some way along the street, far enough from the gate to be out of the guards' line of sight, Focalis spotted their destination in the evening gloom. The doorman had been accurate. A warehouse with a multi-arched brick frontage loomed dark and closed, locked up for the night, the name of the owner emblazoned by the door on a marble tablet. Opposite, a medium-sized bath house had clearly recently closed for the night, for though the door was resolutely shut, there was still a faint golden glow from the windows, and steam continued to rise from the outlets above it. Beyond the warehouse, on the northern side of the street, a rather nondescript insula could have been any ordinary housing but for the sign hanging out front, well-lit and displaying an image that looked physically impractical, though alluring all the same. And between that house of delights and the gloomy storehouse lay a simple single-storey frontage with just a door that stood open, a glow showing from within.

Hope welled up once more. The Mithraeum was occupied, for if it was not in use, that strange and secretive sect would most certainly have locked the place up in darkness. And they clung together like a unit of soldiers, the initiates of the mysteries, for they usually were just that. Which meant that there was no place safer for a follower to take refuge than in the arms of his brothers. Only a madman would take on a Mithraeum full of veteran soldiers, after all.

Something made him shiver suddenly. Despite the rising optimism he felt at the realisation that the place was still occupied and very likely the decanus was inside, something was amiss. He slowed very slightly and listened hard.

'What is it, Dad?' Martius murmured.

'Keep quiet and keep walking.'

As they moved down the street, he listened again. The wind was still groaning around the skies, lamenting the season, and the hum of the city was there as a gentle background sound, along with the very distant murmur of the guards at the gate and the faintest sound of conversation from either the Mithraeum or the brothel ahead. But there was one other sound, so subtle and careful that unless you knew it was there, you'd never hear it.

The man's footsteps were synchronous with those of Focalis, so that the pursuit was almost perfectly hidden. His instinct had warned him, and the moment he'd slowed, it had taken two steps for their shadow to adjust his own pace. A tiny flaw, but a giveaway if you were waiting for it. His mind raced. There seemed little doubt that it was one of

Fritigern's warriors. Where had they picked him up? Had he been watching the house somewhere unseen? Had he perhaps been following them ever since the tannery, but been too slow to stop Focalis taking out the watcher? Or had he been moving in on the Mithraeum but seen Focalis and his son on their own way there, and dropped carefully back? They were dangerous bastards, but Suida was a well-patrolled and controlled city with a sizeable garrison and a strong rule of law. They would be careful to take him on only where the guards could not see, far enough down this street to be away from the gate.

Their pursuer was alone. Only one set of footsteps. Martius had a sword belted at his waist just like Focalis, and he was old enough and tall enough to pass as a young man capable of holding his own in a fight. In fact, thanks to years of being trained, he could do just that. That was probably why the man was hanging back. He wouldn't take on two at once. But Focalis wanted him. Wanted to know about the others here and what their plans were. It was all well and good putting a knife through men sent after you, but they had a large number of men to throw at him, and sooner or later he was going to have to take one alive for interrogation. Perhaps better now, when the chance had arisen.

'We're being followed,' he whispered. 'Keep walking and don't speak.'

His eyes raked the street. There were no side alleys here. He toyed with the idea of sending Martius into the brothel, but winced at the thought. Flavia would spin in her grave and curse him from heaven for doing such a thing. But equally, he didn't yet want to risk putting the lad into a fight. Soon he was going to have to consider sending Martius away for his own safety. And he definitely did not want the lad to watch him torture a Goth for information. That sort of thing tended to put you off people. For now, then, that left only one option.

'Keep going and make for the Mithraeum. The door is open and the light on, so they're still in there. They don't take kindly to intruders, but as soon as they confront you, tell them who you are, and Ofilius at least will vouch for you. Wait there until I join you.'

'I can help.'

'Not this time. Go, and I'll catch up when we're safe.'

Martius, looking less than happy, picked his pace up, pulling out ahead, marching towards that glowing sanctuary. Focalis, on the other hand, slowed again, letting the boy get further and further ahead. Once Martius was approaching the Mithraeum, Focalis stopped altogether. His hand went to the hilt of the sword at his side.

'I give you a chance,' he said, loudly. 'I know your people took the cross when you entered our lands. I know you pray to the Lord, and so in the spirit of Christian brotherhood, I offer you this one chance. Tell me what I want to know, and then turn around and walk away. I will not follow you, nor will I hunt you down as you have us.'

The footsteps continued for a moment, and a shape emerged from the gloom at the side of the street. The man was tall, armoured with a chain shirt, his black hair long and wild, his beard neatly trimmed. He also had his hand on his sword hilt. Focalis could not see his face clearly, other than the flashing of white, sharp eyes in the gathering gloom.

'You cannot take the moral ground here, king-slayer,' the Goth spat.

'What's done is done, and was done in the name of an emperor long dead. Let it go. Walk away. But tell me where the others are. There was one at the house. One or two at the tannery, I'd guess. Where are the others?'

'Close enough,' the man grunted in his thickly accented Greek.

Focalis felt a chill run through him. Had he miscalculated? The sudden thought that perhaps the lamp in the Mithraeum had been lit by one of these men and not the initiates after all leapt into his mind. Surely not? They would not get in if it was locked up, and to take it when occupied by ex-soldiers would be a hard task.

'Where is Fritigern?'

'Fuck off, king-slayer.'

The man's sword emerged from its sheath with a metallic hiss, its gleaming blade catching the meagre light and casting it in flashes around the evening shadows. Focalis gave a single nod and drew his own sword. 'I will be damned for what I did. We all will be. That should be enough for you and your renegade king.'

'You are a liar, a betrayer and a murderer,' the Goth spat. 'You and all your friends. You will all die hard in this life before you burn eternally for what you've done.'

Focalis bit his lip and took a step towards the man, hefting his blade. He'd planned to get information, either willingly or through determined extraction once he'd put the Goth down, but now he was worrying about Martius, and time was of great importance. Another step and he ran. His sword came up, held tight in his right hand, ready to swing down in a brutal crosswise motion. The Goth stepped out into the full light, such as it was, and Focalis saw his eyes follow the rising blade even as he brought his own round ready to parry the blow. What the man did not see was Focalis' other hand.

Even as he leapt into the fight, the sword coming down rather predictably, his left hand pulled that wicked, straight-edged knife from its sheath. His sword met the Goth's and was turned aside, but before the man could retaliate, Focalis' other arm slashed back across. The man's chain shirt had sleeves only to the elbow, and the knife slashed through the mustard-coloured tunic of his forearm, scything deep into flesh. His grip on the blade was tight, and the metal tore free with a spray of blood.

The Goth bellowed in pain, and Focalis wondered in that instant whether the fight would be audible as far away as the gate and its guards. No matter who started the scuffle and whose fault it was, they would both be in trouble if they were caught fighting with open blades in the streets. He had no time to ponder it further, though. He had to put the man down, and fast.

The Goth had staggered back, cursing, his sword shaking in his fingers, for the pain in his forearm was weakening his grip. This time, as Focalis ran at him, he lifted his bloody knife in his hand and brought it forth toward the man's neck. At the same time, he swung his sword the other way and lower, reaching for his knee. The Goth was in trouble. He had only rudimentary control of his own sword, and here came two strikes at once – a killing blow aimed for the throat and a crippling one for the leg. In a panic at his sudden ill-fortune, the man threw his sword in the way of the low blow, and had no choice but to try and deflect the knife with his empty hand. Both failed to some extent. The weakness of his sword arm supplied insufficient force to stop Focalis' sword. Robbed of some of its power, the blow failed to break the knee or hack into the leg, but the two meeting blades did slam against his thigh with muscle-deadening strength. At the same time, the Goth managed to prevent the knife from sinking into his throat, but only at the expense of his hand. The long, straight blade slashed through his palm and ripped the hand up the middle, tearing free between ring and middle fingers so that the appendage flopped into two.

Now the man truly screamed as his deadened leg folded and he fell.

He was out of the fight and stood no chance. Had Focalis the time, he could now, he was convinced, extract any information or confession he liked from the man. But he *didn't* have time. Not only may he have sent Martius into a temple full of Goths, but that last scream must have been heard at the gate, and any time now the city garrison could come pounding along the road. It would take days to argue his way out of his arrest, even if they listened to him, standing over a butchered body as he was. No, they had to go. He had to get Martius, see if Ofilius was there after all, and run before they were grabbed by the guard.

Dropping, he simply slammed his knife into the crippled and agonised Goth's throat, driving the blade through windpipe and muscle and into the man's spine before pulling it free. He rose then, and ran, without a glance back towards the city gate.

Even as he closed on the Mithraeum, his worst fears were rising once more, and they crested with horror as a figure emerged from the temple doorway. The Goth was unarmoured and held a sword in a loose grip, blood spattered all over him.

Martius' blood?

His pulse thundered with panic as he closed on the man. The Goth turned at the sound of running feet and looked up, brow creased. He saw Focalis, and it gave the Roman hope to note that the Goth was wounded, the blood across his tunic apparently his own. While one hand still gripped his sword, the other was clamped to his side, where the tunic was soaked with dark, glistening blood. He looked this way and that, clearly trying to decide between fight or flight, but swiftly realised he wasn't going to get far. He turned, gritting his teeth, and raised his sword.

Focalis was in no mood for any kind of fancy attack now. Martius was clearly in danger if not already dead, and the city garrison would be upon them in no time. He ran at the man and hit him hard, sword knocking away the Goth's blade even as he tried to swing, faltering with the pain this caused in his wound. In a flurry of grunts and curses, he and the Goth hit the filthy stones of the street, the man only saved from concussion against the hard stone because his head happened to hit a large pile of horse manure as he fell.

The wind had been knocked out of them both and, pressed together on the ground, their swords were of little use. Focalis' other hand pushed down, gripping his knife, and the wounded, winded Goth desperately tried to grab the descending wrist, holding the knife away. For a long moment they were locked in that strange embrace, both sword hands occupied but unable to bring their weapons to bear, other hands engaged in a struggle to either drive the knife down into its victim or to keep it away and push it back. Focalis was surprised at the man's remaining strength, given the state of him, and was suddenly glad he was only facing him already wounded. He would have been a harder proposition than the bastard that had been following them.

Knowing he had to break the stalemate before they were both arrested, he did the only thing he could. He rolled slightly onto his left without letting up the pressure on the knife. The man beneath him exploded in a yelp of pain as Focalis pressed on his wounded side. It was enough. The agony distracted the man just enough for his grip to falter, and the knife slammed down into his chest, grating unpleasantly between ribs. The Roman continued to push, angling the blade first this way, then that, maximising the damage. The man cried out again, his sword falling from his hand. He was done, and Focalis was all but out of time. He leapt up, weapons still in hand and, ignoring the dying man on the ground, turned and staggered into the glowing doorway of the temple, heaving in breaths.

He'd never been in a Mithraeum before, though he knew a little about the mystery and its temple. Initiates were very tight-lipped about their cult, but any man tends to open up halfway down a jar of wine, and Focalis had heard enough over the years. He was therefore not at all surprised by the room inside the door. A vestibule for the temple, the room was highly stylised. Up to around knee height the walls were painted browns and greens, in a vague representation of the land, and above that they were daubed in imitation of the sky, arcing from morning to evening, almost powder blue around the entrance he stepped through, gradually fading to deep purple-blue at the door opposite. Birds hung motionless forever in the morning sky, and stars were emerging in the deeper colour near the far door. Pegs at both sides of the room were there to hold the initiates' cloaks, so that they could enter the temple itself in their ritual gowns. No cloaks hung on the pegs right now, but that was no surprise, for the weather had not been bad enough to warrant their use.

His grip tightened at the sound of footsteps, and he turned to the doorway that led into the temple proper, the two rooms separated by a pair of heavy drapes of deep black, sewn with small silver stars. Everything in the cult was symbolic, even the curtains. Focalis prepared himself for the worst as the curtains twitched and a figure emerged from the gloom beyond.

His heart leapt and lurched with a conflicting flurry of emotions at the sight of Martius. That he was standing, walking even, was enough of a relief to completely floor him, yet even as he registered the fact that his son was alive, he also noted the blood all over the lad – soaking him, not just spattered – and far too much to have come just from the man who'd staggered out into the street. His eyes darted this way and that across his son, trying to find the wound, but identifying none. Even as they did, he also picked up on the blood running down his son's sword blade and dripping to the floor in a spotted trail. But perhaps the most shudder-inducing thing was the look on Martius' face. His expression was one of utter horror, his skin almost white, eyes wide and mouth turned down, lip trembling.

'Are you hurt?' Focalis gasped, taking a step forward, sword and knife held safely out to the sides.

He almost collapsed with relief when Martius shook his head, his mouth opening but nothing emerging. The boy was in shock. From what, Focalis could only guess, though seemingly Martius had taken a life for the first time, and that always hit a man hard, no matter how strong he was. Then there was all that blood...

Martius staggered over to the wall and leaned against it. His shoulder left a smear of dark red as he moved, disfiguring the beautiful sky of the painting. Focalis, still aware of the danger they were in and of the likely arrival of the Suida garrison, weighed up the options. He had to go inside. He hated leaving Martius, especially in this state, but the lad should be safe for just a few moments.

Taking a deep breath, he thrust a finger at his son.

'Wait there.'

The boy said nothing. He did not look over-inclined to move anyway. Swallowing the tension, Focalis took a couple of steps and pulled aside the starry-night drapes.

The Mithraeum was a cave. They were all like that. Mithras was in some ways a pagan reflection of Christ. He was an old god from the east, who had slayed a bull in a cave and brought forth light and the world, or some such heretical guff. The details had never interested Focalis beyond being just another god to beg for aid during a fight for your life. But every Mithraeum was designed as a replica of the cave where Mithras had killed the bull, and each was appropriately dark, gloomy and low.

The temple was of simple form. A single room with a vaulted roof, lined with low benches to each side of a central aisle, a painted image of Mithras slaying the bull at the far end, towering above several altars, and statues of what had to be the god's attendants near the entrance. The benches were still littered with the detritus of what must have been an impressive feast, and the room was lit with low, guttering lamps, sufficient to see by, but not bright enough to ruin the subterranean atmosphere of the cave-temple.

What Focalis could not miss, though – and what, despite

the form of the temple, had become the very centre of focus – was the body.

He felt his spirits sink to a new low.

Ofilius was dead. *Very* dead. Focalis had heard stories of the death of the great Caesar, ambushed at the threshold of the senate and stabbed twenty-three times, his body torn and rent and swaddled in blood. Ofilius could have passed for the great dictator. There were so many sword wounds on him it was hard to make out a swathe of untouched flesh. Only his face seemed to have survived unscathed, helping Focalis identify him. Even in death, Ofilius' face bore a snarl of defiance.

And it seemed he had fought his corner, even taken off guard in the temple. Two more bodies were visible a little further along, lying before the altars, hacked and cut, their blood spread out in a wide pool. Ofilius had taken down two of the bastards before he'd fallen to the third. Casting an eye over the scene, Focalis guessed the fight had not been more than a quarter of an hour ago. God, but the decanus had probably still been alive and fighting for his life in the temple while Focalis and his son talked to the doorman on the far side of town.

Martius had clearly been the one to deliver the mortal blow to the third Goth's side, avenging the decanus at least a little. Focalis' gaze fell back to the body in the central aisle of the temple. Ofilius was dead. Ofilius was their leader. He was the man with the plan. The man who would know what to do. It was on Ofilius that Focalis had been resting his hopes. And he'd been so damn close. Had they risen from sleep an hour earlier this morning, they'd probably have found the man here and either swept him away to safety or at least been able to stand with him and fight off Fritigern's killers.

'Shit.'

He stood for some time, contemplating his failure and the body before him, and then realised with a start that it was not over. *Far* from over, in fact. And here he was standing like a moon-struck moron, staring at a body. He had a son standing outside. The guard would most certainly be coming and would arrest anyone they found now. And with two dead here, two out in the street and one in an alleyway opposite Ofilius' house, there was an extremely high probability that a sixth Goth was still at work somewhere in Suida.

They had to leave. Immediately.

Almost immediately.

Signing the shape of the cross over the body, Focalis said a quick prayer for his old friend's soul as he shifted both blades to his left hand. Then, because he was also a pragmatist and knew damn well that Ofilius would have pulled him to pieces over that, he also bent down, fishing out a coin, and opened the old man's mouth, pressing the coin beneath his tongue to pay the ferryman, then closing it again. Maybe God was the only god. Maybe not. The decanus deserved the best of both. In a last moment of respect, he bent and closed Ofilius' eyes, his own gaze falling on the amulet around the man's neck. On a whim that he might pay for with his soul, he took it and tucked it away as he rose once more.

With a heavy heart tempered only by the need for alacrity, he turned and pushed his way back through the drapes.

'Did you see...' began Martius.

'Yes.' Focalis grabbed his son by the shoulder and pulled him out into the centre of the room. 'Snap out of it. We're still in danger. There'll be another of Fritigern's killers out there, and the city garrison will arrest anyone with a blade or spattered with blood. They have to be aware there's trouble by now.'

Still, Martius seemed lost, unfocused. Focalis clenched his teeth. Damn it, but he didn't want to do this. Bringing back his hand, he delivered a stinging slap to his son's cheek. Martius' head snapped round with the blow, but when he turned, wide-eyed, back to face his father, there was a spark in him once more.

'Dad?'

'We need to go. You can mope or cry or panic or pray later, but if we don't go now you'll be doing it in the custody of the city garrison. Come on.'

Grabbing him and pulling him forward, Focalis burst out into the street. His heart faltered once more at a cry from the right, and as he looked over he could see a small group of uniformed men running their way, shouting at them to stand where they were. Focalis considered his options for a moment and a moment only. Martius was still in shock, they were in an unfamiliar city and now being hunted. He had to buy time.

Reaching down, he pulled free from his belt the pouch of silver, bronze and copper coins they had been using since they left. 'Come on,' he said again, and even slightly stunned, the urgency in his tone had Martius springing to life and running after him. Focalis pounded on a few paces, and then turned to the brothel, where two of the women were just visible. On a normal night, they'd be hanging out of upstairs windows or standing by the door, half-naked and trying to attract custom. The violence had driven them inside, but only just, and only for a short while, and the two who would normally be in the street were only just inside the door.

'Evening ladies,' Focalis shouted. 'Free money,' he added,

then ripped the purse wide and threw it into the air before running on. With his son at his heel, he raced down the street as the whores poured out of the building into the open street, unafraid in the face of several nights' takings for free. Twenty paces down the street, he turned and looked back and was gratified to see the entire street blocked by excitable prostitutes and a few beggars who had appeared from nowhere. He could no longer see the city watch on the far side, and if he couldn't see them, it was a good bet that they couldn't see him.

Grabbing Martius with his free hand, he jerked the lad to the right and made for a narrower side street. They continued to run at pace. Focalis spared a moment to look at his son. The lad was still pale and wide-eyed, but a touch of colour was creeping back now, and he seemed a little more purposeful and together. He would be fine in time, if they *had* time. As long as they reached safety soon.

Taking advantage of the time he had bought with the bag of coins, he led them across or around a series of junctions and along a variety of streets of different sizes. He reasoned that the guard had not seen them up close and would only be able to identify them by clothes and blades at a distance. Consequently, as they emerged into a small square between houses where a fountain burbled away at the centre, he came to a halt and told Martius to do the same.

There, he quickly dipped his blades into the water and gave them a rub, shifting the blood and gore from them until they gleamed clean and wet. He then removed his scarf and used it to dry them, sheathing them once more. Grabbing the sword from his son, he did the same with that, and as Martius slid it home once more, his father looked him up and down.

'Both of us are bloody, but you look like you work in a

slaughterhouse. Wish we had our packs with us, but we'll just have to live with wet clothes for now.'

With that, he peeled off his tunic, hissing at the various bruises and pulled muscles from the past few days, and dipped the garment into the already pink basin. There he kneaded and pounded the tunic against the stone side beneath the surface, freeing it from the worst of the blood. Three tries and it merely looked stained rather than bloody. He wrung it out, and then, shivering at the cold, wet wool, pulled it on. Reaching out, he helped Martius out of his top and repeated the process, though his son's soaked tunic took a great deal more work and time. Finally he handed it back, and Martius pulled it on with distaste. He was starting to look a lot more like himself now.

'What do we do, Dad?'

'Now there's no reason the garrison will recognise us as the people from the Mithraeum. We go back to the stable and retrieve our kit-bags. Then we find the nearest hostelry and pay our way for the night with one of the other coin bags. We change into our new gear, which isn't bloodstained, have a hot meal, a good night's sleep, and then we move on.'

'Where to?'

Focalis had been considering that very question as he pounded the blood out of the tunics.

'Titus Odalaricus.'

'What?'

'We find the others. Sigeric is probably the most useful, but he's also one of the furthest away. With Ofilius gone, Sigeric is the best planner and thinker among us. He will come up with something. But between us and him there are several others, and there's strength in numbers. Odalaricus was my best mate

SIMON TURNEY

from the day we joined up. Even your mum liked him. She always said that if I got on her nerves too much she'd run off with him. We go to find him next. He's not far, so we'll set off as soon as the gates open in the morning. Until then we keep quiet and hope nobody notices us. There's another Goth somewhere in this city who is probably looking for us.'

'Dad, I killed someone.'

'I know.'

'Was he a bad man?'

'No worse than most of us.'

'He had a chi-rho on a chain. He was a Christian.'

'Most of them are, son. But you can't let that influence you. If you hadn't killed him, he'd have killed you, and then me. And remember that he was the one who killed Ofilius, too. Harden your heart. It's the only way to deal with such things.'

'I'm not sorry, Dad. That's the problem. I *should* be.'

'No. On this occasion, you shouldn't. Sometimes death is the only appropriate answer. Come on. We need to lie low for the night, and a few cups of wine will take the edge off the shock.'

'And then we find your other friends.'

'Yes.'

'Unless the Goths find them first.'

4

Focalis and Martius loitered in the wide archway entrance of the stable, reins gripped tight, packs once more on the beasts. Down the street, the city garrison was preparing to open the gate for the morning. Already a dozen people, a couple of horses and an empty cart were queued up waiting to leave. Focalis and his son, however, waited out of the public eye, watching the street carefully for any sign of the one Goth he felt certain was still in Suida. None of those queued, nor any of the incidental figures he'd seen in the streets, seemed likely candidates, though the tension remained and would do so at least until they were out of sight of the city.

They had left the small nondescript inn where they'd stayed while the world was still dark and quiet, only bakers and insomniacs out and about. By the time dawn was beginning to show they were waiting outside the stable, and as soon as the owner opened up they moved in and prepared. Focalis had left Martius there, finishing off, while he found shops still opening up and purchased a few supplies, including several new items of apparel, their lesson learned in the blood of Suida. He'd then returned, and they had moved off towards the gate, all the time their eyes and ears alert, and waited for the guards to open up.

Finally, the bar was lifted and the gate opened. More figures appeared further up the street now, the sky beginning to lighten sufficiently to allow clear vision. Still, Focalis waited until he was content that none of the new arrivals approaching the gate could be enemies. One man who was clearly a recently arrived and settled Thervingi alerted him for a moment, but then he spotted the woman and the small boy accompanying him, and comfortably struck the man from the list of potential enemies. No one, Goth or Roman, brought their family on a revenge killing.

Reasonably certain that they were not being observed or followed, he gestured to Martius and the two led their loaded mounts out of the archway and into the street. With ease they slipped into the line, shuffling slowly forward. The guards were busy at the gate, directing the traffic in staggered stages, since a queue awaiting entry had also grown outside the walls. With each shuffle forward, Focalis kept his eyes on the new arrivals. It was, of course, possible that the remaining Goth had been outside the upper town's walls that night and was only now arriving. He subjected every passing figure to scrutiny, and it was only when they had passed through the single-arched gatehouse and moved into the outer city that he felt a sense of relief and allowed a little of the tension to dissipate. Still, he maintained his watchfulness, hand never far from sword hilt, until they reached the edge of Suida, on a different road from that they'd used on arrival, and the last houses of the city were left behind.

They'd walked their mounts through the streets, but now pulled themselves up into the saddle and began to set off purposefully.

'So,' Martius asked finally, 'where are we going?'

It seemed strange to Focalis to hear such a normal question from the lad. Since the events of last night, and the shock they had driven deep into Martius' bones, the lad had been uncharacteristically quiet. There would be a strange, and probably unpleasant, conversation coming, and he was not looking forward to it, so such a banal question seemed a boon.

'Odalaricus. He doesn't have a business as such, like the decanus. He was always quite shrewd with money. Long before Hadrianopolis, he'd invested his funds in three or four businesses. By the time we left the army, you might have said he was a wealthy man already. That allowed him to do a better job than most of us of going into hiding. He became something of a recluse by careful design. All his business dealings are carried out through third parties, so he's very hard to trace even if you know his investments.'

'But you know where he is.'

'I do. Or at least, I hope I do. He's made the trail back to him difficult enough even for me to trace, but he sent me a gift and a message when your mother died. I questioned the courier. He would not tell me where he'd come from, for that was part of his task, but he told me how many days he'd travelled. I worked out how far he'd come in a day and then fished out one of my old maps. I know of half a dozen places that have meaning for Odalaricus, and it wasn't hard to work out which of them was the right number of days' travel away.'

'But you've never been there?'

'When he was a boy he had an aunt in a village not too far from Suida. He used to be sent to stay with her when his parents were away on one business venture or another. The aunt was a spinster, with no heirs. When she died, I never heard what happened to her property, but it seemed obvious that it passed to Odalaricus. I know the name of the village, and though I've never been there, he described it often enough that I can conjure up an image in my mind very clearly. If we travel with reasonable speed we'll arrive not long after sunset.'

They rode on that morning, exchanging only occasional snippets, and it was only as they sat beneath the shade of a trio of cypresses eating a snack on the noon pause that Martius finally broke the silence that had been building.

'Is it like that every time?'

Focalis chewed his mouthful of bread, took a swig of water to wash it down and shrugged. 'Everyone's different. But you'll find it's never quite as much of a shock as the first. If it helps, you didn't actually kill the man. He staggered out into the street and I finished him off.'

Martius sighed. 'No. The amount of blood. It was so dark. I got his liver. He'd have been dead soon. I killed him, even if you put him down. It made me feel sick. When the blade went in, I felt nothing, because I was just panicked. I'd taken him by surprise and he had his back to me. He turned and said something I didn't understand, but he was drawing his sword, so I stuck him before he finished. It was when I pulled out the blade and all the blood gushed out I felt sick. In fact I think I *was* sick.'

'It's not an uncommon reaction, lad.'

'I guess not. But that's not what worries me. What worries me is that even while I was feeling sick there was this weird sense of excitement. As though I already wanted to do it again. Surely that's not normal?'

There was a short silence as Focalis absorbed this

information, chewing more bread and cheese. Finally he sighed. He didn't like this. The lad was having to grow up too fast. He'd prepared Martius to look after himself for the last six years, and even more so since Hadrianopolis, but he'd hoped the boy would have come of age, married and moved on without ever needing to use the skills he'd learned. No boy at his age should have to know what it feels like to kill a man.

'As I said, it's different for everyone. What you experienced might just be a touch of battle madness. Sometimes your blood starts to pump and instinct takes over. It might not have been excitement you felt so much as the natural imperative to fight for your life.'

'Mmm.' But Martius looked less than convinced.

They packed up again a short while later, conversation turning once more to mundane subjects, starting with the geography of Thracia, of which Martius knew little, despite never having left that province. They rode on for the afternoon and, a few hours later, came across a small gathering of farmers and labourers deep in discussion about their wares at a crossroads while the teamsters driving their wagons waited patiently nearby.

''Scuse me,' Focalis began, interrupting them. When they fell silent and several turned to him, the ex-soldier smiled. 'I'm hoping I'm on the right road for the village of Seven Elms?'

'That you are,' one of them said with a nod. 'Keep going. Two hours. Maybe three. You'll wind around a bit between the hills and through woodlands after the next rise, but you'll cross a small river and the road will bring you straight into Seven Elms.'

'Thank you, friend. May God grant you a lucrative day at the market.'

The man gave him a smile and touched his hand to his forehead in gratitude, then went back to his discussion. They rode on, soon entering a heavily wooded region. Just as the farmer had noted, the road wound like a snake between low, forested hills, and dusk was beginning to gather around them as they crossed that river and looked up to the village ahead.

'The house will be on the upriver side of the village. He always used to talk about the watermill that abutted their garden. Come on.'

They entered the village quietly, walking their horses slowly. It was not a large place, just a score of houses clustered around a square with a small church and a meeting hall. The river burbled away behind them, washing over rocks in its passage. Three old men sat on a bench at one side of the square, murmuring in quiet conversation, and the sound of children playing with a dog echoed across the village. It was, in short, an image of perfect rural peace.

At the edge of the square, Focalis nodded a greeting to the old men as he turned and made his way down a lane leading to the north, upstream. Now, he could hear the rhythmic groan and splash of the mill's waterwheel, which suggested he was on the right track.

At the end of the lane, passing the last house by some distance and with the mill, closed down for the evening, off to their left, Focalis smiled to see the house awaiting them. Every tiny detail was oddly familiar from his friend's descriptions, and even though he'd never been here before, he felt he knew the place.

His stomach flipped.

The door of the house was open.

'Martius,' he whispered, reaching out to the boy and pointing ahead.

'Maybe he doesn't live here after all?'

Focalis shivered. It was possible, of course, but he'd have bet everything he had that Odalaricus was here. And it was odd for anyone to leave their door wide open at dusk, let alone a man who had carefully gone into hiding these past few years. He accepted, with a sinking feeling, that the most likely explanation was that they were too late again.

Focalis had always assumed that he or Ofilius would be their first targets and that the others would be safe. That he would have to seek them out and warn or gather them. God above, but it had taken investigation and intuition for even Focalis to pin down his old friend, and he had clues and a head start. How in God's name had Fritigern's Goths managed to find him so readily?

'Wait out here.'

'Dad, I can help.'

'I'm well aware of that, but we don't know what we're dealing with yet, and I can move quieter alone. If there's no danger I'll call you. Stay with the horses. In fact, stay in the saddle. If anyone other than me comes out of that door, kick the flanks and ride for your life.'

Ignoring the splutter of protest, Focalis slid from his own saddle and tied his horse's reins to the fence. In moments he'd untied his shield and unsheathed his sword and began to make his way slowly down the path towards the open, dark doorway, treading carefully, making only the slightest sound, a faint crunch of gravel. He'd toyed with putting on helmet and chain shirt, too, but they would be noisy, inhibiting his senses once he was inside, and donning them would take time, which he might not be able to afford.

There was no sign of life on his approach. The house looked entirely deserted, the passageway inside the door dark and unoccupied. Indeed, the garden had an untended look, and Focalis now began to consider the possibility that Martius was right and his old friend did not live here after all. Perhaps the house was abandoned and derelict, the door open permanently? And the old men in the village had seemed unperturbed, as though nothing was amiss. Of course, looking at the gardens surrounding the house, it would be a simple thing for any subtle killer to approach from across the river without passing through the village at all.

Taking a deep breath, he stepped towards the doorway.

No. Not derelict. It may be cold and dark, but the floor was clean, or at least only as dirty as general wear and tear would make it. If Odalaricus did not live here, then someone at least had, and recently. Careful not to knock the large, round shield on anything, he stepped inside. He couldn't make out any footprints, but then the light was rapidly failing, and it had been dry for days, so that meant little. As quietly as he could, he stepped inside the house.

He could hear the distant murmur of low conversation, somewhere across the house, though not loud enough to make anything out. Eyes locked on the atrium ahead, watchful, ready to catch any hint of movement in the gloom, he took another few paces.

A hand suddenly gripped his sword arm, just above the elbow, and pulled hard. As he cried out, another hand went over his mouth, stifling the sound to a disconcerted mumble. Focalis could do little, surprised and taken off balance as he was, and fell, half-pulled, into the small alcove near the door where a doorman would usually pass his time on duty.

It was even darker here, and cramped, and Focalis struggled to turn and bring his sword to bear.

'Shut up, you fucking fool,' a voice hissed, on the lower edge of hearing.

Focalis blinked. 'Odalaricus?'

'Hush now.'

Focalis stared as the shadow that had assailed him and pulled him into the cubbyhole now removed the hand from his mouth and stepped over him. Odalaricus was thin and lithe, small, like a racing hound, his short hair and close-trimmed beard were pale in the faint light, and he was wearing an unbelted tunic, barefoot. Still, he had a sword in his hand. As unprepared for trouble as the man might have been, those lessons their decanus had drilled into them remained.

Odalaricus ducked back, and now there were fresh voices close by.

'Shit,' whispered his old friend as he recoiled into the alcove. 'They're coming back. Get ready.'

The wiry man leaned close to the corner, around which they could hear Gothic voices in low conversation, and held up three fingers, then two, then one.

They leapt out from the alcove and ran at the two figures in the corridor, who had shields and weapons, but had been expecting nothing at this point, and so all were lowered, unprepared. As Focalis hit the one on the left hard with his shield, barging him against a wall, his old friend slammed into the other. He saw nothing of what Odalaricus did, for he was too busy with his own efforts. A whirl of thoughts went through his mind. There would probably be six. It was an important number for the Thervingi: they sent out scouts in that number, had that number at rituals, a king was surrounded by six guards. And, of course, there had been six sent for Focalis and very likely six in Suida looking for the decanus. Which meant these two would be far from alone. And if they made sufficient noise, they might bring the others running. Fortunately they'd been surprised, and before this man could shout in alarm, Focalis had slammed him against a wall and knocked the breath from him. The man had a chain shirt and an open-faced helmet, and, aware that there was insufficient room and time to take a swing at him, Focalis simply lifted his sword and slammed his fist, still wrapped around the hilt, into the man's head, flattening his prominent nose across his face.

The man let out an 'oof' of winded pain, but Focalis knew what he was doing. He had the initiative and the surprise and he had to hold onto them. Not letting the Goth recover, he changed his weapon grip slightly and struck again, this time driving the egg-shaped ivory pommel into the man's face. The damage was impressive, and he heard the crunch of multiple bones. The man tried to scream, but it was little more than a desperate whimper, half lost beneath a throaty gurgling. Before the Goth could recover from the stunning blow, Focalis struck a third time. This time his sword went up, clanging against the man's helmet at the brow, driving his head back against the wall.

Then he brought the shield up. It was not an easy manoeuvre in such circumstances, but he had the force he required. The rawhide edging of the shield, wrapped around the boards within, slammed into the man's throat, crushing his windpipe and throat apple. It was a killing blow, and though it would take the man a while to suffocate, he would be unable to shout for help while it happened.

Aware that his own victim was only half the problem, Focalis turned to help Odalaricus, only to find that his old friend had skewered the Goth, his blade shoved up through the man's neck and deep into his head. He was pushing up still, as though to lift the man off the ground with the sword, and blood was sheeting down from the wound, soaking both the sword and the arm that gripped it.

Finally, he seemed to realise that the man was dead and let go his pushing, drawing out the sword in a smooth action, allowing the dying man to fall to the floor, where he shook and bucked in his death throes. It had all happened in moments, and with remarkably little sound. As Focalis listened, trying to identify any noise of alarm elsewhere in the house, suddenly Odalaricus gasped, eyes wide, and pointed back past him towards the door.

Focalis spun, shield coming up in anticipation.

Another Goth stood in the doorway, unarmoured and holding a small recurve bow of Scythian-looking origin. He had lifted the bow ready to loose, the arrow nocked, but oddly was not letting go.

Focalis frowned, and his confusion deepened as the man suddenly sighed, his mouth opening, a trickle of dark liquid running down from the corner. The archer's hands spasmed, and the arrow half-fell, half-flew, clattering against the corridor wall a few feet inside the door. As he folded up and collapsed in a heap, both veterans stared. An arrow stuck up from the back of the man's neck, a beautiful shot that had killed swiftly and surely.

The two men staggered back towards the door, and Focalis felt a strange mix of pride and panic flood him at the sight of Martius approaching the door, bow in hand, quiver at his side.

'What the fuck?' Odalaricus breathed.

'I saw him sneaking around in the gardens,' the lad said. 'He had a bow, and once he got near the door, he drew an arrow. I had my bow to hand. It made sense.'

'Who in God's name have you dragged into our little tragedy now?' Odalaricus growled, shoving Focalis roughly.

'That's Martius. You know Martius.'

The other old soldier frowned. '*That's* Martius? Christ, man, but the last time I saw him he was playing with wooden horses.'

'It's been six years,' Focalis reminded him.

'Well fuck me, that was well timed. Good to see you, Martius. It's been a while. Bet you can't remember your uncle Titus can you?'

The lad shook his head, and Odalaricus let out an exaggerated and very theatrical moan of misery. 'Me,' he said. 'How could anyone forget me?'

Martius grinned at the man, and Focalis coughed. 'Can I just remind you that we're in the middle of something?'

'Quite right,' Odalaricus said, suddenly all business again.

'Why were you hiding?' Focalis asked. 'And in that?'

'I was about to go for a bath, when I heard something outside. I came to check and managed to slip into the alcove just as they broke the lock and came in. I was just trying to decide whether to die in a suicidal fight against them all or run like a coward when you turned up. Probably a good thing. Run like a coward was winning by a country mile.'

'Were there six?'

The veteran shook his head. 'Four.'

'Then there'll be two more looking after their horses, probably down by the river.'

'Stay here, with your lad. I'll be back in a moment.'

Focalis watched as the man disappeared back in through the door, sword in hand. The moments dragged out as they waited in the garden. Soon he began to curse his old friend. If they didn't get moving soon, those other two with the horses might well come looking. Focalis was on the verge of telling Martius to wait and going in to find his old friend when the man reappeared at the door. He was fully dressed now, and wiping his sword blade, which was freshly coated.

'Two left,' he announced.

'Maybe we should leave them?' Martius offered. 'Run while we can. Do you have a horse?'

Odalaricus chuckled. 'I have eight. Only one here though. I have stashes of animals, money, gear and more, in a number of undisclosed locations. Quite apart from half expecting to wake up any morning with that bastard Fritigern standing on my scrotum, I've made myself a little unpopular with a number of local business conglomerates. I've been ready to relocate at a moment's notice for years.'

'Good. Because we have to move on, and quickly. I want to gather the old unit again. If Fritigern thinks he can just do away with us, he's got another thing coming.'

'Quite,' Odalaricus agreed. 'Am I the first, then?'

'Not quite. But the decanus didn't make it.'

'Ah, the bastards. But he wouldn't have been hard to track down. I wonder if he was how they found me?'

'No,' Focalis confirmed. 'He only died yesterday. Had we

been a little faster we might have saved him. But he took three of them down in his heathen cave.'

'I'll bet he did. Probably killed one or two with his breath. So next up will be Persius, I presume?'

'It will. He shouldn't be far away, and I have a way to find him.'

'Good.' Odalaricus rolled his shoulders. 'But first let's go deal with the other pair.'

'Can we not just run?' Martius tried again. 'Must we risk another fight?'

Focalis looked at his son. Was he suffering regret at the arrow shot? Two killings in two days could do all sorts of things to the mind of a young, impressionable lad.

Odalaricus smacked Focalis on the arm. 'Have you taught him nothing?' He then let the smile slip, adopting a very serious expression as he turned back to the lad. 'Lesson one, Martius: never leave an enemy alive. They have a horrible tendency to reappear at truly inconvenient times.'

'On that note,' Focalis added, 'all six who came for me are gone, but there's one of those who attacked the decanus unaccounted for. It's possible that Ofilius killed him, of course, and we never found the body. But he may have survived Suida, and it's anyone's guess whether he's gone to report back to the renegade king or whether he's back on the trail, trying to track us down. They seem well prepared, and their intelligence is good. I cannot fathom how they knew about you, unless one of the others has already gone. A few of them might have been able to guess where you were.'

All he got in reply was a harrumph, and Martius frowned. 'Why was your house in darkness? Where are your slaves?'

Odalaricus snorted. 'I only light and heat the bits I'm using.

Tonight it was bedroom and balneum. And I don't have slaves. Or servants.'

'None?'

'No. I hire two locals who come in three times a week to clean and sort a few things out for me. But I don't want to be tied down. Having servants and owning slaves gives you responsibilities. I told you before, I've been ready to run for years now.'

The veteran rolled his shoulders. 'Alright, enough chatter. Let's get the other two Goths. Have you seen them?'

'No. But leaving two with the horses is what they did at my house, and I don't think they came through the village here. The old men in the square didn't look bothered.'

'The only place they could really cross the river and not be seen would be down below the mill. The only vantage point there is from the mill itself. That'll be where they're lurking.'

The three of them, led by the house's owner, crossed the gardens in the direction of the mill, whose wheel continued to turn with ligneous creaks and the splosh and gurgle of water. They angled so that they could approach from the village side of the mill, hiding their presence from anyone down by the water beyond. As they passed the wheel, eternally rotating in the narrow race, Odalaricus held up a hand to stop them. He pressed himself against the wheel and gestured. The other two approached carefully, looked, and then ducked back.

Two Goths stood, looking bored, close to the riverbank. Six horses were tethered on the far side in a grassy meadow, taking the opportunity to feast.

'How's your boy with that?' Odalaricus asked, pointing at the bow in Martius' hand. 'Was the last shot a lucky one, or is he really that good? It's getting dark.'

'Better than me,' Focalis replied. 'And he can loose from the saddle too.'

'They'll hear us coming if we go for them, and there's the faint chance they'll get across the river and to their horses. I don't fancy a cross-country chase at night.'

'I can do it,' Martius replied. 'The light's still good enough.'

'You don't have to,' Focalis nudged, though it was, he had to admit, their best chance.

'No, I'll do it.'

The two veterans followed the lad as he moved along the water wheel, taking advantage of both its movement and sound to mask his approach. Once the two Goths were in sight, the lad looked up and around, sniffing, testing the air. Then he plucked two arrows from his quiver, jamming one between the last two fingers of his left hand, which gripped the bow in its central position. He set the other arrow against the string, then drew it back, lifting the bow, sighting carefully. Three times he changed the angle or direction by such a small degree that Focalis could hardly see a difference, and then he paused, noting where he was aiming in relation to his surroundings, took a series of slow, quiet breaths, then loosed.

The Goth on the left, who'd been fiddling with something in both hands, gave a sudden squawk and disappeared backwards into the river with a loud splash. By the time his companion realised what had happened, and was drawing his sword, looking this way and that in the gloom in an attempt to locate the source of the missile, Martius had the second arrow ready, the need to reach down and pull it from the quiver negated.

The second arrow flew almost in the wake of the first,

the adjustments on his aim being small and already planned in advance. The shaft slammed into the other Goth, who disappeared back into the undergrowth with a cry.

Odalaricus grinned. 'By God, the lad can shoot, Flavius.'

'That he can.'

'Wait here. I'll be back.'

As the man disappeared across the grass in the direction of the bodies, sword out and ready to make sure they were definitely dead, Focalis looked at his son. The shock of his first kill might have been debilitating for a while, but with four notches now, the lad had hardly blinked this time. Indeed, he was paying no attention to the scene, instead counting his remaining arrows.

Perhaps this was a change for the better? Perhaps not.

He was still wondering what to say when Odalaricus reappeared. 'Alright,' the veteran announced, 'let's retrieve my horse, then head across the village and gather some of my things. Then we ride for Persius.'

5

'So how do you know about this place?' Odalaricus mused as the three of them passed a milestone for some provincial town of which they'd never heard. The day's travel from Seven Elms and the barn in which they'd slept had seen a string of such places.

'I'd lost track of Persius within three months of Hadrianopolis. I knew where he'd settled at first, of course, and sent a message a quarter of a year after the battle, when I was putting precautions in place, only to learn he'd gone from there with no forwarding address. I did a little investigation in the civic records office of Augusta Traiana, and after a few weeks' work turned up a document of adoption in which two sons of a woman called Vespilla took a new name. They became Persius Arvina and Persius Artax. I've never confirmed it, but I have the address of the woman and her boys, and it seems certain to be him.'

Odalaricus snorted. 'He got what he wanted then.'

Martius frowned. 'What?'

'He was always jealous that I was so financially sound. I'd made good investments early. Persius, on the other hand, was always broke. Drank far more than was good for him and played dice very badly. Never had two coins to rub together.

Deadliest bastard with a sword you ever met, but hopeless at the game of life. He maintained till the day we parted that he would retire, find a widow with more money than Midas and breasts he could use as pillows and marry her. We joked about it over the years, but I don't doubt for a moment that's exactly what he did. So he disappears and marries this Vespilla woman, gaining a fortune and two heirs. Not bad.'

'Let's just hope Fritigern's warriors haven't been bright enough to trawl through public records for him.'

They rode on for another hour and at a new milestone, marking the point of a junction, they turned and took the side road, following the directions Focalis had learned in years past. Another mile brought them to the edge of a large estate, close enough to the nearby town that they could see the tiled roofs from the hill on which the villa sat.

'Doesn't look too hopeful,' Odalaricus noted as they approached a low wall surrounding the estate. The gate stood open and, beyond it, the drive leading up to the main villa was overgrown and patched with weeds. Carefully manicured hedges to each side had gone wild, growing bushy and misshapen. A small fountain by the side of the drive, not far from the gate, had dried up, leaving just a stagnant mess in the bottom, green and filled with weed.

'How long deserted, d'you think?' Focalis murmured, his hand going to his side and drawing his sword, just in case.

'The best part of a year, I'd say.'

'He didn't enjoy married bliss for long, then. Damn it, but I never thought he'd disappear again. We'd best check out the house, try and work out what happened.'

They rode on up the drive. There was no indication of life ahead, no movement. No smoke rose from the roof, even above the bath suite off to the left, despite the fact that the day was drawing to a close and the weather, while it had remained dry, was grey and more than a little chilly. As they neared, the others drew their blades too, and the three men dismounted near the main entrance. At least the villa's door was closed. No lights, though, and when they paused and listened carefully for a while, only birdsong and the gentle whisper of the breeze filled the air.

'Do we knock?' Martius asked.

His father nibbled his lip. If there were foes inside, hiding, waiting for Persius to show his face, that would very much give the game away, but on the other hand, so would breaking down the door. He stepped over and rapped on the knocker. The sense of abandonment heightened as he heard the muffled echo of the knock rattling around inside the house. There was no one here, of that he was pretty sure now.

'Stay together,' Focalis murmured quietly. 'Looks deserted, but you never know.'

With that, he put his shoulder to the door and pressed hard. The door creaked and bowed and almost gave. Taking a step back, he tried again, this time throwing himself against the timbers. On the second attempt the lock gave and the door swung open with an age-worn creak, slamming back against the wall, sending a small cloud of plaster shards raining down to the expensive mosaic floor. The vestibule might as well have been the gateway to Hades: a dark passageway reeking of dereliction, of mould and mustiness, leading to a pitch-black atrium that could have been the throat of a demon.

Focalis shivered. What had happened to their friend and his new family in the space of two years? After the encounter with Odalaricus, this time Focalis first checked the doorman's alcove, confirming it was empty before they moved inside.

Swords out, senses heightened, the three of them passed along the corridor, taking in the details. The small shrine near the door was intact, if long since disused. No longer a pagan lararium, it now housed a small icon of the Virgin and a mosaic chi-rho. The sense that the place had been deliberately left and locked up increased as they explored. Doors had all been shut. Nothing had been removed, but everything had been tidied away, as though waiting for the owners to return and unpack. All this was discovered in meagre light, for as part of the deliberate abandonment, a thick netting had been stretched across the open roof of the atrium to prevent leaves and birds piling up in the room. The fountain was no longer running in the room's central pool, but given everything else they'd found, Focalis now suspected that rather than having broken through lack of use, the water supply had been deliberately cut off as part of the withdrawal.

'Where is everyone?' Martius asked as they checked room after room.

'Good question. If the whole family had been lost, surely someone would have inherited or bought this place. I think we might want to make enquiries in the town. Clearly there's no one here, friend or foe.'

Odalaricus looked up at the sky. 'Not long before dark. If we head into town it'll be night before we get there. Don't know about you, but I'd be just as happy camping out in here for the night, then going into town in the morning to ask around?'

Focalis thought on the idea. It had merit. If they were planning to keep a low profile, then this might be best. 'Alright.

Let's set up. Looks like we won't be treading on anyone's toes anyway.'

The three of them returned to the entrance, untied their horses and led them through the house, hooves clopping loudly on marble and mosaic floors, and into the overgrown peristyle garden where they could be contained for the night, with grass on which to feed. Focalis pushed the door to, the broken lock invisible from the outside, the house to all intents and purposes still deserted and locked. Satisfied that they were safe for now, Focalis set up one last warning system, a single thread stretched across the dark vestibule six paces from the door at knee height, attached to a bucket balanced on a stool. Almost invisible in the gloom, it would give more than adequate warning of an intruder. No other access to the house was unlocked, and so they were as safe as they could make it, yet still they decided on watches. Martius had ever been an early riser, so he would take the last watch in the hours before dawn. Odalaricus volunteered for the middle of the night, and so Focalis would stand guard when the others turned in.

First, though, they decided they could risk a small fire. It was not as though the fire would damage the place, for the room they had chosen for the night was a small one leading off the peristyle, and the smoke would be drawn up and out. They found a slab of marble and a few bricks and set up a hearth, gathering some of the wood and kindling from the long-disused bath house. It was worth the small risk for hot food and a warm night, given the weather.

They settled into the room, unpacked now and with the horses in sight. The cache they had visited, one of several their friend had set up for this eventuality, had been ridiculously well-stocked, and now Odalaricus poured a cup of expensive wine for each of them while Martius fed the fire and Focalis rummaged in the packs to find the food for the evening meal.

'Why is this king after you?' Martius said suddenly. As his father shot him a look, he flinched, but recovered quickly. 'I know. You killed one of his friends. But that sort of thing does not warrant the efforts he's going to.'

Odalaricus turned a creased brow on Focalis. 'You've got the lad wrapped up in all this and killing Goths, and you haven't told him the story?'

Focalis growled. Damn it. 'I told him some of it. All he needed to know for now.'

The other veteran shook his head. 'No. If he's on the run with us he needs to know everything. Flavius, he *deserves* to know everything.'

'I'm not proud of my past.'

'Who is? That's not the issue.'

'I don't want the lad drawn into my sins.'

'Oh for fuck's sake, Flavius, stop it with the sin stuff. The good Lord will judge us when the time comes, but *hell* exists for the Lord to punish the sinful. He doesn't expect them to do it to themselves beforehand.'

Focalis flashed his old friend a disapproving look, but the man was, when you came down to it, quite right. Whatever the case with sin and its punishment, Martius did need and deserve to know the truth. 'Alright, *you* tell him, then.'

He busied himself with gathering, arranging and preparing a stew of lamb, turnip and onions, waiting for the fire to bloom gold and hot and then arranging two grotesque statues from the garden on either side and balancing an iron poker between them from which to hang the cooking pot they'd borrowed from the kitchens, after a bit of a clean-out. As he worked, he tried very hard not to listen to the old story being related yet again, though he failed at every juncture.

'You know about the Goths crossing the river?' Odalaricus asked the lad.

Martius nodded. 'But just tell me everything anyway.'

'Alright. Well, your dad and I, and the others, were once part of the emperor's scholae, elite cavalry, real posh and well paid. Valens was pissing around in Asia as he tended to do, but we'd had trouble from time to time with the Goth tribes across the Danubius, and fresh rumours had the emperor send a few men to Thracia to support the vicarius and the various generals in command over here. We were part of that force. We were assigned to the comes rei militaris per Thracias, Lupicinus, who was working with the dux Maximus.'

Martius' eyes were widening. He'd had no idea his father had apparently been so important. Focalis snorted. 'Don't get carried away with name-dropping. We were just soldiers, Martius. Just soldiers.'

'*Elite* soldiers,' Odalaricus corrected. 'And of an imperial regiment. Anyway, you miserable old goat, who's telling this story?'

Focalis grunted and went back to cutting up the lamb for the stew.

'There are more tribes of Goths than there are fish in the sea,' Odalaricus continued.

'Try and at least keep to the facts,' Focalis huffed.

'But,' the other man went on, with just a quick glare at his friend, 'for this story only two of the tribes matter. They are the Thervingi and the Greuthungi, allies of old and neighbours in the lands across the river. These tribes had often been our enemy, and very occasionally our ally. That's the problem with borders like this one. Sometimes you have to rely on the enemy to keep other enemies at bay. Anyway, they were being pressured. This new people had come from the north and the east, in the hellish lands towards Serica, and were raiding Thervingi and Greuthungi territory. The Huns, they call them.'

'Too much detail,' Focalis said quietly.

'While the Goths can be ferocious, it seems these Huns are so demonic even the Goths quake in fear when they come. So in the end, the two tribes begged permission from the emperor to cross the river and settle in the empire.'

'And he let them?' Martius said, incredulous. 'I always assumed they just came.'

'He didn't have a lot of choice,' Focalis interrupted. 'He was busy with the Persians. If he'd tried to keep the Goths on the other side of the Danubius, half the east would have been overrun. He came to an arrangement with them instead.'

'They were allowed to settle,' Odalaricus said. 'Even in their original tribal groups, and with their honour and weapons intact. I think Valens hoped that treating them like allies would bind them to the empire and make them join the fight to protect the borders. And, of course, if they're settled and peaceful, the emperor can tax them. Unfortunately, Valens was a man plagued by poor decisions. The worst he made was remaining in the east, dealing with the Persians.'

'So who dealt with the Goths? The dux?'

Odalaricus nodded. 'The dux and Lupicinus. Neither of those men had as much brain as a stewed duck, and both were too greedy for their own good. There were plenty of men, soldier and politician alike, who could have settled the

Thervingi and the Greuthungi in peace and made it all work, but unfortunately the two men with all the authority were fools.'

He leaned back, drained his cup and refilled it, offering more to Martius, who accepted gratefully as the older man went on.

'The Goths were hungry. They'd had to abandon their settlements and farms across the river and start afresh in our lands. Of course, no one was keen on giving up good, ready-worked farmland to them, and Lupicinus and Maximus were not about to anger the populace who filled the treasury, so they allotted the tribes really poor, unyielding lands. Then, just to put the boot in, they demanded taxes from the tribes before they could do much more than get the crops to start growing. Over a few months they extorted everything they could get from the tribes. The Goths were desperate. They were refugees, and they actually didn't want trouble with the empire. They wanted to be part of it. But Lupicinus and his cronies withheld aid from them, starved them, cheated them, and offered help only at unacceptable prices. I saw with my own eyes Thervingi families selling their own into slavery in return for bread.'

'That's horrible,' Martius gasped. Focalis winced. He could almost see it going through the lad's head now. The Goths were becoming the victims in the story. Of course, they *had been* the victims, but that wouldn't help with what they faced now.

'It led to rioting and small fights, trouble between the Goths and their Roman neighbours. Our unit, along with every other one Lupicinus could call on, was required to keep the peace and stop these riots whenever they broke out. In the end,

Lupicinus and Maximus invited the leaders of the Thervingi and the Greuthungi to a conference at Marcianopolis. It was to be a state occasion. A banquet, entertainment, a display of Romanitas for the barbarian. The idiots felt that if they could overawe the kings of the tribes, they could wring from them a better deal than if they met them on level ground.'

Another sip of wine. 'The two kings came to Marcianopolis – Alavivus and Fritigern. I don't think Lupicinus had anticipated those two. They were no cowed barbarians. They came like emperors themselves, with a small army of guards and attendants. Lupicinus refused to allow the entire entourage in, keeping the bulk outside the palace, while a huge swathe of tribesmen loitered outside the walls of the city, waiting for news of an improvement in their circumstances. The two kings would not attend without their honour guard and a small contingent of servants, and the comes was forced to accept the terms. They each came with six of their best soldiers and six attendants.'

'We were there,' Focalis added, as he stirred the pot. 'We were at the meal as Lupicinus' guards, the opposite number of those Goth units.'

'Quite,' Odalaricus agreed. 'For a while it looked like it might all be a success. The kings were actually negotiating, and though Lupicinus was being a complete arsehole, he was remarkably close to coming to an understanding. In a way, one might blame the Goths for the breakdown, though it was our commanders who really fucked it up. A fight broke out beyond the city walls between hungry, desperate Goths and a few local soldiers who wouldn't stop taking the piss. It turned nasty and men died. An alarm went up. The two kings and their guards heard the alarm, and every hand in the palace went to a sword hilt. We could hear the trouble. Still, there was this strange stand-off. We all knew what was at stake. This was the closest we'd come to true peace with the Goths in decades, and the whole future of Rome could ride on what happened that night. So no one drew their sword. We would wait, and hope that the trouble outside could be brought under control.'

'I don't remember it being so reasoned,' Focalis put in. 'Personally, I had my sword half-drawn long before it all went wrong.'

'Anyway, the fact was that it could still have been saved, the situation calmed down. Unfortunately, Lupicinus had had too much to drink. The man was halfway to stupid when he was sober, and after too much wine, he'd gone the rest of the way. He snapped at the kings that he wouldn't countenance such belligerent behaviour from their guards, apparently oblivious that *we* were doing exactly the same. He demanded that they dismiss their guards and send them out of the palace. They refused, of course. No man in his right mind would have agreed to that.'

Martius was nodding, and Focalis winced again. His friend was painting the Goths in too good a light. It would sit badly with Martius next time they met one of Fritigern's killers.

'When they refused,' Odalaricus went on, 'Lupicinus made the worst decision anyone could hope to in that moment. He ordered us to kill the kings' guards and attendants.'

'*What?*' Martius spat out a mouthful of wine in shock, staring at him.

'The emperor's elite soldiers, pride of Rome, the scholae palatinae, were turned into murderers by a drunken commander.'

'What did you do?'

Odalaricus shrugged. 'What do you think? We were soldiers. We were given a direct order by our commander. We drew our swords and went to work. A fair few Romans died that night, but we followed our orders. We got to Alavivus and his men first. They were closer to us. We fought through them, but Lupicinus had completely lost it by then and was screaming at us, telling us to kill the kings, to kill them all.'

Focalis hated listening to the tale. He'd replayed it in his dreams, that and Hadrianopolis, most nights every year since.

'But Fritigern escaped?' Martius said.

'We killed Alavivus and his men, and several of Fritigern's. The man was bright, though. He managed to shout across the chaos and draw the attention of Maximus, who was less drunk than his companion, and I think could not believe what was happening. The dux ordered us to hold, and the fighting stopped. Fritigern offered two choices. Either he would fight to the death, and would guarantee that every Goth south of the Danubius took Roman heads for the rest of his days, or Maximus could order us to stand down, and Fritigern would leave with his surviving men and draw his warriors away. Maximus chose the latter, of course. He didn't want to be the one to send a message to the emperor telling him they'd inadvertently started a war on Roman lands with a powerful enemy who could have been an ally.'

Martius sagged back, taking another sip. 'No wonder Fritigern is upset.'

'I think that word is a slight understatement,' Focalis snorted.

'The war started anyway, that night. Fritigern had no

intention of walking away after what Lupicinus had done. What *we* had done on his orders. They besieged Marcianopolis. Lupicinus did nothing to help matters. He had the bodies of Alavivus and the dead warriors crucified on the walls in full sight of the tribes. I think we'd all have ended our days there had the Goths any real notion of how to conduct a siege. Fortunately for us, they could not overcome the walls, and after a few days they gave up and moved on to easier targets. For months then, even years, they ravaged Thracia. At the time, you were still young, lad, and your dad sent you and your mum down to live near Thessalonika. It was only when your mum died that you were brought back north, but still kept away from the troubles.'

'Can we not talk about Flavia,' Focalis put in, feeling that weight in his heart that always came with her name.

'Sorry, old fellow. Anyway, yes,' Odalaricus went on, 'there's not much to tell after that. In the end, Valens came north from Constantinopolis. He'd rearranged the army in order to provide a sufficient force to take on the Goths. Those of us who'd disgraced ourselves at Marcianopolis, in the emperor's eyes anyway, were demoted and shuffled into ordinary legions. Valens never did make good decisions, though. He was convinced the Goths would crumble under the might of his army, and didn't want to wait for his brother emperor Gratian, who was coming from Rome with another army. He would take all the glory, so he led us into battle at Hadrianopolis, where we were shafted by the enemy like no army in history. The emperor was struck down by an arrow and cut off. Various officers tried to save the day, but it was too late. We'd lost the moment we marched into battle. The emperor was taken to an abandoned farmhouse on the battlefield by his guards, and there they were surrounded and burned to death.'

'And that was it?'

'It was. Gratian came east and managed to start turning the war around, and Theodosius was raised to the purple in the east, leading a fresh army out to help finish it, but we were gone by then. Very few of the survivors – and there weren't many of them anyway – stayed in the army any longer than they had to. We of the old scholae took retirement. We'd served more than our term over the years anyway, and no one was going to try and stop us. We left the army and left the winning of the war to other men. We were done. Your dad limped home and devoted his life to looking after you, and to preparing for what we all knew would come.'

'And it just took peace and the tribes kicking him off his throne to give him the impetus to start it,' Focalis sighed.

'But it wasn't your fault,' Martius said. 'It was the generals who gave the order.'

'Oh, I'm sure Fritigern has plans for Lupicinus. Maximus never made it through the war. I think in truth he probably tried to get himself killed, going out nobly and all that, so that his family would be set up. Lupicinus is more of a weasel. He was cashiered in disgrace for his actions, and now lives somewhere on the coast in rich and reclusive retirement. Fritigern will go after him eventually, but he'll be a harder proposition than us. The Goths hold grudges, lad, and Fritigern more than most. We've always known that he would come for us eventually.'

'And rightly so,' Focalis grunted as he ladled the stew out into bowls. *Sin upon sin, since we were given licence to loot the dead king by Lupicinus, and our houses now are paid for with the gold of our victims.*

'Bollocks,' Odalaricus snorted. 'Your dad thinks our sins were too great. That we deserve what's coming. He'd have given up years ago if it weren't for you. He goes on because of you. For my part, I regret what we did, and I would have liked it to turn out differently, but I also know that refusing an order in the army is mutiny, and the punishment for that doesn't bear thinking about. We did what we had to, and the blame climbs upward from our swords to Lupicinus, Maximus, and eventually the emperor. I regret our part in it, but I will fight to my last breath before I let Fritigern and his killers walk over me.'

Martius nodded. 'Good. I agree. Vengeance is the purview of God, not of men.'

'But the problem,' Odalaricus went on, 'is that there are few of us left, and Fritigern will have hundreds of warriors to call on, if not thousands. He will just keep sending them until we're dead. And that means we need a plan.'

'I was trusting to the decanus,' Focalis replied. 'He always had a plan. Unfortunately, not anymore, and he never passed it on to us. All I can think of is getting everyone together and maybe trying to seek the favour of the vicarius, or even the emperor.'

'Sigeric will have an idea. He was always the clever one. When we get to Sigeric, he'll come up with something.'

Martius frowned. 'Isn't Sigeric a Gothic name?'

Focalis laughed. 'It is. Properly, he should be Sigericus. Herennius Sigericus. His mother was Gothic born, and his dad a Roman officer. It's not unusual, Martius. We've been back and forth with them so many times over the decades.

My own name is rooted in the tribes across the river, if you hadn't noticed. My grandad took citizenship and adopted the name Flavius.'

The conversation then turned to other tribes and the history of the peoples intermingling, which was something of a relief for Focalis. He looked across as they ate and drank, and found himself smiling to see Odalaricus and Martius chatting together, his son and his oldest friend. And though the old bastard had come a bit close to the bone at times with his explanation, he'd done a good job. He'd made it all clear. The Goths were betrayed, and their vengeance was entirely understandable, and while he and the others had murdered a king, it had been on the orders of a drunken lunatic. They may well have been personally responsible for plunging the empire into a six-year war, but the true fault had perhaps not lain with them. Martius had been appropriately incensed and horrified, but he had also accepted that Fritigern's response had to be dealt with. When the time came, Focalis was at least comfortable that, despite everything, Martius would still see the Goths as enemies.

The evening wore on, with them feeding the fire for warmth, now replete with food and already starting on a second skin of wine, and eventually Martius and Odalaricus decided to turn in, rolling up in their blankets close enough to the flames to sleep comfortably. Focalis pulled his cloak around him and changed position in order to give himself an unimpeded view of the peristyle garden and the various doorways that led off.

Ever since listening to Odalaricus reliving their tale, a hard truth had been nagging at him. Whether or not Sigeric could come up with a plan, Focalis had devoted the past few years to making sure that Martius survived – that when this day came, he could get the lad out of the house and away from trouble. And he *had* got Martius out of the house. But he had then brought the lad *with* him, into ever deeper trouble, which was precisely what he'd vowed not to do. Sooner or later he was going to have to send Martius away. As long as Focalis remained a target, Martius stood a good chance of becoming an accidental target.

And there was only one place he could really go. His great-uncle. Flavia's uncle and his family. They lived across the water in Smyrna, far from Thracia and the Goths. Of course, they'd had nothing to do with Focalis since the day he'd been dropped from the scholae into the legions. It wasn't because of their action at Marcianopolis – no disapproval there. It was the ignominy of having a relative who'd been so dishonoured by demotion. Appearance was everything to some people. But he hoped they would not paint Martius with the same brush. The lad was their niece's child, after all. They would take him in, they had to. Once Focalis had gathered everyone, they could make for the coast somewhere and he would give Martius a small fortune in gold and send him off to safety with his mother's family.

His musing was interrupted a moment later by the distant clatter of a bucket on a hard floor. In moments he was up. No need to wake the others, they had not yet succumbed to sleep. Swords were collected, and in heartbeats the trio was up and ready.

Focalis was first out into the peristyle, sword gripped, shield up, senses alert, like a wolf on the hunt. The others were right behind him, similarly prepared as they crossed the overgrown garden and stopped at the end of the corridor.

Focalis leaned to glance around the corner. He could see little in the darkness, but something was moving in the shadowed atrium at the other end of the corridor, a black shape upon black. His tension eased slightly as the figure moved into the open. He could still make out little, but there was no shield and no glint of metal. Whoever it was appeared to be unarmed and unarmoured, which made it highly unlikely it was one of Fritigern's men, but equally unlikely to be Persius. He ducked back and held up a single finger to warn the others the intruder was alone.

The man was walking towards them now, and making no attempt to mask his approach. The steps were light, soft shoes rather than a soldier's boots. Whoever it was, Focalis was satisfied that the three of them were in no great danger. Lowering his sword, yet keeping it bare, he stepped out, his shape silhouetted at the end of the passage. The figure stopped, a shuffling of feet.

'Who's there?' a voice called. A local accent, Focalis reckoned.

'I might ask the same, friend.'

'I am a legally appointed watchman, and this house is not occupied. I say again: who's there?'

It was such an official statement that the veteran could not believe the man was anything other than exactly what he said. To further calm the situation, Focalis sheathed his sword and placed his shield against the wall, holding up his hands in a gesture of peace. 'We are friends of the master of the villa, Persius, a veteran of the First Maximiana. We were surprised to find the place empty.'

The man, seemingly content that they presented no immediate threat, walked forward again, his features coming clear as the night sky caught them. He was an old man, probably older than Focalis, and had the build and the general look of a veteran himself. He had a cosh at his side, a stout length of timber fastened to his belt. Focalis gestured to the others, and they similarly disarmed and then stepped into the open as he backed away into the garden so as not to block the corridor exit for the watchman.

'Not seen your friend for a while then?' the man said, eyes narrow, searching his face, interrogating his features.

'Not for four years, since Hadrianopolis.'

'Then you're a year too late.'

Focalis sagged. 'What happened?'

'Drank himself to death. He was never a happy man, as long as he lived here. Hadrianopolis did for him, I reckon.'

'It did for a lot of people. What of his family?'

'She really did love him, I guess. A month after he died, she opened her own veins. Went to join him. The boys fell out. I say boys, but they're men really. Eighteen and nineteen summers. They live in the town now, but this place is still up for grabs. The parents left no will, and they've been fighting over ownership of the place since the funeral. That's why I keep an eye on the place. Check for looters and squatters and the like. You being old friends and veterans and all, I reckon the old man wouldn't have minded you staying the night. Make sure you put everything back before you leave in the morning, and you might want to donate a few coins to replace the lock.'

Focalis nodded. 'We will, of course. Can I ask where the boys live? I'd like to speak with them.'

'Artax lives next door to the Grapes caupona, house to the

left as you look at it. Arvina has a carpenter's shop on the Canopis road.'

'Thank you, friend.'

The man gave them a last look, a nod, apparently of approval, and then turned and strode back along the corridor, through the atrium and out of the house, pulling the door to behind him. Despite an increased sense of general safety, Focalis followed and reset his bucket alarm in the vestibule before returning to the others. They then moved back to their fire and their blankets, and Focalis set himself up on watch once more.

Sitting and watching the flames, occasionally feeding the fire fresh logs, did little for his mood. The darkness of the garden was populated with ghosts that reached out to him, Persius now among them, a fresh hollowness to add to that he'd felt for years. And the fire was little comfort, for it simply brought back images of a burning farmhouse that had heralded the death of an emperor and the greatest defeat in Roman history, a bloodbath they'd been lucky to escape alive. In many ways, even though it would likely bring the usual nightmares, he was grateful when the time came to wake Odalaricus and roll up in his blankets.

He felt hardly refreshed at all when he was shaken awake by Martius as the first golden glow of the morning sun showed over the roof on the far side of the peristyle. The lad had built the fire into fresh life and already had three pieces of salted pork from their packs sizzling in a pan, and bread warming ready, olives in a small wooden bowl. As Focalis slowly adjusted to wakefulness, his son moved over and shook the third man. Odalaricus awoke, stretching and rubbing his face vigorously. He sniffed, frowned, and then turned to the fire and smiled.

'God, but that smells good. You'd make someone a lovely wife, you know?'

Martius gave the man a weak smile that politely acknowledged the jest, while carrying an undercurrent of 'piss off'.

Half an hour later they were extinguishing the fire and washing out the pots with one of their water skins, the water supply to the house being cut. Respectful of what the watchman had asked, they carefully replaced everything they had borrowed, cleaned up where they'd had the fire and slept, and on the way out left a small handful of coins on the altar with a note explaining that it was for the lock.

Moments later they were outside once more, climbing into their saddles.

'Why do we need to see the man's boys?' Martius asked.

'Courtesy,' Odalaricus replied. 'It looks a lot like the Goths haven't found Persius' house, or if they did, they discovered he died and moved on. But the sons need to be warned just in case. Fritigern is a vengeful bastard, and he might just decide that if he can't gut Persius he'll go after the man's kids. That's one reason your dad didn't leave you at home when he left.'

Martius nodded his understanding and they rode back down the drive. A quarter of an hour later they were entering the outer limits of the small town. Morning now advancing, and the place was coming to life, the streets filled with folk of all ages and genders going about their ordinary business. Focalis found himself wondering what that was like. Just having nothing to worry about but work and life pressures, no grand history or vengeful enemies. Probably not as nice and relaxing as it sounded, he conceded.

They asked directions of a couple of people and found the Grapes easily enough. The caupona was already working, serving up food and wine to those who had not the time to break their fast at home and had to eat on the move. They paused there for a moment, examining the foods in the bowl-shaped dips in the counter. Everything looked fresh and appetising, and so they refilled their supplies, purchasing another jar of wine while Martius refilled the water skins from a fountain. Business complete, they moved to the house next door and studied it for a moment.

Persius Artax was not a wealthy man. The house was poor quality and dilapidated, needing a deal of work to put it right. No wonder they were fighting over ownership of a house worth a small fortune. And there would probably be a solid inheritance waiting to be settled, because of the lack of a will. Handing the reins of his horse to Martius, who stood back in the street with Odalaricus and the animals, Focalis stepped forward and rapped on the door.

There was a long pause, and, finally, shuffling footsteps beyond. Focalis took a steadying breath and forced a smile on his face as the door opened to reveal a young woman with an expression of distaste that was clearly her norm. She frowned at him.

'What?'

'I am here to see Persius Artax?'

She snorted and turned, shouting back through the house, 'Art? It's for you.'

While she waited, she looked Focalis up and down. 'You a soldier too?'

'Not anymore.'

At that point, a young man strode along the corridor and the wasp-faced girl disappeared inside. Persius Artax was a tall man with a pinched face. He wore a dun-coloured tunic and a single plain ring on his marriage finger. His hair was longer than the current fashion, but he had at least clipped his beard short.

'Yes?'

'I am a friend of your father's.'

'I doubt that. My father died when I was four. He didn't have many friends. Fell off a horse into a river in the end.'

'Your *step*-father,' Focalis corrected himself.

'Good for you.'

'You did not get along with him?'

'Would you laud a man who toyed with your mother's affections just for the money, then left her distraught? The man was a shit. That makes you a shit by association.'

'And yet you carry his name?'

'Because I can't afford the legal representation to change it back. Among the other things your shit of a friend did was nullify Mother's will, then die before a new one was drawn up. Now no one gets the money.'

Focalis frowned. 'Could you and your brother not come to an arrangement? Split the money down the middle. And the house?'

He was getting wrapped up in something that wasn't his problem and he knew it, but it seemed such a simple solution.

'Tell that to *Arvina*. Anyway, what do you want?'

'Did Persius ever tell you about our army days?'

'What? No. I tried not to speak to the prick at all.'

'There is a Goth called Fritigern. A powerful Goth with a

fanatical warband. They are hunting our old tent party for something we did before the war. I came to warn your step-father, albeit a year too late.'

'I can point them to where his ashes are if they want to piss on them.'

Focalis was getting irritated now. 'I just felt I needed to warn you and your brother. There's probably nothing to worry about. When Fritigern learns that Persius is dead, he will probably move on and look for the rest of us, but I felt it only fair to let you know. If any strangers come around asking about Persius, other than us, do what you can to distance yourself from him.'

'I've been doing that for years.'

Focalis huffed. 'Well, it's been a delight talking to you. Good luck with your little war.'

The young man gave him a sneer and simply closed the door, shutting them out into the street.

'Looks like our old friend caused a bit of trouble here,' Odalaricus noted.

'Well I've done what I can,' Focalis replied. 'Let's find the other one and then move on.'

As they walked their horses through the town, Odalaricus turned to his friend. 'Where next? After the other brother, I mean. Taurus?'

Focalis nodded. 'Shouldn't be too hard to find. Last I knew he was in Macellum Iulia, just up the road a way. And he should still be around. It'd need a small army to take Taurus down.'

The three of them moved on through the town until they spotted the carpenter's workshop not far from the edge, on the Canopis road. It was a modest set-up, a house with a yard that was given over to storage of both untouched timber and finished items, a single shed serving as the actual workshop. Persius Arvina was far from rich, but certainly seemed to be making a go of it. Indeed, Focalis examined some of the furniture as he once again handed his reins to Martius and stepped in through the gateway, noting the craftsmanship. The man would have done well in the legions, for good carpenters were always valued.

'Can I help you with anything?' a voice called. 'Are you looking for something in particular, or just browsing?'

A figure emerged from the darkened doorway of the workshop, a chisel in his hand, sawdust settled over much of him. He bore a striking resemblance to his brother, although there was considerably more muscle on his frame, and his face seemed less naturally inclined to a scowl. Focalis eyed the various chairs, stools, bowls and so on, and nodded his appreciation.

'Actually I wasn't shopping, but I have a mind to pick up a few things while I'm here. You do good work.'

'Thank you. Feel free to spread the word.' Arvina grinned, and Focalis made the snap decision that he liked this man. 'So if you didn't come for my work, why *did* you come?'

'We were friends of your step-father.'

'Ah. Something to do with the inheritance? I think you'll find it's all in the hands of the lawyers, and given what lawyers are like, there probably won't *be* an inheritance when they're done with it.'

'Actually, no. We didn't know Persius had died until last night. Did you ever discuss his past with him?'

Arvina cleaned the chisel and tucked it into his tool belt, then rubbed his hands together and sat on one of his stools.

'Not in detail. He didn't like to talk about it. But I know it ate away at him. Something he did sent him to drink and to the grave. I know that's caused a lot of trouble for us, but I still couldn't help feeling sorry for him.'

'The problem is that the thing he did, which we *all* did, has had repercussions. There's a Goth chief called Fritigern, with a warband of killers, who's hunting us down. It might be that you're in no danger, given that Persius has been dead for a year, but I thought I ought to warn you so that you could be on the lookout for strangers. Just be careful, especially around Goths.'

'I always am. Just how much danger am I in? Have you told Artax about this?'

'He was a little unconcerned. Your brother seems less content with life than you, if I might be so bold. He sounded extremely bitter about the settlement. I think he blames you for it. I did ask why the estate couldn't just be split down the middle and he told me to ask you.'

'My brother has always been a parasite, frankly. He expected to inherit Mother's fortune and never have to do a day's work in his life. Persius told us both flat that a man was only as good as his own self-respect. He insisted that we work for a living, and if we did, then the estate would be divided appropriately. I had always been good with wood. Mother loaned me enough capital to set up this workshop. I could pay her back now, if she were still here. Artax refused to accept it, though. Persius was not our father, and he never respected the man. I am, I know, being a little obstinate, but I am deliberately not letting him inherit until he does something worthwhile, even though it means I get nothing myself. Selfish, perhaps, but then I agree with the old man, and I have my self-respect.'

'Good for you.' Focalis smiled. 'And I will feed a little funding into your coffers. We need some bowls and cups that are light but durable for our journey.'

'You go to hunt this chieftain?'

'Not as such. We're gathering together, because *he* is hunting us.'

Arvina's brow furrowed, looking past Focalis, out into the street. 'That's your boy out there? Looks like you.'

Focalis nodded.

'And you've brought him with you. Why? How much danger am I in?'

This was uncomfortable, and Focalis shifted his footing as he scratched his chin. 'The truth is that I don't know. A logical man would find that his enemy is dead and move on, but Fritigern is not a logical man. He's a lunatic and a killer. I would like to say that you were safe, but if I was even remotely sure of that I wouldn't have come. Goths can't be that common here, though. Keep your eyes and ears open. Distance yourself from your step-father if you can. Maybe even drop his name from yours. Make yourself hard to find.'

The young man gave him a troubled frown. 'I have built up a business on my name. I may not be province-wide, but I'm proud of what I do, and I don't want to change the name or hide. What kind of life are you suggesting?'

'One that we've been living for years. Listen, I'm sorry that this has come down on you. Most of us didn't have families, so it's not been a problem. My lad has been preparing for this for years. But it's a bastard for you, and I understand that. I wish I could help, but beyond warning you, I can't think of anything else. If we stayed, we'd only attract them, after all.'

'What about the authorities?' Arvina asked.

'They won't do anything. Fritigern has been deposed, but he's still an influential man with the Thervingi and the Greuthungi, and the empire has a very fragile peace with the Goths right now. No governor or officer is going to arrest or hunt a Gothic chieftain without a direct imperial order. The last thing anyone wants is for the war to start up again. I'm afraid we're on our own.'

Arvina took this in with a sober expression, nodding to himself. 'Some days life just hands you a turd and expects you to deal with it, eh?'

Focalis gave a humourless chuckle. 'I live in hope for you. We are making waves as we go. If we make enough noise, we'll attract Fritigern's full attention and he won't bother hunting anyone else. With a little luck all his force will come after us and your life will go on unchanged. Just be watchful.'

Arvina nodded. Focalis found a dozen small wooden items that would be of use in their packs and paid an inflated price for them, exchanged a last wish of fortune with the young man, and then returned to the street. The three men mounted and began to walk their horses out of town. A few hundred yards beyond the last houses, a milestone at the junction marked the road to Macellum Iulia, and the three of them paused for a moment, dismounting and reshuffling their packs with the new wooden implements and food they'd procured in the town.

'Where are we going next, then?' Martius asked. 'Or rather, who are we going for?'

'Taurus,' his father replied, stuffing stacked wooden bowls deep into his pack and replacing the blankets on top of them. 'Big man. Well named. We had no doubt what he would do when we retired. He had only one talent and that was punching people. I once saw him fell a donkey. Since the army he entered himself on the fighting circuit.'

'You mean like gladiators? I thought the games had been stopped.'

'They have in a lot of cities. Some places still hold them. It's not illegal, just frowned on as immoral. But where cities have outlawed the practice, it's simply gone underground. That'll be where Taurus is. He's no great thinker, but he's not daft. He'll have kept himself hard enough to find.'

A distant shout drew their attention and they paused in their repacking to look up. Persius Arvina was jogging along the road out of town, heading their way. As he reached them and slowed, breathing heavily, Focalis stepped out to meet him.

'What is it?'

'I'm never going to be safe, am I?'

'I don't know.'

'If I was going to be safe, you wouldn't have taken your own son on the run.'

That was rather an uncomfortable point, and Focalis winced. 'That's different.'

'I'm coming with you.'

'That's not a good idea,' Odalaricus put in, joining them.

'Why?'

'We're going to be hunted, and we're walking directly into danger.'

'But you think I should sit and turn a lathe and wait for a Goth to turn up at my workshop and spit me? I suspect I stand a greater chance with armed men around me.'

'Your workshop...'

'Can be locked up. I have no family other than Artax, and

he won't even speak to me. At least with you, if you can finish this, I will know it's over and I'm safe.'

'I can't guarantee to protect you,' Focalis replied.

'Nor can you if I stay here.'

'Dad,' Martius said. The three of them turned to him.

'What?'

'You've got to let him come. He's right.'

There was a tense silence. Focalis sighed. 'Do you have a horse, or is there a horse dealer around here?'

'Can you wait an hour?'

'Yes. We'll finish repacking. Get a horse and pack whatever you need.'

As Arvina nodded and hurried back into the town, Focalis sagged. 'He's a good man, but he's no warrior. He's just another civilian we're going to have to protect.'

'You want to pay the price for what we did?' Odalaricus said quietly. 'This is the price. Besides, that chisel looked nasty. He might not be as defenceless as you think.'

'Alright. Let's finish packing while we wait for him, then we go and find Taurus.'

6

It had taken only an hour of travel for Focalis to regret Arvina coming with them. It was not his abilities, for though he may have never been tested in combat, his carpentry had given him sharp reflexes and good muscle tone. And it wasn't because Focalis didn't like the man. Arvina was eminently likeable, and he and Martius had already struck up a good friendship despite the years that separated them, riding together and engaged in conversation all the time. It wasn't even the added risk that came with taking another potential target with them, whom Focalis and Odalaricus would have to protect whenever they ran into trouble.

It was simply that Arvina was so damned slow.

At everything.

It made sense now how good his carpentry was. He was a perfectionist who never did anything without thinking it through thoroughly first, and when he did it, he did it with a finicky preciseness that simply took time. It also explained how they'd all but left town before he joined them. He had spent all that time thinking through his decision.

Their pace of travel lagged.

Whenever they paused to rest the horses, Arvina would fuss around to find the best place with the lushest grass for the animals. Whenever they cooked, the man assiduously checked everything, cleaned and dried everything before and after use, even if they would be using it again in the same meal. At least he would be an attentive sentry when it came to his turn next time they camped.

Oh, and there was his thing about Goths.

Despite his general good nature and positive attitude, the odd veiled comment that had come through in conversation worried Focalis. The man was clearly prepared to do what it took to end the matter with Fritigern and his warriors, which was all very good, but the way he talked with acidic hatred about them carried an undercurrent which suggested a certain xenophobia – that perhaps Arvina applied his opinion about the men that were after them to *all* Goths.

That could be a problem.

It was a positive benefit to be all fired up against the renegade ex-king and his Thervingi killers, but to extend that hatred to their whole race was a little alarming. The war was over, and the vast majority of the Goths to be found south of the River Danubius were actually peaceful allies, people of the empire, and their warbands were officially committed to protecting the borders against those very tribes that had driven the Goths to seek asylum in the first place. It had been surprising how few Goths they had seen so far, but that was going to change a great deal as they neared the coast and the larger cities, especially Marcianopolis. There was a worry in Focalis that the lad would start something with an innocent.

At least that was something to think about later. Right now, they had other matters to attend to.

Macellum Iulia was a mid-sized provincial town in good, flat, wine-producing lands. Before the war it had been one of the more thriving settlements of the province, its wealth and importance born from its position at a meeting-point of three major trade roads and from the wine it produced to distribute along those routes. Then the war had come and, with no high walls or hardy garrison, the city had been one of those unfortunates that had fallen to Fritigern's furious tribes after the murder at Marcianopolis. It had been raided and half-destroyed three times during the following years, never quite managing to catch its breath between disasters. In some ways the place had been yet another victim of Focalis' sins. Their actions on that one night had created brutal consequences for a whole empire. It had now been well over a year since the place had last seen trouble, and already it was beginning to regrow, like some sprawling hedge that has been cut back to the core, but allowed a season to bud anew. Other towns would have given up and moved away, the inhabitants abandoning such an unfortunate place and seeking a new life in other cities, leaving the ruins to decay and grow over. Not Macellum Iulia. The meeting-point was simply too lucrative to leave untouched, and already, even amid the scars of six years of war, the place was clearly becoming wealthy once more.

A stream, too small to even consider the term 'river', trickled from the low slopes of vine-covered hills off to the south, bordering the built-up area, new houses sprouting amid the ruins of the old. There was still a long way for the city to go, though, before it could even consider itself recovered. Just from their approach along the Suida road, he could see the blackened skeletons of two large buildings that had clearly been warehouses, looming over the rubble-clogged stream. Not far upstream a small, new market of half a dozen brightly coloured stalls had sprung up within the shattered remnants of a grand marketplace. Still, only half a year ago the news that reached the Augusta Traiana market, where Focalis shopped, was that Macellum Iulia had been so devastated that only ghosts lived in its ruins. What a change half a year had seen.

'What a strange place,' Martius said as they rode across the tiny, polluted stream and into the edge of the town.

'Oh?'

'It looks sort of ancient and new at the same time. Half ruined and half glorious.'

Focalis had to agree. Every structure they passed was either a burned-out and battle-scarred shell or a gleaming new building of freshly quarried stone or recently felled timber. And refugees from the war huddled in the ruins, while settlers or those with sufficient funds to rebuild their lives moved about the place largely ignoring the misery around them. It was like watching a city haunted by its own ghost.

'Of course,' Odalaricus said casually as they passed through the outskirts, 'it strikes me that Taurus is in little danger.'

'Really?' Martius turned a frown on the man.

'You've not met him. A warband with artillery support would probably find themselves on the defensive after a round with Taurus. The praepositus who led us at Hadrianopolis used to call him "Cataphract". You know what a cataphract is?'

Martius nodded. The heaviest cavalry in the Roman military, clad in iron or bronze from the tips of their toes to the top of their head, even their arms, their horses covered in the same. They were mobile steel monsters, hard to bring down and with a reputation for being able to break any line with a charge. A reputation that had finally been proved wrong at Hadrianopolis, yet the analogy for Taurus was still a good one.

'Sounds to me like we need him more than he needs us,' Arvina put in.

'Precisely,' Focalis agreed. 'It might be hard to persuade him to join us. If he's invested in the fighting circuit he could have made a lot of money, and he won't be over-keen to leave that behind. And I doubt he worries much about Fritigern coming for him.'

Odalaricus nodded. 'But Fritigern's no fool. He probably won't send six warriors for Taurus. He's seen the bastard in action, after all. All it would take, though, is one well-paid nobody with a phial of hemlock. Taurus has his weaknesses, and one is that he eats like a horse, and indiscriminately, because he has no sense of taste.'

'Macellum Iulia banned the fights before the war,' Odalaricus said, as they passed a curved, colonnaded wall broken down to shoulder height that could perhaps have once been a small arena. 'They were trying to promote a new, Christian city for all, attracting trade and culture. The city might have died a few times since then, but the law probably still stands, so I doubt there's official fights here.'

'Then we'll have to be clever and inquisitive,' Focalis replied. 'And this needs to be me and Titus. Just us two.'

'What?' Martius looked worried.

'Just for now. To find him, we're going to have to dig around in the underbelly of the town. That's no place for a lad of your age.' He looked about and fixed his gaze on a building up ahead, on the edge of a wide square filled with life. It had a sign hanging out advertising room and board and, like all the buildings that had a roof in this place, it was new and clean, only a few months old. Which meant that it was a reasonable quality establishment, built to capitalise on the revitalised trade since the peace treaty. He thrust a finger at it.

'That place. Looks like a good place for the night. I know we've got a while before sunset yet, but we might as well get ourselves organised. We don't know how long it's going to take to find Taurus.'

They made their way towards the building and, as they approached the edge of the square, Focalis faltered for a moment. A group of Goth warriors was visible halfway across the market, deep in conversation with a stallholder. It was impossible to tell whether they were perfectly innocent or whether they might be assassins sent by Fritigern, but whatever the case, it put him on guard, and as they reached the inn, he nodded at the square.

'You see 'em?'

Odalaricus nodded. 'More than six, but that means nothing. Our friend might have decided to send half a cohort after Taurus, after all.'

Focalis turned to Arvina and Martius. 'Be alert and be very careful. The trick is to look as though you have not a care in the world and are going about your own business while keeping your eyes and ears open to everything, and being ready to run at a moment's notice. Can you both do that?'

Martius nodded. Infuriatingly, Arvina considered this at length before finally nodding, and the four of them walked their animals through the arch and into the yard beside the inn. Handing them over to the stable lad, they returned to the front door. The Goths in the square were still involved in whatever argument they were having, and it came as something of a relief to Focalis, when they stepped inside, to discover that there was no sign of other tribesmen within. The place was busy, and the four pushed their way through the bustling room to the bar, where the proprietor was busily pouring a small bucket of live eels into one of the hollows on the counter, a fresh delicacy to tempt the customers. So fresh they were still swimming around.

A quick conversation with the owner and the exchange of coins and they secured lodgings for the night in the form of a bunk room the four of them could share. Handing over the room key to Arvina, Focalis regarded the two younger men. 'Titus and I are going to find Taurus. You two stay here. In fact, head up to the room and unpack and stay there. Come down to get food and drink if you must, but then get back out of sight. When we find Taurus we'll come and get you.'

Martius looked less than content at the prospect of the separation, but Focalis had plastered on his parental 'do this or else' face, and the lad knew there would be no argument over it.

As the two veterans turned and marched out of the door, Odalaricus turned to his friend. 'Might have been safer to keep them with us. Your lad has killed people, mate. He's not going to be terrified by Taurus' world.'

'There's a difference,' Focalis replied. 'Killing to save your own life can be brutal and shocking, but it's straightforward. The sort of thing we're going to find is different. You know how seedy and horrible this could get. His mother would have pulled out my tongue if I'd told her I was taking him to the games.'

Odalaricus just nodded at that. Focalis rarely mentioned

Flavia, and whenever he did, it brought a look of pain to his face.

'Where, then?'

'Near water. That amount of blood needs cleaning a lot. Do we suppose they still have an aqueduct?'

'Well they certainly aren't getting fresh water from that stream. You'd be dead in a week if you drank that.'

'But it won't be happening anywhere central. Somewhere on the edge, near water. The southern edge, too.'

'Why?'

Focalis rolled his eyes. 'That's where the hills are, and water flows downhill.'

'Good point.'

The two of them, unarmoured and with only their swords belted at their sides, moved back into the square. There was no sign of that group of Goths at the market stall now, although their disappearance did not ease the tension for the two veterans, for they were still around somewhere. The pair then spent the better part of an hour exploring the southern fringe of Macellum Iulia, walking its streets and taking in everything. A symptom of coming ever closer to the province's larger, more cosmopolitan, cities, as well as the coast, was the increasing diversity of their surroundings. Back in Suida, Goths had stood out. Here, they found at least one figure whose origin was clearly north of the river every other street, as well as easterners from across the Euxine Sea and immigrants from the south. It made it much harder to spot someone who might be one of Fritigern's killers on the lookout, and so the two men found that their senses were heightened, their tension high, throughout their journey.

It seemed that water pooled in the hills to the south, fed

by small streams and springs, and in particular a lake sat in a ring of low peaks just above the city, continually venting by way of a second stream that tumbled down the slopes and through the southern and eastern sides of town, both wider and more appetising in its appearance than the rubble-filled channel to the west. They spent some time wandering the area around that stream, searching for evidence. In similar situations, when they'd been in the army and looking to wager money on illicit fights, one way to track them down was just to look for the blood. If fights were going on or had recently finished, the cleaning up was quite a job, and you could find pink water pooling, or rocks with drips of blood where weary fighters had gone to the stream to wash their wounds.

In this place they found no such evidence, and so settled on the more direct way of tracking down the entertainment. They asked.

They selected the seediest-looking caupona in the southern outskirts of the town, a place where money had been saved by simply rebuilding a ruin, filling in the gaps with new bricks to create an unpleasant, shoddy-looking architecture that belonged to neither the new reborn city nor the ghost of the war-torn one. Both men entered with their hand on their sword hilts ready. This was not a garrison town, and there were no soldiers' bars or watchmen patrolling the streets. Crime could be rife and the respect for a veteran would be considerably less here.

The place was just what Focalis had expected – just what he'd hoped, in fact. No counter filled with delicacies, amphorae of imported rich Chian wine behind, no wealthy merchants and their companions eating a meal close to a roaring fire.

This place had an open room with two trestle tables and a dozen stools. A fire burned, yes, but not in a homely way, merely supplying an uncomfortable, sticky warmth and a greasy smokiness that hung around at the ceiling, just above head height. The proprietor was a surly-looking man with a scar that had almost created a crease down his forehead, and the clientele were about as savoury. In a moment familiar to strangers entering dives everywhere, the conversation in the room drained to an expectant silence as all eyes turned to them, a pair of dice, forgotten, tumbling to a halt across a table.

Focalis ignored the atmosphere and he and Odalaricus strode through the room as though the place was their natural habitat. People like this respected only strength and confidence. Even as they approached the counter, the room remained silent. Focalis leaned on the surface.

'Afternoon.'

'Hello. Whaddya want?'

'Two beers, without gob in them for preference.' To turn the threat into a joke he gave the man a nasty grin. The owner gave them both an unconvinced look, grabbed two wooden cups and dipped them in an open barrel behind the bar. The two vessels landed on the surface with a deep clack, and the brown, flat liquid in them slopped over the sides.

'Six den,' the man said, thrusting an open palm at them.

Focalis fished out the small coins from his purse and dropped them into the man's hand. Behind them, this show had clearly begun to bore the other occupants, for conversations restarted and dice began to roll once more. The barman's fingers closed over the coins, but Focalis' hand shot out and grasped them. The man jolted in surprise, but before he could shout or react, the visitor had pulled his hand open once more and added a larger silver coin to the small pile of copper.

Now he had the man's attention.

He let go and the fingers closed again, this time also on the silver.

'This is a reputable place,' he said in a hoarse voice.

'That's a fucking joke,' snorted Odalaricus.

Focalis shot his friend a warning look, then turned back to the barman. He had put away his purse, but now two more silver coins danced in his hand, moving from finger to finger and cycling round in a little trick he'd used to make Martius laugh as a toddler. The scarred man's eyes followed the movement as though hypnotised, ignorant of Odalaricus' scathing comment.

'I'm looking for entertainment,' Focalis said quietly.

'I know a place,' the barman said, 'but they won't come in here. You have to go there.'

'Not whores, man. I could find them without help, rest assured. No, I'm looking for the fights.'

The barman's tongue shot out, moistening dry lips, eyes still following the coin. 'Ain't no fights in Iulia, friend. Banned, see?'

'I know they're banned. I also know they still go on, and I have two shiny emperors here wanting to join the one in your hand when you help me go to the fights.'

Still the man hesitated. He clearly knew something, and Focalis didn't think he was holding out for more money. He was actually nervous. What of? There were no garrison soldiers in the town ready to leap on him for giving away details. 'I'm not here to stop them. Maybe make a bet and find an old friend. That's all.'

Finally the barman's gaze came up to meet his, sizing him up. The man must have decided that Focalis was on the level, for he took a breath and leaned closer, conspiratorially. 'Used to be held in the old theatre, but the place was levelled in the last attack. Now they're held in an old temple to the Aegyptian gods.'

Focalis nodded. 'Where is the temple, and when's the next fight?'

The man snorted. 'Fights every night, once the sun goes down. Temple is up towards the lake, on the slope by the stream. You can't really miss it. But you'll not get in without the watchword.'

With a swift dip into his purse, Focalis added a third silver coin to the two flipping over his fingers. 'And the watchword?'

'For tonight it's "Achilles".' You want another night's, you'll have to ask that day.'

Focalis stacked the three coins on the worktop. 'You heard of any trouble with Goths in town this past week?'

'Always trouble. Every week. They come to trade, but six years of them coming to kill and steal's hard to forget. Always trouble.'

'Thank you,' Focalis replied and stepped back. He lifted the mug, drank the rank beer and forced himself not to gag by sheer willpower alone. Turning as Odalaricus followed suit, he crossed the room once more and left the place.

'Two hours till dark,' he murmured. 'Just about time to get back to the kids and eat before we go.'

'When we go to the fights,' Odalaricus said, 'take them with you.'

'What? No.'

'Something about this place feels wrong, Flavius. Can you

not feel it? That barman was scared of something, and it wasn't us.'

'It also wasn't Goths.'

'I know you want to protect Martius, but the best way to do that is for him to be with us, not on his own in an inn. I don't think Persius Arvina could protect him.'

'I'll think about it.'

'Do that on the way home. And let me lead the way.'

'Why?'

'Because we passed a shop on the way that sold swords among other things, and I think it's about time we armed young Arvina, don't you?'

The journey back was swift and purposeful, with just a brief stop at a store that held three very used swords, probably looted in the aftermath of one of the town's raids and sold at an extortionate price. The possibility of gathering another of the unit had never felt closer. And they needed someone useful. Thus far his success rate was not high. The decanus who'd have devised a plan to get out of this mess was dead, butchered just before their arrival, Persius, the best swordsman Focalis had ever known, had already been gone a year. Only he and Odalaricus remained of the four they had tried so far. Taurus would be of little use in planning their survival, but if it came down to a fight, their chances doubled with him alongside them. And he'd last been seen here. And the fights happened every night. And if a fight was happening and Taurus was in the city, they knew damn well where he would be.

They returned to the inn, met the two younger men, quickly scoffed down a meal together, and then, armed and ready, left in the last light of the sun and crossed the city once more to

PARA BELLUM

the south, making for that hill and the slope leading up to the lake and the ancient, disused temple.

It became clear, as they passed the last few houses of the town and began to climb the hill close to the small tumbling stream, that they were far from alone in this pursuit. They could see others, individuals or small groups, making their way also. For a supposedly underground fight it was rather obvious to anyone in the area. But then with the lack of a garrison in the city, who would uphold the laws anyway?

The temple was visible up the slope in the evening gloom once they started the climb and passed a certain bump in the rise. Focalis had never seen a temple of an Aegyptian god before. Plenty of pagan temples, mostly disused, but no weird eastern ones. In its general form it seemed to follow the old-fashioned Roman model from what he could see. A precinct surrounded a central temple, the whole thing bordered with a roofed portico. Of course, this place had not been used by worshippers for half a century now, and it had fallen into ruin long before the Goths had come and raided it. The outer compound wall was intact, though patched in a haphazard way with more recent work. The actual temple within must stand on a high podium reached by steps, for even without its roof, they could see its broken column tops over the surroundings.

As they neared the place, people drifting closer, Focalis began to spot dangerous-looking figures, lurking. Men in black tunics and trousers with dark leather armour over their tunics and swords belted at their sides. No insignia, no rank. Not soldiers, and deliberately darkened to not stand out in the night. No one who was not wanted would attend, clearly. Indeed, as they passed one such man, he gave them a searching look and made an unfathomable gesture up towards the ruined temple. Those drifting in made great pains not to get too close to any others, and so, joining the system, Focalis and his friends slowed to allow other arrivals to enter before they came too near. Those guards had the look of the private enforcers generally used by powerful criminals. And illicit games would be the natural fare of such men. No wonder people here were scared. With no garrison it was this powerful man and his private army that made the law.

As they approached the darkened doorway, flanked by a pair of those guards, Focalis leaned towards the two younger men. 'This will be noisy and brutal. Shocking, maybe. Don't say anything to anyone. Try not to touch anyone, even. And stay close to us at all times. Got it?'

Martius nodded. Arvina wore an expression of uncertainty. Focalis couldn't decide whether the young man was having doubts about attending or merely going off on one of his lengthy internal debates before making a decision. They didn't have time for such things now, so he ignored Arvina and turned to the guard as they approached.

'Achilles.'

The man in black shook his head. 'No.'

'Why?'

'No weapons.' He pointed to the swords belted at their sides.

Silently, Focalis cursed. He should have foreseen that. Something like this would be a breeding ground for violence. Of course only the guards would have weapons. He turned to the others, troubled. They needed to get in, and he certainly wasn't leaving Martius out here where he couldn't keep an eye on him. Before he could come up with anything, however, Arvina solved the problem for him.

'I'll take the swords. I'll be down by the stream when you're done. Bet on the big fellow for me.'

Focalis, hitherto concerned about the young carpenter's presence, felt a flow of relief. If Arvina stayed outside, then both the veterans could seek out Taurus, and Martius would remain in sight. He thanked the man, handed over his sword with the others and then, with a shrug to the black-clad guard who nodded and thumbed over his shoulder, the three of them entered.

He'd seen fights in places like this before. The podium at the centre was the arena itself, the steps guarded by four more of the black-clad men. The temple walls and roof were long gone, and what remained was a square of broken columns of varying lengths, a makeshift fence linking them. The crowd of watchers filled the precinct around the podium, while shifty-looking figures sat at tables in alcoves in the surrounding portico, taking money and bets, each accompanied by a couple of heavies to prevent robbery. Off in the corner, a door led away to the priest's quarters, where the fighters would be preparing.

'Do we bet?' Martius asked.

'Yes. It's the best way to make sure Taurus is here.'

With the other two in tow, Focalis fought his way round to one of the bookies and queued until he reached the table.

'Bet?' the man asked without looking up.

'How long are the rounds?'

'Count of one hundred.'

Focalis snorted. 'What are the odds on a win for Taurus in the first round?'

'Taurus is second fight. First fight is Colchis and Pax. Want to bet on that?'

'I'll save my money for Taurus.'

'You won't get rich. Taurus to win first round, two gets you three. I can offer you three to one that he *kills* his opponent first round.'

Focalis heard Martius behind him gasp in shock and willed the lad to shut up. 'I'll take those odds. Three miliarensia on that.'

The man looked up now, sharply. 'Sure?'

'Sure.' Focalis dug in his pouch and found three large, gleaming silver coins and dropped them into the bowl on the table. The man shrugged, swept the coins away into his palm to deposit in some hidden place, and then found two stamps and dipped them on the ink pad before slamming them on a small parchment square. This he shook dry and then handed over to Focalis, who quickly ran his eyes over them to make sure he'd not been stiffed. Satisfied, he turned and led the others back into the press.

'They might die?' Martius whispered. 'I thought gladiators were kept alive because they were expensive.'

Odalaricus chuckled. 'This is not the old days, lad, and these are not gladiators. This is pit fighting. No armour, no blades. But there are weapons of a sort.'

And as they shoved their way through the grumbling crowd to get to a place with a good view, Focalis could see them. The fence that connected the columns and surrounded the ring held clubs at various points, three-foot batons of oak, each of which was stained with the blood of many victims. Indeed, the brown stains all over the podium and its columns made clear just how brutal the fights got.

'Whatever happens, don't shout or scream,' Focalis told his son. 'Close your eyes if you have to.'

The lad had gone a little pale, and he could understand, really. Yes, Martius had taken lives these past days, and not suffered a conscience problem with it, but they had been enemies, busily trying to kill him. Taking a life in a fight of self-defence presented little trouble in the ethics department. Watching two individuals battering each other to death for a mix of entertainment and silver was another thing entirely. Flavia had always disapproved of the fights, and had brought Martius up in the same mould.

They stood, tense, and could sense the fight nearing, for the atmosphere gradually changed, and the number of people both arriving and placing bets dwindled. Finally, the heavy door to the outside world was closed, and the crowd dropped into an expectant hush.

Another door over in the corner opened and the cheering began. Black-clad heavies forced a path through the roaring crowd as two men, accompanied by a scrawny old fellow in a black tunic, made their way to the podium. As they passed by, Focalis took in the details. The men were physically a good match. One dark-skinned, one pale, but both of a wiry, muscular build and average height, both confident in stride and expression.

'Wouldn't have known who to take here, anyway,' Odalaricus noted, echoing his own thoughts. Focalis nodded his agreement. He made sure that Martius was between them, protected as far as possible, as the fighters mounted the steps to the ruined temple and walked around, playing up to the crowd, while the old man gave their names and a short précis of their history. At one comment, his eyes shot to the fighters, the announcer naming Colchis as a warrior of the Greuthungi. His gaze then darted to Martius, whose worried expression had vanished, replaced with one of determination. Focalis studied the pale fighter. He had the colouring of the Goths, for sure, but none of their tell-tale styles, and was perhaps shorter than the average Goth. The suspicion formed that the fighter's history was as fictional as his name. He was no more Goth than was Focalis.

That triggered another glance around at the crowd. He'd scanned the watchers several times since their arrival and had seen no Goths here. Likely they weren't privy to the existence of the entertainment yet. Good. It made their job here a little safer.

A bell clanged as the old man stepped out of the ring, and the crowd roared as the two men raced at one another. Focalis watched the initial meeting. A flurry of blows from both men, fists balled, stamping on feet, punching at face and gut, an attempted head-butt, and then the two fighters were locked in an embrace as they grappled, fingers tearing at one another. They struggled this way and that, hugging tight, and broke suddenly as the pale one sank his teeth into his opponent's shoulder. The darker one cried out and they separated, backing away, the wounded man's hand going up to the bloody mess on his shoulder. Snarling, he flicked a handful of the blood into the crowd, who roared afresh. His questing hand found one of the clubs and tore it free of the fence. In moments he was running at Colchis, who just managed to pull a club free in time to turn aside a blow that might have ended him.

The clubs clonked hard against one another, again and again as the two men swung and parried. The darker one lashed out with a foot, mid-flurry, catching his opponent in the knee and Colchis went down with a cry, still sufficiently alert to lift his club and parry a fresh onslaught.

A bell rang. The two fighters ignored it, still pounding away, until men in black stepped in, sword points levelled at their necks. The round over, the fighters backed away, panting, one still probing the wound on his shoulder, the other limping with his weakened knee. There was a pause, the crowd bursting into conversation, and as Focalis looked across at Martius, he could sense dislike boiling up from his son, not for the fight, but for the one labelled a Goth, the recipient of his hate. He was about to point out to the lad that the man was no Goth, when Odalaricus ruined that.

'The Goth's a goner.'

'What?' Martius looked around. 'But the other one's bleeding badly. Look.'

'His knee's gone. Pax will capitalise on that. The Goth goes down in round two. Mark my words.'

There was no time to discuss or argue, though, for the bell rang once more, and the two fighters moved tentatively forward, eyes on each other. Colchis did now have a pronounced limp. They met in mere moments, and the fighting began again, a flurry of blows with the bats, some of which landed, some turned aside with a clonk. Each blow winded one or the other, but not for long enough to end the fight. Focalis could sense time running out. The bell would go soon, marking the end of another round.

Then it happened. Pax feinted to his right, but as Colchis the 'Goth' brought his own club round to block, the darker-skinned man changed the angle of his blow, his bat swishing past the intended parry and connecting with that same wounded knee. There was an audible crack, and even Focalis, veteran of many wars and witness of a thousand gruesome deaths, winced as the man's leg folded in an unnatural direction, the knee joint permanently shattered. The pale fighter landed on the ground screaming, the club falling away from his fingers. He was done, and as Pax stepped forward to deliver what would probably be a killing blow, to the head, the word 'clementia' rose amid Colchis' shrieks, begging for his life as one hand came up to ward off the blow.

The darker fighter turned a slow circle, a shrug there, asking the audience. The crowd roared back their bloodlust. No mercy for Colchis this day.

The club came down hard. It broke the crippled man's arm, raising fresh howls of agony that only ended with another swing that took the pale man in the side of the head with a crack that echoed across the precinct, sending blood, brains and teeth flying into the crowd, causing their own wounds.

The roar was immense as the crowd jumped up and down, bellowing.

Focalis turned to look at his son. Martius was not shaking. His expression was one of satisfaction. What had happened to that lad who'd felt sympathy for the Goths when Odalaricus had told the tale of their betrayal? But then, since they'd left the last town, Martius had ridden with Arvina and then sat with him for hours at the inn, and it was becoming clear to Focalis that the carpenter had no love for the entire Gothic race. The suspicion formed that Arvina had been filling his son's head with the worst stories of Goths, probably all fiction, since it seemed unlikely the young man had ever met that many of them. He would have to put a stop to that.

Such xenophobia in such a multicultural world could be very dangerous.

He made a mental note to have that conversation with Martius at the earliest opportunity, but for now there was no hope of exchanging words, and so they stood in the press while watchers crowded to the tables around the edge to collect winnings and to place bets on the second fight. At the same time, the broken contestant was wrapped in a blanket and manhandled from the podium, carried back towards the door, followed by the bloodstained Pax, clutching his bloody shoulder with one hand, the other raised in victory, drawing the love of the crowd. There followed a short pause while the clubs were cleaned and replaced, and the podium floor cleaned and dried.

For some time the crowd murmured loudly as all present exchanged predictions and hopes, and then, finally, as the door in the corner opened once more, the crowd exploded in cheers. Focalis' head snapped round, and recognition and relief flooded through him. Despite the press, such was Taurus that Focalis could see him over the many heads of the crowd. He hadn't changed a bit. His expression was serene, that peace that only comes from the certain knowledge that you cannot be beaten. His head was larger than any man's Focalis had ever met. He'd had to have his helmet specially made when they joined up. And his neck was even wider. His hair was still dark, but shaved so short that it looked more like a shadow on his skull. His beard was short, though not quite so much, just too short to get hold of in a fight.

As the new fighters moved towards the centre, they passed fairly close, and Focalis and Odalaricus both shouted and waved, trying to get the big man's attention, but failing because the entire crowd was doing the same. As they came close by, Focalis got a better view, and could see that Taurus, clad only in a loincloth, had lost none of his impressive size or muscle tone in the two years since they'd retired. He was still a mobile mountain of flesh, muscle and bone. Indeed, as Focalis glanced sideways, he almost laughed at the expression of wide-eyed disbelief on Martius' face.

The other contestant, following close behind Taurus, might as well have brought a procession of mourners with him. He was fully two feet shorter than his opponent, and probably the same amount narrower. He had the crazy eyes of a serial killer, though, and there was no fear in his face. He was clad in a suit of leather, decorated with metal studs, covering his torso and arms, and he wore greaves – clearly the organiser of the fight had been forced to bend the rules to give the man a chance. As he looked their way, Focalis caught his eye, and the look there confirmed it. The man was as mad as a moon-struck weasel. A criminal, a murderer and a madman, clad in armour and placed opposite Taurus to die. Focalis was in no doubt who would win, but given the armour, he was revising his opinion that it would not stretch to two rounds. He might lose his bet after all.

He watched and listened as the fighters entered the arena and the old man named and described them. Notably there was no mention of Hadrianopolis or the scholae in Taurus' biography, just that he'd been a man of the legions and a veteran of the wars. The crowd went wild. Taurus was clearly a regular hero and a big hit with the locals. His opponent was introduced as 'Needle,' a name that oddly suited him. It seemed Needle belonged to a tribe from north of Persian lands, but had been so violent that his own people had driven him out. The Persians had captured him, but he'd been so much trouble they'd sold him and he'd come to Thracia as a slave. It might have been as much fiction as the previous Goth, but it made a good story, and it sat well with the mad-eyed killer.

There was a pause as the two men settled into their corners and waited, and finally the bell rang. All three of them craned their necks and pushed left and forward for a better view as Needle gave a whoop and danced around the fence, pulling at the clubs until he had one in each hand.

Taurus walked patiently into the centre of the ring, where he stopped, turning slowly to keep his opponent in front of him. The strange easterner began shouting things in a screechy voice and in some strange, garbled language. Focalis had no idea what he was saying, but from the tone and from his accompanying actions – including grabbing his crotch and making suggestive thrusting motions at Taurus – it was clearly taunts.

When he ran it came as a surprise to everyone. Mid dance and taunt, he was suddenly leaping into the attack, clubs whirling with the expertise of a professional. Taurus hadn't moved. Needle hit him like a small ferret-faced killing machine, both clubs coming round with blurring speed. Focalis watched. Martius was making worried noises. He'd clearly not expected the man to get a blow in on Taurus. But Focalis had watched his old friend's face as the lunatic leapt, and not once did the confidence waver.

The clubs struck, two blows landing simultaneously on the bigger man. One hit his shoulder blade behind the left arm, the other his right bicep. On a slighter man, they would probably have broken bones. Needle might as well have been thumping a rock. Taurus took the twin blows without even a grunt, and as the snarling, drooling killer pulled the clubs back for a second hit, the big veteran took his turn. His hands reached out and grabbed Needle's head, one on each side, and the massive appendages all but encompassed his skull. Without any apparent effort, he lifted the swinging, struggling man almost two feet from the ground, until their faces were level, and even as the now suddenly panicked warrior swung his clubs again, Taurus jerked his hands left, then right, snapping the bones in Needle's neck. The spine seemed to be giving him a little trouble, and he had to repeat the gesture before he was able, with the same stoic look of calm, to tear Needle's head from his body.

The shaking mostly-corpse fell to the ground, blood pumping from the hollow neck, spraying the watchers nearby and making the podium crimson and slippery. Taurus, holding a head with a mouth formed in an O of shock, turned slowly, examining the crowd.

'Who wants a souvenir?' he bellowed, speaking for the first time.

The crowd went wild, every pair of arms reaching for the prize, every voice raised in hope. Then Taurus spotted them. The big man stopped. His eyes always on Focalis, he threw out a finger at one of the hopefuls, and tossed the head to him.

As the announcer dealt with the aftermath and the mess, Taurus strode across to the steps. There was a momentary altercation when two of the black-clad guards tried to suggest he was not supposed to leave yet, but no one in their right mind was going to argue with Taurus for long, especially not after that little display. The huge man stomped through the crowd, hands reaching out to touch him in awe, until he came face to face with Focalis.

'Well, well,' was all he said. He folded his arms, blood-coated hands leaving marks on his bronzed flesh.

'It's happening,' Focalis explained, simply.

'You brought your son to this?'

'We're on the run, old friend. They've found the decanus already, and Persius is no more. I need to find Sallustius, Sigeric and Pictor, but I was hoping you'd come with us.'

'I'm safe here,' Taurus replied. 'My owner has an army. Fritigern's men came for me last week. They never made it through the gate.'

'Your *owner*?' Focalis blinked.

'I ran up debts. Big debts.'

'You sold yourself into the ring? Christ, man, why?'

Taurus shrugged. 'It was easier. I was going to have to fight to pay it off anyway. This way I get room and board free while I do it.'

Focalis growled irritably. 'How much do you owe?'

'Dunno. Was about three hundred solidi. Probably not more than a hundred by now. A few more months and I'll have bought my freedom again.' The big man laughed. 'Then I'll probably fuck it all up and run up debts and start all over again. Such is life.'

'Will you come with us?'

'I can't.'

Focalis sighed. 'If you could, would you?'

The man frowned, chewing his lip. He looked back and forth between Focalis and Odalaricus, and finally his gaze fell upon Martius and stopped. 'You've grown,' he said.

'Soon I'll lose this,' the lad replied, fingers brushing the

SIMON TURNEY

chain around his neck and the pouch of amulets and keepsakes that hung from it, a sign of his childhood still.

Taurus nodded. 'On the run from Fritigern, you'll grow up fast.' He looked to Focalis. 'Has he met them yet?'

'He's killed four.'

'So much for childhood,' Taurus sighed. 'You know that if they got the decanus, they'll get you eventually.'

'And you,' Focalis replied. 'No matter how protected you are, one day you'll eat some bad meat, and there will be an assassin, grinning, watching.'

'What's your plan?'

'To gather the others, and hope that Sigeric can come up with something.'

Taurus nodded slowly. 'If you survive a month, come back for me. I can buy my freedom by then. Look after your boy.'

Focalis turned to the third veteran in their midst. 'Give me your gold.'

Odalaricus blinked. 'What?'

'I know you have a whole bunch of gold solidi in that purse you collected from your cache. You're not half as subtle as you think you are.'

Grumbling, the veteran fished out a purse from his belt and tossed it over. Focalis caught it and found his own, the one he'd taken from his room when they left, his flight fund carefully put away to pay for their safety when this finally happened. Two pouches of gold coins. He held them out. 'That should be plenty to pay off your debt. Try not to use it all. You'll need a horse yet, and it would be nice to eat while we move.'

Taurus looked at the pouches, then at each of them. He was on the verge of shaking his head, and they could all see that, but as he caught Martius' hopeful expression, the fight went out of the big man. He sighed. 'I guess you're going to need *someone* to make sure the lad stays safe. Sure as shit won't be you two ladies.'

With a grin, he swiped the pouches and ambled off into the crowd. Martius began to blabber, but Focalis left Odalaricus to answer, instead watching the big man. Taurus disappeared through that door. Moments later, even over the din the crowd was making, they could hear the faint strains of an argument going on behind closed doors. A voice raised in anger. Two black-clad guards on the door suddenly opened it and rushed inside. One came barrelling back out a moment later, clutching his chest and falling into the crowd. The other soon backed out too, and kept backing away as Taurus reappeared, a pouch in one hand, tunic, belt and boots in the other.

A voice raised in high-pitched fury was bellowing orders inside that room, and the black guards were pushing their way towards it as Taurus rejoined his friends.

'I think it would be wise to leave with haste. I fear my offer did not please him. I left him half anyway.'

'You didn't kill a local crime boss, did you?'

'No, but his arm's going to ache in the cold from now on. Most of my gear's at his place, but I don't think it would be a good idea to go back for it.'

Focalis nodded as they started to push their way through the crowd towards the exit. 'Let's get out of here. I'll make the introduction to Persius Arvina as we run back through town and find our inn. Think we need to get the horses and ride. It's bad enough having one powerful nutcase after us. Let's see if Sallustius has managed to outwit the king so far.'

7

The forest of oak and beech had begun about a mile south of the town and had been an ever-present feature of travel for the night. The road they were following was known in the region as the bandit highway, and with good reason. The wealthy and the mercantile tried to avoid its use, but its nature, connecting Macellum Iulia with Sadame and, ultimately, Constantinopolis, made it far too arterial for most to avoid. Before the war, it had been regularly patrolled, and robbery had been kept to a minimum. Since then, manpower had been scarce, and the road had become a serious threat to trade and to life in general.

Consequently, even the three veterans rode with weapons to hand, eyes constantly on the trees to both sides of the road. The weather had closed in and the sporadic showers and iron-grey clouds that obscured the moon, combined with the darkness itself, made the eaves of the woods truly oppressive, and populated them with continual imagined monsters. Martius and Arvina were as nervous as could be, and even Taurus, who was afraid of little that man could throw at him, was twitchy.

'What do these markers look like?' the carpenter asked

quietly, subdued, as though keeping his voice down was going to save them from bandit raids.

Odalaricus was the one to reply, looking over his shoulder at their young companion. 'Range markers are just sticks with a number of white stripes that denote the distance between it and the artillery. But it's not a range marker we're looking for. That's Pictor when we find him. For Sallustius it'll be a painted doodle. An eagle, a sun and a II. Like this.'

He pulled up his sleeve so the lad could see the tattoo on his bicep.

'Once we've found it, that's when the fun starts,' Focalis advised.

'Fun?'

'Sallustius is an engineer, a practical joker, and a man who delights in ingenuity and in death. It's a horrible combination, even when you're on his side.'

'Maybe we should make camp and look for him in the morning?' Martius suggested, nervous gaze dancing around the darkened trees.

'No. It'll be light soon enough, but we're not sleeping until we're out of these woods and off the bandit highway, no matter how weary we get.'

And they *were* weary. They had left the city and run as fast as they could, for getting on the wrong side of a crime lord could be a fatal decision, and they had clearly done just that in taking away Taurus. They'd needed to be fully clear of his reach before they could relax, but that had then put them on this terrible road and in these woods, which was another good reason not to sleep. When they'd found Sallustius they could work something out. Besides, the less time they wasted, the more chance there was that the others would be alive when they found them.

Another mile passed with no sign of a change in the terrain, no signposts, hints of life or occupation, the only variation the occasional animal track or forester's path that ran off to one side or the other, all threatening and black. The rain began again.

A little later, Focalis opened his mouth to shout a warning, but shut it again, squinting into the shadowy recesses of the forest. He could have sworn he'd seen figures moving as his eyes roved across the endless tree trunks, but by the time he'd nipped back to the spot and focused carefully there was nothing there. It could have been his imagination, and he was certainly tired enough to be seeing things that weren't there, especially in the heightened sense of nervousness they were all experiencing.

Then he saw it again. Deep in the woodlands, some way from the road. Just a hint of movement that couldn't be the trees or the undergrowth – had to be the passage of some creature. Of course, bears, boars, wolves and all manner of fierce, hungry creatures inhabited the forests of Thracia, so it needn't especially be bandits. Still, that was twice now, and twice made it less likely to be his imagination. Under his breath he muttered a fervent prayer to the blessed Mother of God for her favour and protection.

'Keep your eyes sharp to the left,' he said, just loud enough for all to hear over the gentle patter of rain.

'Seen something?' Taurus said.

'Something. Not sure what. Could be a score of angry bandits or a grumpy bear. Hard to tell in this.'

The others nodded their agreement as all kept their eyes on the woods, moving ever southwards.

'Look,' Arvina said suddenly, voice loud enough that anyone within a few hundred paces of the road would hear him. Focalis threw him an irritable glance, but then followed his gesture, and smiled grimly. There it was. A particularly wide and venerable oak tree had died a number of years ago, the entire thing gone above head height, leaving only an immense stump the size, more or less, of Taurus. More or less the same weight probably, too. The old unit insignia was daubed on one side, roughly, stylised so that only those who were looking for it would really see what it was. Added to this, the graffiti had been there for a while and had begun to fade and had run a little in the rain. But it was definitely there, and it was definitely what they were looking for.

'There'll be no bandits here,' Taurus said sagely.

'Oh?' Martius frowned in incomprehension.

'If Sallustius is here, the bandits won't be,' Focalis explained. 'They'll have long learned to keep away from him.'

As if on cue, they all looked up, straightening, the hair on their necks rising in tense nervousness, as a distant howl of agony echoed through the woods.

'Either the bandits haven't learned their lesson, or Fritigern's men just beat us to it,' Odalaricus muttered.

'What do we do?' Arvina asked.

'We? Nothing,' Focalis replied. 'I go and find Sallustius. The rest of you wait here.'

'What? That's foolish. You might need us.'

Taurus shook his head. 'The more of us go in, the more chance someone doesn't come out.'

'The bandits can't be that fast.'

'It's not bandits or Goths you need to worry about. It's

Sallustius.' Odalaricus threw a bag of something over to Focalis. 'Sling bullets. Useful to throw ahead of you, eh?'

Focalis nodded his thanks. 'I'll either be back with Sallustius within the hour or I won't be back at all.'

'That's not a comforting thought,' Arvina said.

With a wave of farewell, Focalis looked along the line of the trees and spotted the track. A deer trail, probably, much like any of the others they had seen in the last few miles. But this one was different. This one had been marked by his old friend. Only five paces from the road he stopped, drew his sword and used it to hack off a five-foot sapling and trim it of growth to provide a light and easy pole. He then sheathed his sword once more. Swords would be of little use, he was sure.

Tying the bullet pouch to his belt, he brandished the stick and began to move, very slowly, like a hunter close to his prey. As he did, he probed ahead all the time. His stick tapped the ground every pace, checking it was solid, waved up and down to make sure even the air itself was empty, tapped the tree trunks and undergrowth to each side. Periodically he would throw three sling bullets ahead of him and only move on when they bounced and came to rest on the ground, intact. Only fifteen paces into the woods, the grass and mulch gave way to an area of muddy ground, and he paused, looking down at it, trying to make out every detail in the near total darkness. Boot prints. Fairly fresh. A matter of hours old, sunset at the longest. And several of them. Heavy boots, and he'd be willing to wager there were six pairs. The Goths of Fritigern.

Keeping his eyes moving about, checking the tracks, yet still testing and probing every inch as he went, Focalis continued to move deeper into the woods. Forty paces in, and he found the first evidence. His probing stick found a length of thin, dark thread, already snapped, hanging loose at what would have been mid-calf height. His gaze went to the tree to which it was attached, and rose, climbing the bole until it found the trap. Someone, and he knew damn well who, had wound torsion cables of thick horse hair between two branches of the tree. The thread must have been strong, for it had clearly held the launcher at the apex of tension until some unwitting traveller had snagged the cable and set off the trap. His gaze followed what would have been the trajectory of the missile and he gave a grim smile as he saw the tribulus, a pointed and barbed iron caltrop, embedded in the trunk of a tree opposite. He reached out to it. It was covered in dried blood, hours old, and more of the blood was spattered across the trunk, along with the scrape marks where another tribulus had glanced off before disappearing into the bushes.

Carefully, more carefully than ever, now he moved on, still testing every step as he went. Hours. The Goths had come hours ago, at sunset at the latest. If they had been moving in a group as the footprints suggested, how come one had survived long enough to scream just now? Was Sallustius playing with them?

A further clue as to what had happened greeted him twenty paces further on. This time he spotted the sprung trap without the aid of the stick. A lily pit, as they used to call them in the army. The pit was a foot deep, the bottom filled with four needle-sharp oak points, looking up to the sky. Two of them were stained with something dark. He grinned. It might be blood, or the Goths might just have shit themselves. The leaf mould that had been covering and disguising the pit now lay between the points at the bottom. As he carefully stepped across the hole, he could see now that the path had picked up an extra trail, this one formed of blood loss, a constant spatter of blood from the crippled victim of the lily pit.

A few paces further on, the trail split, and so did the footprints. Ignoring the one with the blood spatter, he took the other branch, two pairs of boots leading on.

He almost walked into his own death.

This twine across the path at knee height had been spotted by the Goths, and they had carefully picked their way over it. Focalis had almost blundered straight into it, and his heart thundered at the realisation of how close he'd come to utter disaster. Carefully, he too picked his way over the twine and once he was across and had tested the way ahead, he looked back to see what fate he'd so narrowly avoided.

A tree to the right-hand side of the path had been almost sawn through at the base, held in place with the most careful equilibrium of weight and tension. A collection of logs was balanced among the tree's branches. The twine snaps, the tree falls, and all the logs come with it. Focalis tried to imagine the damage just one heavy log would do if it hit you in the head from that height, let alone the tree itself. He shivered.

Twenty paces on he found his first body. The Goth had been wearing a chain shirt, but it had been of little use, for the sharpened stake that impaled him had somehow been catapulted up from the ground and had slammed into him between the legs, driving deep into his torso through the groin. The body was still upright, held there by the stake that transfixed him. Focalis was fascinated by how the trap must have worked, but had little inclination to look too closely and find out. Parts of the Goth that should only ever be on the inside were gathered in a small pile underneath him.

As Focalis carefully stepped round him, he looked back at the man's face and winced. The horror the man had felt as he realised he'd triggered a lethal trap was still there, his expression fixed in death. In passing, he noted a wound on the man's shoulder that suggested he'd been one of the men hit by the flying tribuli back towards the road. They should have taken that warning and left.

Another fifty paces, following the only remaining boots, and he identified two more traps, one that had been spotted and avoided, one that had been more dangerous. A trail of blood from here marked the fact that the last man on this track had been wounded, and recently, for the blood still gleamed. The dart from the trap had been snapped, for its wooden shaft lay in the middle of the path, suggesting that the weighted point remained lodged in its victim.

Still moving with careful slowness, feeling the way with his staff, Focalis continued, pace by nervous pace through the dark forest, the rain now starting to truly settle in and soak him as it pattered off the leaves nearby. It was only because he was so alert that he heard the whimpering.

The man was not hard to find, and for the first time since he'd woken in the villa from that unpleasant dream to find killers stalking his house, Focalis actually felt pity for one of Fritigern's Goths. The dart, launched by some unknown, arcane and devious mechanism, had hit the man in the hip, and he was unarmoured, so it had simply passed into him through his clothes and lodged in muscle and bone. It had ruined his hip socket, as was plain at first glance, and when he'd tried to remove it, he'd done even more damage before the shaft snapped. Now, he was unable to walk further, and would never walk again. He would also be dead in a matter of days. The blood loss was minimal, so he would survive long enough to either starve to death or be eaten by the local wildlife.

'Please...' the man gasped in heavily accented Greek.

'You won't live,' Focalis replied, bleak and straight. 'You're dead already.'

'I know,' the man moaned.

'Shall I help you?'

The man closed his eyes. Then opened them. 'You believe in the Christ?'

'I do.'

'You believe there is this heaven where we will be...'

'I do. My wife waits there.'

'Mine too. Not my father. He blooded to the old gods.'

Focalis nodded, drawing his straight dagger. He gripped the man and pulled him forward, which elicited a moan of pain. Placing the tip of his dagger at the base of the man's skull and, resting the man's forehead against his own chest, he pushed the blade, hard. The man jerked, gasped, died.

He was an enemy, but there were limits a good Christian was willing to go to. A swift death was a better end than to be eaten by a bear.

He rose, wiping and sheathing the knife, and looked ahead. This man had got closest. That meant that any of Sallustius' traps that remained would still be primed. He was tempted to shout the man now, but there was always the outside possibility that there were still Goths, or even bandits, within earshot.

And so he began to move once more, incredibly slowly, incredibly carefully. Perhaps thirty paces further on, he triggered the first trap. As the beam came round at chest height, ready to smash his ribs, he leapt, theoretically out of the way. That he fell *through* the ground, a good eight feet down into a hole should not really have surprised him. He did thank God and the Virgin as he rubbed aching muscles and looked around the pit to see the many sharpened points that he'd missed landing on, only by some miracle.

Slowly, he rose and straightened, being careful not to step on the sharp stakes.

'You don't look like a Goth.'

He looked up. A face had appeared over the edge of the pit, a moon-face, pale and broad, fleshy and clean-shaven with hair that had receded so far it was almost on another person.

'Sallustius?'

'Flavius? What the fuck are you doing in my pit?'

'Getting faintly irritated.'

'I was looking for a Goth. There's a survivor, unaccounted for, assuming there are six.'

'He's back there a way. He's not a survivor anymore.'

'Ah, good. Would you like some help?'

Focalis glared at his old comrade. 'No, I thought I'd stay here for a bit.'

'Fair enough,' the moon face replied, grinned, and vanished.

'Alright, come back.'

Sallustius reappeared, throwing down an arm. Focalis gripped the hand and with a little struggling pulled himself up out of the pit. Brushing himself down, he looked at Sallustius. 'I take it you're ready to leave.'

'Quarter of an hour. Gather my things and saddle my horse. Tell me we're not the only two left.'

'No. The decanus has gone, and Persius died a year ago,

but Odalaricus and Taurus are out on the road with my lad and Persius' son.'

'You have a plan?'

'I plan to find Sigeric and let him come up with a plan.'

'Sound move. I'll meet you out on the road. Don't go without me. And be careful on the way back out. Not all my little surprises point outwards.'

'Fabulous.'

As the pale, chubby engineer grinned and turned, disappearing into the woodland with the sureness of a man who knew where every tripwire lay, Focalis sighed. Good. Another one with them. Just two left now, and then all they had to do was overcome a Gothic warband and kill a vengeful king.

8

'Who *is* this man?' Martius said in a whisper, looking down the drive.

Focalis had to admit it looked impressive. Almost a day south of the forest, they were now at the end of the road to Sigeric's villa, one of the few locations of their unit known publicly, and it might as well have been a palace, or a fortress, or both. No wonder he was not afraid of being found.

'Sigeric was always the clever one,' he said. 'He's only second generation Roman, but he married well and then, when his mother died, married his dad off well too, both to very noble and very wealthy Roman matrons. His blood is mixed, but most of it is lost now beneath the flow of patrician veins, so you'd never know. Decanus Ofilius was a good military strategist and tactician, but if you wanted a real thinker and a real plan, Sigeric was always the man. Look at this place. The Seventh Claudia couldn't get to him, let alone Fritigern and his Goths, or not by a direct assault, anyway. Always good investments, good choices, long-term plans which paid off. The man is rich as Midas, as noble as Pompey and as clever as all hell.'

'Of course, he won't want to come with us,' Odalaricus muttered. 'He's as safe as the treasury of Rome in there. No bastard's going to touch him. Taurus' owner had less muscle, and he was a crime lord.'

Focalis nodded. 'I doubt we'll persuade him, but at the very least he can maybe come up with something useful for us, an idea of what to do next. There's only Pictor left to find, of course.'

'He may have lost his edge,' Sallustius put in. 'I met him less than a year ago. He's a drunk now.'

'He was a drunk when we knew him in the army,' Taurus said. 'Never stopped his brain working, though.'

'All we can do is try,' Focalis said, and the six men kicked their horses into movement and passed through the sumptuous gates of the villa's entrance drive. As they rode along that long drive up to a two-storey palace built in three wings around a courtyard, he peered ahead. It *was* a fortress. Four towers rose from the villa itself, and each bore artillery. Men patrolled the grounds, black shapes in the evening mist, the barely adequate heat of the sun still evaporating the recent rain from the soil and grass.

They were being allowed to approach, that much was clear. Given the number of human shapes out there, if they were going to be turned away, it would have happened already. So they took the failure to expel them as an invite and continued to walk their horses towards that villa. The fact that as they approached every artillery piece across those four towers turned to face them could have been considered a warning. The major alert came, though, as they neared the main building. A small army of private soldiers, twenty strong, had gathered between them and the door. Focalis approached, slowing, the others behind him, and came to a halt in front of some sort of officer.

'I am here to speak to your master.'

'Yes,' the man replied. 'You are Flavius Focalis. You are expected. All six of you may enter. I will escort you. Your horses will be safe out here.'

The six of them exchanged glances, shrugged, and slid from their saddles, allowing the various soldiers to take their mounts. The officer waited patiently until they were all ready, and then gestured for them to follow.

'Come with me. Do not stray.'

The vestibule and atrium were a triumph of moneyed style. A Christian shrine sat to the right, a lararium with some very lumpy and distinctly non-Roman figures opposite. The floor in mosaic told a story of a battle between what might have been Iazyges horsemen and Roman legionaries of maybe a century ago. The distinct impression it left was that the Romans were losing. The mosaic ended at the edge of the atrium where imported African yellow marble took over, surrounding a pool in which a bronze fish spurted water constantly. It was opulence, though tasteful opulence at least.

'Mum would have liked this,' Martius muttered.

'Where do you think your mum got the taste for rich mosaic and marble?'

They were led on through the impressive house, into a more labyrinthine wing, where servants and slaves abounded. Guards were following them at a discreet distance, while the officer acted as a guide, occasionally mentioning a painting or statue as they passed.

At the centre of the wing, where corridors led off, a huge statue, grander than life-size, stood. An imperial figure in archaic armour, a radiate crown on his brow, one hand holding a great bronze spear, the other an orb.

'Who is that?' Martius whispered.

'That is our emperor, Theodosius. Note the chiselled features, the lean figure, the look of shrewd benevolence. The work of the artist, certainly, for I've met the emperor and he looks, acts and thinks like a weasel.'

'He's still better than Valens,' Odalaricus argued.

Focalis shot him a look. 'Valens made poor choices, but he was emperor, anointed by God. This one's just a caretaker who had to step in. A general who got the purple because no one knew what to do when the emperor died suddenly in battle.'

Martius frowned. 'I thought you blamed the emperor for what happened at Marcianopolis.'

'I blame him for putting Lupicinus in command. And I blame him for a rash advance at Hadrianopolis. But he was still my emperor, chosen by God, not by the bureaucrats.'

'At least Theodosius has us at peace,' Sallustius noted.

'But at what cost? This will come back to bite us, be sure of it.'

They became aware that their guide was looking at them expectantly, and followed on once more, leaving the impressive statue behind. Finally they were led to a pair of magnificently carved wooden doors, covered in Biblical scenes. The man threw them open and stood back.

Focalis peered into the room.

Sigeric looked much like his old self, lean and pale, seated with a slumped posture that suggested he had long since stopped caring about appearances. The man had always drunk far more than anyone else in the unit, but it had never, even after a hedonistic night out, affected his performance or his thinking. Focalis was, however, forced to adjust his thinking. Sallustius was right. Their friend's eyes were piss-holes in snow, his face drawn. His arm shook a little on the chair, where he gripped it, and he looked neither well nor happy.

He was alone in the room.

'I wondered when you would show up,' he said, his voice scratchy and quiet.

'Have you had visitors already then?'

'Fritigern's men, you mean? Yes, we've met. I sent them away with a sore arse and told them to come back when they were ready to play like men, not children. They did just that last night, but we still kicked the shit out of them. I'm sorry, lads, but I'm a man now given to solitude. I like my empty palace with all its empty rooms. I think I'll stay here on my own. I would offer to let you stay but... well, I just don't want to.'

Focalis felt his spirits plummet. He'd thought Sigeric might be difficult, but not this bad.

'I will appeal to your logic,' he said, folding his arms. 'You're not as safe here as you think. You won't hold them off forever, Sigeric. If they've failed to storm the place twice, they'll find another way. Poison or suchlike. Staying here is only buying you time, and eventually you're going to have to do something about it. Come with us.'

'Where?'

'Now that's the big problem,' Focalis admitted. 'We were hoping you might have an idea. The decanus did, was working on some plan to resolve it all, but he's dead.'

'I've been thinking on a solution to that very problem for two years,' Sigeric said.

For just a moment, Focalis felt a surge of hope, then the skeletal soldier's lip twisted up into a sneer. 'There isn't one.'

'There has to be.'

'My intelligence tells me that Fritigern has almost a thousand warriors. Even if he can't draw in more from the tribes, that's a *thousand* men, Flavius. Even Taurus there will tire of fighting eventually. There is just no way to take on such a force. It's David and Goliath, but in the real world, Flavius, David always loses.'

'So?'

'So you either accept that we did something fucking stupid and dishonourable and we deserve to die for it, or you run away and keep running. There are your choices.'

'Run away? That's your grand plan?'

Sigeric snorted. 'It doesn't surprise me at all that the idea of running away hasn't occurred to you. Climb on your horses and ride south-west. Eventually, in a few weeks, you'll hit Thessalonika. Take a ship from there, the busiest port in that region. In a month you could be in Hispania or Britannia or Africa, making new lives. Fritigern has had little trouble finding us here, but if he has a whole empire to search, even your grandkids will be dead before he stands a chance of finding you.'

'Is that true, Dad?' Martius asked.

'It might be,' Focalis conceded. He had actually never even considered just running for his life. Nor had any of them, clearly. They had done a pretty good job of disappearing in the wilds of Thracia, but none of them had really considered leaving the province. How determined *was* Fritigern? Taking an army of Goths across the empire would be troublesome, to say the least, and would draw enough attention that they could probably always stay ahead of him if he did come. But he might not. The Goths still had allies and influence in this region, but anywhere else, they would be more out of place than ex-legionaries. A thought occurred to him, and he turned to Sigeric. 'Why not the *local* ports? We're weeks from Thessalonika, but only days from the Euxine Sea. Messembria, maybe?'

Sigeric shook his head. 'No. Play the long game. Thessalonika is far from Gothic influence. The coast near here is flooded with Goths, and Fritigern's probably watching the ports. I doubt you'd make it to sea, and if you did, you would probably be followed. No, you want to go west, not east.'

'I'm not convinced,' Focalis replied. Still, even sallow and drunk as he was, Sigeric was sharp enough to have considered what should have been an option earlier, and to have at least given him something to ponder on. He straightened.

'Sigeric, I'll ask you again. Come with us.' Before the man could argue, he held up a hand and talked over him. 'You said it yourself: he has a thousand men. Say we get to sea and away. That means there's only you to take out his anger on, well, you and Lupicinus, anyway. You've held off his units of killers here, but how long would even this villa hold against a thousand men? And then there's other worries. Fritigern's sly. A poisoned water supply? A single trained assassin? He'll get to you eventually. You're safer with us than even here on your own.'

The man sniffed. 'I'm done, Flavius. If they get me, they get me. It means it was meant to be, and that's probably true.'

He leaned forward for the first time, and there was suddenly an odd, almost desperate energy about him.

'Avoid the Euxine coast. Go to Thessalonika. That's my advice. *Heed* my advice, Flavius.'

Focalis sighed. 'This is your last word?'

'Go with God, old friends, and good luck to you all. *That* is my last word.'

The audience was over, apparently. The guards who had followed them at a distance were now gathered, forming a wall that essentially directed them back to the door, their officer gesturing with one hand for them to depart. With a last look at the dishevelled mess that was Sigeric, Focalis shook his head sadly and turned, leading them out. The six of them tramped slowly along the corridor, that officer moving out front to lead the way again. Soldiers followed once more, the doors to Sigeric's chamber banging shut.

'He's inviting death to come for him,' Odalaricus huffed.

'Had it not been for Martius, I'd probably have been in the same state by now,' Focalis admitted. 'Not all of us have your carefree talent for ripping up a guilty conscience and throwing it away.'

'Fatalistic idiots, both of you,' the veteran snorted. 'Man makes his own destiny. You want to atone for what we did? Do it by living well and for a long time.'

'What do you make of what he said?' Sallustius put in. 'About the ports?'

Focalis shrugged. 'I don't know. It sounds far-fetched that Fritigern would be watching the ports, but then Sigeric could always think me in circles, and we're as close to the coast here as we've been. If any one of us was going to be aware of what's going on there, it's him. Question is: is he still shrewd enough that this information is correct, or is he slipping and relying on guesswork?'

'No,' Odalaricus replied, 'the question is: is there any alternative? Anyone got a better idea?'

As they made their way back to the villa entrance, they mused on this, no one able to come up with a better plan. Unceremoniously ejected from the doors, which were closed behind them, and led to their horses, they looked to one another.

'We need a decision,' Sallustius said.

As by some unseen accord, all eyes turned on Focalis. He chewed his lip. 'First things first, we leave no one behind. That's always been true, and more so now than ever. Pictor needs to be found and, assuming he's alive, brought with us. Once we have Pictor, then anyone that can, or will, come with us is with us. We can do nothing more than that.'

'And where is Pictor? I've heard nothing about the man in the two years since we left.'

Focalis sucked air through his teeth. 'I've never confirmed it, because he's been so far away from me, but I'm willing to bet we'll find him between here and the coast. When we were still serving, he had a girl back in one of these villages. I reckon he went to her when we retired.'

Taurus laughed. 'Pictor had a girl in every village from Rome to Constantinopolis. He couldn't keep it in his trousers for more than an hour. What makes you think this girl is where he's to be found? There could be a thousand of them.'

'There probably were, but this one is the only one he wrote to. I remember that night after Hadrianopolis. The rest of us were getting drunk and tending wounds. Pictor wrote to her. Poured out his heart, he did. I know this because he was wounded and wasn't sure he would make it, so he gave me the letter and told me where to deliver it when he died. Of course, he got well and I gave him the letter back, but one will get you ten that Pictor is there.'

They all nodded soberly. No one felt like joking about their friend's prolific sex life when the spectre of Hadrianopolis had been raised in the conversation. The ghosts of their past killed levity as surely as any spear.

'And you remember where this place is?'

'He made me memorise it. From here, it's about halfway to the coast. And I reckon that decides us on our next move. It's all very well Sigeric telling us to go to Thessalonika, but that's a bloody long way, and we'll be hounded by Fritigern every mile of the journey. When we find Pictor, we'll be a day from the coast, not far from Messembria. It's a gamble, but I just don't see why Fritigern will be watching the ports, and even if he is, just how many men can he spare in each port along the coast? No, something just doesn't ring true about that. I think we try our luck at Messembria.'

'Do you realise how much it will cost to buy passage for seven of us, even without the horses, all the way to some rainy western shithole?' Odalaricus pointed out. 'I don't know how much we can raise between us, but we used half what we had to buy Taurus back. Bit pointless really, since we had to do a runner anyway. But still, we're not particularly rich now.'

'Then we'll have to work our passage to the west.'

'We're not sailors, Focalis.'

'No, but we're all fit and strong, even if we're old. We can pull ropes and wash decks. We can work our way. I don't mind a bit of labour. It's better than three feet of Gothic steel through the ribcage, after all.'

They all nodded at the wisdom of this as they mounted.

'That's it, then. Pictor, Messembria and a new life as sailors.' Odalaricus shrugged. 'There are worse lives. And I know a few old sea shanties already.'

'I'll bet you do, but since you sing like a strangled cat, let's not dip into that stock, eh?'

They mounted up and set their gaze north-east, towards the last of their number.

9

Focalis heard the shot even over the general hum of the village. The late morning rain dampened most sounds, but some noises were so recognisable to a veteran that no amount of background murmur was going to overshadow them.

'You hear that?' he demanded of Sallustius over the hiss of rain.

'Scorpion shot or suchlike. Definitely. Has to be Pictor.'

Martius blinked. 'I can't hear anything.'

'That's cause you weren't expecting it. Pictor's in trouble. Looks like we got here just in time.'

Gesturing for them to follow, Focalis kicked his mount into action and raced into the village. A few folk were about, ahead in the square, though the rain was keeping most people indoors. That and the violence, anyway.

It was not hard to spot Pictor's house. A warrior in a chain shirt, with a colourful shield and a good sword, was lying on the gravel out front of the house's open door. He was already dead, albeit only recently. He was curled around something, lying in a growing lake of blood, and as they slowed their horses and dropped from the saddle, Focalis could see that the man was clutching the bolt that had driven into his chest and killed him. It was not a standard scorpion bolt, slightly smaller and more streamlined, though it failed to surprise him that Pictor might have modified something. Pictor had been their unit's artillerist, aided by Sallustius, and the man was something of a prodigy.

The bolt had killed the man in an instant, piercing his heart, punching through the chain shirt as though it were parchment. His memory supplied him with a scene around a camp fire a decade ago. Pictor holding up a bolt of a style he'd never seen before.

'See? Narrow profile head to help punch through chain links. Why every unit doesn't carry them these days, I don't understand.'

Focalis gave the Goth a nudge with his foot to be sure, but the man lay still, bleeding even in death. 'You two,' he said, pointing to Martius and Arvina. 'Wait here with the horses. Be alert. Be careful.' He pointed to Taurus and thumbed to the left of the house, then Sallustius and the right. The two men nodded and drew their blades, moving off to circle the house and look for anyone else with murderous intent. Then, Focalis and Odalaricus moved towards the darkened, open door.

They could hear shouting in the Gothic tongue further inside, but the rain was clattering on the tile roof of the house and the din was impressive, overcoming most sound. They paid little attention to the house itself as they moved through the vestibule and into the atrium, simply keeping their gaze on every doorway. There was shouting ahead, and they could see shapes on the floor in the atrium, so they paid little attention to other rooms, focusing on the scene awaiting them.

As they closed on the atrium, they could see the scene of carnage in the open room with the pool, rain battering down in the central, open, area. A young boy, dressed like a slave, had been gutted, a sword wound to his belly, his face already grey, eyes and mouth wide open. Two Goths were there, too. One was clearly already dead, for another of those artillery bolts jutted up from his ruined eye socket as he lay still. The other was writhing around, another of those deadly missiles pinning his thigh. He was swearing. Focalis knew only a little of the Gothic tongue, but he knew a few choice words, and he certainly knew some of *these* words.

He and Odalaricus moved into the room and separated, one moving around each side. Somewhere ahead, a familiar voice echoed through the house.

'Get up. Don't make me come and find you.'

Focalis grinned. Pictor was still up and fighting, clearly. With a nod to Odalaricus, he dipped towards the centre of the room. The Goth saw him now and grunted in angry alarm, reaching for the sword that had dropped from his fingers when he'd fallen. Focalis leapt, giving him no time to grab the weapon. His own sword came round in a rough swing and slammed into the side of the man's head. The Goth gave a strangled grunt as the blade smashed bone. Just in case, Focalis reversed his weapon and drove the pommel into the Goth's face four times until he could see brain, then wiped it on the man's sleeve as the body shook and twitched, and then rose. Odalaricus was standing with his back to the wall next to the doorway leading out into the peristyle.

Focalis gave him a nod and then slipped further around the edge until he was on the other side of the door.

'Pictor?' he shouted.

'Focalis? Fuck.'

'If I step out, try not to impale me.'

And with that, both he and Odalaricus emerged from the sides and stepped into the doorway. The noise of the rain, which had become even heavier now, battering tiles and bricks and gravel, was immense. It made Focalis smile to see their old friend. Pictor was standing under a gazebo, a simple leather roof held up by four spears. The rain was not touching him. It had been one of the things Pictor had drilled into them over the years. Artillery and archers were only as good as the weather. Rain made strings wet and stretchy and ruined torsion. Had the man been so prepared for an attack he'd even had a temporary tent ready in the garden?

Pictor, stocky and dark, with curly hair and a beard in a very outdated style, stood beneath the shelter, holding a monstrous machine. Standing on a tripod, the thing was like an old-fashioned scorpion and yet not, for above the runner where the bolt was placed there sat a wooden cannister. He shuddered, realising the machine was pointing at him, even though he was a friend.

Beside Pictor stood a short woman with an expression of solid determination, advancing in years now, but still striking. She had one eyebrow raised and an armful of those dreadful bolts.

'It's alright, Agnes. They're friends.'

Her eyebrow lowered, but none of the fierce certainty left her face. Pictor grinned. 'Target practice. Nice of Fritigern to help keep my hand in.'

'You fucking lunatic,' Focalis said, shaking his head. 'This is not a game.'

'Oh it is, Flavius. And I'm winning. This isn't his first try, you know? The first lot learned about onagers and old-fashioned scorpions.' He gave the murderous machine in his hands a loving pat. 'But I was saving Domnica here for a special occasion.'

That almost made Focalis laugh. Domnica had been the wife of Valens. After he died at Hadrianopolis, the woman had earned the nickname 'the Iron Empress', for she had led an attack against the Goths who'd killed her husband, and maintained a valiant defence of Constantinopolis until Theodosius turned up with his forces. Some said, albeit behind closed doors, that if Domnica had been at Hadrianopolis and Valens sitting in the palace painting his nails, things might have gone very differently that day.

'What in God's name *is* that thing?'

'*Down*,' bellowed Pictor, his grip changing slightly. Focalis had known the man long enough to obey that command without question, and he and Odalaricus hit the floor in an instant as their old friend pulled the trigger. Focalis, from his prone position, stared in shock.

The weapon loosed a foot-long bolt much like any other scorpion, but this thing was *automated*. As Pictor changed the aim, the chain continued to cycle, pulling back the torsion arms as a bolt dropped from that wooden hopper into the slot, then sprang flat, sending it hurtling through the air even as the arms were being pulled back again and another bolt dropped in. The man loosed three missiles in a row in the time an ordinary artillerist would have loosed one and then begun to wind up the tension once more.

Focalis turned, eyes still wide, still hugging the floor for safety in case that monster decided to spit another foot-long death-bringer. He saw the Goth just as the man fell. He must have been in one of the side rooms they'd ignored and followed them into the atrium, else had been somehow hidden in there. He'd stepped up behind them with murderous intent, but Pictor had seen him first.

The man had taken all three shots, one in the neck, one in the chest and one in the belly. He was already a breath from dead, the shaft wedged in his neck enough alone to kill him.

'I love to watch a master at work,' the woman beside Pictor said, leaning in to give him a peck on the cheek. Pictor grinned. 'And that's six. Round two to me.'

As he lowered the arm of the machine, the front rising to point at the tent above him, Focalis breathed a sigh of relief and rose to his feet, brushing the dust of the atrium off himself.

'You are a bloody lunatic.'

'Good to see you, too, Flavius. And you, Odalaricus. The others with you?'

Focalis rolled his neck and stretched. 'Taurus and Sallustius. And a few kids. Ofilius is gone, and so is Persius. Sigeric wouldn't come. How about you?'

Pictor patted the weapon before him. 'Tempting as it is to see how long Domnica would hold against an entire warband, I fear that would be tempting death. I've done this to them twice now. I doubt Fritigern's going to repeat his mistake a third time. Next time they'll come in force and swamp me.'

Focalis nodded. 'I think the only reason we didn't all meet the full force of Fritigern's anger was his need to keep this low-key and not draw the emperor's attention. But now things will change. He's only rid of two of us, and the other six are together and on the move. He's going to start being a lot more direct now.'

'Give me a hand,' Pictor said.

As they followed his instructions, helping Agnes lift the

roof off the spears and portage it towards the door, keeping the rain from their heads, Pictor folded up his artillery and picked up both it and the case of spare ammunition with some difficulty, carrying them inside under the cover to prevent rain getting to the mechanism. Once they were all in the atrium, the stocky man took a deep breath. 'What's the plan then?'

'We're for Messembria. See if we can take ship there for the west. Gaul or Hispania or somewhere where we can disappear properly.'

Pictor nodded and turned to the woman. 'How about it my love? Retirement in Hispania? I hear the coast there is lovely this time of year.'

'Wherever you go, I go,' the woman replied, with a sickeningly infatuated smile. Focalis forced himself not to snort. Only a few short years ago that had been him and Flavia, after all. Who was he to deny Pictor happiness? He toyed with pointing out that she would be a lot safer anywhere else but with them, but then was that still the case? They were a day from Messembria and a ship to the west. Perhaps this was as close to actual safety as any of them had been in six years now.

'Have you got a horse?' Focalis asked.

'Two. And a wagon.'

'Wagons travel slowly. We need to move fast.'

'Until the day you can strap half a dozen artillery pieces to a racehorse, a wagon it is.'

Focalis threw his eyes skywards. 'You don't have to bring them all with you. One will be fine.'

The look Pictor gave him suggested otherwise. 'Leave my children? Never. And there may come a time we need them.'

Odalaricus nodded. 'If nothing else, we can sell them to afford passage.'

Pictor cast his old friend a dark look, then turned to Agnes. 'Are the bags all packed?'

'They have been for years, dear.'

'Then take these two to help carry them and I'll bring the wagon round.' With that, still carrying his beloved weapon, Pictor disappeared. Focalis gave the woman a rather helpless look.

'Come on, then,' she said, with all the authority of a praepositus on a battlefield. Such was the force of the woman that Focalis found himself following automatically without having made the conscious decision to do so. It made him feel better that the same seemed to have happened to Odalaricus. She led them to a room where half a dozen chests and large bags were stored.

'You've been expecting this, then?' Focalis asked.

'We've been packed for two years. All he was waiting for was you lot.' She gave Focalis a very pointed look and levelled a finger at him, holding up the pile of bolts in her other hand. 'He thinks very highly of you lot, and I am not a forgiving woman. You disappoint him once, and you'll have to pull one of these out of your arsehole. Am I clear?'

Focalis blinked and turned to Odalaricus, who was close to hysterical laughter. She turned to him. 'And you. The same holds for you.'

'Dearest Agnes,' Odalaricus said with a warm smile, 'nothing could be further from our minds. In fact, we have dodged assassins and fought armies to get to him and bring him with us.'

SIMON TURNEY

'Good,' she said, and the force was suddenly gone from her as she gave them a pleasant smile. 'Then let's get moving.'

Focalis was struggling ahead of the other two, out through the atrium with what appeared to be two cases full of bricks from the weight, when Martius appeared at the other end of the vestibule, waving wildly.

'Dad, we've got trouble.'

'Oh?'

'What does a Goth warband look like?'

Focalis and Odalaricus exchanged a look.

'Oh, shit.'

10

They gathered outside, where Arvina was still mounted, holding the reins of the rest of their horses. The carpenter was pointing with a sense of urgency, and they followed his jabbing finger out to the west. Focalis felt his gorge rise and the pounding of his heart pick up pace.

Fritigern was coming.

Thus far, they'd only had to deal with small numbers. The deposed king and his renegade warband had largely kept themselves out of it, likely fearing drawing the ire of the emperor. He was possibly already a wanted man, but if he were to properly disrupt the pax of the empire for revenge, he would make himself a target for whatever imperial military could still be brought against him in this over-stretched new world.

The Goths had gathered on the hillside opposite the village, or rather, they were still gathering. It was a huge number, probably as many men as the First Maximiana had fielded on a good day. They were mounted, every last one, which ruled out outrunning them with any ease. They gleamed, dully, in the rain.

'God in heaven,' Martius breathed.

'Quite,' Focalis said. 'We have a few advantages and one major disadvantage. They must have been travelling hard to catch up with us, so their mounts will be tired, while ours are relatively rested and fresh. And there are a lot of them. It will take time for Fritigern to get them together and moving. Also, they are renegades, with no place of safety here, while we are nobodies who can hide nice and easily. Unfortunately,' he added, as a creak announced the arrival of an old wagon around the side of the house, 'we have Pictor.'

'Unfortunately?' Agnes said with a touch of acid, brow arched.

'Because of the damn wagon, not your boyfriend. Don't suppose you could persuade him to leave his toys behind?'

'He'd sooner leave a leg.'

'Then we're in trouble. Even tired, they will be a lot faster than the wagon.'

'A feint,' Odalaricus said.

'What?'

'We draw them off, so that Pictor and his wagon can move without danger.'

Focalis nodded, deep in thought. He turned to Pictor. 'You know Messembria, yes?'

'Of course.'

'Remember that dive down near the docks where Sigeric was sick on a tribune?'

Pictor chuckled. 'How could I forget?'

'Take the main road, cover yourselves up. Look like a farmer and his wife and make for Messembria, you and Agnes. That's less than ten miles. You should make it before nightfall. We'll see you in that dive near the docks.'

Pictor threw him a salute and gestured to Agnes. The two led the wagon round the other side of the house, out of sight of the gathering warband on the hill opposite.

'We assume they've seen us?' Sallustius murmured.

'I would imagine so.'

'Then let's ride like the wind and draw them off.'

As they mounted, Arvina looked at Focalis. 'If your friend is taking the main road, where do we go?'

'We ride directly for the coast, due east. Then we turn north and follow it until we reach the city and meet up with Pictor. With luck we'll lose Fritigern and his men before we reach the sea and won't be followed the last part.' He threw out an arm to encompass them all. 'This is the plan: if we get separated, make for Messembria. There's a shitty tavern near the docks called the Wanton Siren. We meet there. Until then, we ride as best we can. Got it?'

And with that, they were off, kicking life into their mounts, heading east through the village. Focalis looked over his shoulder and was relieved to see the warband on the hill immediately begin to surge forward. He didn't like the idea they were after him, but at least that should buy Pictor the time he needed to get moving without being followed.

As they charged through the village in the pouring rain, looking for their best point of exit, Focalis drew close to Martius. 'Whatever happens to anyone else, you stay with me, alright. You and me, all the way to Messembria?'

His son nodded emphatically, and then they veered off with the others, charging past a surprised looking man raking a vegetable patch despite the rain. It was not a road, per se, but more of a local access or farm track that led out of the village, but it did lead east, and to the east, some ten miles away by Focalis' reckoning, lay the coast and the Euxine Sea.

The gathering, six in total, burst clear of the last of the

houses and rode between two orchards. Focalis looked about. They were as good a bunch to face this disaster with as any man could find. Good old Odalaricus, immense Taurus, inventive Sallustius, his beloved son Martius, and even the thoughtful xenophobe Arvina. And somewhere behind them in the village, hopefully safe, Pictor and his woman. They raced through the orchards and out onto the slopes beyond, and there Focalis looked back to judge the situation. As planned, it seemed the entirety of Fritigern's warband had followed them, for the mass of horsemen poured across the landscape, coming at a tangent in the hope of catching them up. That would hopefully leave Pictor and his wagon time to get clear and make for Messembria on their own. It did, however, draw a thousand angry riders after the remaining six of them.

They rode. As if all the devils of hell were after them, they rode, sparing nothing the horses could give. If they could lose them in this next few miles, they could perhaps manage to run to Messembria without pursuit and find a ship.

He was gratified to note, as they moved across two fields and then back over another rise, that the enemy had begun to separate. Some of their riders were fresher than others, and perhaps a quarter had pulled out ahead, the rest struggling, trying to coax extra speed out of exhausted mounts.

As they crossed that last hill past the village, Focalis took in the land before them with unhappy realisation. From here, the land was as flat as a Gaulish trumpeter, as featureless as a priest's conscience. He could see a landscape of fields that stretched every one of the five or six miles to the coast. Despite the oppressive clouds and the rods of rain coming down at an oblique angle, he could even see, in the very distance, the glimmering blackness of the sea. How would they lose their violent pursuers in such an open, featureless space?

They rode, and as they rode, with Focalis constantly looking over his shoulder at their hunters, another dispiriting truth became apparent. They would not stay ahead for long. Somehow, in some way, he had miscalculated. Either this particular section of Fritigern's horde, who had ridden out ahead of the others, were well rested, or their horses were of hardier and speedier breeds. In truth, the horses Focalis and his friends rode were not of the greatest quality, and they had been ridden hard in the days since this began. It should have come as little surprise that some of Fritigern's horsemen were fresh and fast.

They were going to meet long before they reached the coast. Half that distance, in fact. On the bright side, this was only a quarter of the hunters, the rest far behind, slow and tired. On the unhappy side, that still meant over two hundred riders against their six.

'We're not going to make it,' he shouted through the hiss of rain. 'They're gaining.'

'Do we split further?' Taurus bellowed back. 'Divide their numbers?'

'No. That would still leave each of us with thirty to one odds.'

Sallustius cleared his throat. 'Who's the fastest here at working with their hands?'

Before Focalis could answer, Persius Arvina had looked across and done so. 'That's me.'

'You're fast? How fast could you cut notches in wood and tie rope?'

Arvina gave him a derisive snort, which was all the answer

the engineer needed. 'We keep passing drainage ditches. They're lined with undergrowth and dotted with trees. Next time we pass one, Arvina and I are going to set something up. You need to keep riding, so the Goths don't realise anything's up, but I would like it if you slowed a little so we could catch up with you when we're done.'

Focalis nodded and turned to the others, including his son. 'Keep riding. Halve your pace so we can catch up,' then back at Sallustius. 'You'll need someone to hold the horses.'

The man nodded, and as they rode on, the enemy always worryingly close in pursuit, Sallustius began to unhook two huge coils of thin rope from his horse, guiding the animal with his knees while he worked like only a cavalryman could. 'Catch.'

He threw one coil, and nodded his satisfaction when Arvina caught it without difficulty. Then, moments later, they were closing on another boundary drainage ditch, lined with trees, small bushes and undergrowth. They jumped it as they had the last dozen, but this time reined in on the far side in the cover of the trees. As Sallustius and Arvina slid from their horses, Focalis took the reins to make sure the beasts didn't wander off. He watched with fascination as the other two went to work, stretching out the ropes as high as they could reach, winding them around branches, hacking notches for them to pass through, until, in the space of three hundred heartbeats, the ropes formed a line along the edge of the ditch some seventy feet long, anchored by every tree and shrub on the bank, and held at some seven or eight feet from the ground.

As they worked, Focalis kept his ears open and watched the horizon. He couldn't see the Goths yet, but that was hardly a comfort. In this rain and these conditions, the bastards could be virtually on top of them before they knew it. Then he could hear them. They had to be close. He could hear the drum of hooves and barking in that dreadful language of theirs.

'Come on, you two. We're out of time.'

But seemingly regardless of the danger, Sallustius and Arvina were still finishing off, testing the tensile strengths of parts of the line and tightening them to their satisfaction. Focalis ground his teeth. Sallustius was always a perfectionist, and working with the slow bastard that was Arvina, Fritigern's men would have been in Messembria for a week before the pair were satisfied with their work.

'Leave it, now, or we're all dead.'

To add urgency to his comment, he led the horses over to them and let go the reins so that the two men had to grab their mounts before they wandered off. They mounted and rode in the wake of the others. God, but that had been close. He could see them now, pounding across the land, the leaders only a single field away. The trio of men rode as fast as their mounts could manage, and all three continually craned their necks to look back, trying to ascertain the quality of their handiwork.

He watched their trap sprung, albeit at a distance. The rope was visible enough, of course, but at speed, on horseback, with their attention on the small group of riders they followed, and in the terrible conditions of grey cloud and driving rain, few of them spotted the danger until it was too late.

Focalis watched the disaster. The riders hit the rope just as they were jumping their mounts to cross the ditch. The result was appalling and impressive. In most cases the rope caught the horse in the chest, and in shorter examples, in the face, or even hit the rider. The result was utter carnage. Had the rope been strung out long and straight it would have snapped under the pressure, but the two men had wound and anchored it in every branch and sapling along the edge of the ditch, and so even with the weight of a jumping horse, it held.

Even though they were the enemy, still Focalis winced as horses fell mid-jump, plunging down into the drainage ditch, their riders going with them. It was horribly effective, the rope causing the initial disaster, the dying horses and riders causing more and more trouble for those who followed on. Man and beast together plunged into the ditch, broken bone upon broken bone and worse still as more men and horses fell on top of them. It was like a waterfall of human and equine flesh. Ghastly. Impressive.

A few made it. Of maybe two hundred riders who'd been on their trail they had lost around a third now. Another third, at the rear and given the time to arrest their forward momentum, had stopped and were milling around, shouting angrily. The rest, though, were still coming. Some were expert riders and had managed to navigate the disaster intact, others simply lucky, managing to jump at just the right moment to avoid the rope and those in front of them.

Even as Focalis, Sallustius and Arvina rode on, occasionally looking back, there were still scores of men after them, sixty or seventy at least. Sallustius gave a nod of satisfaction. 'Let me have a think as we ride, and I'll thin them out more.'

'That was magnificent,' Arvina laughed. 'That was... urgh.'

At the strange noise, Focalis turned, his heart lurching at the sight that greeted him. A spiculum, a lightweight javelin of Roman design and manufacture, transfixed the lad in his saddle. He coughed and jerked, blood beginning to run from his open mouth. Some way back the leading figure in their pursuit whooped his triumph, hands in the air in victory for his successful throw, returning a stolen Roman weapon to its rightful people, point-first.

Arvina gasped, and lolled in the saddle. Focalis, shocked, turned to look back at the whooping rider, and then at the young carpenter. He felt an odd hollowness. He'd only known the lad a few days and had, in fairness, been rather uncertain about bringing him along. But he was also Persius' boy, and the likeable one of the two. The one worth preserving. Artax, back in that small town, would now inherit everything and go on to live in lazy ignorance at the cost of a brother who had died saving people from angry Goths.

There was no justice to the world.

It was Sallustius' voice that dragged his mind back to their present situation.

'The boy is gone. Mourn him later. For now, ride.'

And they did. Focalis couldn't stop himself, though, looking over his shoulder, watching their pursuers. The lead riders of Fritigern's band caught up with the dying carpenter on his horse, the beast slow now, milling about, directionless. They made sport of him, which sat badly with Focalis. Even as their enemy he'd had the Christian morality to help dispatch a suffering Thervingi warrior when he found him. The Goths, on the other hand, slowed their own pursuit in order to crowd around the dying young man and throw spears at him, stab at him, hack at him. Blood-mizzle sprayed into the air time and again as they hacked, chopped, stabbed. And each fresh blow brought forth a scream. And each scream cut deep into Focalis. They made him hate the riders. They made him hate Fritigern. They made him determined.

A new goal.

A new purpose.

Even as he and Sallustius rode to catch up with the others, a plan was forming in his head. The rest would take ship at Messembria. Focalis would make sure Martius was with them, and he would note where they were bound. But he wasn't going with them, at least not yet. Somehow, and he had as yet no idea how, he was going to find Fritigern and meet the man face to face.

He'd done wrong. All those years ago, at Marcianopolis, Focalis and his tent-mates had done wrong. He knew it. They all did. But Focalis was not settling now upon retribution, or justice. Retribution and justice stopped with the men responsible, while innocent Arvina had died for the bloodlust of an angry king, and he'd had no part in this but to be unlucky enough for his mother to marry one of the guilty.

No, he was not going anywhere. He would make Fritigern pay for Arvina and for all the others. Persius, Ofilius, even Sigeric, lost to drink and despair.

He glanced back. The numbers were going to be a lot easier from now on. The vast majority of the Goths were now lost to sight, back at that disastrous ditch. More were soon going to have fallen back, for their bloodlust had overcome their sense and they were still busy mutilating Arvina's body. There were maybe a score at most left, actively pursuing them, armed with swords only.

That few close enough that the fugitives might be able to deal with them.

The others had slowed just enough that Focalis and Sallustius were catching up, and of them Martius was bringing up the rear, waiting for his father. As he closed on them, Focalis waved to his son.

'Now's the time to impress me with your Parthian shot, boy.'

Despite everything, Martius gave a grin then, as he reached round and unfastened his bow from behind the saddle, then undid the lid on the quiver attached to the harness. As the remaining five riders closed ranks once more, Focalis, Sallustius and Odalaricus followed suit, unslinging bows from their mounts. Not Taurus. Taurus was never a man for a bow. He'd snapped a couple in training, though.

Archery was a skill not taught to most infantry, but a shrewd commander trained his men in any skill that might help them survive, and among the decanus's lessons to his soldiers was rudimentary bow skill. None of them would ever win prizes for their archery, but it was enough that one arrow placed well could save your life.

He drew an arrow from the quiver and set it to the string, appreciating, now that he'd taken it out in the rain, the hours he'd spent proofing the weapon with beeswax. It would still suffer with the damp in these conditions, but not as badly, and not as quickly.

His first shot was awful, even by his own standards. Loosing an arrow accurately was hard. Doing it from the saddle of a bouncing horse, and turned to face backwards at that, was truly difficult. He felt an odd mix of pride and jealousy as the first couple of volleys from the fugitives fell considerably short of their targets, while the shaft loosed by Martius whipped through the air and thudded into the throat of one of their pursuers' horses. The animal leapt, bucking, and a second horse collided with it, bringing two riders down and out of the chase.

Now, Focalis and his friends loosed with wild abandon, estimating range and lifting to launch their missiles higher for a longer trajectory. They started to find their mark, occasional shafts slamming into horses or men. The hunters began to thin out, dropping away with wounds or injured horses.

'The coast,' bellowed Taurus, still looking ahead and now leading their charge. Focalis glanced forward briefly to see a thin line of sand ahead and the dark sea beyond, surface seething with the rain. He turned back and looked at their pursuers once more. Eight remained, and they were getting dangerously close, for the problem with archery was that they slowed automatically in the process, all attention focused behind them and not on the ride ahead.

'Let's finish this,' he said to the others, hooking his bow back into position and fastening it. The others did the same, while Martius brought another rider down, making the odds that bit more palatable.

The Goths, closer than ever now, were far from deterred by their losses, their faces set in enraged snarls, swords out wide as they raced for their prey, determined to finish the job. They were coming, as was their wont, in a mob, no tactics or plan, just the desire to catch and kill their prey, and that, to some extent, negated their advantage in numbers. Seven against five, but the hunters were strung out, some lagging behind a little.

'Mark your man,' Focalis shouted. 'Centre-left for me.'

Centre left was the closest rider, a man in chain with a bushy dark beard and hair that streamed behind him in the rain. The man looked confident, putting all his weight into the charge. To rob him of both momentum and confidence was the first step. Along with the others, Focalis hauled on the reins, using his knees to turn his horse sharply to face the enemy. This move was unexpected, and the enemy slowed a little in their pursuit, speed now being less crucial, their prey's intentions having clearly changed.

Now Focalis danced his horse forwards, hurrying to meet his opponent. The two moved into a clash, both swords out to their right, both held high, ready to strike. The Roman watched his opponent's eyes. Still confident, still determined. Well, he could use that. Another thing they'd learned in those days in the imperial scholae was how to use an opponent's own skills and abilities against them, to turn enemy strengths into weaknesses.

He loosened his wrist, preparing to take the weak strike. Sure enough, as they clashed, the Thervingi rider swung hard, expecting a solid parry, hoping that with sheer strength he would push past Focalis' guard and gain the advantage. Instead the two swords met, but there was little resistance in the Roman's weak grip, just enough to turn the strike off target, but using the meeting of the blades as a pivot of sorts.

Even as his blade was turning around that of the Goth, so his knees were at work, his horse also turning to the right, a tight circle around the rear of the enemy rider, and in a heartbeat Focalis was behind him on his left. The Thervingi let out a surprised bark, but he was too late to do much about the situation. The Roman was now behind him with his target on his sword-side. Even as he came into position, already his grip had hardened, his wrist strengthened and, as the Goth tried to pull his horse away from this dangerous position, sword flailing uselessly, Focalis swung, this time hard.

His blow took the Goth horizontally across the back, just below the armpits. It was not, he knew with the hit, a killing blow in itself, for the chain armour robbed the strike of the worst, yet it would certainly take the man out of the fight. He may have broken a bone or two, but most surely he had numbed both arms, for the sword fell from the Goth's grip. Seeing the opening for a follow-up, in a fluid move, Focalis swept his long, straight dagger from his waist with his left hand and brought it up and round in a smooth swing, slamming it into the man's neck and then ripping it free in an instant, before the horses separated and he lost the blade, still stuck in its victim.

The man was doomed and, though it would take a while for him to actually die, he was disarmed and in agony, and would be no further danger. Focalis turned, looking for his next target, and only just managed to lurch back in the saddle and get his sword in the way before the growling Thervingi cut a slice off him. Just as he'd come up in the killing zone of his opponent to deliver an unblockable strike, so the next warrior had done the same to him. It had been blind luck that he'd managed to turn the blow. He had the blink of an eye to do something, else the man would get a second strike in like the first, and the chances of Focalis turning that blow twice were slim indeed. There was no time to turn his horse to face the man, and the Goth was coming in so close now he could feel the sweaty heat from him and his horse.

His response was inelegant, but it was all he had time to do in the circumstances. He threw himself backwards, jerking his horse left with his knees so that the beasts collided even as he slammed into the rider bodily. He felt muscles pulling in his waist, where he was anchored into the four-horned saddle, and he would pay for that dearly, but it was better than lying face down in a field with a hole in his back.

His opponent had been taken by surprise. He'd not been unduly inconvenienced, let alone hurt, but the strange and unexpected barge had thrown him and robbed him of the easy blow he'd anticipated. It gave Focalis time to pull away, clear of danger, and as he turned his mount to face the man properly, he was rewarded with an unexpected but very welcome sight. An arrow shaft sprouted from the man's throat, the point punching out of the back of his neck, flights lodged in his Adam's apple. Focalis turned, blinking, to see his son with a satisfied look lowering his bow again.

He looked about. The only fight still going on was Taurus, and that was only because the giant had somehow managed to pull his opponent from his saddle and was bouncing him along the ground, held by an ankle as the man was battered and brutalised by the terrain and occasionally caught by Taurus' hooves.

Only Sallustius seemed to have come off badly, for the man was busily tearing a strip of cloth to bind his upper left arm, which was crimson from the elbow down. Odalaricus, while uninjured, was trying to calm a horse that had taken a glancing blow, a line of red along its thigh. The veteran was grumbling loudly, not about the horse or the fight, but that the blow which had caught his horse had also split one of his saddlebags from which wine was now flowing in a steady stream.

'No time to waste,' Focalis shouted. 'Move. Sallustius, can you tie and ride?'

'Watch me.'

Turning to look back, Focalis couldn't see their pursuers

anymore. Sallustius' little trick with the rope had held too many back and delayed them, and only a few had managed to pull ahead enough to follow them. But the rest would be coming, and soon.

As they came close to the shore they turned, making sure to do so where the ground was thick with vegetation, hiding their tracks in a way that the sandy beach and the flat fields would not. It might slow their pursuit down and confuse them, especially with visibility hampered by the downpour.

They rode along the shore now, with Messembria six or seven miles distant, around the curve of the bay, just visible in the grey as a shape jutting out into the sea.

'Are we safe now?' Martius asked as they rode, as fast as they dare without exhausting the horses.

'Until we are on a ship and out of sight of land, no. Fritigern is not going to give up as long as there is even the hope of catching us. But there *is* a *chance*, now. We've lost them, and if we can get to Messembria, meet Pictor, and book passage before Fritigern's men find us, we can get away.'

'I don't like leaving, Dad.'

'Me neither. Not to be able to feast by your ma's tomb on Parentalia is a heart-breaking thing, and all I've known all my life is the mountains and plains of Thracia, apart from a brief time in Asia with the emperor. But we will learn to love the west, whatever it's like, because no matter what I have to endure, I will make sure that you live to grow old and have your own family. I owe that to your ma. Now come on. Safety is just a few miles away and we've plenty of light left yet.'

Safety for the others, anyway...

And Fritigern's time was coming.

Messembria never changed. A juxtaposed collection of white stone and dark timber buildings crammed, with no concept of organisation, onto what had once been an island, connected to the mainland by a narrow causeway, the whole place surrounded by powerful walls. Messembria was one of the empire's most powerful and busiest ports on the Euxine Sea coast.

They had been to the city a number of times, mostly in the old days, riding as part of the scholae palatinae, escorting one imperial cargo or another to or from a ship, emperors and empresses, princes and princesses, and, on one notable occasion, the emperor's favourite dog with his own mounted escort. Those had been good times, full of humour and glamour, even with the dog.

The last time they'd visited was different. The last time had been around a year before the disaster at Hadrianopolis, and therefore a year *after* Marcianopolis, and already the ghosts of what they had done dogged their every step. As such, the place held mixed emotions for Focalis as they rode around the curve of the bay and towards that causeway. There was the comfort of a place he knew well, the trepidation of the unknown, the sadness of his private decision to leave the others there, the chill of the memory of their last visit, and the hope that it might mean safety for the rest of them, particularly Martius.

The five of them slowed as they approached the causeway, and then reined in and dismounted in the late afternoon light.

'Safety first,' Focalis urged them. 'I can't see the place being full of Fritigern's spies the way Sigeric suggested, but let's not test that theory. Anyone entering the city by land has to cross the causeway and go through the main gate, and if anyone is looking for us, that's the place to start. So we split up. We're less obvious separately. Martius and I will cross first. Wait here until you see us go through the gate, then the next one can join the queue. Once you're inside, make for the Wanton Siren and meet there. There's enough of a stream of people and animals going in and out, hopefully we'll be lost in the mob. Just try not to look like soldiers.'

This agreed by the others, they wished one another luck, and Focalis and Martius led their horses into the queue of sodden locals making their way into the city. The causeway was wide enough for two carts abreast, and so divided comfortably between those entering the city and those leaving, not a surprisingly high number, but then the causeway was always busy thanks to the city gate at the far end, through which they had to filter.

As they sloshed their way through the gathered puddles towards that gate, Focalis' view played constantly over the other people, though he found nothing amiss among them. No one stood out, no one was armoured, no one was watching them. The entire gathering, whether entering or leaving the city, travelled with hoods up and heads down against the rain, pacing as slowly and carefully as they could to prevent treading in a deep puddle and soaking their feet.

It took perhaps a quarter of an hour from standing with the others on the mainland to moving into the shadowed arch of the gate, where a unit of local levies stood in drab tunics with a plain shield and a poor-quality spear. The soldiers were paying little attention to the security of their city, in the manner of bored men on patrol in the rain the world over. They huddled in the shelter of their gate, away from the downpour, and only occasionally lifted their gaze to make sure no invading army was walking past into the city.

It was with solid relief that Focalis and his son passed through the gate and into the city without incident. Once again, the moment they moved into the open, he scanned the roadways inside, where a main thoroughfare led off into the city, while a lesser road passed around the inside of the walls. Hopeful traders had set up stalls on whatever space they could find in the hope of fleecing new arrivals, though most of them hid beneath the canvas roofs of their stalls, trying to keep their merchandise dry while the populace shuffled past this way and that, hurrying to find somewhere out of the rain. Once again, no armoured Goths appeared to be lurking in the crowd, watching the gate.

Gesturing to Martius, he led the way. Only fifty paces along, the road forked into two grand avenues, one marching along the crest of the island, the other descending towards the shore on the southern edge, where even from here Focalis could see the masts of ships standing proud above the roofs.

They passed along the street, curving all the time down towards the water, and Focalis was struck time and again by memories, shops in which he'd spent his imperial silver on those many duty runs to the port, cauponae where he'd sat and drank and laughed with the others, and here on the left, the church where he'd paused habitually to seek the Lord's favour and protection on one mission or another. Martius' gaze was a rapid thing, darting from one sight to another, taking it all in with a sense of awe. The lad had visited Augusta Traiana many times over the years, and had now seen the powerful walls of Suida and the seething mercantilism of Macellum Iulia, but Messembria was something different again, an ancient and thriving imperial port. It was as he pondered his son's wonder that he realised this was the first time Martius had ever seen the sea, or indeed any body of water larger than the rivers back home. Pity he had to suffer what could be such wonderful experiences in such a poor situation, but at least they were alive and well. And once the lad was on a ship, that would be a new experience, too, and this time one he could enjoy in safety... if without his dad.

The walls that surrounded Messembria also cut off the thriving port from the city itself, and here the houses were built up to the defences with no intervening street. They passed the last few shops and another collection of hopeful, if bedraggled, stallholders, and towards that gate. Not through it, though. The port was not their destination this time. A small side street just before the gate led off to their right, parallel with the shore, and even at the junction, Focalis could see the sign.

As they were turning, something caused his hackles to rise, a warning from some unknown source, and his gaze slid towards the port gate. Folk were entering and leaving the city there just as they had been over the causeway, and just as at that other entrance, here local militia stood, bored and inattentive in the protective shadow of the gate.

Here, though, others watched.

Three figures in plain tunics and cloaks, hoods pulled up against the rain, standing by the walls near the gate at three different places. But they were watching. Just observing the street. They didn't seem to have spotted Focalis and his boy yet, which could have been because they were looking for someone else entirely, or could be because, though they *were* looking for Focalis and his friends, they were concentrating on those going in and out of the port, and had not looked this far up the street yet. Roman or Goth it was impossible to tell under a cloak, which not only hid their face, but would also conceal any weapon they might be wearing.

Alert now, he made sure to turn his back on them as they moved into the side street. He mentioned nothing to Martius, for he knew damn well the boy would give them away, looking around in surprise. Instead, he guided them along that street until they were out of sight of the gate.

'Despite everything, I think Sigeric was onto something,' he muttered as they moved through the street.

'We're being followed?'

'No. Not followed. But someone at the port gate was watching the crowd carefully.'

'They could be looking for anyone.'

'They could be. I bet you tonight's meal that they were looking for us.'

The Wanton Siren was the same as any of the waterfront dives in the port cities of the world, with customers spilling out to the street, where they stood in groups, drinking and laughing. Opposite, a stable did good business among those who came with beasts of burden, and, very familiar with the place, Focalis led them in through the wide doorway, collaring a stable lad as he did so.

'I need stabling for one night for these two, somewhere to temporarily store the packs securely, and I'd like them close to the gate, if possible, as we may need to leave at short notice.'

The lad, used to all manner of requests, bowed his head, took the reins and began to make the arrangements as the owner toddled over in their direction, his portly figure giving him a strange swagger. With little preamble he named a price for the night, which Focalis was more than happy to pay, especially since he could see the animals being led into two of the nearest, most convenient stalls.

'We may need access to our packs this evening,' he noted as he handed over the coins.

The man shrugged, his rolls and jowls jiggling. 'Always someone here. No problem.'

'Have you had a horse and wagon arrive recently? A man and woman together?'

'No.'

Focalis thanked the man and he and Martius stepped out and across the street towards that low caupona, where sailors, dockers and all manner of labourers relaxed after their day's work.

'No sign of Pictor yet, then,' he noted.

'Is that a worry?'

He shook his head. 'Not yet. Not for an hour or two. It was unlikely he would beat us here, even going along the main road. Wagons are slow. But with luck we'll get a seat near the windows and be able to watch him arrive.'

'*If* he arrives,' Martius supplied with a worried tone.

'Pictor's not stupid. Pig headed and idiotic, but clever in his way. If anyone can get a cartful of artillery here, it's him.'

'What if they search his cart at the gate?'

'We all carry papers that override such problems, remember? The ones that got us our rooms at the mansio. Of course, that would be more or less announcing our presence, but it would get him through the gate.'

They weaved their way through the crowd, keeping an eye out for watchful strangers as they went, and finally reached the counter, which reeked of fish, for every bowl in its surface was filled with some variety of sea life, either freshly caught or freshly killed. He was trying to get the attention of the busy barman when a subtle waving caught his eye, and he turned.

No wonder he hadn't noticed the owner of the hand immediately. He had, after all, only met Agnes once, and not in the best of circumstances. His heart lurched for a moment at the realisation that she was here alone. Where was Pictor? His worst fears were allayed, though, by the look on her face. There was no hint of the panic he'd expect had she seen her lover in dire straits. She looked carefully casual, which was interesting. Once she knew he'd seen her, she stopped waving and seemed to lose interest in him, turning to examine a wall.

With a gesture to Martius, Focalis shuffled along the bar until he was close to her. Agnes turned again. 'You alone?'

'I think so. What's going on?'

'You're in danger, all of you.'

'Explain, Agnes, for the love of God.'

'He sent me ahead to check the city out before he brought the wagon.'

Focalis blinked. He'd recognised her immediately for

a forceful and clever woman, but to send her alone into potential danger? Pictor was full of surprises. As was Agnes.

'And?'

'Have you seen nothing amiss?'

Focalis' eyes narrowed. 'You mean the three men by the port gate.'

'Three? There were five earlier. That's a worry. I reasoned they weren't looking for me, so I went and eavesdropped. They're on the lookout for you all. They can't know you're meeting at this place, but they're expecting you at the port. I'm afraid we're not taking ship in Messembria.'

Focalis cursed under his breath.

'You use that language in front of your son?'

He gave her a withering look. 'So Pictor is not in the city?'

'No. I left him out by the villas on the mainland, hidden in a barn. He'll not move into the city with the wagon until I return and give him the all clear.'

'Clever. Well done, both of you.'

'But we all need to leave here. Where are the others?'

'Coming in one by one. All but Arvina. We lost him to the Goths on the ride. Damn it, but this causes problems. I didn't believe Sigeric, but he was right. How did you eavesdrop? Where did you learn the Goth tongue?'

She looked at him as though he were an idiot. 'Goths? They spoke good Greek. Local accents, too.'

Focalis frowned. 'So who are they then?'

'Whoever they are, they're not your friends. We need to get out of Messembria, and preferably without being seen.'

'Alright. Go back to Pictor. Tell him to meet us at the third milepost on the Odessus road. I'll make my way back out and gather the others as I go.'

Agnes gave him a nod and left without a word, shoving the tavern's occupants out of the way as she went, scolding them for getting in a lady's path. In other circumstances, he'd have laughed, but now was not the time.

'Who else would be after us?' Martius asked quietly.

'I honestly don't know, but I have no pressing urge to find out. Thing is, we can't go back south or west, because there's a good chance we'd bump into marauding Thervingi. We have to press on the way we were going, which means north along the coast, heading towards Odessus. Maybe, just maybe, we'll be able to take ship there. If not, then we keep going. There are still good ports at Callatis, Tomis and Histria before we reach the border.'

'The border?'

'The edge of the empire.'

'And then?'

'I'd prefer not to think about that. Past Histria there's nothing but the odd border fortress and endless miles of horse tribes who spend most of their time at war with us. For now it's just important to get out of Messembria, safely and preferably unnoticed.'

Without further delay, he led Martius back through the crowded caupona and out into the street. His searching eye picked out Odalaricus and Sallustius making their way towards the stables. Keeping Martius close, he crossed towards the place, approaching the others without openly acknowledging their existence. Odalaricus clearly spotted them, but, realising instantly that they were playing ignorance, turned his face away, making no contact. As he passed his old friend, he hissed a message.

'Trouble. Meet on the Odessus road, third mile.'

And with that, he was past. Even as he and Martius entered the stable, he saw the others turn, as though casually changing their minds, and wander off the way they'd come. With luck they would meet Taurus on that journey and turn him around, too. Suddenly every eye in Messembria felt like a spy for the enemy.

As they entered, the stable lad was still busily settling their animals for the evening, and frowned in surprise as Martius crossed to him and told him they would need them now. Focalis looked for the owner and found him a moment later. The corpulent man was as baffled at their swift reappearance as the lad, but as Focalis held up two gold coins, his focus shifted entirely.

'Gold buys silence, I think,' Focalis said. 'We were never here.'

The man nodded urgently, jowls bouncing, and swept up the coins as Focalis dropped them.

He then stood in the centre of the stables with Martius, waiting impatiently as the lad hurriedly prepared their horses once more.

'Lay down your weapons,' said a voice in elegant Greek, and Focalis turned sharply. Six men stood in the gateway of the stables, and Focalis' whole world turned upside down at the sight. Five of them were clearly those who had been loitering by the port gate, one of them at the centre with his hood thrown back, the speaker, and clearly in command. But it was neither the speaker nor his cloaked and hooded heavies that had shocked Focalis to the core. That honour belonged to the figure of Sigeric, standing next to the speaker, among the watchers.

'What the fuck?'

'Come with us quietly, and your boy can go,' the speaker said. 'He is not on the list.'

'Whatever Fritigern has promised you, I'm fairly sure I can top it,' Focalis said. His sword was still at his side and his fingertips were now brushing the hilt.

'Fritigern be damned,' the man said with disdain. 'Your arrest order comes from Lupicinus, former comes rei militaris per Thracias.'

Focalis' eyes slid from the speaker to Sigeric. 'You?'

His old comrade sighed. 'You have no idea the kind of pressure Lupicinus can exert. I've not been my own man for a year, Flavius. Even falling from grace, he has more power than you can imagine in the region. I did try and tell you not to come here. I warned you.'

The leader turned to Sigeric with a look of anger. 'And that you will take up with the comes, in due course.'

'No man left behind, Sigeric,' Focalis said, bitterness loading his words.

'I had to make a choice. The boy can go, Flavius. Lupicinus thinks he can gain imperial favour again by bringing in Fritigern, and the only way he can stop the renegade king is by taking you out of the equation.'

'He's as fucking deluded as ever. Fritigern hates Lupicinus even more than he hates us.'

Sigeric gave a shrug. 'He's a fuckwit. Always has been, always will be. But he's a fuckwit with a lot of money and influence, Flavius. Your life for your son's. I'll make sure he's safe.'

'You touch my dad and I'll fucking kill you myself,' Martius snarled.

Sigeric gave a humourless smile. 'He's his father's son alright.'

Focalis bit his lip. Six of them was too many to overcome quickly, especially if one of them was Sigeric. He looked his old friend in the eye, and saw something then that intrigued him. The man was drunk, which was clear from the red rims of his eyes and the slight lean to him, but there was something else in his gaze other than the result of too much wine. Pain? Shame? Uncertainty?

'You had to make a choice,' he said. 'Now you have to make another.'

'Oh for fuck's sake, Flavius,' Sigeric snapped irritably, the slight lean gone now as he straightened. 'What do you expect me to do? Pull my knife?' he sneered as his trembling fingers closed on the long dagger at his belt. 'To put it to the man's throat and let you go?'

And with that, suddenly Sigeric was behind the leader, one arm around his midriff, the other holding the razor-sharp dagger to his neck.

Focalis stared in shock. He'd expected the move no more than the leader had, and moreover he'd not considered Sigeric capable of speed, with the drink having such a hold on him.

'Go, you fools,' the man hissed, then turned to the hooded watchers, who had all turned to Sigeric in surprise and uncertainty, hands hovering over their blades. 'I know how much this man means to the comes,' Sigeric said to them. 'First one of you to move signs his death warrant.' As the strange stand-off stretched out, Sigeric gave a wide-eyed meaningful look to Focalis. 'Are you just going to stand there all day?'

Focalis needed no more push. He and Martius grabbed for the reins of the horses and led them swiftly towards the gate, swords drawn now and levelling them at the hooded men, threateningly.

'What are you going to do?' he hissed at Sigeric as he passed.

'I haven't decided yet. I'd not really planned on this.'

'Odessus road, third mile,' Focalis said quietly.

Sigeric rolled his eyes. 'Well now you've gone and done it, Flavius. You can't tell them where you're going. Now we have to kill them all.'

Before Focalis could reply, Sigeric pulled his knife across the leader's windpipe in a smooth move, letting go of the body as it gasped and wheezed, pink bubbles forming at the throat even as blood began to sheet from it. He pulled another knife with a blistering array of insults.

The other four hooded men sprang into action, but the veterans were already moving. Swords in hand, Focalis and Martius let go of their reins and leapt at the nearest pair while Sigeric, a short blade now in each hand, moved on the others.

It was not a fair fight, for their targets had been taken by surprise and unable to free their weapons before they were attacked. Moreover, they were wearing some sort of uniform tunic, but no armour. Focalis' blow caught one across the chest hard, sending him staggering back, ribs shattering, a line of blood blossoming up into the weave of his tunic in an instant. He turned then to help Martius, but the lad needed no aid. His own blow had been considerably less expert, but it had drawn blood and crippled his opponent no less. Martius was no novice to a fight now, and the strange, excited worry that had plagued his son after that first time had long since gone, a professionalism that matched his own replacing it.

He turned the other way to see Sigeric at work. His initial assessment that his old friend was drink-addled was only part right. The veteran was clearly deep in his cups, yet the moment he moved with a blade in each hand, one might have assumed him sober as a saint. And, given the speed with which he'd turned on – and surprised – his companions, clearly his thoughts were far from muddled.

With a windmill-like whirl of twin blades, Sigeric dispatched the last of the hooded men. As a final swipe at the man's hamstring took him down, the second blade plunging into his back and then out again with a spray of blood, Focalis turned to look around. Every figure in view was watching them, the staff of the stable, the denizens of the caupona opposite, and every passer-by in the street, who had stopped to gawp.

'Sorry about the mess,' he called to the owner, and tossed him a handful of coins that simply fell to the flagged floor with a tinkle and scattered around, the man staring in horror at what had occurred in his doorway.

'This was a little public,' Focalis said, turning to Sigeric.

'Oh? I hadn't noticed. Come on.'

With that, the pale, drawn veteran was moving, heading out into the street in the low, golden light.

'Have you got a horse,' Focalis asked, catching up, leading his own beast, with Martius close at heel.

'Yes, but unfortunately, I left him with *friends*. I think I may have to forget about him now. We need to move fast, preferably ahead of rumour.'

'There are others in the city, then?'

Sigeric gave him an acidic look. 'Lupicinus lives in a big villa on the outskirts. He has a small army. And after this, the local garrison will be after us as well. We have to get out and across the causeway before someone stops us. You're fucking bad luck, Flavius.'

'Oh?'

'Only you,' Sigeric sighed as they moved at speed back up that street towards the city gate. 'Only you. I find a conscience catching next to no one else. Only you.'

'Once scholae, always scholae.'

'Oh, give it a rest. You might have brought out a conscience for a moment, but I don't have much of one these days, and you might find that if we land in trouble I'm willing to sell you all out for my life.'

'Ever the thinker,' Focalis snorted. Ahead, he spotted the shape of Taurus moving their way, a head and more taller than anyone else in the street. As they moved, Sigeric nudged him. 'Hang on for a moment.'

As he and Martius paused, looking around nervously, half expecting to be set upon by guards or cloaked mercenaries at any moment, Focalis watched Sigeric cross to where a trader with a cart was unloading. He engaged the man in some urgent conversation. It looked like a barter and the veteran produced an increasingly large pile of coins in his open palm. Still, even heaped, the merchant shook his head. Focalis winced as Sigeric's hand dropped to his side and a moment later the trader was folding up, falling in a heap behind his wagon. Gods, but Sigeric was still quick. He'd never even seen the blade.

As the veteran swiftly unhooked the horse from the trader's cart, someone nearby screamed and Martius stared wide-eyed. 'Did he just do what I think he did?'

'You'll get used to him.'

The lad was still staring in shock as Sigeric walked his new horse over to them, a small, petrified crowd gathering around the dead trader and his screaming woman.

'Think we'd best pick up the pace,' Sigeric said calmly.

'An understatement if ever there was one.'

Taurus' attention had been drawn by the incident, and now he'd spotted the others. Clearly, he realised in an instant that they were in trouble, and was turning his own horse, back towards the city gate.

'How attentive and prepared do you think the garrison will be?' Focalis muttered as they hurried along, leaving behind a scene of death where half a dozen people were shouting for guards and bellowing about murder.

'Not very. Speed over subtlety, then?'

'I think you threw subtlety to the wind when you killed an innocent man for his horse.'

'There's no such thing as an innocent man, Flavius. You just don't know what he was guilty of.'

As they mounted, Martius was glaring at the new addition with a look not far short of abject hatred. Focalis could see trouble brewing there, and turned to Sigeric as they began to ride. 'One day, you'll atone for incidents like that.'

'I'll have to develop a lot more of a conscience before that happens.'

Now they had caught up with Taurus and were riding for the gate. The late afternoon crowd in the thoroughfare was surging out of their path, running to the side of the street as the four riders pounded along the wet flags. As they neared the gate, the bored-looking and slightly soggy watchmen suddenly became aware of the trouble and turned, though in a heartbeat they clearly made the wise decision not to leap in the way and challenge the riders. As they dived to the side, out of the way, they bellowed curses and challenges, but the four fugitives paid them no heed, riding through the gate and out of Messembria. Ahead, people peeled off to either side of the causeway like the sea at Moses' staff, opening up a clear passage for them. Halfway across they could see the shapes of Odalaricus and Sallustius with their horses.

'Will we be pursued?' Martius asked breathlessly, as they pounded along the causeway towards the mainland.

'Maybe, but not fast and not for long. The garrison are infantry, and so, I guess, are Lupicinus' men. They'll not catch us. But somewhere out there are Fritigern and his riders and they're still after us. And once they speak to anyone in this area, they'll know where we've been and what direction we took. We have a head start, but the Thervingi will be on our trail in hours at most. At least it will be dark soon.'

As they reached the coast once more and turned at the first marker, making for the Odessus road, Focalis turned to Sigeric again. 'Alright, we're in a bit of a fix now. There's a thousand or so angry Goths out there with a very focused king. Apparently Lupicinus is after us too, in the hope of buying his own life from Fritigern and his honour back from the emperor. And now word will spread fast from Messembria of what happened here. You were always the planner, Sigeric. What's the plan?'

The man gave Focalis a withering look. 'My plan was to sell you out and live long and drunk in peace. You sort of fucked that all up for me.' He breathed hard. 'I told you before, this coast is no good. I warned you. None of the other ports from here are going to be any better. Lupicinus has influence and money all across the region. Even now, fast ships will be casting off, heading north and south and warning of our approach. Nowhere is safe. I told you: Thessalonika.'

'But that's the way we came, past Fritigern and his warband. Not ideal.'

'Then you're looking at this all wrong. We can't go south or west, because Fritigern's out there. We can't take a ship, because Lupicinus has the ports closed to us. We can't go north too far, because beyond the Danubius there's only angry tribes. I might be alright. I have enough Roxolani blood in me I can probably survive over there, but you lot have no chance.'

'So you're saying there's no way out.'

'Looks that way.'

'So what can we do?'

Sigeric gave him a look, and he didn't like the edge of madness in the man's eyes. 'If we can't run, then there's only one thing we *can* do. Stand and fight.'

12

It had been a tense journey away from Messembria in the last gloomy light of evening. They had moved at speed with the need to be as far from every potential enemy as possible as fast as possible. Now, Fritigern's Thervingi warriors, a thousand riders bent on their destruction, were out there somewhere in the wilds, Lupicinus' private army was seeking them in some insane plan to rebuild his tattered reputation, and the garrison of the city was searching for a group of misfits who had killed a merchant for his horse. It seemed to Focalis that every day of this journey seemed to swell the ranks of their opponents, while narrowing their own options and thinning out their chances.

It did occur to him that some of that was Sigeric's doing, and that things had become decidedly worse since they had met him, but he bit down hard on voicing that thought. Sigeric was trouble, for sure, but whatever he had done, he *had* tried to warn them about the trouble awaiting them in Messembria, and he *had* managed to get them out of a near-death scenario at the stables in town. On the scales of life, he was just managing to balance the benefits of his presence with the trouble he caused.

And when it came down to it, they would need every sword they could find.

They'd caught up with the others on the mainland and raced off to meet Pictor and Agnes at the milestone on the road north. Together once more, and knowing they were likely to be pursued by at least two, if not three of the groups set against them, the need to keep moving was paramount, and yet moving on was the one thing they could not do. Because there was nowhere for them to move on to.

In the end, after a quarter of an hour of violent arguments, some shoving of Sigeric, and some swearing, they had decided to find somewhere quiet and work out their next move. Two miles more from their meeting-point had taken them to the forested hills that brooded over the coast, and, with the rain coming back in force now, being under cover of the trees would serve to hide them not only from angry pursuit, but also from the weather.

They climbed the first slope in the gloom, the road winding back on itself as it rose, trees closing in on both sides, and the second forester's road they saw, they took. The first would be asking for trouble, as any pursuers who knew they had a cart would surely check the first side path down which they could fit a vehicle. The second one wound for some way deep into the woodlands, rising all the time, and from the moment they left the plain, Focalis found himself cursing under his breath, willing the slow beast of burden on, wishing that there was even a chance he could persuade Pictor to leave his artillery. Agnes was right about that, though. There was more chance of him shedding a limb than a weapon.

Deep in the woods, where the darkness was near complete, they finally stopped. They drew up the wagon and stretched a canvas from it, held up with two spears to become an awning, under which they could all huddle without the grape-sized raindrops that fell from the branches blatting onto their heads.

'What the fuck did you have to kill a man for?' Odalaricus snapped, opening the dialogue with a finger wagged at Sigeric.

'I had no horse. He had a horse. We were in a hurry.'

'And now the local garrison is looking for us.'

Sigeric's lip twisted dangerously. 'They're looking for *me*,' he corrected. 'And they won't find me. Now we're a few miles from the city they won't bother chasing us down. I think you're being a little blind here, old friend. Some tin-hat local levies that have no intention of leaving their comfy town are not the problem. In fact, even Lupicinus and his men are not the problem.'

'No?'

'No. They expect you to take ship along this coast. He's keeping a lookout for you there, so as long as you avoid the ports, you'll probably hear no more of him. Your big problem is a thousand fucking angry Thervingi who are scouring the countryside. The moment they find our trail, we're in trouble. So let's not start slinging blame and insults, and focus instead on the problem at hand.'

'Quite,' Focalis agreed. 'Let's do that.'

Odalaricus and Sigeric continued to glare at one another, but finally the former nodded, and they crouched, Pictor and Agnes sitting on the bench of the wagon above them, sheltered by the vehicle's cover and looking down to the others.

'Alright,' Focalis sighed. 'Sigeric painted a fairly bleak but unfortunately fairly accurate picture back in Messembria. We can't try the coast because Lupicinus has men there after us all. We'll never get to sea safely.'

'What about small fishing villages?' Pictor asked. 'I can't see the general having half a dozen killers placed at every cove with a boat between here and barbaricum. Can we not just commission a fisherman to take us?'

Sigeric shook his head. 'Eight people, eight horses, all their kit and a wagon full of artillery. And we need the horses, because if we're emigrating I, for one, do not intend to carry everything I own on my shoulders until we settle. The days of Marius' Mules are done, my friend. So if you want to transport everything, you'd have to rent an entire fleet of fishermen. Unless you're willing to leave your weapons behind.'

'Not likely.'

'Then strike that idea off your list. Anywhere we can hire a ship big enough to carry us all will be under Lupicinus' watch, and the man has a lot riding on catching you. His life is worth less than a shit-sponge at the moment as far as the emperor is concerned. He has money and influence, but he's invested everything he has in stopping us. Not only does he hope the emperor will forgive him and invite him back to court, but he hopes that in giving us to Fritigern he can buy his own life off the vengeful king. He has everything to lose, so he's not going to stop.'

'Alright,' Sallustius said, 'so the Euxine Sea is closed to us.'

'And there's no chance of heading back south or west,' Odalaricus sighed. 'From the timing it seems clear that Fritigern started there, and we know his main force has caught up with us. He was south and west of us, and since he lost us, his men are going to be everywhere. Heading that way, we'll have to go straight through them.'

'Exactly.'

'But that only leaves north,' Martius said, 'and there is no north. Well, there's a bit before we reach the border, but where can we hide there?'

'Precisely,' Sigeric replied. 'We are trapped. The coast is closed to us by Lupicinus, the south and west by Fritigern, and the north by the border of the empire along the Danubius River. We can't run. Damn it, but I'm beginning to wish I hadn't turned on Lupicinus' men. You dragged me in with nostalgia for the old unit, Focalis.'

'But if we can't run,' Martius said, 'what can we do?'

'I told you, back in Messembria,' Sigeric replied. 'Fight.'

'Eight of us,' Taurus snorted, 'including a boy and a woman? Against a thousand Thervingi? I don't even fancy *my* chances when it's more than a hundred to one.'

'That's because you're not using that dried pea that rattles around between your ears, big man,' Sigeric grinned maliciously, tapping his temple.

'Go on, then,' Odalaricus put in. 'How do we take on odds like that?'

'Attrition,' Sigeric said. 'We use everything we have at our disposal before we let them get a sword-length away. We even things out a little.'

'You're talking in riddles.'

'No. I'm not. We need to buy time to reduce the odds, and as we do that, we need to reduce them. Then, when we reach a point where we actually stand a chance... *then* we meet them.'

'And how do we do that?' Pictor put in.

'Well I think you're missing one of the most obvious things,' Sigeric grinned.

'Will you just explain?' Focalis sighed.

'We're being chased by two enemies, yes? Fritigern and Lupicinus.'

'Yes.'

'But the two of them are not working together. They both hunt us individually.'

'So?'

'How much do you think Lupicinus likes Fritigern?'

'He hates him, of course.'

'And the other way round?'

Focalis blinked, a smile slowly spreading across his face. 'Fritigern hates Lupicinus as much as us. Maybe even more.'

'And if the two should meet?'

'Well I certainly wouldn't like to be standing in the middle.'

'So if we can get Lupicinus' private army and Fritigern's riders to bump into each other?'

Now Focalis was grinning broadly. 'I suspect the odds will come down rapidly.'

Sallustius frowned. 'How do we do that, then?'

Now, Sigeric crouched and swept an area of dirt flat, finding a stick and drawing on it. 'Here we are. Here's the coastline to our east, here's Fritigern's men south and west. To the north,' he said, drawing a small representation of a battlemented house, 'what's this?'

'That,' Odalaricus said in a dark tone, 'is Marcianopolis. Best not mentioned, I'd say.'

'You might. But the thing is: we know Marcianopolis. We know the land, the city, the defences. We spent months there in garrison at the palace, and we fought defences there. We're more familiar with it than almost anywhere in the region. That would be the perfect place to make our stand. Ironic, I'd say, too.'

Sallustius leaned in now. 'Are you suggesting we fortify for a siege?'

'After a fashion. I'm suggesting that Focalis and I even the odds a little and buy the rest of you time. And you use that time to take this slow-arsed cart to Marcianopolis and spend a few days setting up surprises for when we get there, since we'll likely have a bunch of howling Thervingi at our heels.'

Sallustius was smiling. 'There's some merit to this, lads. We'd have to take control of the palace there, I reckon, where the dinner was held. From what I understand the place has been considered cursed since that night, and no one but squatters, beggars and thieves are to be found there. Perfect for our needs. With a few days to work with, I can have the place as dangerous as a lily-pit field for a blind man.'

'And I can check out all the artillery positions,' Pictor replied. 'Get fields of fire worked out, position weapons and ammunition and so on. We can make them pay heavily for every pace they take.'

Odalaricus had his eyes narrowed. 'Yes. And with me and Taurus, Agnes and maybe Martius, you'll have all the manpower you need to get the place prepared. Which leaves only one problem.'

'Oh?'

'Well I have no worries about Focalis here. He can ride right up to Fritigern, poke him in the nose and run, and the bastard will follow him into hell's jaws. And Focalis is fast enough and bright enough to get away and to lure him out.'

'So?'

'My problem is leaving Sigeric here to draw out Lupicinus' men.'

'I am by far the best man for that job,' Sigeric replied. 'I know where the men are likely to be found, I know where Lupicinus' villa is, and since I betrayed him in Messembria, he will now want me dead more than any of you. All I have to do is get them to follow me.'

'My problem is not your *abilities*,' Odalaricus growled. 'It's your motives. You've already expressed regret at having joined us. What's to stop you swapping sides again and selling us out to the old bastard? I can just picture Focalis reaching a meeting-point with a thousand angry Thervingi behind him only to find no one there, while you suddenly appear at Marcianopolis unexpectedly with every blade Lupicinus can hire in the province. Face it, Sigeric, you're just not trustworthy.'

The drawn-looking man shrugged. 'You're just going to have to trust me anyway. I can give you my word if you like, though one word is much as good as any other these days. But face it, none of the rest of you stand as much chance of pulling this off as me.'

'He's right,' Focalis said.

'He'll turn on us,' Odalaricus argued, waving an accusing finger. 'First chance he gets, you watch. He'll go home with an armful of gold while Lupicinus and his men come for our heads.'

'There's no real alternative,' Sallustius said. 'He's right. This is the way it'll have to work. And the longer the two of you take, the more time you buy the rest of us to prepare. It's about six days from here to Marcianopolis, if we take the cart. Five at the least. If you can manage to buy us seven days, that might be enough. Every day after that is even better. And try and bring as few Goths with you as possible.'

Focalis looked across at Sigeric. 'You can be in Lupicinus' presence within the day, I presume?'

'I think so, yes.'

'And I doubt it will take me more than a day to find Fritigern's riders.'

'We need to lead them away. Buy more time for this lot to prepare, or we're going to end up right on their heels.'

'So here's what we do. You tell the old bastard that we're running north-west. Tell him we're making for Nicopolis ad Istrum. It's a major garrison town, with a huge supply base. Fritigern would never get in, so it makes sense if you don't think too deeply about it. And it's got to be outside Lupicinus' current influence. Neither of them could afford to let us get entrenched there, so they'll have to come after us.'

'Am I missing something?' Martius asked.

'What?'

'If it makes so much sense seeking refuge in this Nicopolis, why don't we just do that?'

His father nodded his understanding. 'As I said, it makes sense if you don't think too deeply. The chances of us reaching the place are minimal. Even as the bird flies, Nicopolis is maybe a hundred and twenty miles from here. With the wagon we'd be caught on the road by Fritigern long before we got there. And if by some miracle we did, we'd only end up trapped there and unable to leave until Fritigern or Lupicinus found a way to get to us. No, if we can't leave the province altogether and put to sea, the only way to end this is with a blade. Sigeric was right about that.'

Martius subsided into silence with a disappointed look, and Focalis picked up where he'd left off.

'About seventy miles due west of here is Suida, on the road to Nicopolis. Lead Lupicinus and his men to Suida. I reckon it'll take you and the general two days to gather all your men, and two days to get there. Try and time it to arrive at sunset on the fourth day. With any luck darkness will add to the confusion, as well as allowing us the freedom to disappear. While you're doing that, I'll find Fritigern and lead him a merry dance in a wide loop in order to meet you at Suida at the end of that same day. If we time it right, we should be able to set off a bloodbath.'

Sigeric nodded. 'And then we have three days to draw the leftovers back north to Marcianopolis where we finish them off.'

'You make it sound so easy,' Martius said. 'It won't be, will it?'

'It will for you,' his father said. 'You're going with Pictor and the others.'

'No, Dad, I'm coming with you.'

'You're not. Not this time. I want you safe behind the walls of the city, not riding in the open leading around an army of Goths. Your ma would reach down from heaven and flatten me if I took you with me.' He turned to Odalaricus. 'Look after him.'

'Count on that,' his old friend replied. 'Do we get going now?'

Focalis looked up, around the edge of the canopy, a huge drop of rain splattering his forehead. 'I think we're best setting up camp for now. We'll find nowhere better, the light will start to fade soon, and with luck it'll be dry in the morning.'

'And then the hunt is on,' Sigeric said with a weird hint of satisfaction, stabbing the stick into the symbol of Marcianopolis.

13

It seemed strange to Focalis to be more or less turning round and heading back the way they'd come – all the way, in fact, to Suida. This time, though, things would be a little different. The unit had separated at dawn with a clear, if steely grey, sky, and had said their goodbyes. Meaningful ones, too. This was no mere side-trip. There was a very good chance that at least one of them would not return, and if that happened, the whole plan went in the shit bucket and everyone's life expectancy would be measured in days.

Martius had found it especially difficult, which, in turn, had not helped Focalis. The lad had lost his mother far too recently, and now his father was abandoning him to go on some life-threatening chase, leaving him with a bunch of soldiers he didn't know, who were taking him to a place he'd never been, to prepare for a siege.

Of course, Martius knew only half of it, for the rest had been shared between Focalis and Odalaricus once the lad was asleep. Then the full plan had been laid out. Martius was not to be part of this at all. When they arrived in Marcianopolis, the veteran was to make sure, if he had to knock the lad out and drag him, that he was installed in a reputable inn on the far side of the city from any danger, with a newly purchased burly slave to look after him. He would stay there, even if his guard-slave had to also be his jailer, until either news came of the unit's demise, or a tired but safe and victorious Focalis sought him out. If that was the case, they would be able to settle once more in the land of their forefathers. If Focalis and the others fell, the slave would wait two weeks, then take Martius to Odessus, to take ship with a bagful of coins he had left them and sail to Smyrna and Flavia's uncle. Neat. Sad, but neat.

And Focalis would end this, one way or another. If he managed to live through the coming days then he would ride off and meet Martius, reunited and with the chance of an actual future. If he died, then at least Martius would live.

That had been the worst goodbye of Focalis' life, not least because he had to make it sound as though he was definitely coming back, for the sake of his son. And then they had returned to the road, splashing through puddles but grateful that the rain had stopped, at least. The others had turned with the wagon, and with last sad looks had made their way north, while Sigeric and Focalis trotted back down the hill towards the coast. As they rode there was a prolonged silence until finally Focalis broke it.

'Everyone's life now depends on you and me.'

'I know.'

'Odalaricus was wrong, wasn't he? He's not usually wrong about people, but tell me he was wrong about you.'

'He was wrong about me.'

'Because if you betray us, rest assured that I will find you. I will live and get away just to hunt you down.'

'Fair enough.'

And that had been that. Despite the exchange, Odalaricus'

accusations still nagged at him, and he felt no more confident over Sigeric's trustworthiness than before. As they neared the milestone where they had all met up, the two men went over the plan and the timings again, as they had done many times the previous night, and over breakfast this morning. Then, content that at least both knew the plan back to front, they had parted, Sigeric heading back towards Messembria and general Lupicinus. Of course, even without the chance of his old comrade betraying them, it could go wrong in so many other ways. The old bastard could have Sigeric cut down at the door for what he'd done without listening to him at all. Or he could disbelieve Sigeric, for the man was just as clearly untrustworthy to the general's eyes as to Focalis'. Or the proposed timing was out and it would take Lupicinus either longer or less time to gather his men. In fact, every time Focalis thought about it, he noted another way in which everything could go wrong. It irked him that not only was he forced to trust Sigeric in terms of doing what he'd said, but he also had to trust to the man's plan, because planning was what Sigeric did, and because there really was no clear alternative.

Focalis rode openly on the road now. In fact, he'd done almost the diametric opposite of what they'd achieved on the ride from home. Instead of trying to blend in and be all but invisible, now Focalis rode with his shield on display, a chain shirt over his decorated military tunic, the one that he'd kept since his days in the scholae. He had his sword visible, and a good red military cloak announcing his presence and his nature. Now, he *wanted* Fritigern's Goths to find him.

With the upturn in the weather, there were more people on the roads as he travelled, but though he kept his eyes open and paid attention to everyone he passed, it was fairly clear that none of them were the Thervingi busily hunting him, for everyone he saw was either on foot or travelling with a cart, neither of which was likely for Fritigern's riders. He had to constantly remind himself that now he *wanted* to meet them, which was peculiar after so many days of running from them. Every village he passed, he checked for small, gathered groups of horses or strangers in armour, pausing for a quick drink or a bowl of stew in every likely-looking caupona. Everywhere seemed to turn up empty. Where had this safety been when he sought it? He even passed through the village where they'd collected Pictor, briefly checking out the man's empty house to be sure that Fritigern had left no one there. They hadn't.

It was not just dispiriting, but actively worrying as the sun began to sink on that day. A great deal depended on his finding and drawing out Fritigern's forces. If he couldn't find them in time, Sigeric would be in trouble back at Suida with the general on his trail and no opposition to lead them against. The timing of all of this was crucial.

In the late afternoon's dim light, he found himself back at the gates of Sigeric's estate. Again, he'd planned on checking the place to be certain that Fritigern's men were not sitting there waiting for him to come back, but that plan had changed the moment he reached the boundary wall. It seemed that Lupicinus had been swift to take umbrage at Sigeric's betrayal, for the ruins of that palatial villa even now smoked and collapsed in on themselves, the inferno that had taken it burned out perhaps two or three hours earlier. No Goths would be lurking there, then.

Fretting over his failure to locate a force of a thousand riders who were supposedly scouring the countryside and looking for him, he decided on a new tack. Perhaps they were now scouring the coastline, having pursued the fugitives almost that far. Accordingly, he turned and spent the last light of the day riding at speed across land he had already traversed, making for the Euxine Sea. It occurred to him, as the light failed and darkness claimed the land in its shroud, that he was now passing close by those drainage ditches where they had deterred pursuit and where they had lost Arvina, but he had no time to stop. Not now. Time was pressing.

He reached a small coastal village as true dark settled in for the night, bringing a bone-chilling cold, his stomach growling for want of an evening meal. As he closed on the village square, where a smith, a tavern and a general store sat opposite a church, glaring at each other over a small well, he felt his pulse pick up at the sight of a dozen horses tethered on the grass patch near the inn. They were military horses, he could tell from the tack, but he also knew a Goth saddle and blanket when he saw one, and each beast bore just that.

The sense that he had almost achieved his goal enveloped him, and he was tense, expectant, but ready for action, as he slid from his own mount, tied it to a rail a good distance from the Goths' horses, shouldered his shield and traipsed towards the inn. He even left his pack on the horse, trusting that no random villager would be brave enough to try and rob a soldier's horse when he was close by.

He pushed the door open and strode into the place with the swagger of a military man. It was not hard to spot the owners of the horses. Half a dozen locals were clustered around two tables over to one side, as far as they could realistically sit from the visitors without being insulting. The Goths were standing, each one, close to the serving counter, dipping their hands into the serving bowls that the owner should be using to ladle the food into bowls for them. Each had a drink, a variety, from good wine to rough beer to small cups of the fiery brew learned from the Dacian and Moesian tribes. They were laughing and chattering in their own tongue, paying little heed to those around them, including the barman, who looked both nervous and unhappy. He was not about to argue with a dozen Goth warriors, though, and at least despite their poor manners, they were clearly paying well for it, for the pile of coins on the counter would pay for several drinks for all of them.

As he entered, the locals turned to look at him for a moment, then, to a man, they turned all their attention to their drinks, looking down. Trouble between Goths and veterans of the wars had caused violence all over the province for years now, and showed little sign of abating.

It took a few moments for his presence to register over the raucous chatter of the visitors, but finally two of them turned, faces registering surprise. One of the pair tapped another, a minor officer by the looks of it. Focalis tensed, readying himself, fingers near the pommel of his sword. This wasn't a fight, though. He had to let them see him, then run, reach his horse and draw them north-west in the direction of Suida and eventually Nicopolis. His foot tingled with the urge to turn and run, but he had to make sure they would follow first.

To his surprise, the officer murmured something to the man who'd attracted his attention, and the entire bunch went back to their conversation. Were they blind? Stupid? Maybe they were so not expecting the old scholae kit that they simply didn't realise who he was? No, surely not. Surely Fritigern had prepared his riders to be sure they didn't grab the wrong people?

Frustrated, he took a few paces forward. Getting too close could be dangerous, but he needed to...

His eyes suddenly registered something past the entire gathering that changed the situation, and not for the better. Leaning against the wall was a banner, a vexillum bearing a stylised sun over a very stylised eagle. A Roman standard, if one stitched by Gothic hands. Not a banner that would be carried by Fritigern's men, for sure. Once again he'd failed to locate his quarry. These men were innocent settlers, adopted into Rome's military as were so many of the tribes. Probably not even Thervingi.

Sagging a little, hand leaving his sword hilt, he wandered across to the bar, not far from the Goths, and dropped a few coins on the counter, asking for a beer.

'We not to your liking?'

He turned to see that officer looking his way, a grim look on his face.

Focalis sighed. 'I've no problem with you.'

'Then why the looks? I see those looks on men like you all the time. Just because you've been part of the empire long enough to have three names. We were all immigrants once, unless you were born in Rome with a patrician name and a silver spoon up your arse.'

'No offence intended,' Focalis said, then turned to the barman. 'Buy this lot a drink on me. Soldier to soldier.'

He turned, but the man looked no less irritated. Focalis hunched over the bar. 'Thought you were someone else,' he said, by way of explanation.

'Oh?'

'Fritigern's men.'

His ear pricked up at a change in the bar's sound. The Goths, to a man, had stopped talking, and as he turned again, each and every one was looking at him now. 'Only a fool hunts Fritigern alone,' the officer said. 'Even if he fought in the emperor's guard. Fritigern has hundreds, and they're fierce. Fuck it, Roman, but we are a *dozen*, and the moment we saw them, we ran like schoolgirls in kiss chase.'

Focalis' cup stopped halfway to his mouth. 'You've seen them?'

'Not two hours' ride from here. But stay clear of them. They have no love of any Roman, let alone Valens' heroes.'

'Where were they?'

The officer frowned. 'Leave them. Eventually they'll try and get into a big city and they'll come up against a garrison. I just pray it's not Galata, off up the coast. We're part of the new garrison there, and I'd like to enjoy its beer and its whores for a month or two before we're at war.'

'Tell me.'

The officer pursed his lips, forehead creased in a frown. 'They're camped about six miles from here, west of Aquae Calidae. Hard to miss, but you might want to try anyway.'

'You have just made my evening,' Focalis grinned.

'Are you mad?'

'You have no idea.' Focalis tipped out another handful of coins onto the counter and turned to the barman. 'Keep them drinking until this runs out.'

Paying no heed to the response of the Goths, Focalis shouldered his shield and hurried from the inn, crossing to his horse, loading up and mounting once more. He had them. As long as they hadn't moved, he knew where to find them, and if they were already gathered together as a warband, even if they'd gone, they'd have left an unmistakable trail. Aquae Calidae was less than ten miles from where Focalis now kicked his horse into movement, leaving the small settlement and forging out into the dark alone. Ten miles. He could, if he pressed, reach them in an hour, but then his horse would be spent, and the chances of getting away and staying ahead of Fritigern were drastically reduced. No, he had to go slow and steady.

He moved through the darkness along small country lanes and then across open countryside until he met the main Aquae to Messembria road, then followed that in solitude, there being a distinct lack of travellers abroad at such a time. An hour and a half into the ride, he could see the lights of the town ahead, and with another half hour he had skirted around it to the north and continued on, following the directions he'd received.

They were not hard to find, as he'd anticipated. A thousand horsemen take up a great deal of space, make considerable noise and, at night, require a number of cooking fires. He'd seen Thervingi and Greuthungi warbands on campaign often enough during those years of warfare to know exactly what he was looking at the moment the dotted golden glows of their campfires came into view. They had no fear, apparently, for as he approached he could see that the entire force had camped in a bend of a small river, their horses grazing on long tethers with no set corral, no defences, and – something that made him twitch as a military man – apparently no pickets. At the very least there should be men on watch some distance from the camp, yet if they had sentries they were clearly within the range of the firelight. He could see no sign of care taken.

Though there had yet been no official announcement of Fritigern's status as a wanted man – that courier from the mansio when all this started had perhaps failed in his mission – still, surely as a deposed and renegade king, Fritigern must be wary of meeting imperial forces, or even other Thervingi who considered him trouble. Yet he seemed confident enough to set no defences.

Good.

Focalis looked across at that field of tethered animals, and then down at his own sweating horse. The animal was not yet spent, but in a chase against those well-fed and well-rested creatures he would not get far. He chewed his lip, a decision forming. Keeping an eye on the huge encampment, while also being watchful just in case he'd been wrong about the pickets, he skirted the Thervingi until he was on the western edge of the camp, where he found what he was looking for: a small knot of trees on a low hillock. Cover, and a good vantage point. There, he tethered his horse on the far side of the trees where it would not be visible to the Goths when the dawn came, and settled in for the night, wrapped in his blankets.

It was not the most restful of nights. The close proximity of the Goth warband brought on the old nightmares apace, and he raced from one sleeping horror to the next throughout the night, tossing and turning. Indeed, when he awoke, he was disoriented, still mentally back in that old battle, and wasn't entirely sure whether the noise that had awoken him had been real or imagined.

Hurriedly writhing out of his blankets he rose to his knees, blinking away the lingering tatters of dream, and focusing. The dawn was not quite here, but almost, that strange ethereal glow in the sky announcing its approach, and down in the bend of the river the Goths were readying to move.

This was it.

Suida was sixty miles west, more or less, and he had three days' ride before the appointed time. That was a travelling time of just twenty miles per day, a pace the average rider could easily double, let alone if they were angry and involved in a chase. Perhaps they had overestimated the timing?

No. He was content that it would take four days for Sigeric to rouse Lupicinus' army and lead them to Suida, and every day they managed to keep up the chase was another day for the others to reach Marcianopolis and prepare for what was to come. He would have to lead them carefully. On the bright side, serving in Thracia for most of his career, first as one of the scholae palatinae and then as a legionary, he was familiar with the geography of the region, and already a route that would lead them to Suida over a protracted ride of four days was forming in his head. Good. He had the destination, the route and the starting point. All he needed now was the impetus. Riding up to the camp and sticking his tongue out, then riding away was too obvious. The enemy would be wary of such a clear ploy. They needed to stumble across him, to find him as though through their own skill and good luck, not through his actions.

Knowing he had some time, he left the viewpoint, returned to his horse and stowed everything once more. Once he had released the tether, he mounted and then returned to the edge of those trees, watching. It took an hour for the Goths to break camp and begin to move, and he was becoming bored when, finally, they took to the hoof. Tense, anticipatory, he watched.

They began to ride at a steady walking pace in the direction of his viewpoint. He toyed with the idea of waiting there until they saw him, but again that would be suspicious, finding him hovering at the edge of their camp. Fritigern might be a madman, but he was not the sort of idiot to fall for such a blindingly obvious ploy. Crossing to the far side of the copse, he peered into the gradually increasing glow.

A village.

Perhaps three miles away, he could see a small collection of roofs. Would the Goths go round it? No. If they were looking for Focalis and his friends, they would at least send some of their riders to the village to ask questions. And that was where they would find him. Focalis would be in the village, apparently innocent, they would find him there, and the chase would be on.

Satisfied and with a grim expression of determination, he turned to the west and rode.

14

It is curiously easy for a single rider to stay ahead of a large force. For one thing, a lone horseman can traverse narrow ways and difficult spots, where a large army would snarl up. For another, one man can generally find sustenance and shelter fairly easily, while a *thousand* require specific conditions, especially when not travelling with a baggage train. Thus, Fritigern's desires were frustrated at every turn.

It had been an easy matter to look panicked and desperate at the arrival of Fritigern's scouts in the village, to mount up and ride as though all the demons of hell were clawing at his heels. The difficult part had been managing to stay only just ahead and not to race out into the clear. He travelled with a careful guise, putting forth the appearance of a man trying to escape on a weary horse, while in truth his mount was at least as hale and well rested as theirs.

It had been almost laughable that first day, the ease with which he'd managed to stay just ahead and draw them southwest, the beginning of a wide arc that would eventually bring them back north to Suida. Fritigern had sent a vanguard of several score riders out ahead of the army with the hope of catching him, but he simply danced out of their reach, albeit with the façade of desperation, rather than ease.

He could not rest, of course, unless they did. He could not afford to lose them. And so the chase went on throughout the day with only small periods to rest the horses, and even into the dark they travelled. Focalis only reined in, tired and strained, when he knew that the enemy had given up the chase for the day. Try as they might, there was simply no way the army could continue to follow him through the night without adequate rest for the horses, let alone the men. As he saw their camp fires he finally tethered his own horse, though he felt sure he knew what was coming, and so kept the beast saddled and all his gear packed, waiting, fully clothed, in the cold.

The first attack came within the hour. Two riders, searching the area. He'd seen them coming, though, and his response was well-planned and well-executed. The first rider passed around the edge of a high hedge to find Focalis waiting for him with a quickly fashioned spear, a simple thin branch with the end hacked into a ligneous point. The spear took him through the abdomen, and he cried out in agony as he lolled in the saddle. By the time the second rider found him, Focalis was already gone. That second man saw the tethered horse, and approached warily.

A martiobarbulum dart is a heavy thing, and this particular barbed, weighted nightmare dropped from the branch in which Focalis sat and slammed into the top of the rider's head, the point and lead weight cracking the skull and mashing the man's scalp. It was not a killing blow, but it was enough distraction that when the Roman dropped on him with a knife and cut his throat, he had little time to react.

Focalis moved position, then, finding a new spot behind a ruined barn, where he managed a good half hour of shut-eye before the brittle sticks he'd left at both the barn's corners announced the approach of another speculative patrol. The first man crept around the corner, giving a stifled 'urk' as one of Focalis' hands went around his neck and the other brought the knife up into his windpipe. When the second rider, creeping around the other side of the building, spotted the body of the first, he gave a short bark of alarm before Focalis was on him, having followed him around the building, masking his own long strides with the sound of the Goth's short, careful ones. He died just as badly, and just as quickly.

Focalis paused only long enough to make sure he was alone once more, and then moved on, finding another nice, obfuscating patch of undergrowth. Two more Thervingi regretted their curiosity as they fell to the ground with a gurgling thud, while Focalis rose and wiped the blood from both sword and knife.

On the off-chance, he then returned to his original hiding place. It made him smile to see that the bodies of his victims had gone. The Goths had come to find their missing companions and had reclaimed their corpses. Reasoning that they were unlikely to revisit the spot, knowing he had moved on, he once more set up there for the night, laying a few traps of brittle sticks to betray approaching footfalls, and then began to doze off once more.

They had not come again that night, and he had slept surprisingly well. Better, he suspected, than the Goths, who would have been increasingly nervous as the bodies of their scouts continued to roll back into camp. He was woken in the morning by the sound of their horns calling them all to action, and was on his horse and moving long before they. He rode through a small town and made sure to leave ample rumour and evidence of his passing so that inquisitive Thervingi could follow.

In fact, the second day, he made sure to stay far enough ahead that they were having to follow a rapidly cooling trail, though making that trail simple enough to follow. Twice that day he delayed on hilltops and waited with a shading hand over his eyes to be sure that the Goths were still in pursuit. They were, and so he continued each time. In fact, that night he reckoned he had a good hour and a half on them, so he went to work. Finding a spot that would be an obvious choice, he sharpened a few sticks, dug a few pits and jammed them in the bottom – good old-fashioned lily pits which he covered with long, freshly pulled grass. He then moved to another position by a low ridge where he could see, and tethered his horse out of sight behind deep shrubbery.

That night they came in a six, as per Fritigern's norm.

They left in a three, though a fourth was half-limping, half-dragging himself along in their wake, leaving behind the two in the pits that they'd had to put out of their misery. For a moment as he watched their agonising blunders, Focalis had a peculiar insight into what drove Sallustius to do what he did, and he almost laughed at the perverse joy of watching enemies cripple themselves on traps he'd left.

No one else came that second night.

The third day he slowed a little again, and even let them catch sight of him once, just to keep them interested. He had to give it to Fritigern. The man was so driven by hate and revenge, it seemed he would run his men to the end of the world and beyond just to catch one of them.

That night, he laid a false trail in a village where the innkeeper was a startlingly outspoken xenophobe. Once the man learned that Focalis was being hunted by Goths, he was more than happy to play along. For the first time in days, the fugitive had a good, hot meal, several cups of wine, and slept in a comfortable bed. Even as he chewed his way through lamb stew in a back room he listened to hopeful Thervingi scouts asking after a lone rider of the scholae and being told that the man had passed through several hours ago, heading north-west. Focalis' night was all the better for knowing that Fritigern had a score of men out scouring the empty fields in a fruitless search that would keep them all tired and edgy.

Well fed and well rested, Focalis rose before dawn, thanked the innkeeper, tipping him heavily, and then rode out. He paid a quick visit to the Goth camp, just close enough to check on them, and then, with a wide smile, rode north-west, in the direction the Goths believed he'd already gone.

In the late morning, he passed through another village and enquired of an old man with an eye-watering facial disfigurement how far it was from there to Suida. Ten miles was the entirely satisfactory answer. He would reach the place in the early afternoon. Ideally, they would arrive at sunset as per the plan, but to be there within hours of the target was damn good, all things considered, and the only way he could realistically delay things now was to ride in circles and let them try and catch him.

As he rode on, he worked through his plan. He remembered the outskirts of Suida from the last time, when they'd been fleeing at speed. There was a mansio close to the town, on the main road, not a grand affair, but big enough. It was a clear temptation, for an official imperial installation would be a good place for a Roman to hide from non-citizens. It would be a natural place for him to go. Accordingly, he made sure to pull out ahead again today, to leave the Goths behind, so that he could reach the Suida mansio and lay his bait. He needed them to stay here now, until nightfall when, hopefully, Sigeric would turn up with all the trained mercenaries of Lupicinus. Then the fun would begin. So, he would visit the mansio and leave a message for Sigeric, being sure that everyone present heard him announce that he would return in the evening. That way, with luck, he would be able to retreat somewhere secure with a good view and watch the fun. Fritigern would undoubtedly check the mansio, learn that Focalis was planning to return after dark, and then stay in the area, waiting. All he would find would be Lupicinus' men.

Things were working out, and the Goths were close on his trail still. He was feeling elated now as he rode on the last leg of this difficult journey. Though he was well aware that there was another, probably *more* difficult one to come, and that there was always also the significant possibility that his old army friend had betrayed him yet again and not bothered turning up, it still felt like an immense achievement just to have got this far.

That was why he was smiling from ear to ear and feeling rather positive when he discovered that God saved his own special justice for such hubris. Not far past a milestone that labelled Suida as two miles distant, he rounded a bend in the forest road, and the bottom fell out of his world.

Lupicinus' army was already here. Damn it, Sigeric had not only not betrayed him, but the man had been worryingly efficient and had got there early. He tried not to remember that he, too, was early, and it was just that Sigeric was even earlier. He reined in sharply at the corner, side-stepping his horse to the edge of the road so that they were largely hidden by the trees.

Damn it. What was he going to do now? The moment he left the forest, he would be plainly visible to Lupicinus' dark-clad riders, and he had little doubt, given the scholae uniform he still wore, that they would identify him within the first few breaths. He looked over his shoulder, trying to remember the last mile or two of road, which he should have been paying more attention to, rather than congratulating himself on the success of a job he hadn't actually finished yet. He was sure all he could remember for two miles was trees. Like so many of Thracia's roads, this one cut through a forest of some size, and only ended as it reached the cultivated fields outside the city.

Forest, and a road leading back to the pursuing Thervingi. He fretted. He couldn't go forward without walking straight into the men of Lupicinus, and retreating would very likely bring him directly into the arms of Fritigern on the forest road. He couldn't remember any side trails, even logging ones, let alone small village roads. He was trapped between two armies who both wanted him dead.

His eyes darted this way and that. Any time now Lupicinus' men might decide to send out a patrol and come across him. He had to do something, and quick, but what?

Ahead was out. Back was out. That left only the sides, both of which were thick with trees and undergrowth. He sighed, his memory dredging up images of that ride through the woods as he first left the house when Fritigern's killers had come for him. It had been painful and troublesome, and he still had some of the contusions and scars from the ride, even now, so many days later. And he'd been lucky not to be unhorsed the first time. Any rider knows that even if he can force his mount, and it would have to be an exceptionally well-trained mount, into deep woods, the chances of making it through at anything other than a crawl were tiny.

But then he had that advantage this time. Last time he'd been chasing someone, and speed had been critical. Now it was the precise opposite. The longer he lurked in the woodland, the more chance of the two forces meeting without him being caught in the middle.

Issuing soothing noises, he turned his nervous mount and dropped down the agger from the road into the shade of the trees. He found the easiest access, though even that was frightening and dangerous. Cursing, he reached down and found his helmet, hanging by a thick leather thong from his saddle and tucked into the breeching strap, tugged it free and jammed it on, fastening it just in time to turn away the whip-thin branch that sought his eye. His horse was making distressed sounds as he forged deeper into the mass of growth, and he could feel his arms and legs taking a battering as he rode immensely slowly. It came as a tremendous relief when he reached the deeper woods, where the sun and rain found it harder to penetrate the canopy, so the undergrowth was sparse and the trees less dense. He could sense his horse recovering its composure, too.

Slowly, he advanced. Only his innate sense of direction told him where he was going, for there was no way to see sun, or sky at all, from here. He was pretty sharp, though he still prayed to the good Lord that he was on track, and had not got turned around somehow, back towards the forest road. After a while he decided he must have come at least a quarter of a mile, and changed his angle, so that, by his estimation, he was making for the forest edge in the direction of Suida, the mansio, and Lupicinus' force.

His spirits began to lift as there was a perceptible change in the forest ahead. He could sense it thinning. He slowed to an even less hurried walk now, as he began to see columns of white light between the boles of the trees. He was approaching the open land, hopefully in a place where he could once more see the army awaiting him, but this time without another marching along behind him, ready to catch up.

He stopped suddenly.

A figure was just discernible in the trees ahead, the shadow of a human shape amid the shadows of ancient flora. As the shape moved, just a fraction, the glittering of what looked like sunlight on water told of the presence of armour. He remained still. The figure had not spotted him yet, for the stance had not changed, even if he'd moved slightly.

How to approach? Swiftly, on horseback, would be noisy, though probably not enough to draw the attention of Lupicinus' army, but it would also be fast and he might be able to overcome the man quickly. Dismounting, he could creep forward on foot. He might be able to surprise the watcher, but he would also be slow, and that would give the man more time to turn and see him.

He debated, fretting.

'For a supposedly clever man and a veteran of many wars, you are mightily slow and noisy,' Sigeric said as he turned, that shadowy shape coalescing into Focalis' friend as he did so. 'I have no idea how you made it to retirement without decorating the end of a Persian lance or a Thervingi spear.'

'What the fuck?' Focalis let out an explosive breath and walked his horse forward.

'Dismounted riders make a smaller target for the enemy to spot,' Sigeric said.

'What?'

'Get off your horse, you fool. You're almost in the open here.'

Chastised, Focalis stopped and slid from his horse. His questing gaze caught that of Sigeric's, nicely hidden away in an area with deeper undergrowth. He tied his own mount close by and then sidled through the trees to join his friend.

'I half expected…'

'That I wouldn't be here? Yes, I'm aware of that. I'm hoping you're not just out in the woods for a stroll and that you've brought Fritigern and his riders along with you?'

'They're maybe a mile or two back along the forest road. Should be here at any moment.'

'Then let our little play begin. Still about a thousand horse?'

Focalis nodded.

'And Lupicinus sent six hundred men. All he could muster. Still, that should thin all the ranks out rather nicely.'

'The general didn't come?'

'You thought he would?'

'I assumed. How are we going to persuade his men to attack the Goths, then?'

'I've worked on them for a few days. At this point they would eat their own mother in order to get to Fritigern's riders. Don't fear on that count. But no, Lupicinus is not here. He is an inveterate coward and a lazy individual. A drunkard too, even by my lofty standards. He was never going to put himself in danger.'

'Six hundred might not be enough.'

Sigeric snorted. 'They are almost all ex-army. Many

different limitanei and a core of former legionaries. Their leader is a praefectus palatini. To a man they spent their army years fighting Goths and Persians. They know what they're doing.'

'Then let's just hope they stick around long enough for Fritigern to arrive.'

'That shouldn't be a problem. They think I'm in Suida, seeking the latest tidings of you. It'll be hours before they decide I've done something else and wonder where I've gone. By then we should have the show in full swing. Did you bring snacks?'

Focalis rolled his eyes. 'I brought a hungry horse and a thousand angry Goths. You?'

'Wine,' Sigeric replied, unhooking a bulging skin from his belt and lifting it, pulling the cap free. 'We might want to find a seat while we wait. There's a nice fallen trunk over there, and by happy coincidence, that is where the rest of my wine sits waiting.'

15

Sigeric had chosen an excellent vantage point, with a view that took in the mansio in the middle distance and the mass of roofs surmounted by the white walled citadel that was Suida on the skyline, but with a wide panorama of the open lands between, right up to the position where the forest road left the trees and reached farmland.

Thus it was that they saw the moment the two forces became aware of one another. Even without the two commanders – who shared a mutual loathing – being present to trigger a disaster, that very disaster unfolded easily enough, thanks to Sigeric's subversion of the mercenaries, along with their innate prejudices following the war.

Fritigern's vanguard arrived first, and tightly controlled, riding a road that allowed only four riders abreast at a push, three comfortably. The hundred or so Thervingi cavalry moving ahead of the rest of the force poured from the treeline in a constant trickle, but the riders stopped and began to mass as soon as they reached the open. Their front riders had immediately spied the clearly Roman, if not officially army, horsemen waiting for them close by. The Goths formed hurriedly, shields and spears coming up and out, having expected to find nothing, with Focalis hiding in the city or the mansio, but instead stumbling across an unknown potential enemy.

That potential was fulfilled almost immediately. There was the briefest pause from Lupicinus' mercenary cavalry as they spied the arriving horsemen and identified them, but the moment it became clear that they were Goths, something snapped in their number, and they broke into an unruly charge.

As they rode, Focalis tried to forecast what would happen, though it was a difficult prediction at best. The Thervingi seriously outnumbered the Romans, but would be unable to field their full number due to the confines of the forest road, so they would continually pour into the fray in small groups, which made the battle a peculiar one. Moreover, though the mercenaries rode like an angry mob – which initially convinced Focalis they would be of little effectiveness against the Goths – as they rode into the conflict their military training and the bellowed commands of their leader took effect and they changed form, moving into two lines of riders, each four deep.

Focalis nodded his approval at the decision. The officer was good and knew his mounted combat. A wedge was no good here with no solid enemy line to break, while a wide front could envelop the assembling force and contain them. The first, larger, line would deliver the initial charge, while the second would form an effective reserve. And four riders' depth was optimum. More than four ranks risked the horses beginning to press on one another too much, instilling panic in the beasts. Four was still enough for the riders to maintain their position without difficulty. The leader was an experienced cavalryman, obviously, with a record of service against the Goths.

The two forces met with a roar and a crash, a wave of Roman steel breaking on the rocks of Thervingi horsemen. The result was, Focalis had to admit, spectacular. With the Goths extremely understrength and still forming, they were horribly outnumbered and had no momentum, standing their ground while Lupicinus' men hit them like a charging bull.

The spears of the Roman riders slammed into men and beasts all along the line and, with expert precision, the second, third and fourth lines hauled on their reins with their shield hands, pulling their horses up short to prevent a collision, while the front line, formed of the heaviest and best-armoured veterans, went to work.

As the spears broke in their targets, Goth horses bucking and falling, shattered shafts deep in their flesh, stricken riders plucked from their saddles and hurled to the ground with wicked, sharp points, the Romans let go of their initial weapon, drawing swords to begin the real butchery.

For long moments, watching the blood spray filling the air, hearing the screams and bellows of both men and horses, watching pink-stained swords of both sides rise and fall, Focalis thought that just possibly Lupicinus might have this. And if he did, that would solve all their problems. If the Thervingi continued to arrive in a dribble and the veteran mercenaries continued to flay the front lines with little damage to their own ranks in return, they might well be able to overcome and defeat the Goths. And if they did, and Fritigern were to fall, it would all be over. There would be no one left to seek revenge on the survivors of the Marcianopolis murders, and Lupicinus would have his victory to take to the emperor without the need to hand over the men he'd commanded to commit that very murder.

He said as much to Sigeric, who replied with a non-committal grunt.

The man was right in that, for as Focalis watched over the next quarter of an hour, the dynamic on the battlefield began to change. Some bright warrior among the Thervingi had realised they were doomed if they went on as they were, and so they began to pull back into the forest road, leaving a desperate rearguard holding off the Romans.

Lupicinus' men had little choice but to follow if they wanted to press the fight, and they had committed so heavily now that retreating would sit badly with them all. And so the Romans changed formation again, moving into a column three men wide as they followed their prey into the woodland, where they could no longer swamp the Goths. Now it would become a fight that came down to numbers and discipline rather than luck and strategy.

Focalis could no longer see the conflict, for it was taking place within the forest itself, but he could hear it, and he could see the Roman riders at the edge of the woods, massing, waiting for their turn to push into the forest road. Now the result was anyone's guess.

Focalis and Sigeric watched and listened for almost an hour as the fighting went on, attrition wearing down both sides, but it was Fritigern who played the endgame move. Focalis was trying to focus his hearing on what was happening when Sigeric nudged him and pointed. Focalis turned and looked in that direction.

Riders were pushing their way through the woodlands, just as Focalis had done on his arrival, and worryingly close to where they now sat watching. The Goths were forcing a path through the trees in force, at least a hundred of them.

Focalis recoiled, shuffling a little backwards to put an extra tree between himself and them, though to a man they seemed to have all their attention on the woods ahead of them, not expecting to find anyone lurking in the undergrowth. An ambush. A flanking manoeuvre, and likely one that was being mirrored through the woods on the other side of the road, too.

They watched, breath held, as the flood of Gothic riders pushed their way through the woods, assembling near the edge, close enough to burst out at speed through the undergrowth, while not quite in view of the Romans in the open.

A horn blast from somewhere, and the trap was sprung. The Thervingi forced their way through the last of the woods, thick undergrowth and all, and into the open, where they immediately kicked their horses into a charge, swords torn from scabbards. Focalis counted eight riders out of the hundred who fell foul of the terrain, their mounts unwilling to press through the brush, and watched with fascination, half his attention on them, half on the action out in the open.

Of the eight, two managed to drive their unwilling horses through sheer aggression, deep into the undergrowth and out into the farmland, following their compatriots. Four turned their mounts and began to make their way back through the woods as they had come, an easier trip with the path made by the hundred riders initially. The remaining two were in trouble. One had somehow become wounded, blood pouring from his head as he lolled in the saddle. The other was trying to get his friend's attention, barking at him in alarm.

Focalis' gaze slid past, focusing on the field of battle. Near two hundred Goths had fallen upon the rear of Lupicinus' cavalry. While there were, in theory, enough Romans there to fend them off, they were now fighting a battle on two fronts, half their number trapped within a forest path, and this fresh onslaught had come as a complete surprise. As a result, Fritigern's riders were busy flaying the rear of the Roman column before they truly began to react. The men of the Roman reserves were suddenly in turmoil, a panicked chaos as they tried to turn to meet this new threat, dying in droves even as they struggled.

The battle would not last long, and Focalis would not wager a copper nummus on the Romans now. They were lost. The only question remaining was whether they would be wiped out to a man or whether by some chance some might escape to carry news of the disaster to Lupicinus.

'You realise there's no going back now,' Focalis murmured to his friend.

'Was there ever?' Sigeric took a swig of his wine.

'Lupicinus forgave you your transgression in Messembria, obviously, but he won't forgive this second betrayal. He'll want you dead far more than the rest of us now. With us, it was just business. With you, it'll be personal. Even if we survive Fritigern, Lupicinus will put a hefty price on your head.'

Sigeric shrugged. 'I've lost everything, right down to my home, but it doesn't matter, Flavius. I've lost everything before now and I've managed. And unlike you lot, I can still cross the river and call wherever I plant my arse home.'

'You're not a Goth, you know?'

'My father was.'

'You don't look like one. You can't even speak the language.'

'Skohsl þus.'

'And fuck you too. Alright, you *can* speak the language.

You're still not a Goth. Even your breath reeks of Roman wine.'

'Come on. Get your sword. I think we want to be out of here before the fight is over and everyone starts looking for us.'

'How are we going to lead them on from here?'

Sigeric gave an unpleasant smile. 'We leave them a message.'

Focalis drew his blade as Sigeric did the same, and the two of them began to walk through the woods towards the two riders who had become entangled. They had dismounted now, the wounded one bleary and half-conscious, helped by his friend. The Goths only looked up at the last moment as the two Romans bore down on them. Knowing he had no time to draw his weapon and defend himself, the uninjured rider threw up his hands in surrender. 'Not kill,' he pleaded in thickly accented Greek.

Focalis held his sword out, point near the man's neck. 'We have a message for your king,' he said.

Before the man could reply, though, Sigeric stepped close and rammed his own sword into his throat. The Goth choked and gasped, hands gripping and ungripping in agony as Sigeric slowly turned his sword, mincing the man's windpipe and Adam's apple, and then pulled the blade free with a wash of blood.

'What the fuck?' Focalis said in shock, turning to his friend.

'Oh get over it, you're supposed to be a soldier.'

Even as the dying Thervingi gasped and choked out thick blood, clawing at his neck, Sigeric turned and finished off the other one with the headwound.

'We need to leave a message,' Focalis reminded him.

'Yes. We do.'

Sigeric turned back to the rider in the green tunic, who was not protected with a chain shirt, and used his sword to tear open the garment, with some difficulty, as the man was not quite dead and was still convulsing. He pushed the man over, onto his back, and as the Goth finally died and lay still and silent, Focalis watched in distaste as Sigeric pulled his knife and began to carve in the flesh of the man's chest.

Finally he finished, using the dead man's scarf to wipe away the bulk of the blood, and rose, stepping back. Focalis shook his head. 'That was rather unnecessary. You could have told him and then knocked him unconscious.'

They looked down at the letters carved in blood and flesh.

MARCIANOPOLIS

It was, Focalis had to admit, a pretty clear message, if somewhat gratuitous.

'If we knocked him out,' Sigeric explained, 'he might forget the message, or not wake up at all, or wake up quickly enough to gather his mates and chase us. This way the message stays, is clear, and it'll be a while before they find it.'

'*If* they find it.'

'They will. At least some of the other six who got trapped here will have survived and will remember their mates. They'll come looking. Since your lot brought God to the Thervingi, they've taken it on with enthusiasm. They like to bury their dead properly, with a priest present, even if they're in a hurry. Trust me, they'll get the message.'

Still shaking his head in disbelief at his friend's rather callous nature, Focalis followed Sigeric back to the horses as the sound of furious battle continued to echo across the land behind them. Sigeric wiped his blade clean and sheathed it, and the two checked their packs and then untethered the beasts, leading them forward to the edge of the woodland.

'How's our timing?' he mused.

'We've been four full days now. It's got to be more than seventy miles from here to Marcianopolis. Eighty or ninety by the roads. If we push, you and I can be there in two days, but the Goths will take at least three, and that's if they find the message tonight. My bet is that they will search and bury the dead in the morning, and that's when they'll find it. So I'm reckoning the others will have had eight days to prepare, and we'll be with them for the last day or two.'

Focalis smiled grimly as they mounted up, some distance from the fray, and began to trot away from the battle, largely hidden at the edge of the woods. 'Then it's all worked as planned so far.'

'As long as some passing scavenger doesn't eat our message during the night.'

'Absolu... *what?*'

16

'Of course, Fritigern needs to get into Marcianopolis first, before he can get anywhere near us,' Focalis pointed out, as they moved at a stately pace along the road into the city, crawling forward under a foreboding, steely grey sky.

'That, I think, will not be a problem for them,' Sigeric replied, gesturing to the two bored militia standing by the city's east gate. 'The days of Imperial Marcianopolis and the scholae are gone. A man would need an army to enter Constantinopolis or Thessalonika, but this place is half-forgotten and guarded by farmers with rusty spears. I think the emperor would like to forget that this place exists, along with Hadrianopolis. Look at those two,' he added, nodding again at the guards. 'Can you imagine half a thousand angry Thervingi being held up by them?'

Focalis nodded sadly. The city still thrived economically, but its political importance had died with Valens, on the battlefield. Its palace was a haunted shell, its walls guarded by untrained militia. A collection of ambitious bandits could probably take the city without much difficulty.

As they neared the gate, they could see the two guards visibly straighten to attention, and the riders smiled. At least their scholae uniforms were buying them respect. Both men now were wearing the kit they had kept from their days in the emperor's cavalry, and even if the unit had not been in this city for six years now, its uniform was readily recognised.

The white tunic and trousers were decorated not with any old unit design, but with rondels and woven designs in beautiful, rich imperial purple, a contrasting cloak of purple with white decoration. Of course, to call it white after so many days in the saddle was stretching the description a little, but still the imperial connection was unmistakable. And if anyone did not pick up on the purple, the shields slung across the horses' hindquarters made it clear: a purple shield with a golden sun gripped in the talons of an equally glittering eagle, arrayed around a gleaming bronze boss. Again, the few dents and chips in the shields took nothing away from the impact of the design.

As they reached the gate itself, they slowed.

'Sirs.' The native levies bowed their heads in respect.

'Our friends are in the city?' Focalis asked.

'The scholae have taken up residence in the old palace, sir. No one is allowed near, yourselves excepted, o'course.'

'You've been warned what's coming?'

What we hope *is coming*, Focalis added in the silence of his head.

'Goths, sir. Many of them. We've been told to keep a good lookout and close the gates and sound the alarm when they arrive.'

Sigeric shook his head. 'No. When they arrive, sound the alarm, then leave the gates wide and go through the streets telling everyone to stay indoors. Then go find a cellar to hide in.'

'Sir?'

Focalis also turned a frown on his friend. 'What?'

'Do you really think two dozen farmers with spears are going to hold Fritigern out for more than half an hour? And we can't stretch to helping them. And if they try to hold against the Goths, they'll all die. And they'll just piss the Thervingi off and trigger a sacking of the city that'll end up with thousands looted, raped and dead. If they find the city gates open and the populace in hiding, they have no reason to attack anyone but us. God, Flavius, but we need to leave them a signpost pointing to the palace, rather than trying to stop them.'

To this, Focalis could only nod. It was sound logic. And while it meant ignoring a potential obstacle they could put in their enemy's way, he was already a cursed man. What penance would he have to do if he was also responsible for setting hundreds of angry Goths on an unprotected civilian populace?

Leaving the two men looking all the more nervous now, they rode through the gate and into Marcianopolis. The street was so familiar – from memory, but also from six years of nightmare. Focalis closed his eyes.

It was dark, with clouds moving at terrifying speed, scudding across a sickly yellow, gibbous moon. The air was warm but moist, suggestive of an impending thunderstorm. The people filled the streets of the city ahead across the river, shouting, drinking, fucking, a heady mix of excitement and fear.

He could hear the foreigners back outside the gate, thousands upon thousands of voices lifted in that guttural tongue, singing Gothic songs that sounded utterly alien, and not a little threatening. The Thervingi outside the gate, camped before the walls of Marcianopolis, watched carefully by the city's garrison. The scholae and the men of the legions, all here with the dux and the comes. The soldiers looked tense. They knew what was at stake.

The bulk of the city lay ahead, this region separated from the rest by the curve of the river, creating its own isolated island within the walls, filled with the local governor's palace, a grand bath house and a church, along with the townhouses of some of the city's elite. No citizens wandered these streets, the populace kept on the far side of the river by men of the dux, guarding the bridge. Off to the right, that grand palace, rising two storeys, colonnades and fine marble, imperial banners hanging limp in the muggy air, golden light shining from every window, men of four different legions on display. A place fit for a king. Two, in fact, even if they were Goths...

The street was the same, but, then again, it wasn't. It was every bit as deserted now, in the cold, grey afternoon, as it had been that warm, sticky fateful evening, but the atmosphere was different. Marcianopolis was a ghost of itself. But unlike Macellum Iulia, which had been two cities superimposed, one living, one dead, Marcianopolis had never been sacked. It had never been destroyed. It had just been cursed and forgotten, the living becoming ghosts without the grace of dying first. The place made Focalis shudder, and not just because of the memories. It felt like walking into a mausoleum.

The church was still clearly in use, as were the baths, both of them open, smoke pouring from the roofs of the latter, where it coiled up from the flues that heated the complex. On the far side of the street, though, the old governor's palace was different.

The building itself was the same, of course. The colonnade, the fine walls, the bronze doors embossed with designs from a bygone era, now condemned by the Church as pagan heresy – heroes of old, battling monsters while gods looked on. There was no golden light, now, no imperial banners. The windows remained firmly shuttered, the door barred, the whole place clearly deserted. For six years this building had been shunned. No one but desperate and drunken vagrants or children on dares had even tried to enter the place. The palace of Marcianopolis was haunted and cursed, for here murders had been carried out against kings, in the name of a crazed and doomed emperor. Here Christians had butchered Christians on the cusp of cementing a universal peace, and had instead triggered a disastrous five-year war that had shaken the empire to the core, and ruined so much of Thracia. Marcianopolis had survived the war unscathed, but time and the court of public opinion had ruined it every bit as much as a Gothic warband.

Focalis and Sigeric reined in, halfway between the gate and the bridge over the river into the main city. The baths might be open, but there was no sign of bathers. The church might be active, but no worshippers were evident, no voices lifted in song. Only the distant hum of the city across the river and the cawing of scavengers, waiting for corpses to pick over.

They would feast soon enough.

Focalis forced himself back into the present, to focus on the matter at hand and stop wallowing in the past. Much depended on their focus now, particularly Martius' life, which was paramount. His gaze roamed around the street. It looked so quiet and dead.

Unless you knew Sallustius and Pictor.

What appeared to be crumbled stone, fallen from the corner of the church wall, included three white pebbles at a uniform distance from each other. Only those who'd watched artillery in action would see what Focalis was seeing. A distance marker. Three extra turns of the ratchet beyond the first range mark, and a bolt from a scorpion would pin a man to the wall here. He could see other similar marks around the street, threes and twos. And from their positioning, he could also see that they were range markers for two separate weapons, not one.

His gaze wandered back across the street to the apparently deserted palace. Now that he'd identified the range markers, he could see the sources of the danger. Two of the shuttered windows were slightly different, if you knew what to look for. On this pair, the heavy, painted timber stopped just short of the tops of the windows, leaving a gap a hand span wide. No one would expect artillery there, at the top of the windows, some eight or nine feet from the floor. Focalis gave a grim smile as he imagined the firing platforms Pictor had constructed inside, positioned very carefully to give an excellent field of vision along the street over the top of the shutters.

As Sigeric slid from his saddle, also looking around, so Focalis did the same, walking his horse over towards the palace walls. He stopped short, looking carefully this way and that. A drain ran along the edge of the road, beside the pavement, with a pronounced gutter and grates every ten or fifteen feet. They were dry and empty, but the acrid smell of pitch was just discernible in the air, and the closer he got to a drain, the stronger it became. Some trick of Sallustius', clearly.

He reached over and handed his reins to Sigeric and, just in case, stepped high and wide over the gutter. The pavement was flagged with old, heavy stones, and he moved slowly, gently prodding each with a foot as he approached the colonnaded wall. He was not at all surprised when he felt one of the stones begin to give way beneath him, pivoted somehow, the danger invisible to the unwary. Stepping carefully around that stone, he tested others until he reached one of the shuttered windows. They were good, solid shutters, and he put his eye to the crack in them and pulled away in an instant, half expecting something to lance out and take him in the face. When it didn't, he was oddly disappointed.

He leaned closer again. The room beyond the shutters was dark, but he could just see a line, a thin rope stretched horizontally across the gap. What it might do he had no idea, but was equally disinclined to test it. A thought occurring, he glanced up, at the top of the colonnade. A decorative architrave ran along the top of the columns which were interspersed between the windows, and he was not at all surprised to see nets of something half-hidden in the gloom behind the columns.

He tried not to think about what might happen if he accidentally triggered one now, and moved carefully, watchfully, across to the next window, one of the two slightly truncated for artillery. This set of shutters, he noted with satisfaction, was a different proposition. There was no gap between, beneath or beside them, only above. He gently, carefully, pushed them, stepping swiftly aside. They were as solid as a church wall, reinforced impressively from within. Pictor and Sallustius had made good use of their time.

With a nod to Sigeric, he moved towards the gate to the old palace, continually testing the flags of the pavement and finding another loose one in his path. The gates were bronze and fit for a fortress. It would take a battering ram to get through them, or a runaway cart at least.

'I know you can see us,' he said. 'Care to let us in?'

There was a momentary pause, and then the left of the two bronze portals crept open with an ominous creak. The interior was as dark as the rooms behind the shutters, which took him by surprise. Focalis tried to picture the palace layout, conjuring it up in memory.

The Kings of the Thervingi and the Greuthungi, brothers in arms, moved into the gateway through the open bronze doors. The men of the legions stood to either side, armed, but with swords sheathed, eyes watchful, expressions wary. Ahead of the kings came two men, a herald of some sort with a banner and a horn, and a priest who, for all his Christian symbols, looked so like a druid of ancient times that it was hard to see him as anything but a barbarian. Behind the kings came their retinue, several nobles in rich dress, each haughty and stern-looking, and then, bringing up the rear, six Thervingi and six Greuthungi, each the highest valued of the tribes' warriors, a military escort for their leaders.

They passed beneath the long arch and out into the wide gardens of the palace. Torches and lamps lit the place as fountains gushed and tinkled, manicured lawns and hedges forming a veritable maze between white-chip gravelled paths, statues of beasts and maidens rising in marble glory in the stifling evening air.

Flavius Focalis, rider of the scholae palatinae, stood with the others on the far side of the garden, close to Lupicinus, their commander, watching the Goths arrive. The dinner would be held in the grand summer triclinium of the palace, a great, apsed room that looked out over the gardens towards the south wing and the main gates.

The kings had arrived to discuss the future of the fragile peace...

The palace was arranged as a square around the gardens. The gates stood in a two-storey wing of individual rooms, mainly used by guards, servants and slaves, and as storage, including the main barracks of the garrison. The principal structure of the palace, with the governor's own residence and all the rooms of state, stood on the far side of the garden, that great windowed apse of the dining room, facing onto the open area. To the left lay the impressive private baths of the palace, and to the right, closing the square, lay the library, the private chapel and the stables.

What struck Focalis immediately was that, once through the gates, there should be an open, unobstructed view to the gardens. He was also a little surprised to find the gates opened so easily. He'd not even heard a bar being lifted. What was Sallustius playing at, the inventive arsehole?

He scanned the darkness, but could see hardly anything but the small square of light cast inside from the open door.

'Hello?'

'Walk around the edge,' came Odalaricus' voice from somewhere, echoing eerily in the darkness. 'Halfway around, you'll find a ladder. Climb it. Don't deviate from the course. Stay at the very edge.'

'Horses can't climb ladders.'

'You'll have to leave the horses. We've sealed the place.'

Focalis sighed. He didn't like the idea of turning the beast loose – he might need it – but there seemed no alternative. If Odalaricus said the place was sealed, then the place was sealed. With Sigeric nearby doing the same, he stripped his helmet, shield and three bags from the horse, then gave it a pat on the rump to send it trotting off down the street, hoping it wouldn't stumble into one of his friend's traps. His shoulders and arms strained under the weight of the bags and armour as he stepped into the darkness and turned to his left, pressing himself against the wall and edging carefully around. Behind him, Sigeric did the same.

It was a tense journey, finding the corner of the arched entrance and then turning and following further until, with considerable relief, he found a ladder by the simple expedient of walking into it in the dark.

'I can't climb with the bags.'

Something smacked into him, and he felt around with difficulty until a rope with a hook on the end almost concussed him. Grunting irritably, he hooked all his bags to the device, including his shield by its shoulder strap, and waited until they disappeared upwards in jerky movements. Once they were safely out of the way he began to climb. The gatehouse was quite high, and despite being surrounded by impenetrable blackness, his bowels told him all he needed to know about the drop below him by the time he found an aperture and pulled himself through it into an attic room lit by just a small window.

Odalaricus was crouched next to his packs, grinning at him.

'Special, isn't it?'

'Couldn't have left a path open until we got here?'

'There was no guarantee you *would* get here.'

'Dad!'

Focalis' attention sharpened as his eyes shifted to a shape in the gloom. 'Martius?'

'I... I hoped, but I just didn't believe.'

Focalis' eyes shot back to Odalaricus. 'He is supposed to be safe.'

'Have you ever tried to take a man's son away from him. It's not damned easy. He's fucking determined, Flavius.'

'You *know* what's coming.'

'Then *you* persuade him to go. He kicked *me* in the balls.'

Focalis, tension enveloping him, scurried past his packs and threw his arms around his son. He was furious, absolutely livid, that Martius was still here, and yet embracing his boy made him tremble at the knees, and he knew in that instant he couldn't send the lad away again. He spent long moments in that embrace.

'We have to win this, Odalaricus.'

'Oddly, I had that in mind myself.'

Behind them, a voice called up through the hole. 'Would someone like to lower the rope again?'

As Focalis hugged his boy tight, Odalaricus returned to the ladder top, hauled up Sigeric's gear, and then waited for their friend to climb the ladder. Once he'd pulled himself through the aperture, Odalaricus and he retrieved the ladder, sliding it across into the attic room, and with a waggling of the eyebrows, crossed to the wall and pulled on a rope that wound around a pulley before disappearing into the floor. As he tugged, Focalis could hear the palace door closing. Sallustius was an ingenious bastard from time to time.

'So what's with the gate? You've blocked it off, I see.'

Odalaricus nodded as he crossed the room and opened a door to a narrow flight of stairs. Light flooded into the dim attic room. 'Yes. Properly, too. Stone and mortar. It's walled in and bolstered. The room inside is littered with caltrops, and we have a few surprises ready for when they're trapped in there.'

'You've been working hard.'

'Sallustius is a slave driver. And Agnes, too. She's cruel, and nearly as weird as Sallustius. Between them they've almost made me feel sorry for the Goths.'

Moments later they were traipsing down the stairs, struggling to carry the kit-bags and shields in the narrow space. 'I take it the other approaches to the palace are defended? Fritigern is unlikely to try just one angle.'

'Two sides are protected by the river, but we've put some additional work in there too. The last one could be a problem. The roofline is level with the city wall and they're only twenty feet apart. Scaling ladders or ropes could just reach from the one to the other. I think that and the street side are the two to concentrate on. Sallustius thinks so too.'

They reached the bottom of the stairs and emerged into the gardens, once beautiful, fit for a provincial governor, now overgrown and ruined, partially by time, but mostly by the efforts of the defenders. Most of the garden was now a shallow pit, the earth piled up against the wall built across the gateway, an embankment in support, preventing the possibility of breaking through it with any ease.

The others were gathered in front of the great apse of the summer dining room, and Sallustius heaved a sigh of relief at the sight of them.

'Tell us,' he said as they approached.

Focalis looked to Sigeric, who cleared his throat. 'All went pretty much according to plan, surprisingly. Lupicinus is still lurking in his villa, but his small mercenary army met Fritigern's warband near Suida. The result was brutal. We didn't stick around to count the survivors, but I'd be surprised if more than half of Fritigern's men made it out.'

'Five hundred men is still a lot,' Taurus murmured.

'It's a lot less than a thousand.'

'True.'

Sallustius gave a weird smile and patted Agnes on the shoulder. 'And with everything we've done here, a hundred to one odds might not be enough for Fritigern.'

'We left a fairly clear message about where to find us,' Focalis said. 'Unless a hungry bear ate the message.' He glanced sidelong at Sigeric. The others frowned at him. 'Never mind. With luck they're on their way here, probably two days behind us, I reckon.'

'Two days?' Sallustius grinned. 'Excellent. I have time for a little more preparation, then.' Clapping his hands and rubbing them together, he gestured to each of them. 'Alright. Odalaricus? Use the wall exit, find a handcart and start shopping. The smith on Water Street does excellent work. I want the fixings for a whole load more darts, and two hundred caltrops. He should be able to provide some of that today, and the rest by late tomorrow. I put in an order for more pitch with the merchant down on Euxine, but I didn't think it would arrive on time. Looks like it might, now. Chase him up, and pay for and collect it if you can. There's a timber merchant just inside the Danubius Gate. I was going to plunder the palace rafters for more pointed stakes, but if we can get them brought in without having to demolish our fortress, that would be handy.'

'That all?' Odalaricus said with a sarcastic tone.

'No, but that's enough to get you started. Once you've sorted that, come find me and I'll give you more jobs. Pictor,

you take Sigeric and Focalis around the place and familiarise
them with everything we've done, including all your artillery
positions. Taurus, you and Martius start work on the gardens.
I want this shallow pit changed. Dig and fill, so we can create
a ditch in a U around the door into the main palace. That's
our fallback position when they breach the wall or street
approach. They'll not get across the water, I think.'

'And what will you and Agnes be doing?' Taurus said
meaningfully.

'We will be planning the next step of defence.'

With nods and murmurs, the group split up to go about
their assigned tasks, and for the next two hours, Focalis
and Sigeric followed their friend around the palace, trying
to take in the details of everything that had been done to
prepare for the onslaught. Each of them had been assigned a
place in the defence and a series of conditions to meet before
they fell back to a secondary and then a tertiary position.
Martius, of course, had no specific tasks, for he was not
supposed to be there, and Focalis struggled with the decision
for a while. The clear favourite was for Martius to find
somewhere secure in the main building and hide, waiting it
all out. If they lost the fight, the enemy might not find him,
since they would not be looking for him. But then, he also
considered the possibility that the safest place was beside
his father and, perhaps selfishly, this latter won out in the
end. Focalis' place was to oversee the gate approach from
the attic room and, once all the surprises there had been
sprung, to climb to the roof and move west to help defend
that position from the city walls. Once either the gate or the
west roof was breached, they were to fall back to the trench
in the gardens and hold the last approach. Once that went,

any survivors would defend the main palace building, room by room, until it was over. Simple.

The rest of the afternoon, while there was still light, they helped dig and consolidate the trench in the garden that would help defend their last position. For now, long beams were thrown across the ditch as they worked, so that the defenders could cross from one side to the other without trouble.

Through the afternoon, Odalaricus came and went on shopping and delivery errands. Access to the palace for now was through a smallish window in the western wall, leading out from the library, which had a solid shutter defence ready to block it at a moment's notice, and timber and jars of pitch among other things were slowly fed through the hole into the palace.

As darkness fell, Sallustius the slave driver called a halt to the work, for every muscle on every man and woman ached from their day's work. Martius, Odalaricus and Agnes produced a meal, and the entire group gathered together in the grand triclinium to eat, the need for sentries largely redundant. The city garrison would blow the alarm the moment Fritigern's horde hove into view, and half a thousand cavalry make a noise that's hard to miss, even from a distance.

After the meal, each of them moved to a watch-post on the roofs where they were close to their defensive position, ready. Eight of them anticipating the coming cataclysm, Sigeric and Taurus watching over the water from above the palace baths, Pictor and Agnes the city wall approach, Sallustius and Odalaricus on the main palace roof, and Focalis and Martius over the main gate. Each roof was pitched and tiled, but each had a balustraded walkway around the edge, studded with pedestals at even intervals. Last time Focalis had been here, each of those pedestals had sported a statue of a hero or a god. Now they were gone, but whether through looting and damage or through some scheme of Sallustius', he had yet to determine.

Father and son settled for the night, half alert but foregoing sentry duty through exhaustion, given the warnings they'd get from the garrison anyway. Finally, after some time looking at Focalis and apparently working his way up to it, Martius spoke.

'I have to take my place when they come.'

'No.'

'I can play my part, Dad.'

'No. I want you safe.'

'Then we need every hand added to the defence. Dad, I'm nearly old enough to join up. In less than two years I'll be of age. I'm a man now, and you know it. And it's not like I haven't proved I can do it. I've killed, and I can do it again. I know you want me to be safe, but I'm a part of this already. Agnes will fight with Pictor, and after him I'm the best shot here, and you know it. I can be of use. I'll not put myself in extra danger, but it gives us all a better chance if you let me do what I can rather than keeping me hidden.'

Focalis sighed. The lad was right, of course. He couldn't send Martius away. He wouldn't go anyway, as he'd proved when Odalaricus tried. And God knew, they *would* need every hand. But he would make sure that Martius was as far from direct danger as possible at all times.

They sat there in silence for a while, the chill forcing them to pull their blankets tight around them. Though he really should sleep while Martius watched, Focalis found that slumber would not claim him as he sat thinking. Finally, Martius spoke again.

'Will it ever stop, Dad?'

'Yes. One way or another, in the next few days. Either we'll be gone, or Fritigern will.'

'I meant for the empire, Dad. When the emperors are raised to power, the people shout "more fortunate than Augustus, better than Trajan". But they aren't are they? In *their* day, the empire grew. They conquered and expanded, and the peoples beyond the borders were frightened of Rome's power. Now, we have those tribes inside the borders defending us from other barbarians. The Huns push the Goths into the empire. What happens when the Huns reach the border? And who's behind them, pushing? Will the Huns be the next to want in when they're driven south?'

'You think too much,' Focalis murmured, and turned over.

Martius made a noise suggesting that this was a far from satisfying answer and shuffled further into his blankets. What he'd said, though, had somehow wormed its way into Focalis' thoughts, and he now found himself thinking on the same matter as he drifted slowly towards sleep. Was this the new norm? And if it was, what was the difference really between Goth and Roman? All Christian, all fighting the same enemies, and with remarkably little difference in appearance.

He fell asleep, cursing his son's infectious intellect. He could do without more appreciation of the Gothic people, given what was coming.

17

Flavius Focalis heard his decanus bellowing an order, a hoarse and desperate cry in the press, lost amid the tumult of war. Ofilius had a powerful voice that could suppress any commotion, and yet here, in this disaster, it was little more than a whisper of hope. Focalis tried to turn to see the man, to see if he was gesturing, had some great plan for survival, but there was neither room nor time. If he took his eye from those before him, he would die, and there was no doubt in him over that.

The Thervingi warrior roared as he brought down his long, straight blade, hammering at Focalis' shield, leaving great rents and dents in the brightly painted surface, numbing his arm with shock after shock. He struggled, heaving Sallustius – who was so close the two kept clouting one another – away in order to bring his own sword to bear. The battering on his shield continued unabated, and he took it as stoically as a dead man standing could, waiting for the moment he knew would come, as long as he survived long enough to recognise it. Then it came. The warrior, exhausted by his own relentless assault, paused for breath, bringing his sword back and up.

*

The dream was changed though, this time, for the blow and counterblow that would lead them inevitably to the last inferno moments of an emperor never came. Instead, somewhere across the battlefield, a horn blew, a sound that was at once dreadfully familiar and totally unexpected. This was not how the dream went.

In a heartbeat, Focalis was blinking awake and leaping out of his bedding, crossing to Martius, who continued to snore lightly beneath his blankets. The horn was blaring with urgency in the waking world, cutting through the early morning light. Dawn was here, the first golden rays gracing the fields of Thracia... and so was Fritigern.

As Martius started awake, realising what must be happening in those first bleary moments, Focalis crossed to the edge of the roof and looked down the street. The local levy guardsmen had fled the city walls and the gate already, leaving the latter wide open and inviting for the Thervingi. Four of them, still clinging to their spears, were running down the street past the palace, sounding a horn in warning, racing for the bridge that would lead them across into the heart of the city where they could warn the populace and seek a place of refuge. It was highly doubtful, if Fritigern and his men managed to deal with their prey, that they would cause any trouble in the city. With the peace treaty in place, doing so would put them not only against the combined might of Rome, but also against their own people.

Straining, hand shading his eyes, Focalis peered off past the running men. The city walls and gate obscured any view out across the flat lands beyond, and he could see no sign of the Goths, nor if he leaned forward and tried to see through the arch itself. Turning, he looked across the palace, but could not see the others for the pitched tiled roofs. They would be up and readying themselves.

'What do we do, Dad?'

'Get yourself ready. Sallustius left me a list. We don't need to be in the chamber above the gate until they look like breaching the door. Then we get down fast. First thing is to try and keep them back. We watch them approach, but if they start sending arrows up here, keep safely below balustrade level. I'll tell you what to do as we need to do it. Alright?'

Martius nodded, looking nervous, and the two of them moved a little along the rail, eyes still locked on that gate.

They heard the Goths before they saw them, a mob outside the city. Then, after a curious delay, six riders, nobles by their dress, emerged through the gate, slowly, warily, shields up, eyes peeking out below the brow line of good solid helmets. They rode into the city, walking their horses along the empty street, looking this way and that.

They knew the place, for rather than continue along to the bridge and the city itself, they stopped outside the bath house door, looking across the street at the palace. Had those men been the ones with Fritigern at that dinner? Had they been the warriors who had crowded around their king as they watched Alavivus and his men cut down by imperial soldiers at a peace conference? This would not be a happy return for them, but they would be looking to shed blood themselves this time.

They were checking out the situation, clearly, for there would be no need for the Goths to bring their horses in. Focalis chewed his lip. There was no chance that they could be persuaded against their course of action, for if they had come this far, they intended to see it through to the end. Still, it was always worth giving peace one last chance, and it was the Christian thing to do. Focalis rose, becoming clearly visible over the balustrade, and opened his mouth to offer them a peaceful conclusion, asking them to turn and leave without further violence.

No words emerged, for just as he stood, there was the slap-and-clatter of artillery loosing and one of the Goth nobles was plucked from his saddle and slammed against the wall of the baths. The dying man stared down in shock at the heavy bolt protruding from his chest as he slid down the wall to the flagged pavement and lay in a shaking heap, a red smear down the bricks behind him marking his path.

The other five reacted with shock, then turned rearing, panicked horses, and raced back for the gate. Pictor made it clear to them that nowhere in the street was safe, for even halfway back to the line of the walls, a second rider gave a cry of agony, an artillery bolt lodged in his spine as he fell forward over his horse's neck.

Focalis stared. Oh well, it appeared that Pictor had declared war on behalf of them all.

'Be ready,' he told his son. 'But try to relax. They won't be back for a while now.'

'Why?'

'They'll have to dismount and corral their mounts. They can't storm a building on horseback. They'll do that, and then there'll be a lengthy discussion as to how to get to us. Fritigern and many of his warriors know the city and even the palace. First, he'll send scout parties to the other city gates and they'll come through the streets and check the approaches across the river. Sallustius assures me that's not a feasible approach, but Fritigern needs to check them anyway. And then he'll have men positioned over there to stop any of us escaping over the water. Then, I reckon he'll take control of the city walls and look at the chance of getting across to the roof there. Odalaricus and Taurus are on there at the moment. But if they decide to check that way in, it'll take them time to get together ropes and ladders, so I doubt they'll even attempt that before noon. I reckon in an hour he'll have men everywhere, though, and then they'll decide that the direct approach is the clear one. Then they'll come and we'll have a fight on our hands.'

As the riders disappeared through the gate, the two of them stood at the rail and watched. For some time nothing happened, though the sounds of cavalry organising and encamping outside were clear enough. Pictor finally popped up through the hatch onto the roof and sauntered around to their position with his thumbs hooked into his sword belt.

'I was about to try and negotiate,' Focalis grunted without turning.

'I negotiated for you, Flavius, and my way they're now two men down.'

'Good shots, though.'

The man simply nodded as though this were a redundant piece of information. 'We caught a glimpse of riders in the distance from the other side of the palace. They're skirting the city and coming from the other gates. They'll not try the water, I think, and if they do they'll get surprises. You know what you're doing?'

'Think so.'

'Good. We'll be on soon enough.' And with that, he was gone again.

They remained in position for some time, waiting, watching, listening. An hour more had passed before movement drew their eye, the sun now above the level of the walls, so that looking in the direction of the gate was eye-watering, despite the paleness and greyness of the light. Figures began to emerge on the walls, hurrying along them, keeping low. And well they might. From behind the wicker screens that had been raised on the roof there, Odalaricus and Taurus began their onslaught. Focalis could not see them work because of the angle of the roof, but the result was visible. The arrows loosed by Focalis' oldest friend whipped out through the morning air and found a number of targets. He was no Apollo with a bow, but he remained the best shot in their unit, and the enemy were close, poorly covered and numerous, so it was hard to miss. Man after man hurtling along that wall would suddenly stiffen and topple to their death. And interspersed with the arrows came the martiobarbuli, hurled with some accuracy by Taurus, the one man who through sheer muscle could be relied upon to get a dart across such a distance with power.

After a short barrage, a new sound began, announcing that Pictor had joined them on the roof with his machinery of death. Focalis could hear the rhythmic clatters of his repeating scorpion bow as it loosed bolt after bolt fed from the wooden hopper. For the first time, Focalis started to consider the possibility that they might even win as he watched two men in every three that emerged onto the walls die in agony. Of course, when he thought about it, perhaps fifty men had gone up there, which was a fraction of the force Fritigern could call upon, and each barrage was costing them precious ammunition. Still, it was an encouraging start.

After a time, the shots faded and the clattering ended as Pictor moved to a new position, for the Goths had taken control of the city walls and were in cover now, safe. As they waited, Focalis located the small bag with their emergency provisions, and buttered bread to keep his and Martius' strength up. With a little salted pork, they stopped the growling of bellies, and were just washing it all down with a cup of wine when a new noise drew their attention. Tense, they watched the first Goths emerge through the city gate. They had learned from the scouts the danger of simply riding along the street, and had adopted the ancient testudo notion after a fashion, for as they came out into the street they pulled tightly together, attempting to create a complete shell of shields as they moved along the shit-stained flags towards the palace.

It was a nice idea. Not good enough, though. A shield could protect from slingshot, and might or might not stop an arrow or a dart, but an iron bolt shot from torsion artillery was another proposition entirely. Focalis watched the front of the mobile shield-wall pass Pictor's subtle outer marker. The artillerist allowed them to walk on for a while, letting them reach the second marker to reduce the range and thereby increase the power of the shot.

Twin thuds announced the loosing of bolts, and Focalis remembered then that there were two windows with artillery positions. Had Pictor trained Agnes in their use? It seemed quite likely, knowing their old friend. Two bolts hit the advancing Goths simultaneously, and both punched through the shields as though they were but windows, slamming deep into the press of bodies within. The advance faltered in an instant, each shot finding multiple victims within the fictitious safety of their shields. That was not the end, though, for, aware that they were already in danger from the artillery, they simply burst into activity, running into the fray.

'Here we go,' Focalis said, watching more and more armoured bodies pouring in through the city gate and flooding the street, racing in their direction. 'Go over to the pedestal marked with white. Can you see the rope?'

Martius nodded and hurried over. The rope was wound and tied on a metal hook in the stonework, from which it disappeared through a freshly cut hole in the edge of the roof. In Sallustius' usual peculiar fashion, he'd not given any details of the defences he'd prepared, marking them on his list as 'Surprise I', 'Surprise II' and so on.

'What does it do?'

'No idea, but it says here to free it when the first score of men get to the colonnade. You can do that?'

'I can.'

'Be careful. They might have archers.'

'I know what I'm doing, Dad.'

Still keeping half an eye on the boy, Focalis kept low and looked out over the balustrade. Judging the distance, he crouched and collected a handful of martiobarbuli from the pile against the slope of the tiles. Gripping them in his left arm, he hefted one in his right hand and then changed his mind and his grip. Holding all seven so that the points looked up at him, he gripped them like a bundle of rods, then bent, bringing them down to the level of his knees.

Satisfied that the range was now adequate, he tensed, put all the strength he could into his arms and rose, flinging the bundle up and out with every ounce of power he could muster. The seven darts, heavy iron and timber weapons weighted with lead, hurtled up in a sharp, high arc and then, at their apex, turned, the weights flipping them and then dragging them down with gravity, back to the earth below. Focalis grabbed a second handful and moved closer again, seeing the odd gap in the mass of men that his missiles had caused. Below, inside, the artillery clattered again, and small pockets of Goths fell away with the shots. The hidden weapons were powerful but slow, since each was crewed only by a single person, either Pictor or Agnes, with no help loading or winding. Three times Focalis repeated his barrage of martiobarbuli, until only three darts remained in the pile, which he decided to save.

They had done immense damage already, and yet the numbers coming at them did not seem diminished. The flood came on. Focalis watched, counted, glanced at Martius. He was about to tell the lad it was time when Martius suddenly released the rope, which he had already untied and unwound.

Unable to resist seeing what happened, Focalis risked peering over the parapet, just in time to view the effects of Surprise I.

The nets up in the shadows behind the columns all along the palace façade suddenly emptied, the rope holding them closed having been freed. The nets contained rubble. A demolished wall from somewhere in the palace had given up its existence for their defence, and smashed lumps of stone and brick, each jagged and heavy, the size of a bunched fist, dropped some twelve feet onto the heads of the first men to reach the colonnade. The result was impressive. In a score of years in warfare, Focalis had never seen so many shattered skulls and smashed brains in one moment.

The attack faltered then, waves of men halting their forward surge, unwilling to be the next victim of Sallustius' traps. Indeed, the entire attack stumbled and then broke, the street's mob pulling away from the colonnade of the palace. They were swiftly reminded that a street-width was not a safe distance as a fresh pair of artillery bolts slammed into them, each impaling a victim and sending them barrelling back into their friends, knocking over piles of men. In a dozen more heartbeats the street began to clear, as Goths moved back out of artillery range. Some crossed the bridge into the town, others retreated into the safety of the city gate. More pushed their way into the baths or the church across the street, where they could still watch the palace.

'Is that it?' Martius said, a wide grin plastered on his face.

'That was their first push. That was to test us. They got a lot more of a battering than they were expecting, I'd wager.'

'We must have killed over a hundred men.'

Focalis nodded. 'That's a significant number, but we've also used up a lot of ammunition and several of Sallustius' surprises. I think we'll manage a second assault like that, if I read my instructions right, but after that things will get harder and nastier.'

But at least there was breathing space. The enemy, safely back out of range, made no immediate attempt to repeat their disaster. One brave soul tried to leave the church and run for the gate, but he'd barely made it out into the street before an artillery bolt slammed into his back, pitching him forward into a street littered with bodies and washed with blood.

An hour passed with no fresh movement, and eventually Pictor reappeared.

'Update for you. Odalaricus has taken an arrow wound to his left bicep. It's been bound and it's quite nasty, but not life-threatening. In fact, I think it's just made him angry. You don't see Odalaricus angry often.'

'No. How's it going elsewhere?'

'Alright. I left Agnes on the artillery below and went to help with the second wave. Another group tried to come across the river, but that was pretty much an instant disaster. They tried the old trick of paddling across on their shields en masse, but we'd set defences in the water. Sallustius is a devious prick. We spent six hours in the water the other day, and in boats, driving posts down into the riverbed. We drove them down so the top was half a foot below the surface, then wound ropes around them in a weird sort of net. After the first half dozen Thervingi drowned just now, trying to untangle themselves in the ropes, the others decided it was a stupid approach and swam back to the far bank. There, they learned they were within bowshot from the roof, and half the survivors from the water got an arrow in the back as they ran for cover. I don't think they'll try the water again. Shame, really, as I was looking forward to them finding the iron spikes in the palace-side riverbank. Still, I think they'll spend some time taking stock now before they try something new. If Martius comes downstairs, we're cooking up a quick stew, and I'll give him a bag of replacement darts. Last supplies, though.'

Focalis nodded. 'I think we're going through ammunition fast.'

'Tell me about it. Agnes and I are spending every moment we're not at the machines trying to put together new bolts from the supplies I ordered, but it's a struggle, and we'll run out soon enough. My only hope is that we've picked off enough by the time we run out of surprises and ammunition that we can face them man to man.'

'Amen to that, my brother.'

Focalis waited then, watching the empty street, littered with bodies, while Martius fetched some of the stew and the replacement martiobarbuli. There was a long pause in the assault. He could quite imagine Fritigern, somewhere out there beyond the walls, raging and shouting, pushing his men around for their failure. He would be angry beyond belief. But he still had hundreds of men – Focalis couldn't even say *how* many hundred. The next assault would be more dangerous for the Romans, and every push made them more tired and reduced their ammunition.

He watched the sun climb the vault of heaven, and it was almost noon when there was new movement. Hastily constructed screens were being lifted up onto the city walls and then carried out and positioned opposite the palace, protecting the Goths on the walls from the missiles of Taurus and Odalaricus. Then, Focalis watched massive plank edifices being raised, temporary timber bridges that could be lifted and dropped over the gap. The second assault was about to begin.

'What are they doing?' Martius asked, peering off at the walls.

Focalis explained their next move, and winced as he saw the look in his son's eyes. 'No,' he said, in anticipation of the question.

'You have to let me join in.'

'No, I don't. It will be hell over there. Our place is here, as Sallustius said, watching the street. What happens if they come again while you're over at the wall side?'

'You deal with them. C'mon, Dad. You know I'm the best shot in the whole palace with a bow. They need me over there, and Odalaricus will make sure I'm safe.'

'No.'

Focalis stared in astonishment as Martius gave him a hard look, one eyebrow lifted, and gathered up his bow and quiver from the ground. 'If their roof falls now, we're all dead. How is stopping me helping going to protect me? I'm going, Dad.'

Focalis was on his son in that moment, grabbing him, trying to pull the bow from his grip. Martius clenched his teeth, hissing with the effort as he tried to break free of his father's grip. 'Let me go.'

'No.'

'Dad, you're going to have to break my arm to stop me.'

'I won't let you go.'

'You don't have a choice,' Martius snapped. 'I'm going. You want to stop me, you're going to have to hold onto me all the time, because the moment you let go, I'm gone.'

Gasping with frustration, Focalis let go of his son and stepped back. He realised only now that tears were streaming down his face. 'You can't. I can't lose you. I lost your mother, I can't lose you. God above, Martius, but if it weren't for keeping you safe, I'd have gone to face my maker years ago.'

'And a great job you did of keeping me safe,' Martius spat, turning his back and marching off towards the roof exit.

Focalis stared in bleak horror at his son's retreating back. He made to move, but as he lunged, fresh sounds reached him from the street, and he turned to see men beginning to file out of the buildings in which they'd been hiding. Clearly Agnes had been left on her own with the artillery once more, for only one of the emerging warriors found himself staring down at the bolt that had punched deep into his abdomen and pinned him to the bath house door frame. Then they were coming.

Focalis turned and stared longingly at the empty doorway. Martius had gone, descending and crossing the gardens to the library and the staircase that led up to the roof to help defend there. The small part of him that remained the cold, professional, dispassionate soldier knew that the boy was right, and that lending his considerable skill to the defence there was also increasing the chances of his own survival. The large part of him that was a father and a widower raged against the boy for going. He roared, though with rage or with pain he could not tell, and turned, wiping his tears away with a cuff as he watched the men flooding towards him across the street. They surely could not hope to do any better than last time, but they would act as a distraction from the main event, keeping Focalis and Agnes busy and pinned in position, unable to help defend against the real struggle.

This time he did not take armfuls of darts. This time he took fierce and angry pleasure in hurling them individually at chosen targets. He watched as the weapons smashed into his victims from above, their impact huge, gravity and weight only adding to the power of his muscular throws. He would never be an archer, but with a dart he was deadly, and he knew it.

A head smashed open, the heavy point and lead weight cracking the skull like an egg, allowing the missile to mash what lay inside. The man collapsed to the ground, shaking wildly, dead, but mobile. Again and again his darts found their targets, pulverising Goth heads, taking men out of the fight one by one.

He only realised how much danger he was in when the arrow came. In his rage he had been standing at the balustrade in full view of the enemy, and some Thervingi with a bow kneeling in the church door had taken careful aim.

The nose guard of Focalis' helmet saved his life, for the arrow was expertly launched at his face and only chance or the grace of God turned his head at the last moment, the tip of the missile clanging off the bronze. Even then he thought he was a goner, for the arrowhead, deflected, slid across in front of his left eye, slammed into the top of his cheek and almost punctured his ear, wedged between the bone of his skull and the metal of his cheekpiece. The white-hot fire of a flesh wound raced across his face, and he cursed as he undid the thong beneath his chin and pulled the helmet away, the broken arrow falling to the rooftop, blood running down his cheek. He staggered back, realising he was still in danger even as a second arrow whipped through the air, worryingly close to his head. Gingerly, he reached up to his cheek and immediately wished he hadn't. The pain was intense, much like any flesh wound he'd taken in half a dozen battles in his life, but the fact that his probing fingers touched bone without the protective layer of skin and flesh in between caused bile to rise, and in moments he was throwing up violently. Still he probed, making sure there was nothing critical. There was bone, there was a lot of blood, and he seemed to be missing that piece of his ear he didn't know the name of, that little bit from the cheek that covered the earhole.

Pain and blood, but nothing that would kill him, as long as he managed to stop the bleeding, which, of course, would have to wait until the next lull.

As he winced and dabbed at his cheek with his scarf, he became aware of new noises.

Carefully, he crept back towards the balustrade, his eyes searching out the archer. He could see the man, but for the moment the archer was not looking in his direction, his eyes instead on the façade below. Focalis took the risk, leaning forward to look over the edge.

Another of Sallustius' traps had been triggered, for the side of the street close to the colonnaded front was an inferno, flames erupting into explosions of liquid gold up from the sewer grates. Dozens of men had been caught in the inferno as the pitch that had flooded the drains was lit by some unseen hand. Now, they charged around the street screaming, the fire clinging to them like liquid glue, burning deep into their flesh and impossible to extinguish. Every now and then one would bump into someone else who'd not managed to get out of the way in time and the conflagration spread. The result was horrifying, and caused far more damage to enemy morale than any amount of falling rocks, well-aimed darts or hidden artillery. Once again, as had happened with the falling of the rubble, the hell-fire that consumed one entire side of the street, hiding their objective and spreading towards them in the form of mobile, screaming corpses, caused a complete failure in the attack. The Goths surged back across the street, more to get away from their blazing companions than from any fear of the defenders. Focalis watched with distaste as the terrified Thervingi fled into the church and the baths, slamming the doors behind them, barring the way to their screaming brothers. Similarly, up and down the street, men ran into the gateway or onto the bridge and presented a phalanx of long spears, to hold their friends at bay and preserve themselves from the blaze.

The secondary attack on the palace front had failed as quickly as it had begun.

Focalis stood back, breathing heavily. He could faintly hear action over on the far side of the palace, where the main fight was going on, but the noise was overlain by the ever-decreasing screams of the dying burn victims in the street below. One by one the shrieks disappeared, becoming hissing, bubbling and cracking sounds. One particularly agonised poor soul had escaped fatal damage from the fire, but the burning pitch had clung to his legs from ankle to thigh, and he was finished. He would live, but he'd never walk, or even stand, again. Focalis winced as a thud echoed from below and a heavy ballista bolt took the crippled man in the head, smashing it back against the flagstones and putting him out of his misery. Focalis staggered over to the roof hatch and yelled into it.

'Agnes, save your ammunition.'

But he didn't know whether she heard him, and he was half in agreement with her. They were the enemy, yes, but some things transcended war, and in other times he might well have aimed that shot himself.

He was uncertain for a moment. As the last cry died away in the street it seemed highly unlikely there would be another push, at least until the blazing pitch in the gutter faded and cooled. Even after it died, of course, the ground itself would be red hot, the stones cracking and sizzling with heat. He was almost certainly free to go around to the far side and check up on Martius. Sallustius had made it clear that for his various plans to work, no approach should be overlooked, eyes always on the enemy, and Focalis would be unpopular if he left his post, yet he was very much redundant right now.

As it happened, he was saved the difficult choice of deciding family over duty as the pain and the shock from his wound finally took their toll and he passed out, crumpling to the rooftop in a heap.

18

The world returned slowly. Focalis flicked one eye open – the other seemed unwilling to comply. At first, he wasn't sure that he was actually awake, for it was just as dark and silent in this world as in the one behind his eyelids. He blinked a few times in an attempt to resolve anything: the darkness, the disorientation or his monocular vision. It came as something of a relief when the other eye popped open on the third blink, having been glued shut with something. Another couple of blinks for good measure.

Then everything returned with a bang as the pain hit again. White-hot agony around the right side of his head, his ear, his temple, his cheek. As the pain slowly ebbed, not vanishing, but returning to an insistent throbbing, he reached up gingerly, the faintest gossamer brush of a touch in an attempt not to aggravate anything. He found some sort of linen-type material covering his cheek. It moved slightly to the touch and that made the pain return for a moment, so he let go and sagged back.

The dark was now crystalising into something different, not the plain black of unconsciousness, but the dark shapes of a room. He was inside. Carefully, very slowly, he turned his head. He could just make out shuttered windows, but there was no light visible in the cracks around them, just a lighter darkness.

'He's awake.'

The voice was a woman's. For a moment he was utterly confused. Flavia had gone, years ago. Unless he'd finally come to meet her? Then he remembered the imperious tones of Agnes, Pictor's woman, and connected the two readily. He was still alive, then, and still in Marcianopolis apparently. And at least Agnes and one other lived, for she was speaking to a third party.

'He's always been a tough old bastard.'

That voice was Odalaricus. Something about it worried him, though, and it took moments to nail down what that was. His old friend was ever a jocular man, quick with a quip at Focalis' expense. For Focalis to have suffered such an injury and yet apparently with no permanent damage, he would naturally expect Odalaricus to be ripping into him from the start. Instead, his old friend's voice was solidly serious, worried, even.

'How long have I been out?'

He jerked in alarm as a shape suddenly loomed over him, and though he realised immediately it was Odalaricus, the pain flooded him once more with the movement. Each time, though, the pain was a little easier and a little less. As he returned to consciousness properly, he was managing it naturally.

'The sun is gone,' Odalaricus replied. 'Just less than an hour ago. There's much to catch up on. Can you sit?'

'Let's find out.'

With some difficulty, Focalis lifted himself from the bench to a seated position. The movement brought on a worrying amount of nausea, though did not overly stress the pain. Once he was sitting, he looked around slowly, so as not to aggravate his wound.

His heart sank at the sight. The room was dim, lit only with two small oil lamps, but his eyesight had now adjusted enough to pick out details. Agnes was playing nurse, and it had seemingly been her who had patched his face, for even now she was working on her own hand, hissing in pain at her prodding. Odalaricus had his left arm in a sling, and behind him, in the doorway, Sigeric was leaning heavily on a stick.

Worse was to come, though, as his eyes fell on a huge shape. Taurus lay still and silent, his massive bulk soaked with blood.

'Is he...?'

Odalaricus nodded. 'Two arrows in the belly, and one in the neck. Then he went backwards off the roof. He's a mess. Stopped breathing half an hour ago. We took a battering today.'

Focalis fixed him with a look. 'Martius.'

'He's fine. Actually, he and Agnes are the only two pretty much unscathed.'

Relief washed over Focalis as his old friend sat beside him. 'He's been worried,' he said. 'And upset. Something about an argument. You'll have to go to him.'

'In a moment. Tell me about this,' he added, pointing to his face, 'and about the afternoon.'

'Your wound's nasty but no real damage. Your ears don't match anymore, but the rest will heal if we live long enough. Agnes couldn't do a lot about it. She's no capsarius, but she's done what she could. We found honey and linen, so that's what you've got. Leave it be and hope is my advice. We managed to locate henbane and poppy but we couldn't work out how to get it in you while you were asleep.'

'No painkillers.'

'You're going to hurt.'

'But henbane and poppy will affect my reflexes and judgment. Can't afford that tonight.'

'The past five hours have been difficult,' Odalaricus continued, nodding. 'They pulled back from the main gate once the fire hit them, and they've not had the guts to try there again, and they stayed safely across the river, but they made a big push from the city walls. We actually had two boarding bridges across to us at one point, but we managed to get rid of them. It was in hacking the second one to bits and sending it down to the street that Taurus fell. They managed to get enough archers onto the walls and the gatehouse that they could keep us down, and we had to show ourselves to get rid of the bridges. It was pretty nasty, but we made them pay heavily for it. The bodies are three deep on that side of the palace now. The fight went on all afternoon in bursts, and it was only when the sun started to set that they let up. I think they were just hungry. We've been able to hear them since nightfall. They're still outside the walls on the whole, camped and raucous. I think we're all hoping that this is it for the night. They have to be tired after all that riding and then a day's fighting.'

Focalis shook his head, regretting it instantly as the throbbing increased. 'No. I guarantee you that Fritigern kept a reserve in camp for the day. He's wily, and he knows that if he can keep us busy for the night, most of his army can recover, but we'll be shattered.'

'Sadly, you're probably right. We've been trying to predict

their next move. The closest they've come is from the city wall, and Sallustius thinks they'll try that again, because all they need is to build some new bridges and then they can get that close. Sigeric, on the other hand, reckons they'll try a frontal assault again. He says that now the fire has gone and the nets are empty they can get right up to knock on the door.'

'And they will have been watching, so they know we've not replaced those traps.'

'Exactly.'

'I agree with Sigeric. They'll come up to the gate again, but this time they'll come from every side at once, in order to divide our numbers and weaken the main defence. Not tonight though. They're settled in for the night. They'll send enough men to keep us awake and busy, but the main army will be resting up for a big push.'

'We need to rest our own, no matter how difficult, else we're fucked tomorrow. We'd planned on three on, three off in two shifts, one watching the street, one the city wall, and one positioned at the north-west corner to see over the river on both sides. And each needs to have a wicker screen and some sort of missile weapon. Sallustius still has a few little tricks ready, too, which will help keep us safe, hopefully. For the first half of the night we have Pictor and Sallustius on the main approaches and Martius watching the river, the safest position for him.'

'Well I'm awake now, so Martius can go rest.'

'Just go steady. You're injured, remember?'

Focalis rose, somewhat unsteadily, and padded across the room, sparing the broken, bloody shape of Taurus a brief, sad look. Already Fritigern had cost them too much. Persius and Ofilius, Arvina and now Taurus. Focalis' determination had waned somewhat in the busy days since that desperate race to Messembria, but now it was back. Fritigern could have walked away at any time, and what he was after was no longer justice, but revenge, pure and simple. Whatever happened in the next day or so, only one of them – Focalis or Fritigern – was going to leave Marcianopolis.

He paused momentarily to thank Agnes for her work, which made her go all coy and blush, something that seemed weirdly girlish and out of place on the woman who had been loosing iron bolts into angry Goths only hours earlier.

'I'll send you up something to eat shortly,' she said, indicating Pictor, 'after this.'

Sigeric joined him, limping somewhat as he leaned on the stick. As the two left the room and entered the garden with its killer ditch, Focalis pointed at the man's leg. 'Bad?'

'Temporary. Got hit with a flying rock. No bone sticking out or anything, but the consensus is a fracture, so I'm using the stick to save damaging it further.'

'So long as you can fight.'

'You're a bottomless well of sympathy, Focalis.'

'You're not a sympathetic character.'

'My talents lie elsewhere.'

'Go hit the sack. You'll be needed later.'

'Keep your eyes open. They've been quiet for two hours. They'll come again any time.'

Separating from Sigeric, who lurched off with his stick, Focalis returned to his earlier position above the gate, where he retrieved his small pack, bow and quiver. Unfastening the container, he peered inside. Seven arrows. That was all, and he doubted there would be many to spare around the palace, especially for a man with a fairly poor archery record. Sighing, he shouldered them and descended once more, crossing the ditch in the garden by the easily-removable wooden planks. The main palace rooftop he'd only visited once, never during the old days, and just in that brief tour when they first arrived a couple of days ago. Consequently, it took a few goes to find the right door that led to a narrow staircase which climbed to the roofline, switching back and forth as it ascended. He emerged into the open night air and appreciated the difference from the garden below. Down there the night had been dark, but temperate, sheltered by walls on all sides. Up here, a breeze sent a chill through him immediately, but the darkness was far from absolute. Marcianopolis went on, torches and lamps all around the city creating a faint golden glow to the purple night that looked somehow majestic in its imperial colours. Gold and purple, just like the emperor. Just like the scholae palatinae. He spotted Martius immediately and felt a surge of pride along with the relief. The boy could have been any veteran soldier. He sat on a chamfered stone hugging one knee, bow and quiver to hand by his side, eyes on the city beyond the balustrade while remaining safely back and out of the clear view of enemy archers.

'Martius.'

The lad's head snapped round, and he was up in a moment, scurrying over, face bright and beaming. Still, Focalis noted, the lad ran ducked, keeping out of the sight of archers, though it would take an expert bowman to land an arrow from so far away and below with any accuracy. Focalis let out an explosive breath as his son hit him at full pace, arms wrapping around his father's waist and gripping so tight, the old man worried for a moment that his breath wouldn't come.

'I knew you would be alright. Agnes said she wasn't sure, but Odalaricus said you'd survived much worse, and I knew you would be back. Does it hurt?' he added, looking up at his father's partially-covered mangled face.

'Not as much as some wounds I've had. It'll fade. I might not look pretty anymore.'

He smiled, which hurt, while Martius rolled his eyes. 'Dad, you've never looked pretty.'

'*Now* I'm hurt.'

'I'm sorry about before. I know I should have stayed, but it just seemed the only thing to do. I'll not leave you again. How do you feel?'

Focalis shrugged. 'If I pull a face it hurts like hell. Otherwise it's just like a bad ache. And thanks to that knocking me out for a few hours, I'm feeling better rested than I have in days. Which reminds me. I'm here to take over. You go sleep. You've had a busy day.'

'No. I'll stay with you.'

Focalis considered arguing for a moment, but knew it to be a futile gesture. 'Alright, but try and sleep anyway. I'll wake you if there's trouble.'

Settling himself into position where his son had so recently sat and watched, Focalis propped up his bow and quiver nearby. Martius found blankets from his pack and wrapped up against the chill in the lee of his father and the steep pitch of the roof. Silence descended, and it was a true silence. The city glowered in quiet, unable to live its normal life for fear of the small pockets of renegade Thervingi in the place, watching the palace, and the large force outside the walls.

'Dad?'

'Yes?'

'Will Fritigern come for us?'

'He already is.' Focalis frowned.

'No, I mean the king. The ex-king. The enemy. Not his men.'

Focalis mused on this for a moment. 'I think he'll have to in the end. If his men fail, then he will come. If he doesn't, he can't finish it, and I don't think he could stomach that. And he won't raise more men. Deposed, he has no money or authority, and any Goth who was willing to ignore the peace treaty and go with him has already gone. Once this warband is destroyed, he's alone. And if he comes, I will put a blade through his black heart, my lad.'

'I've hardened myself to the fact that he's the enemy, Dad, and that he has to go. But really, he's just a victim in this. We all are.'

All except Lupicinus and Maximus.

'I know.'

Martius fell into a thoughtful silence, and Focalis waited for the next question, but was rewarded instead with the lowest of gentle snores. Trying not to make any noise, for the lad had done more than anyone could have asked and needed his rest, Focalis leaned forward to look over the balustrade. From this height and angle and with the lack of sun or moonlight gleaming off the water's surface, he could see the defences his friends had put in the river. They covered roughly the middle third of the narrow flow, the central part. He could see the tops of the posts and the coiled ropes wound around them all, the entire length of the river around the two sides of the palace. Moreover, here and there he could see the shapes of unfortunate Thervingi warriors bobbing and wavering with the current. Even by leaning over and opening himself up to enemy shots, he was unable to see any visible work on the near bank.

The Goths were visible, though. Only in small pockets. Men spaced out here and there along the riverbank in groups of half a dozen. None of them were asleep, or even resting. Each group stood watching the palace. For the better part of an hour, Focalis watched them watching him, and he was almost starting to doze with the tediousness of it all when the noise began.

It started as a long, deep grumble. A 'hoooooooooooo' that sounded from every throat. It took only moments to realise that the sound was not coming from the watchers across the water alone. It was far too loud. They had joined with every Thervingi and Greuthungi voice within earshot, including those on the street and those outside the walls.

'Hoooooooooooo... HA!'

Silence.

It was, Focalis had to admit, unnerving. It was a Gothic adoption of the Germanic barritus battle cry, something that was not uncommon among Roman units charging into battle. He knew how it would go, and he knew the effect it could have on a waiting enemy.

'Hoooooooooooo... HA HA!'

A little louder this time.

'Haaaaaaaaaaaa... HOO!'

The final syllable was almost enough to send plaster dust scattering down from the parapet.

Focalis stood watching, listening, then realised that Martius was awake again, wide-eyed and fearful. 'Ignore them. They're trying to unnerve us.'

'It's working.'

'Keep down.'

As Martius did so, Focalis grabbed his bow and pulled an arrow from the quiver.

'Haaaaaaaaaaaa... HOO HOO!'

Martius was up again, then, a hand going over his father's. 'You're going to kill one?'

'Seven, if I can. Let's turn the fear back on them.'

'Then let me do it, Dad. I'm trained. I'm a good shot. You couldn't hit Africa with half an hour to aim.'

Focalis frowned at the jibe, but the lad was right. 'Then pop up, loose, kill one, and then drop again.'

'And then move to a new position and do it again?'

'Exactly. Keep them guessing.'

He held out his bow and quiver, but Martius ignored the weapon, taking only the arrows. He swept up his own bow and looked up and around, sniffing the air. When he was clearly content with the position and conditions, Martius nocked the arrow to the bow.

'Hooooaaaarrrr... HOO HOO HA!'

Focalis had to admit that he was impressed. Martius suddenly stood, making himself visible to the enemy, but the arrow was already in place, he had tested the conditions, listened to the voices to identify targets and so, as he rose, the string came back and was released in one smooth move. Focalis followed the track of the arrow even as Martius dropped below the parapet.

The war cry was going to be one voice quieter now, as one of the nearest Thervingi clutched his abdomen and toppled forward into the water. The group around him stopped howling and dashed back into cover. He could see Goths moving this way and that, trying to identify the source of the arrow. They would spot Martius fast next time. With a fierce grin, Focalis rose from the parapet. Voices of alarm called, and all eyes turned to him. At that moment, ten feet further down the roof Martius suddenly rose and loosed. This time the arrow missed, but only just, and another small group pelted back into safety.

They repeated the manoeuvre a third time, and this time Martius' arrow caught the man in the head, sending him crashing back to the riverbank. This time, the enemy were unwilling to stand any more, and all along the river, those small units retreated to the cover of walls, watching. Martius crept back along to his father and the two watched and waited, taking turns. It took almost half an hour, that war cry still going on at the far side of the palace, before one of the hidden Goths made a move. Ducking out from a wall, he hurried across to the body of Martius' last victim. With no urging needed, Martius simply rose, arrow already in place, drew, adjusted and released. The unlucky Thervingi clutched the shaft protruding from his neck and fell forward to land with some irony on top of the body for which he'd been running.

It went on like that for the next couple of hours, as evening slowly turned into night. Every now and then one of the Goths would be taken by bravery or stupidity or both, and venture into the open, and half the time either ended his days on the ground with an arrow in him or staggered back with a limp or a dangling bloody arm. The rest of the time was not much better for them, for even if Martius missed, the shots were close enough to send them scampering for cover in a panic once more. Eventually they stopped trying, and Martius went back to sleep, though with his bow still close to hand.

It was past the middle of the night when the next move occurred, and it was one that Focalis would never have expected. Along one of the streets on the other side of the river, a dozen Thervingi were bringing something by cart, and, as it came closer, Focalis swallowed with fresh nerves. Where had they found a catapult?

He woke Martius now, and they gathered their things, taking all but their weapons and putting them inside the door to the staircase, ready to run. They moved back to that position where they could see the enemy without being too open and watched with dismay as an onager was removed from the cart with some difficulty and manhandled into a position facing the two Romans. Goths were no practisers of siege-craft. It had been their undoing in more than one campaign that, when faced with good Roman walls, they were usually pretty much powerless. This was new.

It came as a small relief that no ammunition basket was unloaded. Wherever they'd acquired a Roman siege weapon, they'd apparently only found the weapon itself. After a small, heated argument, sadly outside even Martius' bow range, four of them went over to a wall formed of mortared river boulders and began to take it apart – slowly, thanks to their lack of appropriate tools. Each time they found a brick or a rock bigger than a man's fist, it was brought to the men trying to work the catapult. It was fascinating to watch, and Focalis almost burst out laughing as something down there went wrong – a man ended up getting an arm trapped, screaming for help, and was then beaten senseless by his friends to shut him up.

Finally, they had it ready, dropped a rock into the cradle, stood back with reverential looks, and pulled the lever. The rock made a half-hearted arc through the air at about head height, bounced on the ground and disappeared into the water with a plop.

The next hour was curiously entertaining, watching the Goths slowly getting the hang of the onager. Within an hour they had cobbles and bricks hitting the palace wall. They were far smaller than the ammunition a Roman artillerist would have loaded, which would have required two men to drop in the cradle, and the hits were doing little more than cosmetic damage, but Focalis had to remind himself that should they hit a man with one of those, it would almost certainly be fatal. Moreover, now that they had the technique, their aim was improving, the thuds gradually climbing the palace wall towards the roof.

'Time for a shift change,' a voice called, and they turned to see Odalaricus standing in the doorway.

'I'm half inclined to stay.'

'Oh?'

'They've found an onager, and they've been learning how it works for the last hour or so. You might want to be careful, though. They've just about got it right, and the roofline's going to take a pounding now.'

'Go get some sleep. Four hours it'll start getting light, and then we'll be looking at the big one, I reckon.'

Focalis nodded, clapped a hand on his friend's shoulder, and led Martius to the door and to relative safety down the stairs. They found a room in the main building that had once been a very well-appointed bedchamber and, while Martius tried to make things comfortable, ignoring the muffled occasional thuds as the Goths pounded the outside of the wall with rocks, Focalis crossed to the window looking onto the garden, ready to shout to the others and let them know where he was when he needed waking. His words died in his throat as he spotted Agnes standing by the plank bridge over the ditch with a panicked look. She caught sight of him and threw out her finger.

'There you are. I've been looking for you. Sigeric's gone!'

19

It took Focalis only half an hour to search. Every room was checked, but with no sign of Sigeric, and finally they located a window on the city wall side where the shutters had been forced from the inside. He cursed, but had to admit that, despite everything, he was not entirely surprised. Sigeric had made it clear from the outset that he was out for himself alone, and only nostalgia and Focalis' persuasion had dragged him into all this. They found his packs in one of the rooms, with all his scholae uniform inside. The man had slipped out in plain dress.

Focalis had slept a dispiriting sleep then for a few hours, plagued as always by the old memories and dreams, and had risen with the dawn, the change in the light enough to wake him. Besides, the ache in his face was almost continual, and if he accidentally rolled over so that the wound was beneath him, he woke with a start and a sharp pain.

Committed to the day now, he dressed, armed himself in full kit, though without his helmet for obvious reasons, and with Martius in tow made his way down to the garden and then, spotting a figure high up, climbed the stairs to the roof above the library and chapel. The weather seemed to be on the turn again this morning. The light was good, but there was an oddly amber glow to everything, and the clouds boiling in the sky to the west presaged a storm. More, the air itself was building to an uncomfortable clamminess.

Atop the roof, Sallustius looked tired, standing and watching the walls intently, glancing around for a moment as Focalis appeared.

'Morning.'

'Morning. What's happening?'

'Major mobilisation out beyond the walls. I think they're coming for a proper push this time. This will be the one to win or break, I think. When this wing or the main gate falls, we all need to be on the far side of the ditch with the bridges removed, and the moment we're in danger there, we withdraw into the palace wing and fight a last defence.'

'You speak as though we've lost already.'

'I'm just being prepared. I've a number of little surprises half-prepared in the main wing. Given that I can't see us holding the walls beyond the afternoon, I'm going to devote the next hour or two to getting them ready, so that we can use them when the time comes. You need to be prepared above the gate. You have the list?'

Focalis nodded. In his pack was a series of notes scribbled on wooden sheets, Sallustius' instructions and reminders. They all had them. The man was a menace. There was even a sealed note from the man marked 'last ditch' which he'd been instructed to open only at the end.

'Then let's get into position. I don't know how long we've got but we'll have to do something about food when...'

He broke off mid-sentence as they both became aware of shouting. Moving around the roof to get a clear view across the central garden of the palace, they could see Odalaricus waving. Between the waving and the not-quite-audible shouts, he was pointing off towards the bridge that led over the river and into town.

'What on earth?'

'Who knows?' Sallustius shrugged. 'Get into position and you should be able to see whatever it is.'

Nodding and beckoning to Martius, Focalis ran back into the stairway and pounded down the steps, across the near edge of the garden, past the gate-block embankment and into the south wing, up the stairs once more, heaving in breaths. Shuffling around the pitch of the roof, he found a place where he could look down the street into the city, checking first to make sure there were no Goths lurking with bows in the shadows of the buildings opposite.

He peered off at the bridge and squinted.

He frowned. It hurt.

Goths. More Goths, but these ones were on horses. They'd not seen a mounted Thervingi in the city since they first arrived. There were five riders, and they approached with an arrogant confidence. He looked around. There were three martiobarbuli still left over from yesterday, and Martius still had arrows. They could probably take down those five riders before they reached the door, but the way they were so open and casual was far too intriguing, and Odalaricus had drawn attention to them without sounding panicked.

He peered at them again, and as they came into better and better focus, blinked in surprise.

He'd not expected to see Sigeric again, and even if he had, it would have surprised him to see the man like this. He and the four other riders were not elaborately uniformed, just armoured in chain and with a sword and a shield in a leather cover. There was something naggingly familiar about them. As Sigeric closed on the palace, he looked up.

'Get that gate open and the ladder down before Fritigern's men come and find us.'

In a heartbeat, leaving Martius on watch, Focalis dropped down into the room below, above the gate. In the time he'd been here, he'd now familiarised himself with the room that was to be his responsibility, and it took only a moment to find the hatch and the ladder. Lighting two lamps for ease, as quickly as he could, he pulled open the hatch and slid the ladder down into the darkness below. With difficulty and care, he held the lamp in one hand as he descended the ladder and edged around the walls to the gate. It may have been openable by rope for ease when they had still been expecting friendly visitors, but since the Goths had arrived, the gate had been barred again, and so Focalis struggled alone with the heavy beam, levering it out of the sockets, and then hauling open the great wooden door.

Outside, the five riders had already dismounted. Sigeric reached up and gripped him by the shoulders. 'You look fucked.'

'Thanks,' Focalis replied drily as Sigeric pushed past into the gate. 'What happened to you?'

'Went for a walk.'

'Who are *they*?' Focalis asked, waving a hand as the men slapped their horses and sent them away.

'Don't you recognise them? You're the only one who might.'

'Stop talking in riddles.'

'When we met up at Suida I told you about my trouble getting Lupicinus to agree, and you told me about your search for the Thervingi. You told me about a dozen Goths heading to Galata to take up garrison duty there.'

Focalis tried to frown, but that just hurt too much. 'The ones from the inn. The ones who told me where to find Fritigern's men?'

'Exactly.' He paused in his explanation, then, to tell his four companions how to edge around the room and climb the ladder, and once they were off, he turned back to Focalis as they closed the gate and lifted the bar back into its sockets. 'I thought we needed fresh intelligence, and I knew if I told people I was going you'd all argue and complain, so I went anyway. You'd be surprised how easy it is for a man in nondescript clothes with my features, and a command of their tongue, to slip past Fritigern's men. I went out and had a good look at their camp. I was about to come back when I heard someone mention Odessus and Galata. That brought to mind the men you'd spoken of. Galata's only twenty miles from here, so I stole a horse and went for a ride. Luckily their horses have been well rested while they attacked us, so I got to Galata in about an hour and a half.'

The bar back in place, the two men collected the oil lamp and made their way back around the edge towards the ladder, as the last of the Gothic auxiliaries climbed up. As they moved, Sigeric continued his explanation, in a near-whisper so his voice would not carry to his companions. 'I can be quite persuasive, but I'm an even better liar. I told them the bounty on Fritigern's been authorised.'

'You what?'

'They're not officially on the muster rolls at Galata yet, so they could come and help out without being classed as deserters. Most of them weren't interested, but these four were won over by the possibility of a chest full of coins if we can take Fritigern's head.'

'And when they find out there's no reward?'

'Well *I'm* not going to tell them. Are *you*? It's a bridge I'll cross if they're still alive when this is over, but they'll have done the job by then. Tell me four men won't be of use.'

'Of course they will be,' Focalis replied as they reached the ladder and Sigeric began to climb. 'Tell me about the enemy camp, then.'

'I tried to get close enough to get access to Fritigern himself. One knife to the throat and I could have ended this immediately. Sadly, he's not leaving his tent unless he has to, and he has six of his best men with him at all times. Numbers-wise, I think you'll like the news. I did a rough count, and I reckon they're down to about two hundred men in that camp now, and that's all. Even overestimating the number in the town, there can't be two hundred and fifty left.'

'That's still a lot.'

'But it's coming down all the time. When you left my house it was more than a hundred to one odds. After we engineered our meeting at Suida, we were down to about sixty to one, I figure. From what I've seen, we've pared that down now to nearer twenty to one. That's a hell of an improvement, Focalis.'

He nodded. When it was put that way, it really was. Even twenty to one sounded horrifying, but Sallustius and Pictor were not done with their work yet, and they could at least halve the odds yet today, unless something went horribly wrong.

'Plus,' the man added, 'we took down about two dozen on the way back in on the other side of the river. Their sentries are useless. They're only watching the palace, so from behind they fall easily.'

Removing the ladder once they were up and sealing the hatch, Focalis extinguished the lamps and made his way back up to the roof, leaving the doorway open for swift access. Sigeric nodded a quick farewell and escorted the new arrivals down and across the palace to find Sallustius, who would assign positions and roles to everyone. Martius watched them go with a brow furrowed in confusion.

'Sigeric has a habit of the unexpected,' Focalis explained. 'He's found us some allies. Whatever you do, don't mention gold around them.'

'Why?'

'Let's just say they're here under false pretences.'

As he broke out some cold breakfast from their pack, Focalis explained about the new arrivals and where Sigeric had been. It should be a warning sign, he suspected, when potential odds of twenty to one made the lad smile with relief. They spent perhaps a half hour sitting quietly, discussing almost anything but what was to come. Finally, mid-chat, he held up a hand and listened carefully.

His chest tightened a little. This was it. The horn he could hear blasting in the distance, outside the town, was definitely a Thervingi signal. He straightened, checked the hang of his chain shirt, adjusted and tested his belts, slid his sword and dagger out of their sheaths and back in to make sure they would not stick at a critical moment. Stretching and limbering up, he then tested Martius in the same manner. As he finally checked over the belts, he fixed his son with a look.

'Your safety is all. You know that?'

'I do.'

'So you don't do anything to put yourself in danger. You make sure you live. And even if I fall, you know what you're doing?'

Martius nodded again. 'Sallustius showed me the best hiding place. It's an old sewer access to a drain that's no longer in use.'

'You get there and you stay there until the palace has been silent for a whole day, yes?'

'Yes, Dad.'

'And then?'

'And then I take any money I can find and head for Odessus and try to find my great-uncle in Smyrna.'

'Good. But I don't intend going anywhere anyway. I will sell my life for a very high price, Martius.'

They straightened and moved to the parapet, glancing first across the road and then, content no archer was targeting them, up the street at the city gate. The enemy was still marshalling outside.

'We should pray,' Martius said.

Focalis nodded and, since he said nothing, Martius began to speak in pious, reverent tones.

'Lord, be with us this day, within us to purify us; above us to draw us up; beneath us to sustain us; before us to lead us; behind us to restrain us; around us to protect us.'

'Amen.'

'Amen.'

As Martius stood, head bowed, Focalis cleared his throat. 'Sol Invictus, prostátepsté mas.'

Martius looked up sharply, shock and panic filling his face at his father's words.

Focalis fixed his son with a direct look. 'Any god in a storm, lad, any god in a storm. And not just the unconquered sun. Mithras and Zeus-Jupiter and Mars-Ares.' To add weight to his words, while he held the chi-rho at his throat in his right hand, his left lifted the amulet he'd taken from the body of the decanus in Suida so many days ago, raising the silvery carving of the god slaying a bull to glint in the morning light.'

'We shall be cursed,' Martius breathed.

'What do you think this *is*, lad? Do you not think I'm already cursed? I shall pay my penance in the afterlife as always. It will just be a little longer and more painful now. And if the priests are wrong and Mithras is still watching us, then I shall happily take his aid.' A new sound drew his attention, and he turned. 'I think we need to leave comparative theology till later. They're coming.'

A movement caught his eye and he and Martius stepped back into cover as a pair of archers emerged from the bath house opposite and began to loose up at them. Martius nocked an arrow.

'Can you do it?'

With an expression of prideful certainty, Martius looked up, sniffed, rose, loosed and then ducked again. There was a cry of pain from across the street. Moments later he repeated the action and then stayed up. 'It's safe.'

Pride swelling his chest, Focalis stepped forward to stand with his son. The two archers lay in a heap beside the doorway from which they'd emerged. Other warriors were lurking in the darkened door, unwilling to be the next to fall to the lad's arrows. More were waiting in the church, but soon they would find courage, for the sound of the army on the approach was clear. Hundreds of boots crunched on gravel and thudded on stone, and in mere moments they began to emerge from the city gate. There was no doubt now that Fritigern had committed. He'd made some strong pushes yesterday, yet even at the worst, he'd still been testing them. Now he intended to finish this today. There was no man held in reserve. All the Thervingi were coming. As they crunched down the street, closing on the palace, so more came out of the church and the baths to join the throng, other warriors flooding along the city wall to threaten that side.

'How many arrows do you have left?'

'Six.'

'And I have three darts. Once they're done we have three baskets of stones to tip over the edge, and then we pull back. The moment we're out of ammunition, we move below for the next stage. Got it?'

'Got it, Dad.'

'Loose at will, then, lad.'

And Martius did just that. As the crowd of figures in armour moved along the street, massing outside the palace and joining with the men from the baths and the church, the boy drew and released, drew and released until his quiver was empty, each shaft vanishing into a crowd that was simply impossible to miss. It was also impossible to see the result, but every missile had either wounded or panicked someone, for no shaft could miss that mob. Once they were a little closer, as Martius moved to the first of the baskets and heaved it upwards with a grunt of effort and some difficulty, Focalis grabbed the three martiobarbuli and cast them upwards, letting them fall as they may in that crowd.

As they both worked, Pictor and Agnes were committing to their own onslaught below, for while arrows and darts rained down from the roof, huge artillery bolts launched out from the shuttered windows, ploughing furrows through the mob in their passing, maiming and killing with ease. If she lived, when this was over, Focalis was going to throw his arms around Agnes in a most undignified manner.

The Goths were massing, yet they had not yet crossed the edge of the road and moved against the walls of the palace. Every mind among that crowd would be recalling the disasters of the past day, falling rocks and burning pitch, and if any man tried to block out that image, the grisly evidence of their failure littered the street in the form of crushed skulls and blackened corpses with the skin sloughing from them in the warm air. It must be appalling down there. Even up here, high above, the smell of carnage, burned pork and opened bowels was eye-watering. To be directly among it…

'They're about to come,' he said.

'Really?'

'I can see them tensing. They're not happy about it, but they're waiting for a signal. I think we need to get below, to the gate defence. Those doors are not going to last long under that pressure.'

'The baskets?'

'Let's do them together.'

And they did just that. Though the baskets of stones were far too heavy for a man to lift and do more than tip down over the parapet, with one man on each handle, the weight was much more manageable. Together, they swung the basket back and forth three times, letting go on the third, container and all. As the thing swept out into the air, it rolled over and over, and its contents scattered. Rocks and bricks, much the same as those that had been held in the nets, hurtled down into the crowd, followed by the empty basket. Many of the warriors had enough warning to get their shields up in the way, the rocks smacking into them and bouncing off into the crowd with little more than bruise damage. A few, though, found their targets nicely, and in more than one place Focalis could see a man staggering around in the mass, wailing and clutching his head as blood pumped up through a shattered skull, soaking him to the feet. Twice they repeated the procedure, each time causing mayhem and carnage. Indeed, the enemy's order to advance went unheard the first time, the horn call missed entirely under the clattering and thumping of bricks bouncing off boards and skulls.

Focalis and his son looked at one another. The roof around them was done with. All the darts had gone, two quivers were empty, and the baskets cast. There was little more they could do from here, but they had to have dropped more than a dozen in the process, and the artillery bolts were still coming from below. By mutual unspoken agreement, father and son raced for the door into the stair that led down into the dark room above the gatehouse, as well as down to the gardens below.

As they emerged into that room, long and wide, but low and with a flat ceiling, Focalis pointed left. 'Light the lamps.'

While Martius grabbed the flint and steel from the shelf by the door and ran around the left, pausing at each lamp to light it, Focalis did the same to the right, and gradually oil lamps burst into life, guttering with an orange light that slowly filled the room, giving it an eerie, Infernal glow. The last lamp lit, Focalis produced the thin wooden sheet with Sallustius' list, tapped it and looked around, checking the room. Using the checklist, he found the four amphorae leaning against the wall, safely away from the lamps and, with Martius' help, located the four holes that had been knocked in the room's floor and then covered with thin flags. These they slid aside to reveal the cavernous dark of the gateway below. With an access now to the room underneath they could hear the pounding and battering as the Goths, who had finally reached the palace itself, made a spirited attempt to break down the timbers and gain access. Ignoring the noise, the two of them dragged amphorae across one by one, using the sacks of mud from the garden that had been left here for this very purpose to wedge them upright, one beside each hole, precisely one jar-height in distance from the aperture.

The pounding on the gate below was now louder, and there were tell-tale groans and cracks coming between the blows. With a quick glance at Sallustius' checklist, he and Martius then removed the seals from the top of the amphorae. An acrid smell rose from each opened jar, and Focalis quickly leaned away. Martius gagged as he popped clear a seal.

'What *is* this?'

'Engineers call it bitumen. It's a lot like pitch, but more liquid, when it's warm, anyway.'

And it *was* warm. The air of the morning was sultry with pre-thunder heat, which, when added to the twelve lamps lighting the room and the low height of the ceiling, made this attic uncomfortably warm. Just to be certain, Focalis nudged one of the opened amphorae and noted the contents moving in response.

'I don't want you to do this,' he said.

'Dad?'

'Taking the life of a man who's trying to kill you is one thing. And I know that's what these men are trying to do, but burning is no way for a man to die, and I don't even want you to see it once, let alone have it on your conscience so that you see it every night for the rest of your life.'

'Dad, you need the help.'

'No I don't. You've helped me get it ready, and they're almost in. Go to the stairs and wait for me.

'Dad...'

'No. Go.'

With a look of near defiance, Martius gathered his things and left the room. Once he was gone, Focalis looked around. The four jars were in position and ready, the gates were about to give. Focalis checked the list one last time, and then crossed to the far side and collected one of the oil lamps from the shelf. Crossing back to the middle of the room, he placed it nearby, carefully on the floor.

He will rain down fire and brimstone on the wicked and scorch them with his burning wind.

Somehow even the psalms were little comfort now.

Tense, he crossed to one of the amphorae and waited, listening. It did not take long. Seemingly only a few moments after assuming his position, he heard the enormous crack and thud of the gate finally breaking, the noise amplified by the large empty chamber below. Still he waited. Maximum damage, maximum coverage.

He will rain down fire...

The gates were torn aside, and the Goths flooded into the darkened archway, a passage some twenty feet square which had once led straight into the decorative gardens. The confusion and consternation of the invading Thervingi was audible as they entered the dark room only to find the far end completely sealed with a new stone wall. Within mere moments, the roar of triumph turned to a wave of confusion and then became cries of pain. The front ranks of those pouring into the room swiftly found the spiked, hooked caltrops scattered across the floor, and as the barbed menaces tore through their boots and embedded themselves deep in the flesh of the invaders' feet, they tried to stop moving further into the nightmare, but there was nothing they could do. The ranks of Goths behind them, unaware of what awaited and still believing themselves triumphant, were pushing on, trying to get inside, driving the front lines ever further into the field of caltrops.

Focalis leaned forward and peered down through the hole. He could just make out, in the light cast from the broken gate, a sea of humanity ebbing and flowing in confusion and pain below.

Time.

Another step back and he pulled away one of the bags of mud, carefully tipping the jar. His aim was good, and the distance perfect. Though a little of the sloppy bitumen spattered the floor around the hole, most of it began to belch and slide into the aperture, raining down onto the heads below. Swiftly now, he ran to the next jar and did the same. This one fell short, and some of the liquid pooled worryingly on the attic floor. Focalis cursed when some slopped onto his shin as he desperately nudged it closer so that the contents now went down the hole. In truth, he really *could* have done with help, but he knew damn well that this was a moment that he would revisit in nightmare for years to come, if he lived, and he would spare Martius that horror. Fortunately, the third and fourth jars went over with reasonable accuracy.

As he moved over to the lamp he'd left carefully on the floor, he could hear the subtle change in the noise from below.

The murmur of confusion overlaid with cries of pain had shifted now to anguished moans and howls of fear. Even those who had no idea what bitumen was, or what was about to happen, would have seen or heard of the inferno in the drains of the main street the day before, and the crisped corpses still littered the street. They could have little doubt what their fate was to be.

With a silent apology for what he was doing, Focalis gingerly picked up the guttering lamp, careful not to get it anywhere near the bitumen that had sloshed onto him. Crossing to one of the holes, he dropped it through.

The conflagration never happened. He peered down through the hole with a sinking feeling. The lamp had gone out in its descent. The enemy were starting to pull themselves together below. Those at the back had realised what was happening and were retreating into the street at pace, while those trapped inside, coated with bitumen and impaled with caltrops, were staggering, hopping and lurching with the desperate urge to flee.

Time was running out. Focalis, breathing shallow to avoid inhaling too much of the heady atmosphere of bitumen and burning oil, hurried over to the side shelves and located two more lamps, taking one in each hand. He then carried them back to the holes, careful not to spill on his legs, as that would undoubtedly be the end of him and, with less care now, he dropped both lamps through one hole, trusting to quantity.

God was with him. The Lord did *indeed* rain down fire. Or at least a servant of the Lord did.

One lamp extinguished in the fall, but the other smashed on the stone flags between the feet of the panicked, surging Thervingi. The effect was instant, the liquid accelerant having spread across most of the room now and coating many of those within, the very air itself almost ready to ignite. The din rose immediately, the roar of the fire itself meshed with the screams of his victims. He had no time to watch, even had he the urge, for the very floor upon which he stood was also covered in bitumen, as were his shins, and the room was warming rapidly. Soon the attic would be on fire, and then this whole wing would burn down.

One last job on his list from Sallustius, though. He had no idea why it was there, but he trusted his old friend, and so as instructed, he grabbed the pole, a handle from an old broom, which leaned against the wall near the door, and crossed to the middle of the room, gingerly treading amid the spatters of fallen liquid, and reached up. The beams of a section of the tiled roof had been sawn through and hinged in the past few days, and it took just a prod with the handle to push open a section of the roof so that it fell back and allowed daylight and fetid air to stream in.

Focalis almost panicked then. As the air rushed in, so the fire in the room below, suddenly given a through flow of air, roared into fresh life, racing skywards. He could even see the flickers of flames not far below the level of the holes through which he'd poured the bitumen, sparks rising and tumbling in the air.

Desperate now to be out of this stench of acrid fuel and burning meat, especially before it reached any flammable part of himself, Focalis ran for the door, ducked through it and pulled it closed behind him.

As he descended, finding Martius part way down, he took a deep breath of the relatively clean air, and then coughed solidly all the way down to ground level. That was it. He'd just burned a bridge. In a matter of hours the entire palace wing facing the road would be a charred remnant and the Goths would be inside. The hope was that he'd brought the odds a lot closer, with probably fifty Thervingi trapped and burned in the gatehouse.

As they emerged into the gardens, he could hear the sound of fierce fighting at roof level over near the city walls. The Goths were still coming, determined, from two sides. Today, the palace would fall. The only question now was whether they'd survive it.

A shout drew his attention, and he turned the other way, his heart lurching at what he saw. Pictor and Agnes were trying to put all their weight against the door that led into the artillery rooms, forcing it shut as angry Thervingi pounded on it from the far side. God above, but the enemy must have got through the shutters and overrun the rest of the wing while Focalis was dealing with the gate. He and Martius rushed over to add their weight to the others. As he did so, two new and unwelcome sights greeted him. The look of despair on Agnes' face sent a quiver of hopelessness through him, and the reason for it was far worse.

Pictor was done for. A blow had managed somehow to penetrate his chain shirt, which hung in shreds and tatters from the waist down, coated with blood. The man himself was already a deathly grey colour, the blood drenching him to the soles of his feet, and he was using only one arm to try and seal the door, the other holding in the coils of his belly that were constantly trying to slither free onto the ground.

Sallustius had, of course, been prepared for the fall of any part of the palace, and all the doors that had once been lockable from the inside now had bars and sockets on the outside, in the garden. As the door slammed into place, Pictor and Focalis holding it there, Martius and Agnes lifted the bar into position, and only when it was secure did they step back.

Agnes' eyes were brimming now, as Pictor turned and, lacking the strength to walk any further, fell into Focalis' arms.

'It was good to fight with you a final time, brother,' the stocky, bearded man said with a sad smile.

'May God take you to his hallowed halls, my friend.'

And, as though that wish absolved him of all responsibility, as though he had been waiting for those words, Pictor slumped, shuddered twice, and collapsed to the ground, still and silent.

Focalis turned. He'd half expected a wail of anguish from Agnes, but then he'd come to know her somewhat over the few days they had been together, and such a response was not her way. Instead, a steely look of anger was rising in her.

'The wing has fallen,' he said. 'The fire may well take the two sides as well, but I think the main building will be safe. We need to pull back beyond the ditch.'

'Shouldn't we go and help on the roof?' Martius asked.

'No. Sallustius was clear. And if the enemy get out of the roadside rooms into the garden, and we're on the roof, we'll be trapped there. But I'm not leaving Pictor to be ravaged. Help me carry him inside.'

With Agnes displaying a worrying look of determination, Martius and Focalis picked up the body, trying not to gag as coils of his intestines slid this way and that, and began to carry him towards the planks over the ditch. Focalis marvelled at the strength of Pictor's woman as she hurried across and, without shrinking from the gore, heaped his innards back into his belly and held them there as they carried him to the last refuge, in through the great door, and laid him on an old dusty table in that very banquet hall where they had last met Fritigern at a peace conference six years ago.

Leaving Agnes with the body to deal with her grief, Martius and Focalis stepped back out into the garden. The air was close now, truly warm and damp, hardly a breath of wind anywhere. The clouds had slid over above them, dark and brooding. They stood for a time, watching and listening. Smoke was boiling up from the roadside wing, black-grey coils melding with clouds of a similar hue above. The pounding on the door they had sealed had stopped. Likely that entire wing had caught the blaze now, and they'd had to pull back from the inferno. The enemy could wait it out. Even burning in the dry, the enemy would find their way clear into the gardens long before nightfall. If the storm broke and the rains came in force, the fire would not last, and their access would be all the faster.

His attention was caught by movement and noise, and he looked left. Figures were emerging from the doorway by the library. Odalaricus, Sigeric, and one of the soldiers he had brought from Galata. Three? That was all?

As they reached the gardens, they turned and barred the door, rolling barrels and throwing sacks of mud against it to block it further. That done, the three hurried over to join Focalis and Martius. Sigeric was all but dragging his injured leg now, his stick lost somewhere. Odalaricus was wincing with every step, blood visible in numerous places, the sling that held his left arm soaked crimson. The auxiliary soldier had blood matting his hair, though it did not seem to be hampering him. Given Agnes' wounded finger and his own headwound, that left Martius as the only uninjured figure among them.

The others tottered and limped across the planks, and Focalis sighed. With Agnes inside, their numbers were now down to six, none of them at full fighting strength. He had no idea how many Thervingi were left, but the situation was starting to look bleak. As Odalaricus crossed at the rear, and he, Sigeric and Focalis moved to haul the planks in and remove the only easy crossing from the garden, he cleared his throat.

'Sallustius?'

'No. Gone. We couldn't even bring his body, as he went over the edge and down to the street outside. They have the roof above the library now. They took one of the Galata lads alive. I can only hope they're sparing him the worst, what with him being Thervingi too, but I'm not hopeful.'

'Can you estimate their numbers?'

'I don't know. Fifty? Sixty?'

'And probably the same on the street side. Maybe a hundred left, then, if we're lucky. That's still a lot to face with just a ditch.'

'More than just a ditch,' Odalaricus corrected him. 'Sallustius had everything prepared right to the last stand. Pictor's last scorpion and his polybolos are both stored inside. Where is he?'

'He didn't make it. Agnes is with the body in the dining hall.'

'Damn. We're getting all too few, old friend.'

'We are. I suspect Agnes can use the weapons, though. She seems as skilled as he was. And I think she's ready to tear them apart with her bare hands now.'

'Sallustius set a load of last defence traps. We'll bring their numbers down a lot further before they get close enough to use a sword. Here.' He held out a tablet scrawled with another of Sallustius' lists.

'What is it?'

'The list of all the ammunition held for this moment, such as it is, for defending the ditch. You and Martius bring it out, and Sigeric, Yungeric and I will bring the wicker screens round. Time to prepare. We have just a few hours now, I think.'

There was an ominous crack, and above them the storm finally broke.

20

Whether it was the fault of the inferno that raged for two further hours, ravaging the roadside rooms despite the rain, or perhaps something superstitious among the Thervingi about fighting in the midst of the storm, or even simply the fear of wearing iron in the open with lightning around, the Goths had withdrawn en masse and waited out the day.

Rather than give the paltry half-dozen defenders time to prepare, however, all it did was allow them more hours to fret and wait. They had swiftly readied themselves in every way they could, for Sallustius had already set everything up in the preceding days, and so they waited under cover of the main palace block: Focalis, Sigeric and Odalaricus rotating duty, keeping watch at the large window of the dining room.

Even had there been no storm, no booms and crashes like gods of old hammering anvils beneath the earth, no flashes of dazzling silver, no rain that hammered down like rods – even with blue sky and singing birds – little could have lifted Focalis' mood. Just being in this room was like living in a ghost of the past. Everywhere he looked carried a memory.

The dusty, torn old lectus on which Martius lay, dozing lightly...

*

Lupicinus looked up, eyes pink, shaky hand sloshing wine from the rim of his cup, stupidly undiluted, too strong for this situation. 'What is that commotion?'

An officer of the numerus manning the palace walls cleared his throat. 'There seems to be some sort of altercation beyond the city gate, sir.'

'Altercation?' the general asked, eyes screwing up suspiciously. 'That sounds like a battle.'

'It would seem that the Thervingi are attempting to enter the city by force. I gather there has been fighting, a number of deaths.'

'Are we in danger?'

'I do not believe so, sir.'

'Then they need to be taught a lesson. Filthy barbaroi filling Thracia with their horrible tongue and their Arian heresies.' His wine slopped again. Focalis looked across at Sigeric, who he knew also to follow the Arian teachings that the emperor had adopted despite counsel otherwise, and then to the decanus, who was watching Lupicinus carefully. The decanus had his hand on the hilt of his sword, which was unusually provocative in these circumstances. Had he read something in the general's face?

Focalis felt the world shifting around him, a strange feeling of dread creeping over him.

He closed his eyes to the tables where Alavivus had reclined with his retinue, focusing on the present, for he had no desire to live through that moment again.

339

'We have movement,' Sigeric murmured from the window.

Focalis strode over to join him. The rain had stopped finally, just as the light faded, and yet the enemy had waited still, letting the shroud of night draw across the place, remaining on the periphery. The garden was a quagmire. Little grass or foliage had survived Sallustius' preparations anyway, but with hours of hammering rain, the mud had become slick, soft and sucking, dotted with puddles. Even from the window, Focalis could see the occasional flicker of a reflection on the water that filled the bottom of the ditch surrounding their last position. His eyes rose to the far side of the garden. The door to the stairway beside the library was open. It had been forced at some point during the storm, and now figures were on the roof above, moving into the stairs, ready to descend and finish their work. Other shapes were faintly visible in the darkness, moving among the charred ruins of the gatehouse wing. The last Thervingi were coming for them.

They had managed to bring Fritigern's numbers down from around a thousand to perhaps a hundred, which was a feat for which the decanus would have showered them with praise. And it did raise the spectre of hope, until one did the maths. Even counting Martius and Agnes, they were but six defenders, and the main defences of the palace had fallen. They were now making a last stand, and it was sixteen to one.

The hope died once more.

Focalis turned to find Agnes. She was seated on a lectus close to the body of Pictor which remained on a table, white and still. That seat had once been occupied by a king...

★

Fritigern rose. He was a shrewd one, and Focalis had spotted that from the moment Lupicinus had given the order. In fairness, Alavivus may have been as clever, but he'd never had the chance to show it. As soon as Lupicinus had started screaming his command to kill them all, even as the decanus questioned the order, Taurus had closed on the king. Lupicinus spat bile, something akin to panic in his eyes, confirming again and again his order to kill the guests.

Alavivus had no chance to rise, let alone defend himself. Taurus' blade ripped through his fine tunic, a great gout of blood slopping across the table before him, the blade pulled back and then thrust again, robbing a king of his life. Before his guards could react, those of the unit nearby had leapt into the fray, and Alavivus' men were cut down even in the process of drawing their swords.

Fritigern had been preserved by luck alone. A unit of legionary soldiers, another part of the Roman military presence, had been nearer Alavivus, and their commander – clearly a man of principles and morals – had paused too long, not believing his ears at the command to slay guests. By the time Focalis and his friends were moving on Fritigern, the second king was rising, his own fingers dancing on his sword hilt, his entourage similarly preparing.

'Think fast, Flavius Lupicinus,' Fritigern said, holding up a warning hand to the approaching men of the scholae. 'You have broken your word, abandoned the principles of xenia and committed murder – regicide, no less. You have me trapped, but I tell you this now. Before the last of us falls, your liver will hang from your belly and you will be bleeding your last.'

Lupicinus was close to apoplexy with rage, but Fritigern

persisted. 'If I die here, who will calm my people? I can guarantee you that if I do not walk out of this palace with my head high, every last Thervingi and every last Greuthungi south of the great river will make it their lives' work to kill every Roman they can find. Your move, Lupicinus. Are you prepared for war?'

And Lupicinus was. He was already shrieking the order to kill.

Maximus, however, stupid, greedy, dangerous man that he was, knew not to poke the wasp nest, and stepped in front of the comes, holding up his hands, calling the men of the scholae to stand down.

They had done just that, but in that moment, as Focalis caught Fritigern's eye, he knew that the Thervingi would kill every last one of them before they agreed to another peace.

Focalis opened his mouth to trot out the lines he'd been preparing, asking Agnes to put aside her grief, for they needed every last hand on a hilt now, but he'd no need for such words. The moment he looked at her, she turned, looking back at him, and he could see the steely resolve in her eyes. She answered with just a nod, rising and crossing to the centre of the room.

Pictor's pride and joy, a scorpion bolt thrower he'd always referred to as simply *Nike*, stood ready. A machine that he had taken on when they'd fallen from imperial favour and been reassigned to the Prima Maximiana, Nike had been continually improved and tweaked by the clever artillerist. It had an ingenious gear mechanism that cut the time required to wind back the torsion arms hugely, one single turn of the handles setting the machine ready for loosing. There were sadly only six bolts left, but Focalis was in no doubt from the look on her face that Agnes would make good use of them all. As she began to set up the machine, the others checked their weapons once again.

They had discussed it all. Agnes had the artillery, as she was the only one likely to make effective use of it. All the remaining arrows, eleven in number, had been given to Martius, who would remain at the window with Agnes. Once he was out of ammunition, the lad was to run to the drain cover and get into his hiding place. The three remaining men of the scholae, along with the soldier from Galata, would step out front and defend the ditch as long as possible from behind their wicker screens, pulling back at the last moment to the doorway, and then defending, falling back room by room. The apse windows were an obvious weak point, but Sallustius had told them not to worry immediately about that. It was all in the instructions.

'Here they come,' Sigeric called, and, taking deep breaths, the four of them stepped out of the door and into the garden.

Thervingi were pouring from the ruined wing opposite and from the stairwell of the chapel wing, gathering, facing them. The four soldiers stood, fingers dancing on hilts, watching. Someone had miscalculated, and that was immediately clear to Focalis. There were more than a hundred there, maybe even twice that number, as the last stragglers joined their fellows in the garden. Thirty to one, he thought with despair clawing at the edge of his consciousness. With a sigh and a nod to the others, he found a position behind one of the screens. At least they had darts still, and with Martius' bow and Agnes' scorpion, they could whittle down the numbers further yet.

Moreover, there was little evidence of ranged weapons among the gathered Goths.

The gentle tones of Martius saying a prayer for them all drifted from the open windows of the dining hall, filling the silence as the last Thervingi fell into place. There was no mistaking the intention now. They were all here, nothing held in reserve. They knew they had their prey trapped and outnumbered, and this was to be the end of it.

'Ready,' Odalaricus called, as the lad's prayer died away.

Then, with a roar, the Goths came. They ran across the garden, though their speed was hampered by the slippery slick of mud left by the defensive works and the storm rain. Without the need for a command, the defenders launched into their work. With a clack and a thud, the first of Agnes' iron bolts whipped out through the windows, between the defensive screens, and ploughed into the ranks of Goths, taking several down at once. Martius' first arrow took a warrior in the neck, sending him falling back, and each of the three Romans behind the screens threw a handful of martiobarbuli up into the air, high and far, to come down among the massed ranks of the enemy.

Still they came. Twenty had to have fallen in that onslaught, and yet their bodies were trampled by their comrades in the rush to overwhelm the defenders. Halfway across the garden now, the Thervingi were hit once more. Another of Agnes' bolts, another of Martius' arrows, and the remaining darts the veterans could throw.

Each of them now resorted to their secondary weapon. As the Thervingi closed on the ditch and slowed, working out how to best cross the obstacle, each of the four defenders reached out to the three spiculi that stood jammed into the earth behind the screens. Two to throw, one to use as a spear.

But they had time, for the ditch was a powerful obstacle, and the first of the Goths to try and cross quickly discovered *how* powerful. He slithered down the wet, muddy side into the ankle-deep water and, with a roar of triumph and encouragement to his fellow warriors, ran forward. His leg sank into the water and the oozing mud beneath, where it found the sharpened point of the stake driven into the bottom, impaling his foot. He howled with agony, transfixed in place, but his encouragement had already done its work, and all around the ditch Thervingi were hurling themselves down into the water, only to discover that those sharpened points were everywhere. Men were bellowing in pain now, all around the ditch.

As the advance faltered and slowed, Focalis and his three companions selected targets uninjured in the press and cast the lightweight, barb-headed spiculi. The three experienced Roman veterans, trained in their use over the years, each managed to put their weapon into the target, while their Goth auxiliary companion managed to graze his as the javelin whipped past and into the mud. As they threw their second, all four this time finding a mark, Martius' arrows continued to thrum out from the windows behind them, the rhythmic clatter and thud of the artillery followed each time by an iron bolt that ripped through the gathered crowd like Moses at the Red Sea.

Then, as the enemy regained their momentum, pulling their injured men back out of the way and carefully fumbling forward through the opaque water and the sucking brown mud, the symphony of missiles ended. The last arrow in Martius' quiver whirred through the air into a man's arm, and the thuds and clacks of the artillery died away into silence. Only one spiculum remained available to each man behind the screens.

'When do we fall back?' the Goth auxiliary hissed.

'At the last moment,' Focalis replied, 'when we've done what damage we can. Hold them to the ditch.'

With difficulty, the lead runners of the Thervingi reached the near side of the obstacle and, roaring, weapons brandished and shields up, began to advance on the defenders. To begin with, dealing with them was simple. Each of the defenders covered a length of the ditch, stabbing out with their spears, shields propped behind the screens now. Finding targets was not difficult, with the Goths moving so slow, dealing with the sucking mud and the slippery slope, and even their shields were only so much use. Man after man died trying to get up the slope. But then they were coming in larger and larger numbers, and Focalis was having to leap this way and that to counter each climber, finding time now only to lance out protectively, rather than to find an opening for a kill. They were now holding back a tide, and it was only a matter of time.

Then the line broke. The auxiliary, Yungeric, fell to a well-aimed thrust from below, stiffening and toppling forward into the ditch filled with his enemies.

'Fall back,' Sigeric bellowed as Thervingi began to crest the rise there, an entire stretch of ditch no longer defended. But the command was easier given than followed. Focalis found that he could not simply turn and run, for without stabbing out at the enemy he would likely be cut down in retreat. Instead, he found he had to give ground a foot at a time, stabbing out continually to keep the enemy at bay as he backed away from the ditch. Moreover, he had no time to retrieve his shield from behind the screen, and glanced at it with dismay as he was forced to leave it and move carefully, edging back to the door of the main palace wing. Taking a single heartbeat to glance around, he realised the trouble they were in. The other two were having to move exactly the same, retreating slowly, shields left, but while they were doing that, Thervingi were flooding from the ditch where Yungeric had been, and would cut them off.

'Bastards,' came a snarl from behind, and it took Focalis a moment to place the voice, for the fury and the bile in it stripped it of all Agnes' femininity. Risking death from any coming blow, he glanced over his shoulder, eyes widening as he did so.

Pictor's woman had emerged from the doorway of the palace, that great automated polybolos in her grip. How she was holding the damn thing at all was impressive, given that it was commonly shot from a tripod. How she maintained her grip on the great heavy weapon with each shot that whipped from the runner as the next dropped into place from the wooden hopper was astounding.

Focalis fought with renewed vigour as, even watching his opponents carefully, he could see out of the corner of his eye man after man thrown back off to their left, heavy bolts thudding into them with impressive regularity.

They were going to make it. He was close to the others now as they converged on the door. Only as he stabbed out and stepped back did Focalis realise that Agnes was not coming with them. As they stepped back, she stepped forward, continually bellowing imprecations like a sailor and killing with impunity.

'Agnes!'

Realising what was happening, Odalaricus tried to reach out to her, but as he did, he took a stab wound to the shoulder, crying out, and was forced back again, further from her. She was trapped now, surrounded. Focalis could see her over the heads of the enemy as he retreated. She snarled and loosed shot after shot, and then there came nothing but hollow wooden clacks as the ammunition in the hopper ran out. Focalis saw her fall to a blow from behind, and then they were on her, swords rising and falling. Momentarily she reappeared, roaring, soaked with her own blood, hardly recognisable as human, let alone as Agnes, a knife in one hand, and then she was gone again, this time never to reappear.

Focalis tried not to grieve, there wasn't time. If they lived through the next hour, he would pray for her soul and honour her memory. Right now, it was enough to make sure no one else died.

They reached the door. Odalaricus was through it first. Focalis and Sigeric made last jabs with their javelins, and then slammed the weapons into the enemy, letting go and dropping back through the door. Odalaricus slammed it, but the enemy were pressing on it, feet in the way, desperately heaving to keep it open. Sigeric put his shoulder to the door to add his weight, while Focalis drew his sword now and stabbed into any limb or appendage that found its way into the doorway. Finally, as the legs were pulled back with shouts of pain, the portal slammed shut, and Sigeric slid the bar across.

A cry of alarm from Martius drew Focalis' attention, and the call was followed by a sound like a building collapsing. With Odalaricus and Sigeric at his heel, he ran through the antechamber and into the great dining room. Behind them,

Sigeric lifted the slab in the doorway and reset Sallustius' trap there, one of the few left until the last moment.

The great apse of windows that looked out on the garden from the dining room, of course, made a tantalising, easy access for the attackers now that they were over the ditch, and the windows were open and inviting, left that way for the artillery to shoot through. The Goths may have thought the approach safe. They'd soon learned otherwise. As half a dozen of them had clambered in through the window, eyes on young Martius who stood at the rear of the chamber, they'd snapped Sallustius' taut thread, releasing the nets up in the ceiling. Clearly the lesson they had learned in the main street had not stuck, for the half dozen men inside had died badly under an avalanche of falling masonry. But that had not been the end of it – the same tripwire had been connected to a second net full of stones, this one balanced on the parapet above the building, which had showered masonry down on those still outside.

'Back,' Focalis shouted to his son, pointing to the door opposite the one through which they'd entered. As Martius backed away, Focalis opened his mouth to warn the lad, but he had remembered anyway, stepping wide across the slabs, with a little hop across the barely-visible tripwire. Then he was gone, through the door and into the rear rooms of the palace. The other three, aware that it was only a matter of time before the main door broke or the enemy felt brave enough to try the window again, followed, using the same odd little dance to avoid Sallustius' traps. Passing them by, the four survivors shut the door and barred it, backing further away.

'How many left?' Odalaricus said between heaved breaths.

'Less than half,' Sigeric replied. 'Sixty? Seventy? Eighty? Hard to tell.'

'Sallustius' surprises will take more, but there are still too many.'

'Martius, you need to get to your hiding place.'

'Not yet, Dad. I can help.'

'No you can't. Hide. That's an order.'

For a moment, he worried that Martius was going to argue, but with a bleak, panicked look, the lad stepped away into the next chamber. One more room. One more set of traps, and then they were trapped like rats and it was all down to sword against sword, at which point it was only a matter of time.

'We did our best,' Odalaricus sighed. 'And no one could have done what we did. We turned Fritigern's force from an army into a handful. Shame the bastard himself hasn't shown up. I'd have loved to finish what we started.'

Outside the door there was a loud rumble and a collection of screams as men stumbled into another trap, and then a series of thuds punctuated with howls, evidence of the last tripwire being broken. Hammering on the door announced that the Thervingi were now almost on them again.

'Come on. One more room, then we sell ourselves dearly.'

And with that, they backed away, following Martius into the last room, skirting around the edge, knowing that Sallustius had one more surprise left for the enemy, his revenge from beyond the grave. The last room was a decorative one. In the days of the pagan gods it had been a nymphaeum, for the great basin in the centre of the room was still adorned with discoloured and broken statues of nymphs and sea monsters. It had not seen flowing water in years and was now dry and

full of detritus. Off to the left stood the drain where Sallustius
had decided Martius could hide, a stone cover shaped like a
misshapen grinning face currently slid off to one side. Martius
was already in there somewhere. Another tripwire had been
partially set here, but Sallustius had apparently run out of
time and manpower, and the last net had not been filled or
raised, sitting empty off in the corner. A large pile of broken
stones, presumably intended to fill it, stood near the manhole
and the broken fountain, much of it having come from the
latter.

'I hope there is a heaven,' Odalaricus said with a sigh. 'I
shall look forward to seeing you all there.'

'If there's a heaven,' Sigeric replied with a snort, 'there's
fuck all chance of *us* going there.'

Focalis let out a barked laugh as he closed the final door and
slid the thin bar across, the last defence, and one unlikely to
hold for long. Sure enough, in a matter of a hundred heartbeats
there came a tremendous crash and a lot of screaming from
beyond the door, and then, soon after, battering at this last
portal. The game was over.

'Dad.'

They turned, to a man, to see Martius emerging from his
hiding place. He was dusty and covered in filth.

'Get down,' Focalis hissed. 'We'll cover the drain. Don't
make a noise, alright?'

'Dad, this drain leads outside.'

Focalis turned to the others. 'I thought Sallustius had
checked all the drains?'

'It was blocked,' Martius said breathlessly, 'but only with
mud and plants. I can see the outside. It just needs a bit of
digging.'

'We still can't run,' Odalaricus said.

'Why?'

'It won't end. We'll just end up being hunted again, and this time there are only three of us and the lad, with no clever engineer, no artillery, and hardly any money. They'll never stop until we're dead, you know that. If you want Martius safe, we have to stand our ground. Let the boy run.'

Focalis nodded, turning to his son as the battering on the door increased in volume and intensity. 'Dig your way out and run. We'll hold the room and seal the sewer.'

It occurred to him that he had a last instruction to read from Sallustius, the sealed one for this moment, but it was with his pack somewhere out there beyond the attackers. He sighed. Perhaps it was how to set this last trap. Perhaps it was about the sewer exit. Whatever it was, he'd never know now. He looked at the pile of masonry, then to the others. 'Can we shove that into the hole? Block it? The sewer's only crawling height. Shouldn't be hard.'

Sigeric straightened. '*I* can.'

'We.'

'No. *I*. We have a way out here, Flavius.'

'No,' Odalaricus said once again. 'I told you, Fritigern will never stop while we live.'

'Or while *he* does.'

'What?'

'Have you not seen the opportunity here? Fritigern's men are in the palace trying to kill us. Fritigern isn't. He'll be safely back in his camp outside the walls with only a few men. All you two have to do is follow the lad, get out, go and find the bastard and put a blade through his heart, and it's over.'

Focalis blinked. 'With the three of us…'

'Not me. Someone has to stay, fill the hole with rubble and put the lid back on, otherwise they'll still be right behind you.'

Focalis looked at their old friend. He wanted to argue, but the man was right. One of them would have to stay behind. 'I don't know what to say.'

'Nothing. I may be only half Roman, but I'll die like one. Now go.'

'But...'

'*Go*, Flavius. That door won't hold for long.' And with that, Sigeric was already limping to the pile of rubble, pushing the heavier pieces towards the hole. Martius had gone again. With just a shared look, Odalaricus clasped their old comrade's hand and then dropped into the hole, moving onto hands and knees and following the boy, hissing with pain every time his damaged arm bumped the side.

Focalis gave Sigeric a look. He didn't have words for what he needed to tell the man. The veteran gave him a weird smile. 'I know. Go with God, Flavius.' And with that, the man gave Focalis a shove. He staggered backwards towards the hole and then, with a heavy heart, jumped down into it and followed the others. As he shuffled along in the darkness, following the sounds of Odalaricus and Martius ahead, he could hear the rumbles and crashes as Sigeric filled in the passage behind them.

They were down to three, but things had changed. Back in the palace they had been four men trapped and doomed, now they were three, but with a chance and a purpose. They had to get out of the sewer and out of the city and deal with Fritigern before the palace fell and the Thervingi searched it and left. Fritigern had to die before his army returned.

21

Somewhere back in the palace, the last fight would be going on. By now, Sigeric would hopefully have dropped sufficient masonry in to block the channel and replaced the cover. By now the bar on the last door would have given, and the Thervingi would be in the room.

Focalis could imagine it, though he wished he couldn't. There had been times over the past weeks when he'd despaired of Sigeric, had found himself devoid of trust, and yet the man had proved himself in the end, had stood by them and even bought them time and a chance. On the balance of souls, Sigeric had not come out wanting, may the Lord give him peace.

Focalis could hear nothing of what was happening back in the palace. Quite apart from the three hundred paces of tunnel they had crawled through since leaving the palace buildings, their ears were continually assailed by the scrabbling, heavy breathing and muttering of Martius ahead. There was nothing they could do to help, the tunnel being wide enough for only one man, and the lad being the one at the front, so the two veterans waited, tense and expectant.

The air in here was cloying and fetid. Even though the storm had come and gone and had cleared the air, in this narrow passage all they could smell was their own sweat and the thick scent of fresh earth and damp plants. It was stifling, hard to breathe.

Gradually, though, as Martius worked, the air began to move a little, an evening breeze drifting in from ahead, from the end of the tunnel. In fact, gradually, the light began to seep in too. It was, of course, dark out there, and still relatively cloudy, and yet after a quarter of an hour trapped in a lightless sewer tunnel, even the purple darkness of night was like the blazing of the sun, throwing shapes into relief, allowing Focalis' eyes to pick out the odd detail.

He was beginning to fret, to worry that the palace had fallen entirely – that every room had been searched, their absence confirmed and the sewer identified as their escape route – when there came a huff of triumph from ahead, and a sudden pull of air and flash of dark light as the shape of Martius no longer blocked the tunnel end. Ahead, there was a splash. With a growl of triumph, Odalaricus followed, dropping from the tunnel mouth. Focalis, breathing in the fresh air of watery evening that wafted his way, pulled himself along the tunnel and looked out.

The sewer emptied onto the riverbank behind the palace, close to the city wall. He frowned. The river had been fitted with defences all around the palace to prevent crossing by the Thervingi. How had the other two not come to grief dropping into the water? And clearly they had not, for they floundered, laughing quietly.

He looked this way and that, focusing on what he knew to be there. With a little concentration, he could see it. The sharpened stakes on the near bank stopped two feet from the outlet, and the stakes with their ropes continued mid-stream, but the area of the near riverbank had been kept clear. Focalis gave a grim smile and looked up at the cloudy sky. The unread last instruction. Somewhere beyond those grey scudding shapes, in the glory of God's heaven, Sallustius would be laughing.

'Thank you, you daft old goat,' Focalis snorted.

The man had been coy about all his work here, keeping the surprise of his traps even for his friends, but as a final surprise, he'd set it all up, and that was now clear. Sallustius had known about the escape from the start. He had kept the river defences clear of the exit, had positioned by the access sufficient rubble to block it, and had then shown Martius where it was so that he was prepared when the time came.

Taking a breath, Focalis scrabbled down from the unblocked tunnel mouth into the waters of the river. After the warm, thundery heat of the day, the effort of battle, and then the cloying air of the sewer, the cold water of the river felt like a balm, and Focalis pushed his way up to the bank with a little regret, following the others. There would be no one across the river to watch them now. No point in having scouts and pickets out when the fight was already in the palace, after all. Consequently, they moved along the riverbank below the line of the palace walls with little difficulty, openly and readily. As they reached the corner of the palace, with the city walls looming ahead, Focalis reached out and took his son's shoulder, pulling him back as he and Odalaricus edged to the corner and peered around it.

The street between the palace and the city wall was quiet, empty of life. Though not empty of bodies, by any means. In fact, by Focalis' estimation, a man could quite easily walk the entire length of the street to the city gate without touching stone, simply by stepping from body to body, such was the evidence of the hard fight there. But there were no enemy watchers to be seen, either on the ground or up on the walls. All the remaining manpower Fritigern could muster would now be tearing the palace apart, stone by stone, looking for the last two survivors from the scholae. Any time now they would come to the conclusion that the sewer was the only possibility, and would either begin to clear the blockage or trace the course and look for the exit. Either way, Focalis and the others would need to be long gone before they appeared.

'Which way?' Odalaricus murmured, looking back and forth along the walls.

Focalis mused on the problem. The simplest, of course, was to hurry down that alley and through the open city gate. It was quite possible that they could do that without bumping into wandering Thervingi, with all their attention fixed on the palace interior. But all it would take was one sighting, a warning given, and then in moments they would be hounded by dozens of angry Goths. No, the city gate was still too dangerous.

They could make for one of the city's other exits, but that would mean either crossing the river with its obstacles or hurrying back to the bridge and running the gauntlet, again risking falling into enemy hands. Only one exit remained.

'The river gate.'

'I had a feeling you were going to say that. Come on, then.'

Preparing themselves, already exhausted and now facing further exertion, the three of them set off once more along the riverbank, keeping low just in case anyone had climbed to the top of the palace roof and was looking down towards the water.

Marcianopolis' water supply came from a series of natural springs that bubbled up into a sizeable lake within the northern end of the city. The small river that flowed in through the city walls created an island within, and then disappeared out through the defensive circuit again, serving only as a drain and sewer system. Passing through the defences at each end, the river flowed beneath a low arch in the walls, the tops of the arches only just above the surface, the walls channelling the flow through the aperture. To prevent the arch being used as an unauthorised access for rowing boats or swimmers, iron bars lanced down from the stonework into the water. The bars, however, only just penetrated the water, stopping a foot or two beneath. Other cities had encountered issues with water-gate grilles that sank down to the riverbed, for floating detritus and weed would gradually collect against the bars until it turned into a dam, dropping the water level inside and creating an impromptu lake outside. Bars covering the top were enough to deter the vast majority of attempts, while not risking such blockages.

The three fugitives hurried ever closer to the walls. There was a very definite change to the sounds they could hear from the palace now. What had been a hum of triumph tinged with hate had become more a melody of frustration and anger.

Odalaricus reached the water gate and took a deep breath, then ducked beneath the surface and disappeared for a while. Focalis and Martius waited, tense, listening to the ever-increasing frustration in the search for them back in the palace, eyes continually straying back that way. After what seemed an eternity, Odalaricus burst from the water on the far side of the gate, heaving in lungfuls of air. As he coughed, he pointed down.

'Deeper than I thought. Be ready.'

As he moved off to the riverbank outside the city, Focalis tapped Martius on the shoulder. 'Go now.'

His boy needed no further urging, taking a deep breath and pulling himself down beneath the water. Focalis stood, tense, waiting. A shout from back in the palace area made him turn. Figures had emerged around the far corner of the palace, following the riverbank beneath the walls. There could be little doubt that they would be looking for the exit of the sewer pipe, and they would find it any moment now. Once they did, their gaze would rove this way and that along the river, and time would be up.

Out of options, Focalis took a breath and dropped beneath the surface just as one of them turned to look east along the river, toward the walls. Focalis gone, he would see nothing more than a little rippling on the surface in the dark, which could be fish or random eddies, or any of several everyday things.

The narrow river was about as clean a waterway as Focalis had ever come across. The flow came from the confluence of six streams, each formed from a spring, the furthest not more than ten miles north, none of which flowed through more than a tiny hamlet. Consequently, as he dived down into the river, eyes open, he could see everything pretty clearly – the riverbed, a mire of mud and weed, the city walls, stone driven deep into the bones of the land to either side, minnows darting this way and that, as though panicked and unsure of their destination, crayfish scuttling in the murk, and there, iron bars descending perhaps halfway to the riverbed, ending in dangerous-looking points.

With some difficulty, battered and bruised and weary to the core, Focalis pushed himself down. Though it was not far, still the increased pressure beneath the water was making his face hurt beneath the honeyed bandage, and he wondered if some terrible rot might infect the wound from the water. Worst of all, as he reached the bottom of the iron rods and dipped beneath them, his chain shirt caught on one of the points, and he struggled, the breath beginning to burn in his lungs as he thrashed to free himself. Lights were starting to burst in his eyes, flashes and spots as he desperately fought, holding in the very last of his air.

When he freed himself it was with little relief, for it was then he discovered that he lacked sufficient strength to pull himself back up to the surface. The sheer weight of the chain shirt he wore pulled him down even as he fought to push upwards. The dancing spots in his eyesight were becoming steadily worse, and he knew he was going. It was bad enough struggling to rise, but now he was also having to use every ounce of willpower he had not to breathe in, for that would be an end to it all.

There was a moment of extreme panic then – or, in fact, two of them. Firstly, the realisation that he was about to die and there was nothing he could do about it, and then secondly as he fell flailing, and the water rushed past at speed. Then his mind focused, telling him he was in the grip of his friends and being hauled to safety. He burst from the surface like a leaping salmon, and opened his mouth, pulling in air with relief. Still, he only allowed himself one such breath. They were not out of danger yet, and now, with Goths searching the riverbank, they had to minimise the noise and disturbance they made. Odalaricus was cursing and rubbing his damaged arm, all the activity doing little to help.

Indeed, as the three of them pulled themselves back from

the riverbank, against the outside of the city walls, Focalis caught a momentary glance of those Thervingi searching back inside the city. With that, the three of them hurried up and away from the water, sodden and dripping. Focalis and Odalaricus knew about the gap beneath the water from the days they had formed part of the temporary imperial garrison here, but it was unlikely the Goths had any such knowledge. And in the darkness there would be little or no trail to follow. Eventually the Thervingi would search as far as the city wall, but it seemed highly unlikely they would investigate further. It would appear at first glance that the water gate was blocked, and so they would not assume the fugitives to have made their exit that way.

Turning their attention instead to what lay ahead, the three of them moved a safe distance from the walls, where they could not be spotted by anyone searching at the water gate, and there rested for a moment, breathing, shaking the last of the excess water from their bodies, testing swords in sheaths to make sure they still drew with relative ease, and taking in their surroundings.

It was not hard to spot the Thervingi camp. The Goths had been outside Marcianopolis for two days now. Hundreds of horses were corralled to one side, while a sea of tents surrounded half a dozen campfires. There were, notably, no guards on the horse corral, nor were there pickets around the outside of the camp itself. It would appear that the brutal level of attrition Fritigern's army had experienced since first sighting their prey had now reached such a critical level that they no longer had sufficient manpower for anything other than the search for the survivors. That was something to be proud of, if nothing else.

'What now?' Martius muttered, wringing out his tunic hem.

Focalis turned to him. 'Now we split up.'

'Dad?'

'I know. You did well, son. We'd not have lived through that without you. But it ends there. I'm not taking my son into the enemy camp. What happens next is for Odalaricus and I to deal with. God willing, we'll walk away from this, but I won't risk dragging you down with us.'

'Besides,' Odalaricus put in with a meaningful glare at his old companion, 'you have an important job too.'

'I do?'

Focalis frowned at his friend, but Odalaricus ignored him, patting Martius on the shoulder. 'When this is done, we still need to get away. There'll still be plenty of Goths who might feel like chasing us down. We need you to find the three best horses in this lot and lead them over to the farm over there. You see it?'

Martius glanced at the buildings some distance away and nodded.

'Wait there with three horses, and we'll meet you there. And before you leave the corral, untie every rein.'

'Every one?'

Odalaricus nodded. 'Every one.'

With just that short exchange, they sent Martius off towards the unguarded corral, while Focalis and Odalaricus turned and made towards the tents. As they closed on the Goth camp, they could still hear the growing anger and consternation from inside the city walls as the Thervingi searched in vain for the vanishing survivors.

'I'm guessing we don't have a plan?'

Focalis threw his friend a look. 'Sigeric was the planner. Him and the decanus.'

'So the plan is to run at the enemy screaming, and push steel into his gut until he stops moving?'

'Something like that, yes.'

'Subtle.'

Yet as they neared the outer tents, it did actually seem feasible that they might finish this. The camp was all but silent. They could hear the odd voice here and there, but they were single ones, and scattered wide. The camp was almost empty, every available man searching the palace for the survivors.

'Aren't you going to get all contrite and pious over this?' Odalaricus murmured.

'What?'

'Well you've been full of remorse and the certainty that you'd be damned for what we did to Alavivus. Is killing another Christian king not going to send you over the edge?'

Focalis' lip wrinkled. 'Two different things. That dinner was a conference of peace. What Lupicinus had us do was murder, plain and simple. Fritigern, though, is hunting us, and killing the guilty and the innocent alike. I knew he had to die the moment Arvina fell, but watching Agnes go too? No, Fritigern has earned it. I will not even pray over his corpse.'

'Well put. Come on.'

Moving between tents, they gradually made their way towards the centre of that great camp. The Goths had learned a few things from their Roman neighbours and hosts over the years, one being the value of an ordered camp, and those tents were in neat lines around a central command area. Indeed, but for the lack of defences and the absence of weapon stacks, the camp could easily have been a Roman one. Even the tents were of Roman origin, taken as prizes throughout the long war, including the larger officer's tent visible at the centre, where their leader would be found. Perhaps the one giveaway as to the true nature of the camp was the standard. Whereas in a Roman camp, the vexilla of the army, the shining standards and eagles, flags, imperial likenesses and even crosses would rise in a small forest, here only one standard rose, and it was high and powerful.

The image of the Thervingi's ancient war god, Teiws, remained the focus of the standard, even now that the tribe entire had accepted Christianity. That the bloated, misshapen god with the skull-like rictus face seemed to have been crucified and was wearing a thorned crown did not dismiss the wickedness of the pagan symbol. Other decorations hung from the standard, too, but it was the hideous Christ/Teiws that leered its dead grin across the camp from the top of the staff.

The two men stepped out from a tent and immediately pulled back. Two Thervingi sat outside a doorway skinning an animal, conversing in their thick dialect. Focalis looked to Odalaricus, who pointed back the way they came and then at his friend, then thumbed his chest and pointed the other way. Focalis nodded, and the two men slowly slid their knives from the sodden sheaths, then stepped away. In a matter of heartbeats, Focalis had moved around the tent and was peeking out towards the two men, who sat just six paces away, each intent on the carcass between them. Above and beyond them, he spotted Odalaricus similarly appear at the corner. The man nodded, and with a steadying breath, both men turned the corner and ran.

The two Goths had no chance. They were entirely

unprepared for this sudden attack. Each wielded a skinning knife, but each was cross-legged on the ground and intent on his work. Neither even looked up in shock until the two Romans were on them.

Every soldier, even a good God-fearing one who obeys the commandments, found a way early in their career to somehow settle the need for violence and death in the service of emperor and empire with the scripture's flat prohibition of killing. As it was with Focalis, who, in the privacy of his head, apologised to the Lord for what he must do, even as he did it. His hand rounded the Goth's head and slammed down over the mouth, cutting off the surprised squawk and muffling it to an inaudible squeak as his other hand drew the blade across the man's throat. The blood from the killing blow washed out, soaking the half-peeled fawn they had been working on, and Odalaricus' own attack was the mirror image, albeit one-handed and so with a little more noise. Deed done, they did not even wait for the thrashing to stop before dragging the bodies back into the tent behind them, and then the deer too, just to remove any immediate evidence of activity from a casual passer-by.

As they moved back out between the tents again, they passed through the glow of one of the campfires, and Focalis caught sight of his hands, both soaked up to the wrist in blood. His trousers and boots were similarly drenched with the stuff. He and Odalaricus looked like creatures of nightmare.

Good.

They were.

Closer they came, until finally, in the gloom of a cloudy night, but illuminated by the flickering light of campfires, they saw their goal. Fritigern's tent was separate from the others, but although the camp was almost empty, the wily king had retained his guard of six men. Four well-armed and clearly experienced warriors stood outside the tent, beneath the rictus grin of their pagan Christ standard, but six was the number to watch for, and that meant without a doubt that two more lurked inside.

Frustrated, Focalis chewed his lip. Two against seven was workable when you had the initiative, as he'd had that first night at the villa, but here the enemy were alert, at least partially anticipating trouble, and the best of all the men on whom Fritigern could call.

'Shit,' Odalaricus hissed, clearly having reached a similar conclusion. 'What do we do now?'

'Divide and destroy. Like Caesar with the Gauls, or Agricola in Britannia. We split up.'

'What?'

'You run out there, show your arse to them, and run like a bastard. Make sure they see who you are. They're looking for us, and I'm willing to bet Fritigern's put a hefty price on us. They'll follow you. That leaves me with fewer men to deal with.'

'And why that way round? Why are you getting to face him while I run?'

'Because your left arm is in a sling and damaged, you clot. You only need your legs to run, but you'd be in trouble inside. I'm fine.'

'Half your head's missing.'

'Like Taurus, I don't use my head all that much. Come on, you know that's what we have to do. Give them the run-around for a bit, then lose them and meet me at the farm with Martius and the horses.'

Odalaricus glared at him for a while, but the silence he maintained said that he knew Focalis was right. If he could draw four of them away, it would give Focalis a fighting chance. 'Don't fuck it up,' was all he finally said, jabbing a finger at Focalis.

'There goes *my* plan of walking in and giving him a sloppy kiss. Fuck off and run. Do something useful.'

The two men gave each other a grin, which Focalis instantly regretted. His face felt more or less numb now unless he prodded it, or smiled widely. With a nod to his friend, Odalaricus drew his sword, dropping his knife, only one arm free, hefted it for a moment, and then moved two rows of tents over to be far from his mate.

Focalis watched from the corner of a tent. In retrospect, Odalaricus didn't have to be a soldier, he could have had a convincing career on the stage. The silly old bastard crept out of a line of tents into the open in front of the command area with such an air of innocence that it was astoundingly suspicious. He turned as Fritigern's guards noticed him, his mouth forming into a highly dramatic O of shock, and let rip a nervous fart he must have been holding in for some time.

'Oh shit,' Odalaricus said, loudly, then put his feet to the turf and ran like a champion race horse, away down the main camp thoroughfare towards the city gate. Almost as if they were working from a script on a stage, the four men outside the tent looked at one another in astonishment, and then burst into life, racing away after the running Roman.

Focalis watched them go, listening carefully. The tapestry of sound told him a great deal. The dullest threads in the background were the shouts and murmurs of the men still searching the palace and the streets of Marcianopolis for the two survivors. Above that was a second layer, formed of an Odalaricus who really had missed a career entertaining children on the stage, for he bellowed humorous obscenities as he ran, calling the Thervingi a number of anatomically unlikely things. And along with that in the weave came the four voices of his hunters, calling back and forth in their own tongue as they tried to cut him off, only to find that the wily old soldier had already cut across a line to escape their clutches. Once or twice he even heard Odalaricus shout, which he knew was to attract their attention because they were in danger of losing him. Then, finally, there was the top layer of threads, and these came from the main tent.

It had been a long time. After six years most voices would be unrecognisable, but not this one.

You have me trapped, but I tell you this now. Before the last of us falls, your liver will hang from your belly and you will be bleeding your last.

That had been to Lupicinus the night of the fateful banquet, but while these words were different, the voice had not changed one iota. Fritigern was speaking to his two remaining guards. One was ordered to check on the disturbance outside.

This was the moment. That moment when a battle could be decided. There were three men to deal with, but one was separating. Divide to kill.

He hefted the knife in his hand. He needed a missile. It was too far across the open space to the tent. The man would have time to give a cry of warning as Focalis ran at him. He wished to God he'd trained more with thrown blades, and that the one he prized was better weighted, for he knew his straight blade to be hilt-heavy. Still, it was all he had, and he was out of time. He stepped from the line of the tents just as Fritigern's headquarters opened and the Thervingi warrior emerged. He took half a dozen steps forwards, eyes on the road down which his companions had run, towards the sound of flight and desperate pursuit. The man hefted a sword and had a shield at his side, but he had not immediately spotted the extra danger coming at him from his periphery. As he realised there was someone there, he turned, his mouth forming into an O to shout in alarm, sword coming up, shield coming round, but he was too late. Focalis' knife was already in the air, and the Roman was now pulling his sword free with a menacing squelch as he ran.

It was not a great attack, and far from a fatal wound. The knife, predictably, had spun wrong, mid-flight, and the weapon was square-on as it hit him. Focalis' throw, though, had been good, and the weapon, even if it wasn't point-first, hit the man square in the face. The flat of the blade and the bronze guard smacked him between the eyes. It was enough. The man was stunned, just for a moment, robbed sufficiently of wits to prevent him crying out or fighting back. He floundered, blinking, staggering, and before he could even fall, Focalis was on him.

He hit the man hard, before his wits could return, driving him over and down to the ground, where his sword came up and then back down. On top of the man, there was not enough room to pull his long, heavy sword back and stab, and so he slammed it down in a chop. His own strength, depleted as it was, combined with gravity and the weight of the blade, was enough that he heard the distinct crack as the man's skull broke. Still stunned and now with a ruined face, the Goth could do little more than gasp as Focalis pulled his sword back, turned it side-on, and gripped the tip with his left hand. When the next blow came, it was that of a butcher, not a warrior, one hand on each end of a sharp blade as he drove it down into the neck.

Even as the man hissed and bubbled into death, Focalis was up once more, sword in his free hand, drenched in blood, looking like some demon summoned up from the pit. He could hear urgent murmuring inside now. Fritigern and his last guard knew that something was happening outside. The moment Focalis stepped through the door of the tent, they would be on him. He would not get close enough to kill quickly with a sword. He looked about the blood-soaked ground. There was no sign of his knife. It was dark, the blade was dulled with blood, and it could have ricocheted away or be buried beneath the dying Thervingi. He needed a missile...

Or something with a long reach.

It took only a few moments, and he slowed his approach briefly, in order to listen hard to the voices inside. He knew Fritigern's, and so he could tell the other was the guard. Fixing the voice as a rough position within the tent, he charged through the door, weapon levelled.

In actual fact it was a fantastically stupid manoeuvre, and he was lucky not to have died in its initial execution. Only luck or the grace of God could be thanked for any success. The long pole-standard with its hideous Christ/ demon became tangled in the tent door fabric as they met, and only sheer force, the momentum Focalis had built up, kept it going, tearing the tent door clear and taking it with them as he ran. The last of Fritigern's guards could not have been more surprised if the angels themselves had descended to give him a talking-to. The pointed tip of the standard took him in the chest. Even his chain armour was not going to save him from this, as Focalis ran, the great stake with its flapping tent-leather decoration ramming him so hard that the blow drove him back across the tent and into a wardrobe full of armour. There the blow smashed his ribcage and pulverised his innards without having to break a link of chain. Focalis let go of the standard, the butt of which fell to the ground. As he turned, he noted how the leering rictus of the Jesus/Teiws was almost peering up at the man it had killed as he coughed his last, pinned to the wardrobe with it, blood trickling from his mouth and down his chin.

Focalis turned, weary.

Fritigern looked old.

He remembered the Goth king well. It had only been six years, after all. At that dinner the man had looked to be in the prime of life, eyes sparkling with intelligence and wit, form lean and muscular. This Fritigern looked like a shadow of that man – could be his father, even.

'I know you,' the Thervingi said, eyes narrowing. His accent was so imperial, his Greek so fluent he could easily have been born in Athens.

'Yes, you do.'

'You have surpassed all expectations.'

'If that's a compliment, save it.'

The man shrugged. 'Alright. You realise I can call on plenty of men with just a shout.'

'No, you can't. The last of your men are busy. No one will hear you, and by the time they do, you'll be dead. You should have walked away. At any time you could have forgotten about us and gone your own way. It's your own bloody-minded need for revenge that's brought us to this. Yes, we killed Alavivus, and yes it was wrong, especially under a flag of peace, but you know it is the command that orders the hand, not the hand that wields the blade, which is to blame. And you also know that your people's actions outside the wall were the trigger. It was a massive, and I mean *massive*, fuck-up all round. We shouldn't have done what we did, and Lupicinus and Maximus will rot in hell for their part in it all. But that's the point, isn't it? You follow the one true God now? You understand salvation and damnation. What we did will earn us our own little corner of hell. So why spend all your time and energy dealing with us?'

Fritigern's expression did not change. 'You believe this is just personal anger? You think I am such a fool as to devote all my energy to the destruction of eight men for dispatching Alavivus? Ha. Had I known how stupid you all were, I could have saved myself so much time.'

Now was Focalis' moment to frown. 'What?'

'Alavivus was a fool, and slow. He was almost as drunk as your master that night. Why else do you think he was so easy to kill? *My* people were starving and *your* people just hastened the problem. And when we fought to hold our own, you tried to subvert us all, to give us hope, to dangle a future in front of us while crippling us. Alavivus fell for your lies, and half the tribe would have done. I let you kill him, because it was exactly what we needed to incite my people. We were going to fade and die if we didn't fight back. What you did that night *got us* fighting back. And God, Roman, but we very nearly had your empire on its knees. Six years of destruction. We even burned that fat sack of shit Valens. And we could have done it all, but my people became tired again. That dangled promise of a future started to look good again. My own people sued for peace. After the Romans sold our children for grain, raped our women, starved and humiliated us, then killed one of our kings, still my people wanted that Pax Romana.'

Focalis blinked. 'They made peace and they kicked you out.'

'Fools.'

'And you... God Almighty, but you and Lupicinus are a pair.'

Fritigern's expression darkened at the comparison, but Focalis sneered. 'You are. Lupicinus used all his power to try and sell us to you to regain his place in the empire, and you've devoted everything you have to killing us, just to regain power among the Thervingi. And what will you use it for? Another six years of war? Twelve? A hundred?'

'Rome lies. Rome cheats. Rome should die.'

Focalis flexed his wrist. He was tired. Really tired. He could do with a week's sleep and a warm bath. But somehow there was a reserve of strength he hadn't known he had, that was surfacing with the realisation that he'd had things wrong from the start. For years. One blow. That was all he needed. He was almost close enough, too. Could he edge just a little closer without it being obvious?

'I knew I was damned for what I did to Alavivus, and had it not been for my son, I might have bent my neck to your blade. Only when you extended your anger to innocents and killed those who travelled with us did I decide you needed to pay for all of this.'

A tiny step forward even as their eyes remained locked. 'But now I realise that I have nothing to atone for. Nothing. All this time, I had focused on my own sins, and had not realised how we have been played from the start by you and by Lupicinus.

You're both serpents. We killed a king, but you were the one who offered him up. And now you have to meet the Lord face to face, not for what you've done, but for what you *will do*. I could still let this go. Make peace. But I cannot let you start up the war again. The war is done, and good riddance to it. We have peace. Your people are finally comfortable, serving *with* us, protecting what we can *all* share. You *will not* ruin that.' Another shuffled step.

'And you continue to show your foolishness. You delay in the end just to learn the truth. And now I hear the approach of my people. They have failed to find you in the city, and now they return, and you lose. It's over, Roman. Don't you see?' Last step.

Focalis moved so fast that the Thervingi king never saw it coming. One blow, a single swing of the blade. For a moment, Fritigern seemed to think nothing had happened. Then he looked down. Blood was sheeting from the cut across his neck. He looked up in shock, which was a mistake, for the blow had half-severed his neck, and his head lolled back as though about to separate from his body.

'The punishment for a traitor is beheading,' Focalis said flatly, and swung again.

This time the blow smashed into the exposed spine, shattering the bone. The head, already half-separated, fell away to the floor with a bony thud. The body crumpled and collapsed in on itself. Focalis stood and watched for only a few moments. He could hear the boots of Fritigern's Thervingi returning, and there would still be enough to overwhelm him. Instead, he ducked to the back of the tent and heaved at the bottom edge, pulling up the leather until there was sufficient gap, then dropped and rolled through it. He was barely out, letting the tent leather drop again, when he heard the warriors burst in and find their dead king, so recently executed that his blood still flowed in torrents.

It was over.

With a strange sense of release and the lightest heart he had felt in years, Focalis set his sights on the distant farm buildings and ran for his life between the tents.

22

Focalis' mind wandered back over the events of the last three days as he waited. It seemed almost unreal. Fritigern was dead. It was over. Perhaps fifty at most of the man's warband had survived, but they were tired and dispirited, and now without a purpose. They had been the king's men, devoted to his plan to retake his place among the Thervingi and restart the war, but without Fritigern there was no point. They would go their own way now, find somewhere to disappear.

It was over.

Soon, Focalis would return to Marcianopolis and find the bodies of his friends, making sure they were given proper burials and raising memorials to them, but not yet. He had to leave adequate time for the Thervingi to leave first. They may have lost their purpose, but he couldn't imagine bumping into them would be good for him.

With just moments to spare he'd made it out of the Goth camp. As planned, he'd raced away through the corral, and as he'd pounded across the turf, he'd slapped animals on the rump, shouting, causing panic and chaos. He'd almost fallen foul of the animals, having survived an army of angry Goths, for their panicked stampede began while he was still crossing the corral, and he felt battered and desperate as he burst into the open and raced for the farm buildings.

He'd found Martius there, waiting with three good-looking beasts, all saddled ready. No Odalaricus, though. He'd really hoped his old friend was up to it and would survive, but the man had been wounded, after all. There was every chance he'd been picked up by the other Thervingi as they returned from the city and the palace. He and Martius had waited as long as they could, and had only given up hope with a heavy heart when the Goths began to round up the scattered animals and search in the direction of the barn. Then, he and Martius had slipped away in the darkness.

'Is it over, Dad?' the boy had asked.

'Almost.'

And that had been that. Martius never asked what remained. He knew, for there was only one loose thread now. They'd covered the forty miles to Messembria by noon the next day with several short stops. There, Focalis had led them back to that same inn, the one where they'd all been supposed to meet – the Wanton Siren. Martius he settled into a room there, and paid the innkeeper rather handsomely to make sure the lad was not bothered by the more rodential of the dive's denizens. The horses were stabled, and Focalis set about watching his quarry, returning during the evening for a meal with the lad and to sleep in a bed, catching up at long last. There were far better inns in the city, but this was their old dive, and there was always hope.

The next morning he chose his place, and in the early afternoon, he chose his time.

Lupicinus' villa was no longer a fortress. The man had almost emptied his vaults in a vain attempt to see them all dead with his stupid quest for power, and his force of mercenaries had met their end almost to a man against Fritigern's riders at Suida. All that remained at the palatial Messembria villa were a handful of fat, lazy guards and a household staff of slaves and freedmen. Getting into the grounds had hardly been troublesome.

Crossing to the bath house was similarly easy, just a quarter of an hour after the former comes rei militaris per Thracias had slipped in for an afternoon dip. Boots off, no wooden clogs on. No armour worn, and no sword belt. Just a blade in hand, silent and easy. Creeping through the bath house not an issue. Just one slave on duty, and swiftly dealt with. Not a kill, though. Focalis was not like those men. The innocent should live, and so he simply smacked the slave on the back of the head with his knife hilt, knocking him unconscious for the duration.

Lupicinus was a weasel of a man, and now, with half a decade of the pariah's life, he looked more like one than ever. The man lounged in the water of a hot bath some eight feet across, a circular affair decorated with mosaics that harked back to a time of sea gods and monsters. He was naked and poorly-shaven, thin and skeletal with scruffy hair, and the rodent look clung to him even bare-skinned.

Lupicinus looked up with a start.

'Who are you?' he demanded. 'How did you get in here?'

'Don't you know?' Focalis replied idly, thumbing the blade of his shining knife. 'You really *should*. If you're going to devote so much effort to killing a man, you should at least commit his face to memory.'

'You.'

'Quite. I expect you'll be pleased to hear that Fritigern of the Thervingi is no more. Less so, I suspect, when I explain that you won't be around to capitalise on that.'

'You have no right to judge me, soldier.'

'Oh, I'm not judging you. God did that, and I'm afraid that on the balance of sins, you come up rather wanting, Flavius Lupicinus. The blame lies firmly on your shoulders. You are responsible for half a decade of war that killed an emperor and almost ruined the empire. You and Maximus. Greed and stupidity. The new emperor should have ordered your end the moment he came to power. That's the problem with government-appointed officers, you know? They don't get the lesson a true soldier learns in his first year of war, a lesson that lies at the heart of this entire bloody nightmare.'

'Which is?'

'That there is nothing more valuable than peace.'

Lupicinus' hand reached out, along the side of the bath, where his towel sat folded. He gripped the knife that lay atop it and brandished it, rising slightly in the water, so that only his lower half remained submerged. 'I've not been unarmed since Marcianopolis. And you might think me a noble appointment with no military skill, but I trained with the best. You are injured. Tired. You'll not find me an easy opponent, soldier.'

Focalis smiled, and it was not a pleasant smile. 'What was it you said at Marcianopolis? What was the order you gave? "Kill them. Kill them all".'

Lupicinus' brow furrowed, then shot up in alarm. The tip of a blade emerged from his chest, blood spurting up round it, spraying out into the bathwater, leaving artistic curls of pink in the blue. Lupicinus stared downwards in shock, agony now gripping him, his own knife falling away into the water.

Odalaricus left the blade where it was, and rose from the bath side behind the old general.

'This time, happy to obey,' he said, with a smile every bit as feral as Focalis'.

Lupicinus coughed, gouts of blood flowing from his mouth and adding to the steady increase of red staining the water. Focalis nodded at his friend. It had been his one hope. If anyone survived, they would surely know to meet at the Siren as planned. He'd held out hope for the survival of Odalaricus, and even of Sigeric. And he had put off this last move in the game as long as he could, knowing that his friends had every bit as much right to this as he. Odalaricus had arrived, tired but in high spirits, this very morning, after having spent a day hiding from furious Thervingi, then stolen one of their horses and ridden for his life.

As Odalaricus wandered around the side of the bath and fell in next to his old friend, they watched as the jerked breaths from the old man gradually subsided, and the light went out of his eyes, the flow of blood into the water slowing as his skin took on a waxy, grey look. Not until he had left this world, and begun his descent to the hell that surely awaited, did the two men turn and make their way back through the baths, stepping over the unconscious slave and pausing briefly to slip back into their boots.

'What now?'

Focalis shrugged. 'I don't think there's any reason to hide anymore. My home's still standing, but I don't know whether I want to go back. The place is nothing but memories of Flavia and of years of waiting for the Thervingi to come. I think Martius needs to grow up somewhere new. Somewhere different. Positive. Might see if I can sell the place and move abroad. I've spent everything I had, but the house is worth a bit. What about you?'

'Mind some company when you go? My house is worth a bit too, and we only emptied two of my caches, remember? I have hidden pots of coins in a dozen places yet. Where will we go though?'

Focalis smiled. An image of Pictor grinning at his wife popped into his mind.

'I hear Hispania's nice this time of year.'

Author's Note

The world of fourth-century Rome is to some extent alien to me, and this is the first time I have explored the empire beyond the cataclysmic time of Constantine and Maxentius. Of course, those books were written with my good friend Gordon Doherty, whose familiarity with late Rome is far, far greater than mine, and whose flagship series Legionary is a mainstay of military fiction for that time. But for me, the research, the planning, and the writing of *Para Bellum* has been an epic voyage of discovery.

Forget the legions and shield-walls, the testudos and pila, the gladii and praetorians. Forget prayers to Jupiter, Greatest and Best, forget Marius' Mules and senators and tribunes and centurions. Forget everything traditionally Roman in the layperson's eye. The Rome of Flavius Focalis, based in Thrace in the late fourth century, would be almost as alien to Julius Caesar as it is to me.

We are exploring a world where Christianity is ascendant, in which gladiators and paganism are not banned quite yet, but are anachronistic and unpopular. This is a world where the border between Roman and barbarian has blurred almost to a point of indistinguishability. Now – as Martius notes on that night before the battle – the emperors are not engaged in conquest for the glory of Rome, but more in trying to hold together the unravelling strands of an empire under immense pressure from without, and slowly collapsing from financial trouble and an ever-increasing military-centric attitude within. This is AD 382, and the events that trigger this story are as viable an answer as any to that age-old question: What caused the fall of the Roman Empire?

In truth, there was little more that Valens could have done than let the Thervingi cross the river and settle in Thrace. He was already involved in an empire-threatening situation in the east, fighting Persians, and could hardly spare the manpower to eject thousands of Gothic settlers back across the River Danube. Indeed, he seems to have granted the Goths unrealistically favourable terms, presumably because he was at the time in no position to argue with them, and indeed needed the additional manpower for imperial security.

The result was Goths more or less allowed to settle in their own tribal groups within Roman lands. And despite everything, that could well have been a successful decision. Taking one of the biggest tribes of enemy Goths from across the river and adding them to your own military might sounds like a win, after all. And as part of the deal, the Goths would take on the emperor's religion as their own, so they would now all be brothers in Christ.

Not all the blame for the ensuing disaster can be attributed to Rome. I have not elaborated on the matter in this text as it is of peripheral importance to my story, but it seems the Greuthungi were not invited along with the Thervingi, instead taking the opportunity to do so without permission.

Having a foreign tribe enter your lands without permission is, after all, tantamount to an invasion.

What then happened we will likely never have a full handle on. It is distinctly possible that the Goths were initially given everything they needed, rather than being stiffed by the Roman authorities. It is possible that the year had a poor harvest, and it is *that* which led to the hunger among the tribes, rather than Rome deliberately giving them poor land. Though that is, of course, also a possibility. Many of the contemporary accounts blame the Goths themselves for committing acts of violence and driving the Romans to deal harshly with them. The account of Ammianus Marcellinus, however, is generally considered likely to be more accurate than those alarmist and more clearly biased writers.

Whatever the cause of the Goths' hunger, Ammian lays the blame for what happened firmly in the hands of the two most powerful Romans in the region, comes rei militaris per Thracias, Lupicinus, and the dux Maximus. Ammian directly accuses the pair of criminal corruption and almost predicts the fall of the western empire, decades before the event. He tells us of this dreadful moment with the line "There [in Marcianopolis] another, and more atrocious, thing was done, which kindled the frightful torches that were to burn for the destruction of the state."

In that line he is talking of the infamous dinner, which we will come to shortly. First, though, we must look at the culprits. We are told that the Goths were starving, and appealed to the Roman authorities for help, and that Lupicinus and Maximus responded by releasing food to them at an extortionate price for personal profit, the trade so appalling that the Goths were selling their children into Roman slavery in return for grain.

Oh… did you not hate Lupicinus enough in my tale? Bet you do now.

The result was predictable, really. Two Gothic tribes were fully armed and inside Roman territory while the bulk of the Roman military was elsewhere, and they had been cheated and wronged. They inevitably went on a rampage across Thrace, taking what they needed, largely unchecked and unopposed. This was the start of the Gothic War. Then, in an effort to halt the disaster and reinstate control, Lupicinus hatched the idea of inviting the two Thervingi kings, Fritigern and Alavivus, to a grand dinner at Marcianopolis where peace could be discussed. I have more or less retold those events, paraphrasing Ammian through the mouths of my characters. Trouble kicks off outside the walls, and drunken Lupicinus makes the disastrous decision to send his men to kill the kings and those who escorted them.

This, of course, is where my characters come in, and where we more or less depart from the historical record for our own story. If you wish to read more of the time of the Gothic Wars, once again, I direct you to Gordon Doherty's Legionary series that covered the era, including the battle of Adrianople and the fall of Valens.

Our story begins after that fateful conflict, once the dust has settled, the war is over, and the Goths are now, irrevocably, part of the empire. Yet it is a fragile peace. Alavivus has now been dead for years. Fritigern, the other Thervingi king, is deposed from his position as part of the peace accords. He then disappears from the historical record. We have no knowledge of what this clever, dangerous, ambitious war leader did, once deposed. It seems highly unlikely that he took this lying down and simply retired to grow cabbages as Diocletian had. It also seems unlikely that a man who had led a nation for years of war would go alone. He would undoubtedly harbour grudges, have grand plans, and take many warriors with him. That is part of the root of this story: the untold tale of Fritigern's last days and demise.

On the Roman side, the emperor Valens had also died, and a new, apparently more effective emperor had managed to turn the tide and was on speaking terms with the Thervingi and Greuthungi. Maximus is not mentioned in sources after the dinner, and Lupicinus only in the immediate aftermath. Their fates are not known. It has been postulated that Maximus is the same man as Magnus Maximus, the usurper in Britain a few years later, although if this was the case, it seems likely that at least one surviving work would connect the two. As an author's conceit, I pared down the villains, for it is always too complex and less satisfying for a novel to have a group of villains rather than a core. As such I had Maximus dead since the war, and Lupicinus in retirement, something of a pariah, which seems extremely likely, given his culpability and the change of emperors.

It was reading of the meal at Marcianopolis that first gave me the idea for this tale. It struck me that such a largely unknown event in history (because I'm fairly certain the majority of laypersons, even those with a keen interest in Rome, are unaware of The Meal) had such far-reaching and cataclysmic effects for the empire. And I didn't want this to be the story of the war and the finale at Adrianople, despite my grounding in war stories. I wanted this to be a personal tale in which the reader could appreciate the less grand effects that awful evening had on history: the world the Marcianopolis dinner brought about, and the aftermath.

SIMON TURNEY

I toyed initially with a tale that pitted either Lupicinus or Maximus directly with Fritigern, but the problem with that is that they all come across as villains in some fashion. Fritigern is the 'noble savage', a Vercingetorix or Arminius or Caratacus, and I didn't want this to be a tale of a wronged Goth hero (although that is a juicy tale awaiting the telling, I guess). Maximus and Lupicinus are clearly greedy and sickening human beings and I could not make either of them a hero. All my potential cast were villains.

Then it occurred to me. Who were the men who did the actual deed for Lupicinus? Are they culpable? After all, the excuse 'I was only following orders' has been heard on the lips of some of history's most horrifying villains. Yet to some extent they are exonerated by being the blade, rather than the hand that wields it. Therein, I realised, lay my heroes, or possibly anti-heroes. And they would not be popular. With anyone. Fritigern, who had only just managed to avoid dying on their swords by his sharp wits and silver tongue, would hate them as much as any man. Maximus and Lupicinus, fallen from grace, would have little love for the men who would be a reminder of their failure. The emperor, who had been nowhere near the debacle, would be appalled at them. They would be lucky not to be executed or cashiered. And as men who'd then been shuffled into obscurity, they could eventually become a target for one of those enemies they had made.

This, then, became a story of revenge. Of an angry, disinherited Goth king seeking out the men who'd murdered his brother king at a supposed peace conference and had almost done the same to him. It became a story of those men's flight and preparations, their fight to survive in a world in which they could rely on nobody but themselves. And only once the story was underway did the extra motivations of Fritigern and Lupicinus come to light: the war-mongering of one, and desperate need to rebuild of the other.

I made my heroes an eight-man unit (with their assorted hangers-on). Each man is different. Each has dealt with what they have done differently, and each sees their guilt a different way. It has ruined some, even killed some. It has made others determined. The portrayal of these men is partially based upon models I already know well from earlier Roman periods, but has been greatly tweaked with the colour of the fourth century. This is not a time of red tunics and segmented armour, of huge rectangular shields and old-fashioned weapons. Hence the arrival of the martiobarbuli, a very real piece of late Roman military hardware, of chain shirts without the old doubling on the shoulders, of light javelins (spiculi) and of decorative long-sleeved white tunics. For those interested in delving into the military of the time, Osprey Publishing do a good range of books on the different units, including one on Roman v. Goth. This is a world which has more in common with what we now think of as Byzantium than ancient Rome.

Those with an astute eye for a plot and a good movie knowledge might spot a number of influences here. During the time I plotted this tale, among the movies that cropped up were *First Blood*, *The 13th Warrior* and *Mad Max: Fury Road*. Elements of all three have definitely wormed their way in.

My locations for this story are a mix of invented sites and of historical places. Clearly Marcianopolis is a true place, now the Bulgarian town of Devnya. Of the ancient city little remains, barring the amphitheatre and a mosaic-rich villa, neither of which has any bearing on this tale. The layout of the place is largely conjectural. Since it served temporarily as an imperial capital in the years prior to this, it seems certain there would have been a sizeable palace there. I have placed it specifically within the loop of the Devnya River within the city's eastern wall, following the logic that places the imperial palace of Antioch on an island separate from the urban mass even while within the city. The layout of the palace is my own conceit, and if to the reader it sounds more like a Medieval castle than a Roman palace, there are good reasons for that. This, remember, is very late Rome, and a glance at the structures from this era makes a precedent clear. Constantine's fortress of Divitia clearly resembled a Medieval castle far more than anything from antiquity, and Galerius' palace at Gamzigrad-Romuliana is a fortress-palace on a most impressive scale.

Messembria is now the coastal city of Nessebar on the Black Sea, an ancient place built on a virtual island, connected to the coast by a narrow causeway. The landscape of this tale around Nessebar is easy to track on Google Earth, from the fields where Persius Arvina fell (farmland north of Pomorie) to the forested slope where the party split (just east of Cholakova cheshma).

The surviving remnant of ancient Suida is the fortress, now a ruin that lies on the hillside on the northern edge of Sliven. The positioning of a lower city on the slopes south of that walled enclosure is conjectural, but highly possible. Other sites in the book are largely fictional, their descriptions based upon locations chosen through Google Earth as being in roughly the correct position geographically. The only other site used in the book that corresponds to a true place is

Macellum Iulia. The name and history of the site are entirely my own devising, but the geographical descriptions are based upon the Bulgarian town of Karnobat, which has unearthed evidence of occupation in the period.

As a last note, you may notice in this book a marked difference in character naming from my other Roman works. This is, again, an effect of the date and location of the book. *Para Bellum* is set in the land of Thrace, which would have been principally Greek-speaking even earlier on in the Roman era, and so the presence of names like Persius should not be a surprise. Names like Odalaricus and Sigeric are quite clearly non-Roman, and yet with the gradual profusion of Gothic, Sarmatian, Germanic and other external blood slowly spreading through the empire, it should not be a surprise that these 'barbarian' names also become the norm. Some of late Rome's most famous characters exhibit more barbarian nomenclature than Roman, such as Flavius Stilicho, Ricimer and Fullofaudes. The days of the tria nomina (the three names) are gone, so it is extremely unusual to find anyone with a name like Marcus Decimus Brutus. Another element that is hard to avoid is the Flavian profusion. Many late Roman appellations are formed from a native name preceded by Flavius, which goes some way to explain why Odalaricus, Focalis, and Lupicinus in this tale are all Flavii. This was quite simply way too common.

So that's it. *Para Bellum* is over. This is a standalone book, so no need to wait for a sequel. This was just a single tale that I felt the greatest urge to tell, and Nic and Greg at Head of Zeus were wonderfully enthusiastic enough to agree to publish it, fabulous people that they are. Soon we will be back to our regular schedule of book series, but there will be at least one more standalone to come, for there is another tale that I am twitching to tell, and the heroes at HoZ are even more enthusiastic about that. I'm sad to say goodbye to Flavius and his son and friends, but it's always fun to move on into the unknown, and there are wonderful characters waiting to be built.

See you in the past.

Simon Turney, June 2022